I0526160

The Immortal of Degoskirke
Tales from the Netherscape - Book Three

By Michael Green

Cover art by Alexey Rudikov

1st Edition

ISBN: 978-1-950593-05-7

To the timeless voices,
You nameless members of that fallen class.
You, who give fright with your honesty,
who endanger your futures for need of truth.

To the careless farseers,
You, who tumble into ravenous wells,
Your eyes glued to the stars,
Even as you fall.

Table of Contents

Chapter 1: First Steps

Looking ahead, Andy saw two broad towers flanking a gatehouse. One was built of brick and painted deep crimson with golden borders, while the other was plain, hewn stone draped in flowing banners that featured monograms and credos written in Latin and English. These banners were unique, with no uniform color or shape among them.

Andy glanced at Ziesqe and was unsettled by the sight of Dr. Ropt. Though his human self was less intimidating, Andy knew what lay beneath.

Ziesqe fretted with the collar of his robe. He put a hand in his pocket and produced a heavy orb. Bumps rose across Andy's arms. The orb was gray, not purple.

"It's the lenses; now you see what the average human sees," Ziesqe said, anticipating Andy's question. "Calm yourself, and look ahead. Act bored, and do not open your mouth at the gates."

Andy nodded, distracted by a pair of riders, garbed in ornamental robes and bearing short swords, mounted on their monitor lizards. Exiting the city, they lumbered past the carts, towards the broad expanse of ruins. Andy sighed, mentally adding giant lizards to his list of ridiculous sightings.

"Why not ride horses?" Andy asked, waving his hands at the lizards.

"Thank your side for them as well. Horses refuse to take a rider in the Netherscape—some contrivance of the Dead God. So, we improve the monitor to take their place. One more strike and riposte on the chessboard of the Gods," Ziesqe droned, sick of waiting in line.

Andy's cheeks bent with wry disbelief as the improved monitors passed into the distance.

The long line of carts traversed the gates one at a time, as inspections were conducted, and tariffs paid. Andy tried to follow the proceedings, only to find himself perplexed once more.

Closer now, Andy inspected the banners and pennants. He read one, white fringed in gold, "Greek Idealist," and then a jagged crimson, "Egalitarian Redistributionist," and finally, a blue fringed in white, "Peace and Parlay Party." There were still several others he couldn't make out. Above one banner, the Egalitarian Redistributionist at the moment, hung a shoddy wooden crown, painted gold. The bulky crown sat on a spoke jutting from above the banner.

Andy watched as a man with a long pole carefully moved the crown from above one banner and placed it on the spoke above another. An approving murmur rose from the carts. The hundreds in line watched with trepidation, understanding some significance that mystified Andy. The man with the pole kept his eye on another, who stood atop the tower and occasionally called down to them.

"What's going on over there?" Andy asked.

Ziesqe groaned. "This city's eccentricity is what. I see it's spilled out beyond the walls."

Since Ziesqe was no help, Andy continued his

vigil. He saw that the groups of curiously dressed people about the base of the tower also changed position with the crown above. This was all in contrast to the tower on the right, which featured no banner. At the base of this tower, stood a couple in heavy robes; one bore a plain canvas stretched on a staff.

"Can you believe it?" A trader with a large pack walked up alongside their cart. "This was a Braid gate, at ten percent, for months! Now it looks like the Redbaggers are making a run. The Anarchists are also trying to stick their foot in; you'd think they'd give up—only us merchants like them."

Ziesqe grunted.

The man laughed. "Been out of town for a while, I see." His gaze lingered on their robes. "I can exchange those for something newer, if you like." Ziesqe didn't bother looking up. The man continued, "Hmm...well, good luck with the tariff. The Redbags cut you at forty percent, but if we're lucky, the Anarchists might wave us through," he concluded sourly, before walking ahead of their cart.

Andy sat in perplexed silence as the line inched forward. He watched the caller atop the tower and, as they neared the gate, heard him cry, "Redbag!" Groans rose from the crowd, and the owner of the cart ahead cursed as the crown moved to the Redbag's banner.

A pair of men, clad in leather armor and holding red burlap sacks, approached to inspect his cargo.

The robed men from the right-hand tower also

conducted a quick inspection. One stood ahead of the cart with the plain canvas on its staff and snapped his fingers for the merchant's attention. He shook the staff and canvas and the merchant looked. Seconds later, the robed man was satisfied and stepped aside.

The right-hand inspection was over in moments, but the Redbaggers took far longer, finally relieving the merchant of several barrels.

His tariffs paid, the merchant cursed his way through the gate.

The men with red bags gazed at Andy and Ziesqe. "No dawdling, or skipping to another gate; we'll chase you, and make you pay the parasite's privilege."

Their cart rolled forward, but a voice called down from above, "Braid!"

The crown moved positions, and the men with red bags stepped aside disappointedly; one whined at the other for wasting time with threats.

A woman, wearing an open, blue pea coat and sporting a gray wig above her young face scoffed at the retreating Redbaggers and approached with her clipboard. "Manifest?" she inquired, before inspecting the cargo. The robed figures also began their inspection.

Ziesqe handed over his papers and produced two small bags of coins from the folds of his robe.

"Bolts of cloth, jars of dye, loom parts..." The woman drew calculations on her paper, and then counted the coins, before stamping the documents. The robed figures returned the papers, took the money, and watched closely as they walked the canvas and staff ahead of the cart.

"You there," a robed man called out to Andy. "Eyes here," he said, shaking the staff.

Andy saw nothing.

The robed men stared for a long while before finally stepping aside.

Ziesqe tugged on the reins, and they rolled into the gatehouse.

A cheer from within was suddenly overwhelming.

"This pointless display of adolescent posturing may satisfy your starved egos, but consider the damage you do to the people of Eighth Gate! The lines of the merchants are a mile long! Look, here comes one now!"

They passed through the gatehouse and entered the city. A massive crowd filled with humans, ychorites, brutox, even goblins and mice craned their necks toward Andy and Ziesqe.

The speaker, wearing tight breeches, a haggard gray wig, and with his coat at his feet stood on a stage, covered in so many stains of various colors, that it resembled a rainbow in places. His arms rose, revealing sweat stains and his chest heaved with the exertion of performance. Above the stage stood a placard bearing the name: "Eighth Gate." Another golden crown dangled on one of many banners here; currently, the Peace and Parley Party bore the crown. Many books, some massive, others barely a few pages, dangled underneath the banners, held in place by chains. Goblins cheered from second story

5

gutters on nearby buildings—box seats to creatures their size—and tiny stands, resembling flower boxes large enough to accommodate hundreds of mice, jutted over the stage.

The wigged man also wore a stiff board, covered in glittering coins, on his chest. He held his hand out expectantly to Andy and Ziesqe. "Good merchants these, who by the toil of their days enrich themselves and our city in turn. Twice the latter, for they are robbed at the gate, and then when they lay their goods at our markets. Their struggle against each other lowers prices for all! You, fair merchants with robes so old, did our city greet you as friend or another foe? Did you meet a Braid or a Bloody Bag?"

Ziesqe was silent, but Andy happily raised his voice, "A Braid!"

A chorus of cheers went up, and the speaker gestured widely, as if Andy's statement was proof of something.

A man in red, also bearing a full chest of glittering coins, pushed forward onto the stage.

"Pish, posh! You would imply their poor clothing a consequence of us, you benighted lovers of the poor, had he met with a Red Bag at the gate. Where is that touted reason of the reasonable? You levy, like we, but not as well. Take stock, Eighth Gate! Your timbers split, and the line outside this gate is proof that the Braids are letting you down! When grumblesome merchants such as these fester in droves, there can only be prey for them! Your flowing blood calls them to this gate! Your good nature lies trampled in the gutter, spat upon by

6

those who call no land home!"

Another, angrier cheer went up. A score of mice, perched on the board with the banners, were avidly counting. Andy turned to the crowd, and saw countless hands waving colored strips of cloth. There was suddenly a preponderance of light red, as opposed to navy blue. Andy also spotted a few black ribbons clenched in tight fists.

"Red Bag!" A mouse on the board called out.

The mice moved the golden crown from the Braid banner to another, that bore the name Egalitarian Redistributionists.

Andy observed the watcher on the tower, knowing that the crown outside would be changing as well. It all made sense now.

Astonished, Andy laughed. At first, he felt judgmental, but was then struck by sadness. It was undoubtedly insane, but the sight of their faces, their rich cries and waving hands, felt like evidence of something more.

The Braid took center stage again. "Nay, nay! What hate! Do not go down that path! These, who travel so far across the purple blight, are doing what we will not! Our gate's popularity, yes, even the love the traders have for this sacred entrance into the Free City, is not to be insulted by jealous children, who cut purses and spill concord forever! And for what? A few petty coins! Coins that keep the merchants alive and coming back! It is hate in this man's heart! Hate, that he is not brave enough to see the work of his sinews blossom or wither at mere turn of sky! Freeze the hate in your veins, and see how bedecked they enter our city! Wearing plain clothes of ten seasons hence! How rich do you dream these others, Red Thief? How rich are these, who love our city and enter, heedless of any petty fashion, to tend to that dream which bares fruit only in Degoskirke?"

Spectators were crying and waving the blue ribbons. "Braid!" Called the mice, and the crown changed locations again.

Ziesqe had pulled the cart to the side of the road, allowing those entering through the gate behind to pass. They noticed a slew of angry merchants.

"They got hit with the red bag," a man pushing a cart bearing crispy chicken said at the sight of the newcomers.

"So, this is just normal here. They live like this," Andy whispered.

Ziesqe gave Andy a weighty glance, not unlike his teachers after they had finished a lesson, before flicking the reins. They rolled on; Andy turned in his seat to watch the arguments continue. A man in black leather armor took the stage, but the crowd booed so quickly and angrily that Andy couldn't hear him.

"It's clear that we need newer clothes. Fashion must be a recent cause for concern," Ziesqe mumbled, half to himself.

"Yes, it's been brought up more than once," Andy agreed.

The buildings in Degoskirke proper were raucous and varying, akin to the ruins outside, though kept to a marginally higher standard. Most were three floors, but a few stood taller, and occasional wrecks testified to the freeform building standards. A few mansions, with iron fences and gardens, occupied whole blocks. Banks, museums, and posh restaurants clustered in pockets about those mansions, though these pockets were only intermittent. Additions, akin to after-thoughts, jutted from structures here and there. Extra rooms or towers, built for creatures of mouse or goblin size, rose awkwardly from human-sized tenements, like branches or paper-clipped notes. Many had their own rickety stairs, leading into the gutters of nearby buildings or roads, and, as Andy watched these, he saw a microcosm of the large streets. Mice moved their cargoes in small carts, or by way of pulley systems, akin to a network of clotheslines reaching through the lanes they had cut in the gutters or alleys.

The raucous yelling faded as they rolled down the bumpy street. Hardly five minutes passed before they came upon another curiosity. Painted lines covered the ground, winding between buildings and across streets ahead of them. Andy noticed two gangs, armed with scrapers, paint brushes, and cans full of paint, facing off. Most of the members were about his age. Both gangs wore ramshackle, wooden and scrap-metal armor. One boy even had a dented pot strapped to his head. Both sides were mottled with flecks of white-wash. They hooted and shook their implements, each side daring the other to action, while a tired vendor of fine water sat between their battle lines.

Ziesqe reined the cart to a halt, giving Andy the chance to watch. They were still for a long time, as each side inched toward the other. Andy noticed that one side had the words "Eighth Gate" painted on their equipment, while the other read "Clemson Downs".

"Scrape!" An Eighth-Gater cried, before lunging forward with his long-poled rolling brush.

"Go around!" The leader of the Clemsons yelled and pushed his people into action.

They were trying to scrape away the other side's paint.

"This stall is ours!" One voice yelled out.

The tired stall owner barely looked down at the flying globs of paint spattering his inventory of water jars.

Suddenly, two Eighth-Gaters left the fray and chipped at paint near a building.

"They're feinting!" Was the reply.

The struggle around the vendor ceased, and the opposing sides tripped each other with their equipment as they rushed toward the new front. Andy laughed as one fellow took a rolling brush to the face. He fell over backwards, but quickly regained his feet and ran after the action, thoroughly striped.

Andy's laughter continued as he watched children from both sections of the city relieve the painters, taking up their equipment. Fallen painters were dragged off and scrubbed. Andy was surprised to see smiling faces behind the occasional bloody nose.

What the hell is wrong with these people?

Ziesqe gave Andy a curious look.

"Is the whole place like this?" Andy asked.

"Almost. About ninety percent of the city functions in this manner. There are a few holdouts."

"How have ryle never been able to take the—hey!" Andy grunted as Ziesqe jabbed him in the gut.

"Careful now, that kind of talk will get us killed," Ziesqe muttered, smiling towards the paint fight. "Just grin like an idiot. I'll answer your question shortly."

Andy did as he was told, and they moved on.

"Degoskirke is free for several reasons," Ziesqe spoke quietly. "First, they despise us. You recall the Exegesuit priests at the gate, and their canvas? That canvas was to keep us both out; we, however, were ready." Ziesqe scoffed. "Of course, if ryle were to come into ownership of this city, we would never allow this—vexing—comedy. It is laughable to the point of tragedy. How can I explain?" Ziesqe was silent for a moment. "You surfacers have a strange love for creatures that cannot propagate. Those cream and coal bears—what are they? Never mind, but you must keep them alive out of a bizarre—or misplaced—sense of pity. Some of us feel the same way about this city."

"But here you are, trying to conquer it."

Ziesqe laughed. "Perspective, boy. My heart has been cursed, plucked like a string by your Dead God, centuries before I was spawned. I have a weakness for this place, this living zoo. It's Viqx who would burn it to the ground, in her search for an enemy. Look here," Ziesqe pointed to another wide plaza.

Thousands of creatures filled the area; some on roofs, the mice, in their box seats, and the goblins, leaping from the shoulders of taller creatures. A sign proclaimed the area "Clemson Downs." A woman in a sparkling robe stood against a particularly tall goblin and a brutox with a strange device mounted to his back. The contraption was a conglomeration of brass horns, whose stems terminated at a spot above the creature's head, while their throats pointed towards the audience.

"Give back, they say! What preconceived conceptions and faulty precepts they stumble upon," The woman, wearing something akin to a toga, cried with a wild expression. "If you truly cared to give back, you would melt your excess coins and pave the streets, and thereby raise the value of all money in the city. All these other schemes only benefit this parcel. Of course, you won't melt the money, but do not speak falsely! There is no giving back here, only foolish attempts to line pockets. Wait for the Greek Idealists to complete their audit, and consider a more—considered plan."

"Idle Greeks!" The goblin spluttered. "Waits forever-evers for no plan! The shiney speaks! It says to make new goblin inn for the great calling and gambling of many other such goblins! The shineys put down will return many times over!"

The goblins let loose a raucous huzzah. A group of them, once calmly resting atop a hefty beetle, found themselves swatted by the brute as they cheered riotously.

"Look at this!" A small, tinny voice echoed over the crowd.

Andy hopped off the cart and approached the stage. Now he could see a mouse balancing on the brutox's head. The mouse was speaking into the amplifying contraption, which worked fairly well.

"Look! The goblin plan is as substantive as their courtesy, which is to say, it simply doesn't exist!"

The tall goblin guffawed rudely.

"The builders of Clemson Downs have come into prime information regarding future migration into the city. We believe, very strongly, that a new inn would be the best option for our excess funds!"

"It's the samey as my plan!"

The goblins in the audience booed and hissed, pulling on hair and ears—not always their own—in protest, resulting in several airborne goblins.

"It isn't! Our plan is substantive, built on evidence, whereas your plan is a bold-faced cash grab, based on nothing but idiotic exuberance!"

The woman laughed. "Indeed, the mice are known to increase property value, through their improvements and tinkering. Think now, would that not also cause landowners to raise their rents on your many fine institutions? The mice are famous spendthrifts, whereas the goblins spend money they don't have. It is clear that the taverns, repairmen, vigiles, and all renters would benefit far more from a goblin presence than a builder's."

Is she just up there arguing for the sake of it?

The audience broke out in a chorus of

grumbling.

A moment later, Andy saw green and white strips of cloth raised to the sky. The brutox-mounted mouse shook his head. His brutox did likewise, and as he moved, Andy saw hundreds of silver coins glittering, embedded in his carapace. Andy wondered if the coins belonged to the mouse.

The mice on the board communed for a moment, before one called out, "The goblin tavern shall be constructed! May the God that doesn't exist have mercy on your souls!"

"No editorializing!" A voice yelled.

"The cost is four Sici, split!" the mouse concluded.

The brutox bearing the mouse peeled four coins from one of its many plates and handed two each to the goblin and the woman. The mice near the hanging banners made changes to a large book chained under the sign reading: "Clemson Downs." From where he stood, Andy could read the name of the book: "Local Laws of Clemson Downs." Underneath the title were the words: "Tampering is punishable by popular demand."

Andy returned to the cart.

"Another law added to the books. It looks like the goblins have realized that they need to employ better speakers to make their points for them. The Greek Idealists are ironically cynical and a good pick," Ziesqe mused as the crowd became excited for a new debate concerning the border painting strategy.

"Can anyone get up there and speak?" Andy

asked.

"Certainly, but if the crowd finds against your stance, and you cannot afford the cost—"

"What do they do to you?" Andy asked.

Ziesqe laughed. "You think they have a set punishment?"

Andy blinked.

"Wait—that's worse!"

Ziesqe nodded. "It doesn't happen often. At least it didn't when I was here. You will find small arguments—more practice than anything else—on the side of the road. These are often young people, sharpening their teeth on each other for sparse audiences. That's how all the great speakers got their start."

"But what about the groups? There are banners standing for the Braids and the Red Baggers."

"New groups, built on new ideologies, may spring up and find their tenets nailed to a board— or sewn into civic being—as the Braids see it. They call this form of popular governance the Archatian system. A complete amateur can speak, and win, and win again. People will want that wisdom ratified, so they can live it. An amateur would need a faction name, not to mention a small army of quick-witted followers to keep others at bay, particularly when out for dinner or visiting the Warrens, where the Archatians train and organize."

"So, the arguing never stops?"

"Occasionally it does. If I see a concord, I'll point it out."

They rolled further into town, passing another

melee between border painters, and then another rambunctious stage.

"Take the reins," Ziesqe commanded, when they were halfway down a silent street.

Andy did so, and Ziesqe fiddled with his eyes.

A moment later, Ziesqe looked up and around. His glance rested here and there, and he seemed to be reading. "We'll have to head towards the Warrens and the Panforum. You'll need to drive. If anyone asks about me, just tell them I'm drunk. Under no circumstance can anyone in crimson robes look into my eyes. They will give me away, just as yours would."

"But why take the lenses out?" Andy asked.

"There are signs my people have left. They will lead us to a friendly house. Now, let's get moving."

Andy flicked the reins and they drove further into town. Ziesqe feigned drunkenness, muttering to himself and swaying from side to side, his eyes scanning the surrounding buildings and signs all the while.

Andy learned to keep to the right of the road as they approached the center of town. The traffic grew denser the further they went, until they were finally caught in a jam at a crossroads. Two men, owners of a pair of entangled carts, argued in the middle of the street. Casks of beer off one cart had rolled into the street, blocking traffic, while fallen sacks of milled grain from the other lay split open, spraying puffs of white into the air as people and carts scrambled over them. Many were cheering as the two men argued, even though it wasn't a proper debate on the stages.

A pair of guards in gleaming plate armor broke up the argument and angrily unclogged traffic, stopping just shy of flogging the men to get their carts off to the side of the road. As the traffic cleared, Ziesqe tugged on Andy's sleeve. "Pull over up there. I think we've found something."

Andy only saw a tall building. Five floors high, it loomed over its neighbors—a bakery and fine cobbler—in more than height; it was ornately decorated, with gilded foliate swirls adorning the facade. Guardstox stood watchful at the gate.

"What is it?" Andy asked, moving the cart to the side of the road, despite a few complaining pedestrians.

"It's a counting house," Ziesqe answered, carefully settling his robes. "A merchant, or possibly a group of them, own this establishment. There is a certain marking under the first-floor windows. To you, it would appear as two, four-spoked wheels, overlapping each other."

Andy stared, trying to spot the symbol, but saw nothing.

"My ychorons didn't do a very good job of dressing us." Ziesqe paused. "If you haven't already learned, in this city, they are all ychorites, not ychorons. Do not forget that, or you betray yourself." Ziesqe read the confusion on Andy's face. "The only difference is that ychorites are free, and ychorons serve. There are some speculations about physiological changes—but never mind that. You need to watch our cart while I make some trades."

Ziesqe shuddered. "Merchanting again. It's been many decades, and I still despise it...but I can't look like a fool."

Ziesqe reached into the cart, lifting out a pile of cured leather sheets. He sighed heavily before carrying his burden into the cobbler.

Andy sat in the cart and watched the pace of the city. People rushed by with carts and baskets. Others rolled barrels that sloshed with their contents. His jaw dropped when he saw two extravagantly dressed women riding side-saddle on another pair of monitor lizards. Even the locals bent their necks to watch, but Andy realized that the monitors alone did not warrant the attention.

Those women have teal skin.

Andy watched as they rounded the corner.

"I'll talk to a maiden someday," a young man said longingly.

Andy spied a few circles of aggressive young bravos. They idled about, many polishing the luster on a single silver coin sewn onto their jacket or vest. These budding debaters eyed one another hungrily, though none dared to risk their coins.

A group of brutox marching in circular formation appeared. Something was obscured in the center of their circle. Soon they approached the bakery and parted. Inside, Andy saw a lithe, lightly-plated brutox, of the beetle type, that looked like a female, particularly in the delicate and flowing silk robes. Her robes featured long bars of green and yellow, crisscrossed with white stars. He realized that she was a brutox queen.

Insults and heckling filled the air. "Queens! We don't stand by royalty here! If you think so little of yourselves, go back and serve the ryle!" "This behavior is a stain on our city! You insects are true to your name!"

The queen's guards only reacted when someone went towards the bakery door.

"What? So, we aren't equal? I can't go into the shop while she's in there?" An ychorite yelled at the guards, who simply held him back.

The queen, finished with her business, emerged with a piece of paper, which she hid away in her robes. The group encircled her, and they moved down the street, occasionally colliding with a protester.

As the crowds dispersed, Andy noticed movement above a building. He saw a floating rock tied to a roof across the street. It was familiar, and when he saw the propeller on one side, he realized what it was.

It's a cyclostone, part of a mouse city!

He had the sudden urge to abandon the cart, climb up the building, and hunt for the mice.

I wonder if the mice up there know me. Are they from Sentinel's Watch? I should at least talk to them; they might know where I can find Titus and Taptalles.

Ziesqe was nowhere in sight.

Maybe I'll walk over, just for a moment.

With one leg out of the cart, Andy paused as he caught sight of a goblin picking the pocket of a human. The human had stared too long at a display of shoes in the cobbler's window. Andy sat back down.

Not willing to give up, he waved at an idle ychorite. "Pardon me."

"Pardon you indeed, bare-chested fellow. Dost thou seek to match words?"

Andy raised a brow. "No, I don't think I can afford it."

The ychorite and his friends, a pair of young humans, laughed unkindly. Their other companion, a mute mantis, stared, placid and still.

"Of course! You can't afford the inevitable loss of trying to cross words with the rising star, Mascutio!"

Andy glowered, trying to get a word in, while the ychorite continued praising himself.

"Hey—listen—damn it, shut up!" Andy blustered.

The ychorite finally silenced, though he looked confused.

"I just need to know about the cyclostone over there," Andy said, pointing.

"A bit crude. That isn't how it's done here. You listen politely, and then I listen politely, and then I take it easy on you—though after that little outburst, I might not," Mascutio said, slightly flapped.

Andy rolled his eyes.

One of Mascutio's human companions spoke up. "I think he's talking about the mouse rock."

"Ah," Mascutio replied. "Why didn't you say so?"

Andy regretted opening his mouth.

"A few mouse rocks have started appearing over the city. I wonder how the officials levied their tariffs if they just flew over the walls," Mascutio mused.

The humans laughed. "A good trick, shame they can't haul much cargo on those things. You could make a killing," one said.

"That's not what I'm asking. What I want to know is where they come from," Andy said, struggling to keep his voice calm.

"What do I look like, a bloody-bagged stone diviner?" Mascutio said.

"Look, would you please go to the building the cyclo—mouse rock, is tied to, and ask around for me? I'd do it myself, but I have to keep an eye on the cart."

"Ah ha! Here lies a foundation for a bit of a scrap, don't you say, boys?" Mascutio was suddenly excited. "We argue. If you win, we discover this information for you. If I win—you must—buy us all a drink at the Nook."

"The what?"

"The Nooked et Alcoven. It was the only mouse tavern I could think of. I've always wanted a sip of that blue beer they're famous for," Mascutio replied.

"Fine," Andy said, though he had no money.

"All right!" Mascutio did a little hop and stretch, as if for a race.

"Debate!" One of his companions called out.

Dozens of idlers and busy pedestrians stopped and rushed over to watch. Andy gulped at the sudden attention.

"Very good! Go on then; I'll give you the advantage—only fair. State an opinion," Mascutio projected his voice and put his hands on his hips.

Andy drew a blank, and his face flushed.

Finally inspired, Andy insisted, "You first."

Mascutio scoffed. "The dearest fair-weather friend is less than the most anonymous moral man."

Andy's face twisted in puzzlement. "What? How can you know if an anonymous man has morals?"

The audience laughed at him, but Andy didn't know why.

Mascutio turned toward the crowd, grinning foolishly, before rounding on Andy. "Twice the lesser of two halves is just shy of half whole."

"What?"

The audience laughed again. Many were shaking their heads and grumbling about sportsmanship.

"Take it easy on the boy, he's not from 'round here," a voice called out.

Mascutio raised a hand and called for silence, before his final argument. "Half a breech is just short."

Andy gawked at the absurd statement, and the audience clapped for Mascutio's performance. It seemed conclusive; Andy had been thoroughly thrashed by the foppish ychorite, though he had no idea why.

A few coppers flew to Mascutio. His companions gladly picked them up.

"You need some practice," he said to Andy, grabbing him by the wrist. "But at least you didn't cry. We'll have that drink at the Nook, oh— tomorrow, at evenbell." He reached into the cart and inspected a loom component before taking it. "I don't know what this is, but I expect you want it back, so be there."

Mascutio and his friends recounted the finer points of the triumph as they left. "You'll have a second Sici any day now!" "That was glorious!" His friends fawned, though the mantis was still silent.

And I've learned nothing about the mice...

"Well done," a stern voice said.

Andy turned to see Ropt watching him, his arms folded carelessly across his chest.

"You saw that?"

"I did. At least you didn't cry."

"I didn't even get a chance to argue! What the hell was that?" Andy blustered. "Half a breech is just short?"

Ziesqe laughed so hard, he started coughing. He settled himself and climbed into the cart before speaking, "It's a quip. It's customary for the younger generations to tarry with quips or follies before a proper argument. More experienced debaters don't bother. If they say, 'half a breech is just short,' and you're quick, you say, 'I put on my just short, doubled twice, in the morning, like the rest of you,' or, 'just short is still all naked.'"

Andy climbed up beside Ziesqe and shook his head. "I still don't get it."

"A single short is one quarter a pair of breeches, or pants, as you call them. A doubled short is called a pair of shorts. Doubled again and you have a pair of breeches. It's a foolish joke, but the point is fluidity, grace, and effortless reply. There was no proper debate because you failed the preliminaries."

Andy leaned back in the cart and sighed.

"While you were losing our stock, I learned a fair bit. The ryle here are cloistered, afraid of change, and will not work with me, at least not easily. We must create an opening. For the moment, they are our opposition." Ziesqe pondered as the cart continued down the wide street. "I can make something of this."

They rode to a vast and circular open-air market. Ziesqe had called it the Panforum. Ziesqe asked a few questions of passersby, and eventually they halted outside the clothier corner. A few dozen shops all competed for attention on the lane. Ziesqe hopped out of the cart and approached a woman wearing a toga. She bore several dozen coins, Sici, arrayed in bracelets on her arms. Ziesqe spoke with her assistant and purchased a piece of paper. A few clerks at the shops spotted his transaction, and Andy watched as they spread the word. Almost immediately, several shopkeepers emerged, approached their cart, and examined their wares.

Ziesqe ordered Andy to drive the cart to a small stage at the end of the lane. Once there, Andy carried the stock up to the stage, one piece at a time, and Ziesqe auctioned it off.

"I'll take care of auctioning for a ten-percentage, sir," a lithe goblin, wearing a checked jacket and pants, interrupted.

"And you'll miss bids, accidentally selling my stock too cheap to friends of yours in the audience. Walk away, or I'll have my boy drown you in the fountain," Ziesqe said calmly, unrolling a bolt of fine silk.

The goblin blanched and almost ran.

Andy soon grew tired of carrying everything first to the stage, and then out to the buyers, though he quickly became familiar with the currency. Silver pieces were called ludma, and were distinct from the debating Sici, by being far smaller. The occasional gold piece was called a seculon. He even saw iron bars presented as currency, though Ziesqe scowled at them, and Andy didn't learn their name.

Ziesqe concluded by auctioning off the cart and bruton.

They left the stage as the cart rolled away with its new brutox owner. Before Ziesqe could open his mouth, a woman carrying a large ledger appeared. She wore an ebony ruff and a fine orange tunic fringed in black lace. A pair of similarly garbed mice sat, not on her shoulders, but on each side of her ruff.

"Would you like to change all that coinage for larger denominations?" she asked.

Ziesqe took a heavy breath.

She cracked a slight smile as the mice whispered in her ear. "I see you're tired. I'll only charge two ludma, no need to haggle."

Ziesqe huffed and then nodded. They left the clothier street, and approached a prominent and ornate wooden building, reminding Andy of the gilded counting house from earlier, only larger. The sign outside read: "Mercantile Guild of Degoskirke - Panforum Headquarters."

"Let's count the money there; you can give the Merchant's Guild their cut as well. You don't want to be on the wrong side of the statutes, or you'll be barred from trading in the Panforum."

"Or worse," Ziesqe added. "I didn't realize I had a guild agent in the audience."

She smiled, and the mice stared suspiciously at them.

"People find this to be a friendlier way of enforcing local laws. The Panforum is our parcel, after all. Imagine what might have happened, had you conducted that little auction in any other part of the city."

"What would have happened?" Andy asked.

She gave him a curious look. "First time in the city, lad? Hmm, well, if you had tried to cut the Guild out of this sale, you would have wounded yourself. The red baggers, or worse, had eyes on you and your cargo from the moment you entered the city. If you had tried to start a sale somewhere else, they would have stormed—" Ziesqe interrupted with a wave.

"Storming, rushing hundreds of members into a plaza and forcefully changing the local laws in a flash."

She nodded and continued. "In your hour or so of auctioneering, they would have run the parcel's tax through the ceiling and bled you dry. The guild keeps merchants safe from that kind of legal thievery, here in the Panforum. Look at the peace knot," she said, pointing to a plaza that was unlike the others.

The sign read "Panforum," but only one book hung there, and there was no audience. White ribbons stretched across the plaza and met in the middle of the stage in a knot. A red wax seal held the knot closed and a handful of armored guards kept watchful eyes over the stage.

"That is a concord, the sealed ribbon—or, as she calls it—a peace knot," Ziesqe whispered to Andy.

A guild-mouse interrupted. "You aren't grumbling, are you? I've seen people robbed to the tune of ninety percent in some cases. Enough to run you out of business forever. You should be grateful that we're here for you."

"Indeed, we are," Ziesqe said.

The other mouse chimed in. "Foreign merchants have a tendency to be afraid of the guild, but we are your friends. If you join, we can cut your rate down from twenty, to fifteen percent."

Ziesqe rolled his eyes, and whispered to Andy, "This is why I hated being a merchant." Then, loudly to the guildsfolk, "Yes, that's why I came straight to the Panforum. Give me a moment with the lad, before I join you inside."

The woman smiled. "Of course, I'll have a table set up for us, and some tea, or coffee, if you prefer."

The guildsfolk went inside, though a few armed brutox, also in guild-livery, kept a respectful distance. Ziesqe led Andy around the side of the busy building. "I need to get those lenses out of your eyes—"

"But—"

"Listen, just keep your eyes down and no one

will notice, at least not until you want them to. If you see crimson robes, turn the other way." Ziesqe glanced around before handing Andy a small bag of coins. "Spend it in the pursuit of our ultimate goal."

"But why?"

Ziesqe shook his head. "You need to climb Panobscura Talionis," he said, before pausing for a moment. "I believe they call it the Guilt now. Ask for directions. Or follow signs."

Andy stood in numb silence.

"Climb the pillar. There are still pieces of Argument sitting in plain sight, though they are guarded. Ignore those, for they are paltry, and find a way to the Cogito, the largest of them all. You must take it. The Exegesuits will recognize your eyes, and if they suspect what you are doing, they will not hesitate to capture or kill you."

"This is what Zava asked me to do. You aren't going to ask me to wear the Casque?"

Ziesqe shook his head. "No. I foresaw the need for this action. What I did not foresee was your reasonable attitude."

Andy wondered if he hadn't made a mistake.

"What do I do? Once I take the Argument, I mean?"

Ziesqe scoffed. "Stay alive."

Andy's eyes widened.

"Escape the Exegesuit guards, and don't be bashful about using the Argument. You might want to keep an eye out for your holy symbols, which is why I am removing your lenses. Those symbols will have gone unnoticed, since your eyes were shielded, but once unmasked, you might see something."

That wasn't reassuring.

"How? How are we going to do this? It's impossible. Even if I find a piece of Argument, how can we take the city peacefully?"

Ziesqe blinked. "Your eyes see an insurmountable task." Ziesqe paused, his face thoughtful. "My old master told me that true intelligence—its ability to see into the future, is as much a hindrance as it is an enabler. There are thousands of ryle bearing greater intelligence and capacity than mine, but where are they?"

Andy scowled, uncertain of the answer.

"They are hampered by the same foresight that has undercut you. You see the impossible mountain, where a simpler man only sees his foot taking a single step. In this way a thousand idiots will die scaling the mountain, all by accident, while the great intellect will sit at the base, decrying the task."

Captivated, Andy listened.

"Only two types of people can scale the mountain. One: the thousandth idiot, who just by sheer accident, failed to fail. Or, two: that rarest of all types, the genius, who sees what is great in the idiot, and alloys it with the foresight of intellect. Do not fear the thousand steps; each one is simple to you. Do not let time flex and unfurl, like a dragon, to kill your resolve. Strike it down with a thousand fearless steps."

Andy was silent.

"I will wait for an hour, every day at noon, by this building. Return to me, and we will take the next step."

Ziesqe took Andy by the shoulders and pointed him towards the pillar called the Guilt.

"There is the first step. You will know what to do."

Chapter 2: The Hunt

Chimerax stared deeply into the sink hole. The thick jungle sat just back from the fissure, allowing intermittent light to shine down from above. He considered the fuzzy apes dogging him from the branches.

My ryle is down there.

He tasted the air and found the faintest hint of precursor. He had followed it for what felt like days, with the apes following and occasionally attacking.

Here I find a sunken limestone cavern. It could be quite deep. But my hairy pursuers—are they mindful enough to collapse the entrance?

Chimerax grinned, remembering his vast store of Counter and the godlike memory of one third of his persona.

I'd hate to waste Counter blowing my way out from under ground. But, would it be a bigger waste to kill them all right now? The noise might alert my ryle, provided he's still alive down there.

Chimerax morphed into his bipedal form and walked the distance to the sink hole. The apes moved softly from tree to tree, not far behind.

Chimerax relaxed his body and floated. He flexed two nerves in his hand and summoned light. Floating down into the cavern he saw no immediate trace of the ryle. He looked up at the breach, and watched the silhouettes of the apes circle the hole. He waited for the sound of a crash but heard none.

He descended to the bottom, which was lined with thick moss and livid with neon-colored frogs, who hopped away from the surprising new light source. Chimerax cast his eyes across the space, hunting for some detail.

There.

A sheet of moss atop a boulder had been ripped apart. Something had climbed there.

He moved closer and saw more disturbed or crushed plant material.

He's here.

Chimerax took a deep breath and worked through the many scents in the cave.

There's the precursor again, and—stale sweat.

He flew towards the damage, following the trail, which led down a side cavern.

Maybe it's time for the Sight.

Chimerax moved the Counter from his hand to his eyes, which now shone purple in the dark.

No need for light.

The cave all around took on the otherworldly wireframes of letters and numbers. Lights pulsed here and there as creatures moved in the darkness. He saw a swirl in the air. It told him that a draft was coming from the right.

No, not a draft.

He floated and followed the faint swirls.

Tucked away between two boulders in the dark lay the bulbous and destroyed body of a once powerful ryle.

The body still breathed, if slowly, perhaps in a comatose state.

Chimerax saw the purple cord that ran through the ryle.

He is drained of Counter, yet polluted with unrefined precursor. It's keeping him alive, but he is barely cognizant. If he dies, the corruption will take his body and turn him into an abomination, like Xyth.

"Ryle," Chimerax spoke in the darkness.

The ryle shuddered.

"I spoke to your cobalt ravager. Even in death, the creature was loyal."

"Death dream, leave me in peace."

"What is your name?"

The ryle coughed up a ragged laugh. "I speak to the shade of death, very well. I was once, Puktifa, a nothing ryle from a part of the scape that no longer exists. But, by the end, I was a General."

Chimerax tried not to laugh. "General of what?"

Puktifa scoffed. "I built something few ryle would attempt, for fear of shame. I was a mercenary warlord. I lent my blade in dozens of campaigns before I finally settled a captured fortress when my employer couldn't pay. My warriors do not call me lord and do not dress me in the morning. They are proud, like nothing you can imagine. I have earned the title."

"Well, General. Who would you fear most?"

Puktifa's eyes shot open. He heaved in a breath and tried to pull himself up against a boulder.

"Don't waste your energy. The precursor has almost turned you into a mindless husk."

"Did Ziesqe send you?"

Chimerax was silent.

"The bastard left us for dead—who are you? What is this place?"

He's feverish, barely alive.

Chimerax gave the General a quick slap, but he continued to mutter and repeat the same questions.

Nothing for it.

Chimerax laid a hand on Puktifa and forced the taint out of his body, while gifting him a trace of pure Counter.

The bulbous lumps on his body receded as a stream of black ink ran from the corner of his mouth.

"General."

Puktifa coughed up more of the ink and slapped himself a few times to clear his head.

"I've been talking—who's there?"

"The Maelstrom has come for you, General."

Puktifa reached for a weapon.

"Please, don't make me kill you, just to bring you back to life. It will only waste time."

"Fine. I knew this day would come. Any ryle can only climb so high before they are called. I've been afraid, till now."

Chimerax laughed. "You presume—many things. Let's start with your plan. If it matches what I've learned, I'll consider pulling your bloated corpse out of this hole."

Puktifa grimaced in the dark.

"You said it yourself, they left you to die. There is no treason in speaking."

Puktifa sighed. "Ziesqe was the mastermind. The rest of us simply supplied our forces and capitol. The plan was originally a simple matter of applying pressure, in the form of the next Caspian, onto Xyth. We hoped that he would use his clout with the Maelstrom to have us overlooked for ascension to act as wardens for the boy. We also would have accepted the Xyth treatment."

"Xyth treatment?" Chimerax scoffed. "Xyth was an abort-ascend. That isn't special treatment; he failed to endure the transcendence. His punishment was to rule, forever, in the scape."

"It doesn't sound like punishment to all of us."

"I've looked into it, and it would seem that you had Caspian after all. How did that turn out?"

Puktifa laughed, painfully. "He got loose. We thought he was just a boy, that even the Voice of the Dead God would be weak in such a young body. Boqreq knew though, he knew the plan would fail. He wanted to present the boy directly to the Maelstrom, but the rest of us were too fearful to enter the City."

"Tell me about your compatriots," Chimerax said.

Puktifa described the principal ryle of their organization. He mentioned Kal, Veloiz, Viqx, Boqreq, and Ziesqe, and what each brought to the table.

"Ziesqe was the leader," Chimerax mused.

"In a sense. He brought us together, even though Boqreq was most senior in age."

"Resourceful oligarchy. A shame you played with fire. Do you want to know the sad truth, General?"

Puktifa bowed his head, a shame filled curl to his tentacles.

He already suspects.

"The sad truth is that only two of your six were called to ascend. You were not one of them."

Puktifa was silent.

"Everything you built is gone. Your warriors, who never dressed you in the morning, your magnificent ravagers, all ending in a fate worse than death."

"Go on then! Take me, or kill me!" Puktifa snapped.

Chimerax chuckled. "I'm giving you a chance. A way to start again. All you have to do is tell me where your old compatriots are now. What was the backup plan? All generals plan for failure, plan a retreat. Have you done any less?"

"It was a stupid alternative as well, and I don't know if any of them survived Hyadoth. I might send you on a pointless chase."

"They escaped the city, by ravager."

Even though the cave was pitch black, Chimerax's Sight discerned the questioning look on the General's face.

"An eyewitness account assures me."

Puktifa nodded, a look of admiration about his eyes. "Ah, the Maelstrom has its ways, unknown to mere spawn. The plan, in case of failure, was to retreat to Degoskirke, first for safety, and then to attempt capturing the city."

"Ludicrous."

"Indeed, it seems that way, but he has several options available for this plan. I would have opposed them all at the outset, as would Boqreq and Veloiz.

Kal would have sided with Ziesqe, who impressed her so with his ambition. Viqx, of course, favored war in the first place. If they all survived, save my vote, they would likely have gone to Degoskirke. Ziesqe's first plan, before we agreed to go to Xyth, was to use the boy, in any of various possible ways, to help subvert and conquer the city."

"I see. Could your combined forces have taken the free city?"

"Absolutely not."

Chimerax laughed. "Why not?"

"I toured the city once, years ago and in disguise, but even then, I kept an eye on the local soldiery, their walls, and on the hotly contested sewers. Despite their apparent division, they would unite to fend off any ryle incursion. But more than that, the rogue brutox queens would be the most dangerous deterrent to any attack. They are the city's true insurance."

Chimerax considered this. "I would agree. Even if all the ryle in Pansubprimus pooled their strength, it would still not be a certainty. What made Ziesqe so brave? You wouldn't call him stupid, would you?"

Puktifa scoffed. "Not that one. He has vision, and two primary plans. Both are largely the same, save one detail: who is in command of the boy's body. If following the safer plan, he would use the boy to divide the secular city from the elements that still keep secret faith with the false-Argument. He planned to personally save Degoskirke from the boy, who would be motivated to cooperate and surrender at the opportune time. Then, before an attack, he would use local humans or goblins, or any mercenary that wasn't a brutox, to round up the queens and kill them. If these coups were achieved, he would dash into the confused city and give them an apparent peace. This is the safer plan, less approved by Ziesqe, as it lacks the security of the other."

"It's a shame; if he had succeeded without destroying Hyadoth, as putrid of a place as it was, he would have been rewarded by the Maelstrom."

"Wait until you hear the dangerous alternative," Puktifa whispered.

Chimerax was still and expectant.

"If he runs out of options, or suspects that you are coming, he might repeat Hyadoth. If the boy doesn't cooperate, or he believes that he has sufficient leverage, he will unleash the Usurper."

"You think he would have learned his lesson," Chimerax said, growing disgusted at what he was hearing.

"Ziesqe is afraid, but sure of his genius. He sees utility in the dangerous alternative. He will hide before summoning Caspian, hoping the Usurper will ravage Degoskirke, before turning on the City in the Sea, which rests not far. This will distract the Maelstrom from his treachery. He will rise from hiding, and using similar schemes, take the city. His reasoning: a weakened Maelstrom will more likely forget his failure in Hyadoth and allow him peace, governing a newly conquered Degoskirke. With this time, Ziesqe will contrive another crisis that only his continued existence can solve."

Chimerax considered this plan doubtful. "These are ill words," Chimerax said. "Is there any evidence to verify what you have told me?"

"We are in Euboia now, if my memory serves. Ziesqe's famous palace, Zentule, is not far. If he intended on attacking Degoskirke, there would be activity in his holdings. His forces would likely muster from Zentule."

"One last detail, General. The boy; you haven't told me much about him. Besides being weak or helpless, what were the signs? How did Caspian manifest?"

"The Casque. An old possession of a long dead Caspian caused his early manifestation. But we had signs before. We spoke to a being claiming to be Caspian, while the boy slept. These conversations are what convinced myself and the others. This Caspian wasn't fully realized and it was more like talking to a broken ego. Ziesqe tried to make an arrangement with Caspian through the sleeping boy."

Chimerax heard this and stood in disbelief. His body trembled with outrage. Purple flame burst out in patches on the ground and on the cave walls. The air seemed to roil and pulse.

Puktifa heard the muscles flexing, saw the flames, and stood as tall as he could, never looking away, ready to die.

After a moment, the flames calmed. "A ryle attempted to bargain with the Voice of the Dead God?" Chimerax asked.

"Hearing the voice of the Usurper enflamed Ziesqe's ambition. He felt himself raised, and among the heroes of legend. He believes he can control Caspian—reason and bargain with him even."

"Releasing him was crime enough! What cowardice drives ryle to such unimaginable treason? Caspian cannot be controlled! He is our enemy! His every thought, a poison! His every action, turned to the destruction of your kind." Chimerax paused, and took a heavy breath before continuing, "Part of me knew Xyth, we fought together once, and now he is broken beyond reason and nothing will end his suffering. The land surrounding that place will be blighted for a hundred generations. The creatures that crawl out of that festering sink will infest Euboia until the next cataclysm, and you, General, had a hand in it. You stood by while a ryle consorted with the Usurper."

Puktifa stood ready.

Damn him. I admire his fearlessness. He would have ascended easily. Now he must be broken.

Chimerax rested a hand on Puktifa's face. The General flinched, but did not cower.

"You would do well to scream." Chimerax nearly liquefied him, but then paused.

They stood in tense silence.

Maybe something different for one so brave.

Chimerax felt that obscure and ancient third of his being, the dragon, working unknown forms of holy creation. Where his skin touched the General's face, blazing purple script appeared and waved and smoldered like crisping paper.

The General changed. His body thinned and he sprouted hair from his pallid scalp. His tentacles receded, and his face grew a nose. Moments later, the change was complete.

A young man stood there.

The human felt his face.

"What? No! No, this is too much!" Puktifa slammed his fists against Chimerax and was startled at the pain, but Chimerax only watched the man's face. "Make me right again or kill me!"

"I promise you a chance to regain some of what you have lost. You will never be called to ascend. This is a gift, young human."

Puktifa fell to his knees.

"You have all your old talent and knowledge, but you will never wield the Counter, no, nor the false-Argument, yet you might regain some of that lost glory. Though I would be careful if I were you. There is a horde of apes outside this hole. They might take you as one of their own, or possibly tear you to pieces, but, if you make it past them, who knows what awaits?"

Puktifa clawed at his face and pulled at the alien hair, shaking his head in horror.

A punishment fit for the ryle and for the crime. It is up to him how to see it. Is he cursed or blessed? Even I do not know.

Chimerax floated up and out of the cave, the groaning cries of Puktifa echoing less and less as he ascended.

Once out of the hole, Chimerax reached out and

caught an ape by the throat. The thing had tried to leap at him with a sharpened rock.

Dozens of others screamed in outrage.

Chimerax snapped a finger and the air became heavy. All sound dulled and deadened until there was silence. The other apes were terrified. They turned and escaped into the jungle.

"There is a man down there, go help him."

Chimerax released the quivering ape and ascended higher. When he was finally above the trees he looked into the distance.

Zentule isn't so far. Let's have a look there, before Degoskirke.

Chapter 3: Ascending

Andy felt self-conscious without the contact lenses. He tried to keep his eyes glued to the floor, but a moment later he bumped into a brutox, who grunted and pushed by. He found himself in another raucous plaza. Luckily, all the attention was on the speaker.

Andy kept to the edges of the crowd and tried to slip by. He had nearly pushed through before a party of goblins were suddenly underfoot.

"Ey! Watch it tall'un!" one shrieked at him.

Andy cringed. He had stepped on the goblin's foot.

"Sorry!" he said, trying to get away. He locked eyes with a pair of the surprised goblins and felt suddenly mortified that they knew what he was.

Andy backed away and felt the imagined hands of guards grasping him by the shoulder. He had seen a patrol a few minutes prior. Again, the guards wore polished plate armor and bore halberds and massive, wavy swords. They were large men, made taller with plumage in their helms. All this, mixed with their considerable armament, lent them an air of intimidation to which he was unaccustomed.

Despite his fear, no shouts or calls rang out. Minutes later, he crossed the street to avoid another patrol, which comprised a handful of armored guardsmen flanking a woman in red robes. The woman reminded him of the people he had seen at the gates.

He chanced a quick look at the guards as they passed and noticed that a pair bore ornate long guns.

Guns? Metal tubes on wooden stocks can only be one thing, but they look nothing like any gun I've ever seen.

Andy stopped at a crossroads to get his bearings. The roads in this part of the city were generally built over a grid, but fallen structures and sudden walls or elevation changes made for more turns and guesses than he expected. Andy waited until the street was almost empty before looking up. He scanned the horizon for the impossibly huge pillar. It was nowhere in sight.

How did I lose something that huge? It's probably behind one of these buildings.

"Oh, wow," a female voice said, from over his right shoulder.

Andy nearly froze.

A pair of younger women had just left a shop, not ten paces away, and they were both gawking at him.

Why did he take my lenses out? He should have just shown me how to do it myself!

"I haven't seen a robe cut like that since my brother was accepted into the Apuiline, oh, five years ago, I think."

"Don't gawk, it's rude, and he's so young," the other girl whispered. "He's poor, probably from the Wreck, or beyond. Let's not ruin his first trip to the city."

Andy rolled his eyes at the issue of clothes again. He turned towards the young women. "Excuse me, could you show me where I could get something new to wear—nothing too expensive."

The women shared a laugh. Andy looked behind them and saw why.

They just came out of a clothier's shop.

"Come on then. I don't have anywhere to be," said the first woman, a brunette with a pointed face.

Her friend, a dark-haired woman with piercing blue eyes and startlingly red lips reached out and grabbed him by the arm. "We'll have you breaking hearts in a bell's breadth."

Bell's breadth? An hour maybe?

Andy almost resisted, but their smiling faces disarmed him completely.

"Let's dress him as a guildsman, I love their collars, and the tunics."

They entered the clothier's shop. A large woman wearing a simple, if well-made, blue dress looked up from her work in surprise. "Don't tell me you've burst a seam, Shel, you've just left a moment ago!" She spotted Andy. "And who's this? Pull him out of the sea, did you? I suppose you took that robe off a dead man in a shipwreck?"

Shel laughed, "He isn't a mer, Gilda. He's just a scamp."

"I'm—" Andy opened his mouth, but Shel instantly had a finger against his lips.

"Don't tell us, you little fool," she said, sounding cruel, but with a smile on her face.

"Well, what'll it be, lad? A few outfits? Something for labor in the city? I know old Madj back at the theater might could use a lad with your looks. Why don't I set you up in something dashing?" She stood up and turned toward the shelves, before a serious look came across her face. "And how would we be paying for any of this? Shel, Belle, have you taken up charity?"

Before the women could speak, Andy held up the small bag of coins.

Well, I can't go around looking like an idiot, and these women seem like good people. I'll be dressed properly, and I might learn something. This is money spent in pursuit of our goal.

They all stared at the little bag.

"I don't take copper dags here, my dear," Gilda said, coming over to inspect the bag.

Andy spilled the contents out onto the counter. The women gasped. The coins were all gold and silver.

"My lord!" Gilda sputtered.

"Is it a lot?" Andy asked.

"Who did you kill?" Belle replied.

Shel laughed over Andy's sputtering denial. "What a man of mystery." She played with his hair for a moment. "I've got it! You've fallen in love with a maiden of the Sunken Temple. You saw her going to pray in the waste, where you grow bloody heart-root with your destitute parents. Now, you've run away with four generations worth of family savings to make a new life, debating in the city, all the while you hope to see her lovely face again."

Gilda cracked a sarcastic smile, while Belle shook her head and spoke, "But, he can't have taken his family's money. They have to die in a vicious brutox raid, or a freak skybreak, anything terrible really, otherwise he's just a thieving traitor."

"Oh! But that's so awful. This way he can redeem himself by debating across the city and earning enough Sici to buy the family estate back from the evil ryle lord, who then betrays him anyway, and he's stabbed in the back, but then he's tended in a secluded grove by his love—"

"Is she always like this?" Andy asked Belle.

"She's tying the knot soon, and I don't think it's everything that she hoped for," Gilda said, butting in.

"It is everything I hoped for! It's only—well, I miss the romance."

Gilda raised a brow and spoke up, "Right. That aside, we still need to know what the young hero of mystery needs his new clothes for. I could see if Madj would take you on as an apprentice for some of this coin. It's a good career, and you'd have idiots like these fawning in less than a year."

The women huffed, but didn't argue.

Andy felt surprisingly disarmed by all the women. He almost agreed, but resisted. "Maybe I'll be an actor one day; I have something to do first." The women shared wide eyed glances, but Andy continued before they could start up again, "I just need the clothes to blend in with a crowd. I need to look normal," Andy said.

Gilda rolled her eyes, "Aye boy, fair enough, but what's your trade? Are you a mason, a chef, a merchant?"

"Oh," Andy said, before he realized that he wasn't sure what he was. Instead of pondering overlong, he simply said the first thing that came to mind. "I'm a criminal, or I will be at least."

The room went silent.

Andy cringed; he meant it as a joke.

Andy felt a hand turn him around to face all three of the women. It was Gilda, she and Belle stared at him. Shel stepped back, confused, at the sudden change in tone.

"What is it?" Shel asked, staring at Andy in turn. "Oh, he's a bit naked. Gilda, be a dear and fetch a pair of nightroots; I'm behind myself."

Gilda stared for a moment longer before rushing off, but Belle just stood there, her mouth slowly slackening.

"What on earth is wrong, Belle?"

"Boy," Gilda said, rushing forward with a small purple carrot. "Eat this, now."

Andy stepped away from them. "What is that?"

"What is that?" Belle repeated, with an almost angry look of disbelief plastered onto her face. "Where are you from?"

Gilda tried to offer Andy the carrot again. "It's for your eyes; you've gone a bit naked. Or do your people go like that out in the blight?"

"Of course they don't; the ryle hunt them down! Everyone knows that. How did he get past the Exegesuits like this?" Belle asked.

"Oh, you two are making such a fuss, he's simply forgotten to take one! It's his first time in the city."

Gilda held up the carrot.

Andy shook his head.

"It's for your eyes, boy, it'll put them back to

normal. You can't go walking around the city like that. We're a bit more understanding, near the Guilt, but anywhere else—"

"It'll change my eyes? I won't be able to see?" Andy asked.

That choice of words made the women step back.

Gilda nodded.

"I can't do that right now," Andy replied. "About the clothes," he prodded slightly.

The women were silent.

Shel seemed annoyed. "What's wrong with you two? He's just a stupid boy!"

Belle slapped her. "He's the damned Voice, you idiot!"

Gilda muttered something to herself, before looking up and speaking, "Yes, the right clothes, I don't have the armor, but I can pull everything else together."

"He isn't the Voice," Shel insisted, raising a hand in retaliation.

Belle pushed the hand aside and leveled on Andy, seriously. "How did you enter the city?" she asked.

"I came in through the Eighth Gate," Andy said, suddenly feeling nervous.

Belle shivered, her body poised to flee the shop.

"Thousands of people come in through the Eighth, don't be such a child, Belle," Shel said, lowering her hand, though a tinge of doubt rang through her voice.

The two younger women shared a long look

while Gilda rushed around her shop looking for something.

"How are you such a romantic about everything else, but so stupid about this?" Belle asked.

Shel was silent.

"Thieving I, through the Eighth Gate, fly!" Belle spoke, as if from memory.

"To Panobscura Ta-a-lionis!" Gilda sang as she started work on a familiar-looking cape.

"To hearth and Guilt, I, naked, fly!"

"Sisters, bare up my mantle, and I'll call the bla-a-ade!"

"With God's word by my side!"

"Bearing violet eyes, I-I-I will never die!"

Shel sang with the others, though she was still unconvinced. She grabbed Andy and searched him. Andy didn't resist. "So he refused to cover up, that doesn't mean—" she pulled out his pockets. "Look, no Argument. It's not him."

"Also, no Sici, either," Belle countered.

She means the coins the debaters trade and wear. They call those Sici.

"What are you doing, boy? After we get you dressed, what are you doing?" Shel asked.

"I'm going up the pillar—"

"Which one?" Belle demanded.

Andy shied away. "The Guilt."

"And what are you doing there?" Shel asked slowly.

Gilda looked up from her work, and the women stared in fear and expectation.

Andy sighed, not sure what to say. *I'm getting sick*

of this whole Voice of God thing.

You'd best get used to it.

Andy froze in shock.

What? What the hell was that?

The women saw his expression.

Andy bolted for the door, but Shel reached out and grabbed him.

"Don't go yet! If you're—well, you need to be clothed."

Andy shook with fear, his eyes looked for the source of the voice, but there were only the three women.

They didn't hear it. If I even ask, it might upset them more. I need to get dressed and get out of here.

Gilda appeared with the clothes and placed them on the counter. Andy laid a hand on the familiar pile.

I've worn this before. Pythia—she put these clothes on me. Only, she put armor over them too. It's the same outfit, only made by a different hand.

"This cape doesn't deliberately snag on things, does it?"

Gilda shook her head.

"How much?"

"Call it gratis," Gilda said. "Ladies, we have to dress him."

Andy sighed as they walked him to the changing area.

Under other circumstances he would have been embarrassed, but Andy felt an urge to rush.

How can I rush? I have no idea what I'm doing. It would be like rushing into traffic, and won't these clothes make me stand out?

Andy gritted his teeth as they tied the cloak over his shoulders. He recalled Pythia putting the cloak on him. A sudden rage boiled over. He shook and nearly ripped the clothes off.

"Is this a common outfit?" Andy asked, a fragile edge in his voice

The women looked at him in the mirror. They were suddenly afraid.

"Of course it isn't," Gilda answered, unsure.

"Didn't I ask for something to help me blend in?"

Silence.

"I'm not the Voice of God!"

Gilda and Shel ran from the changing room.

"Is this a test?" Belle asked.

Everywhere I turn, I feel like something is waiting for me. Something is putting these clothes on me, and doing this to me. I can't go home, and I can't leave! I must walk out of this store wearing this damn outfit again!

Andy felt his hand hurt at how tightly he was grasping the collar of the cloak. He released and heard the fabric flex.

He looked up into Belle's face and saw fear.

Andy scoffed. *These three women are running and cowering when a few minutes ago they were laughing at me.*

Andy chuckled, but felt a tear threaten to well up. He brushed it away and left the changing room. He found his money bag and left a gold coin for Gilda, hoping she wouldn't take it as an insult.

He looked around, but didn't see her anywhere. He wanted to apologize, but no one was there.

Andy left the store and turned left up the street. His feet moved almost by instinct. He felt his breath deepen, and a smile snaked its way onto his face.

He looked up at the windows and saw faces looking down on him. He heard dozens of whispering voices as he passed. People cleared the street as he came. He saw a group of guards distracted by a sudden fistfight, right as he walked by.

He made another turn before looking up at the pillar.

Here it is!

He craned his neck to take in the full dimension of the Guilt. The massive, craggy column of natural stone looked encased in a polished white finish. Twined grapevines and the bent wings of songbirds rose in deep-cut relief on the alabaster surface. Andy felt that a story, never seen by the people within, was carved all the way up the edifice.

A dozen guards stood on the road that led to the wide snaking path which traveled up the Guilt. Andy saw that the base of the column had been ringed with a ramshackle wall, to separate it from the rest of the city. This was the only way onto and off the column.

This is the way in, but it's watched. How am I supposed to get by? They'll spot me for sure.

Andy looked over at the guards. He spotted more ornate guns.

A moment later he heard a loud hiss.

"Watch out!" a guard yelled, pushing one of his fellows to the ground.

A gun fired, and then another, and finally a few more. Andy saw one go off. The strange mechanism spun sharply, before sparking and firing.

People panicked and raced in and out of the Guilt.

Andy looked down and saw his right hand was lifted. His fingers had bent in a strange way.

What?

He shivered, lowering his arm.

Ignoring the feeling of violation, he raced past the guards, who were busy inspecting their weapons and yelling at each other about misfires.

Once past, Andy turned up the curving path. Guards stationed inside the Guilt nearly knocked him over as they ran towards the sounds of firing. Andy ignored them and kept on.

Minutes later, with the excitement died down, his thoughts drifted back to what he had seen his hand doing. The gesture reminded him of Pythia trying to fold the Juncture. She had raised her hands and held them like that.

Andy was startled by a score of young, smiling faces.

"This way," said a small boy.

They seemed insistent that he follow them, but Andy ignored them and pushed through.

I don't need any more weird help, or scared people, or stupid songs.

Andy remembered the Casque. He remembered being crushed down into the smallest corner of his mind as another being piloted. He recalled seeing out of his own eyes, but also being unable to direct them. Andy shivered again and nearly slapped himself as he felt the urge to break down and cry. He paused for a moment and looked out over the city. He was hundreds of feet up.

He realized that his legs were throbbing. He felt his thigh muscles and realized that they were as stiff as rocks.

How long have I been climbing?

Andy had been leaning over the rail on the right-hand side of the path. On the inside of the path, was the body of the guilt. Occasional alleys and paths led from the corkscrew path into the body of the pillar, and whatever was inside. He saw a few young faces staring at him from a window. None of their expressions were alike.

Andy ignored them and continued on.

Not certain where to turn, he tried to recall Ziesqe's exact words. His thoughts were a blur and he knew that he should feel lost and scared, but despite that, he felt something he could only describe as, powerful.

As his legs pumped up the steepening path, he thought back to Letty, the Caspians, and his mouse friends.

I wonder what they're up to. Hopefully I'll see Titus and Taptalles again. They're supposed to be in the city. The others though—I might never see any of them again, or my parents.

Andy's thoughts drifted back to all the faces he had seen. He remembered Thrag, and his mind lingered on memory of the man.

Andy stumbled.

His hands reached out, but he still smacked his head into the stony path. He tried to pull himself up, but found that his legs refused to hold any weight. Andy felt his thighs. They were shaking.

He pulled himself to the rail and looked out over the city.

Oh, God.

He slowly pushed away from the edge. He was far higher than he had expected.

My legs are dying, but I barely feel it.

Andy felt the urge to cry again. He knew people were looking. He sat against the rail and manually lifted his knees, so he could hide his face behind them.

A few small tears fell.

I should be in school. I should be afraid. I'm not right anymore—

He kept his eyes closed for as long as he could.

Am I going to die? Should I be dead already? Maybe this is hell. Climbing a tower, and not realizing it, not seeing more than a few seconds, when you have been climbing forever. Is this hell?

Andy felt a tap on his shoulder. He cleared his throat and wiped his eyes before looking up.

"For you." A small girl held out an apple for him. "Since you made it."

A few other children stood nearby. They seemed cautious, but carried food and water-skins.

Andy accepted the apple. He took a large crisp bite, and nearly wept all over again. It was delicious. The speed with which he ate calmed the children.

"Come on, sit with me for a minute," Andy said,

reaching out for a water-skin.

The children looked back and forth between one another before they sat with him.

"What's in this?" Andy asked, as he downed the whole water-skin.

"That was wine," a shy girl mumbled.

Andy laughed like an idiot before taking a second apple.

"I almost don't believe you, little girl. The last time I had alcohol, it tasted disgusting."

"This wine's for you," she said, sheepishly. "It would kill anyone else."

Andy tensed and looked down at the apple he had nearly finished. The apple looked normal. It had tasted far better than any he remembered.

He recalled being in the Juncture, after having food and drink that Pythia had given him; he had felt the same then.

His body tingled with elation. His muscles buzzed with the need to work. He felt a grin trying to break out onto his face, but he knew that something more had happened.

"What do you mean, little girl? Why would this wine kill anyone else?"

"It's moon wine—any who drink it, die," she said, plainly. "You have made proof."

Andy took a deep breath and felt nothing at this news of poisoning. He saw the children, saw silver cloth bracelets tied to their arms, and felt this must mean something. He saw a score of nervous parents peeking out onto the curving pathway.

The Acceptance. This pathway up the Guilt is the

Acceptance.

The parents watched from the windows of a closed temple. He saw boards nailed over the pediment, but someone had painted over these boards.

The Caesura.

Andy stood. The children did likewise, they seemed expectant, and motioned him towards the temple. The heavy doors opened, and he stepped inside.

The chamber was long, narrow and poorly lit by lamp light. Banks of seats ran down the left and right sides of the chamber. At the far end stood a tall podium overlooking a font.

A piece of Argument! But it's so tiny.

Andy saw the floating orb and nearly ran towards it.

The parents and children walked with him to the orb. Looking beyond the podium, Andy saw that the rear of the chamber was heavily damaged. The walls had been mostly demolished, and a debris strewn path led to another room beyond.

Andy reached out and grasped the Argument, which, to his dismay, was much smaller than his original had been. He wondered if it would work.

He tightened his grasp on the pea-sized marble. A weak glow appeared.

He tightened further, and the blade flickered momentarily into existence. He had an urge to twist his hand and flex his fingers. As he did so, the flickering blade shortened into more of a dagger, and solidified.

"The blood is strong," a few voices whispered at the display.

Andy cringed and released his grip, before turning to leave.

The people, surprised by this, tried to direct him further into the chamber.

"Why? I have what I need."

He tried to evade them, but suddenly felt nervous. Andy wasn't sure what to do; every step he took towards the exit made him feel worse.

"Maybe I'll just take a look."

Andy went with them to the damaged wall. He was surprised when they would only go so far. He produced a glow with the Argument.

There was a creature lying on the floor in the chamber beyond. He nearly jumped at the sight before realizing it was dead.

What the hell is going on here?

The creature had the torso of a woman and the body of a lion. She had wings, which splayed out helplessly on the floor. Her hair fell across her face, and Andy saw she was motionless. He was most surprised by her blood, if it was blood. A trail of flickering letters lay pooled around her body. Occasionally, a symbol or letter would crisp off the pool and float away, smoldering as it went.

Andy shook his head.

He felt a sting of pain when he leaned in closer and saw a tattoo running up her right arm. The tattoo looked like a few paragraphs of text written in different languages.

Andy stepped past her body and saw, on the far

wall, a door surrounded by fine clockwork gears. The door was flame-scorched and covered in scratches. Andy saw small plaques above each gear. He noticed that they were also scorched. He walked around the room, inspecting the gears.

Let's just take a second, before I use the Silversight.

Andy spotted a shining letter on one of the less damaged plaques. He rubbed the plaque clean and sighed as the char wiped away. There sat the letter T.

Andy went around the room, cleaning the letters where he could. He found Latin and Greek letters, as well as a few unfamiliar symbols. The whole contrivance struck him as another puzzle.

Andy held the marble up to his eye and wasn't surprised when it disappeared and the Silversight remained.

He walked over to the door. The sight showed that it was held in place by hundreds of locked bolts. He looked closer and saw silver threads running through the mechanism in ways he couldn't understand, but he realized that not all the locks were engaged, only a dozen or so kept the door sealed. In his attempts to open the door, he made a few mistakes, and realized that when the wrong gear was turned, several bolts locked, while others unlocked.

I need to take my time. Every time I mess up, the locks reset.

Andy located the correct levers as he had in the ossuary. He was careful around the woman-creature's body. It struck him that she was something out of mythology. Andy felt a lump in his throat as he stepped past her again. He wondered how she died.

A few minutes later, Andy had flicked the last lever. The door popped. He paused for a moment and tried to make sense of the letters that corresponded to the gears.

They make no message at all. Most aren't even English characters.

He felt the urge to dismiss it as another trick, like the one he experienced outside the Juncture.

If there was a greater test, why would the door open for me?

Andy scowled, staring at the gears, before finally giving up and going for the door. He found it unlocked and pushed it open. The space inside was cramped and cylindrical. He realized it was an elevator.

Andy stepped onto the round platform and saw another lever at waist height. He summoned the dagger before raising the lever.

The cylinder shot upwards without a sound or delay. He felt the speed pushing him down. There was an almost instant stop, and he lifted slightly off the floor.

He left the elevator and found himself in a rocky nook. He heard rushing water nearby. He stepped forward and saw a glittering silver light reflecting off the rocks ahead. There was a sharp left turn, and Andy had to cover his eyes before the overwhelming silver light. There was a piece of Argument, enormous and dazzling.

Andy felt his heart leap as he stepped out of

the narrow rocky hall into a much larger cylindrical space. The round room contained the massive orb, which floated a few feet off the floor. A torrent of rushing water poured from the roof, about twenty feet up, over the Argument, and then onto the floor, where it drained as quickly as it fell.

Andy saw the sheer walls rising at least twenty feet, before terminating in a carved stone rail. The space between the rail and the ceiling was filled with steel bars. It seemed like the orb was trapped inside this large, cylindrical cage.

Andy stood, overwhelmed by a surge of awe.

He saw his right arm reaching for the orb and struggled to stop it.

Andy stepped forward and nearly slipped.

The floor is covered in coins!

He saw copper, silver, and even gold coins lining the floor. He was so awestruck that he hadn't seen them.

Andy felt like grabbing a pocket's full. He even bent to grasp a handful of the shining coins. He listened as they slipped through his fingers and clattered to the floor.

It wouldn't be right.

Andy smiled as the last of the coins fell and clicked against each other.

He heard a loud tap and looked up. A guard with a musket leaned against the rail, looking the other way, while a second guard, with a halberd, approached. The noise of the water was so loud that Andy couldn't make out what they were saying.

Andy saw his arm reaching for the orb again.

What the hell?

He resisted and stepped back.

He heard another tap as the guard lent his weapon against the bars.

Andy shied away and hid behind a rock.

He felt the ground crunch as the coins slipped and pushed against each other. He saw a piece of cloth sticking out from under the coins. Andy pulled on the cloth and saw it was quite long.

There's a message here: "Cogito, purifier of Degoskirke, for your enduring patronage we give endless thanks. We will not curse the day when you are called to serve."

Andy dropped the banner.

This is for the Argument. It has a name, Cogito. It must purify the water that the city uses. They were thanking it, as if it were a person.

Andy couldn't help feeling the urge to reach out and touch the Cogito.

This is the one Ziesqe told me to find. But I need little more than the small Argument I have now. I can draw a dagger and use the Silversight. If I take this, I might hurt the city.

Andy remembered the first Argument, and the mouse town of Cair Fromage. He regretted what happened to the mice and felt responsible. He couldn't take the Cogito.

"There!" a voice cried out.

The guards had spotted him. A musket fired and a pile of coins to Andy's right exploded in all directions.

Andy rolled away and towards the rocky hall that led to the elevator. A fearful urge told him this might be his last chance.

Andy ducked back into the hall and looked out at the Cogito. Another gunshot grazed the stone near his face.

He backed away and went towards the elevator, but found it gone, and no friendly button stood out to summon it.

Andy's legs shook as he fumbled at the closed door, searching for anything that might call it back.

He summoned the dagger and prepared to fight the guards.

What the hell can I do with just a dagger? They'll kill me!

Andy looked back into the Cogito's cell. He spotted the guards unlocking a panel of bars and readying themselves to descend the circulars stairs into the pit full of coins.

There's no way out. They're going to shoot me!

Andy froze. All he could do was wait for the guards to come down and find him.

"How'd he get in?" A guard yelled.

"I don't give a damn how he got in; the punishment is death!" Another responded.

Andy looked out onto the Cogito. Everything in his body wanted to race out and touch it.

Now! This is your last chance! Take it now!

"No! I won't do it!"

Andy felt his limbs move. He lunged towards the Cogito. He tried to resist and pulled against the force driving his legs, but he only succeeded in falling to his knees, out in the open.

This is it. I'll die here.

"There!" a guard yelled.

Andy didn't look up. It was all he could do to keep his arms and legs from racing forward. He heard heavy footsteps on the coins. The slick crunching made his skin crawl.

"This is how it has to be," a guard said sadly.

Andy heard a click, and the spin of the clockwork mechanism.

He heard a crack, but felt no pain.

There was silence.

Andy looked up and saw an orange burst hung in midair. A round bullet floated a few inches from his face. The water pouring over the Cogito had frozen in place. He stood and felt the carpet of coins sticking firmly, also frozen.

Andy saw something moving on the other side of the massive Argument. He circled and saw a shadow, like a moving body obscured by glass and water. It looked to be a walking form, like his own.

On the far side of the Argument he came face to face with Caspian.

Caspian wore the same clothes, and blackened armor. His face was neither sad nor disappointed, nor was it proud, but it somehow conveyed all these emotions. Andy was afraid and ashamed, but more than that he felt something he had never experienced before.

I hate this man.

Caspian smiled.

"You've put me through my paces."

"I'm not taking the Cogito. I'm never putting that helmet on either. Just unfreeze time and let them kill me."

Caspian sighed. "A coward—"

Andy looked away.

"No, too far. A coward wouldn't have made it so far, but that's the problem, isn't it? You've struggled through far too much, in such a short time. It's jaded you. Now you reject my help, after everything."

Andy furrowed his brow. "You've never helped me! You're a killer!"

"I've been with you from the beginning. Don't you remember?"

Andy felt a burst of memory overwhelm him. He saw Dean for the first time and then he was at the gallery. He saw a silver glow.

Flex the muscles around your eyes, they will focus around the halo.

Devoid of even annoyance, Andy obeyed the command. The glow focused as he tensed his eyes. The statue came into focus.

"I've been with you since this moment."

Andy remembered rushing around the corner with Dean and grazing the statue. He remembered feeling something, even then.

"I've been slowly awakening with you."

"The whole time! You've been in my head since then?" Andy yelled.

Caspian nodded, and Andy's sight shifted back to the Cogito.

"When Thea saw you, she suspected. She wasn't certain, but she sensed it—she sensed me. She was hoping to make the transition easier by taking you into the Juncture. She expected to find one of my possessions there. She didn't know what still lingered in the dark. Though her plan to draw me to the surface did succeed, I wasn't present enough to reach through. Poor girl, she's probably still in there, tearing her hair out."

"Pythia is sick. What she does to her students is wrong."

Caspian laughed. "She's a few thousand years old, Lysander. Come back and talk about right and wrong after just a century. I'm sure you'll find her methods a far cry from what those students would have suffered, if left on the surface. Though naming her school, Caspia, was in poor taste."

Andy shook his head. "I'm not going to change my mind. Not about Pythia and not about you."

Caspian inclined his brow. "Thrag recognized me in you, and even the traitorous ryle saw something. They know and understand what you do not, Lysander. You speak with the Voice of the Dead God. Do you know what that means?" Caspian paused, but Andy was silent. "Do you believe that you killed that mantis? Did you winch that crossbow on the beach? Did you grasp the Argument, when you thought it aflame? Could you have survived a fight with that bloated failure, Xyth, in his disgusting city? Could you have stood to run away from your family on a bare hunch? Did you have the strength to subdue the cyclostone, Cygnus? Did any of these feats cause you a moment's doubt?"

Andy was silent for a long while. "Yes, they did."

"And why?"

"Because each was beyond me."

67

Caspian crossed his arms. "Without me, they were. I guided you through those trials, to this end alone. You chased after Lysette—I knew where she would be taken. You moved towards her, but why? Does your heart stir for her? Is your child's honor so pronounced? What moved your two feet so far? Do you think the ryle—those coward fools—would have unchained you last night, if it were not on my word?"

"No."

"Now, look here. There are men with wheel-locks. You said a moment ago that you stood no chance against them. Indeed, their bullets are coated with a mixture that will not allow a wound they cause to be healed. Even if you knew how to call up a shield, or better yet, coat your body in armor, those bullets could pass right through. This is how they keep the empowered ryle out of the city, but it is also how they keep any Seers from picking up a piece of Argument."

Andy felt a question form. "It is known that every piece of Argument is guarded?"

"They guard the critical pieces, at least those they know of, and they have for ages. These men stand guard here on the order of the Exegesuits. The robust temple of atheism that, though despicable, keeps the city from crumbling further into degradation."

"Ziesqe must have known the Cogito would be guarded. He sent me up here to take it and cause a distraction—" Andy trailed off into suspicious thought.

"There's a lad. Use that brain."

"He knows that if they shoot me, I can't be healed?"

"Possibly."

"He planned that I would die here."

Caspian shook his head. "I would like to let you believe that."

"What? That isn't true?"

"He expects violence far grander." Caspian gestured widely at the Cogito. "Reach out and claim it. You will know everything I know. You are afraid, and remember what it was like with the Casque, but, with time, you will learn to blend your thoughts and experiences with my own. Your understanding of the surface will be invaluable in our next campaign."

"Our campaign?"

Caspian smiled.

"What's your goal?"

Caspian laughed. "The same goal I've had since I inherited the Voice. Exterminate the ryle, and peel their parasite God from the spine of reality. Just touch your old weapon."

Andy looked over to the Cogito. "So much Argument. You could do almost anything with it, but wouldn't the city suffer if we took it?"

"It would. Panobscura Talionis would crumble into ruin, and this purifying source of water would dry up. In time, Degoskirke would finish sinking back into the sea."

"So, all these people, even the ones who worship you, who expect your return, they would all die."

"Again, you lack the breadth of perspective. Join

with me, touch the Argument, and I will show you why it must be this way."

Andy reached out. The impulse to take the Argument was immense, but the faces and voices of the people below filled his thoughts. The lively trade and passionate debate. He remembered Hyadoth. He felt the desire to strike fear, to make Ziesqe pay, but knew it was wrong.

"I will not be a wild killer. Unfreeze time and let them finish me."

"Lysander, the people of this city live in humiliation. Your kin in the purple waste live in worse. Your families on the surface are slaves! The millions with Seer blood scattered across the Netherscape all live in constant fear. Change is cataclysm! It is the greatest possible end for these sad remnants. They will look up and see that your ascension is just! They will see the cavern burn with silver light! The ryle and their servants for miles in every direction will molder and crumble at the sight! We will travel to the surface and awaken the billions there! The sky will fall and our old enemy will stir! He will remember what it means to feel fear!"

Andy stepped closer. He felt the warm glow coming from the Cogito. He wanted it more than he had ever wanted anything. He wanted to kneel before Caspian, before his thousands of years, before the infinite depth of his knowledge, and before the certainty in his fearsome eyes. Andy bit down on his cheeks and tasted blood.

"No more half measures! No more

preservation! I have been soft, but today we grasp Cogito!"

Andy felt his stomach clench as a terrible question came to his lips: "How many times has this happened?" he asked.

"This will be the last."

Andy lowered his hand and shook his head. He felt a tear streak down his face at the sickening revelation. "Your words are moving," Andy paused, tears falling, "but it will be a repeat of Hyadoth. You love glory and slaughter. You do not deserve to be worshiped."

A loud crack, almost like laughter, rang out. Andy spun around and saw a dark purple shadow flash over the stone. Caspian growled and vanished in silver light.

The ground shook and the air burst with ringing explosions. In an instant, the water was flowing again. A bullet struck rock, and the guards stumbled in the violent shaking.

"What's happened?" "He's vanished!" they yelled.

Andy saw that the stairs were unguarded. He rushed towards them and climbed, not looking back. The bursting concussions rang out, but it sounded to Andy as if they were coming from outside the pillar, like thunder or lightning outside a building. On the last stair, Andy heard one of the gun mechanisms firing.

The ground shook, and the bullet missed its mark, ringing against an iron bar.

"After him!" a guard yelled.

"To hell with that! There's a damned skybreak!" the other's voice was almost drowned out by the violent banging.

Andy looked around, trying to spot a way to escape. He saw an outer rail that opened onto the wide Netherscape. He rushed to the rail and looked out onto the massive city, so far below. The colorful cavern ceiling was barely a dozen feet further up, though the colors there were now flashing between purple and silver.

A burst made his eyes flex in pain. Flashing silver and purple lights shot into and out of existence. They cracked against each other with such force that the whole Guilt shook.

He heard people down below screaming. "Skybreak!"

The two lights exploded at each other and instead of bursting apart, they held in place. The air around them flashed with moving figures and the burnt-out silhouettes of images. Andy tasted something acidic in the air, and then heard rasping cracks. He saw fields of dark purple and silver grow out over the surface of the Guilt. The silver and purple drew closer. Finally, they grew over the rail. Andy stood back and saw that the fields comprised small, rapidly growing crystals.

It's like frost, but it moves like it's on fire.

The purple frost was pushed away from Andy, and the silver caught him. It grew up his arms and legs. He tried to run, but felt the Argument shaking. He opened his palm and saw the orb. It flashed, and burning fields of crystals rushed into it.

Andy stood in amazement, as the tiny orb grew and grew. The crashing and banging outside finally faded away. Moments later, his orb was the size of a hefty snowball.

Andy grasped it and the blade appeared. It was huge and almost too bright to look at.

"All clear!" A guard yelled from in the pit.

Andy saw a gate off to his right. He ran towards it and sliced a way through. On the other side he was met by crowds of people trying to collect the fields of crystals that had grown all over the walls and floor. They were using anything they could to brush the thin layer of crystals into jars or bags. Now and then someone would cry out as their bare skin came too close to the crystals.

Andy was careful as he pushed through the masses of people. Only a few looked up to be startled by him and the blade.

Andy smiled like an idiot and released his grip. He looked for the path down the tower, but only found a ragged stairwell close to the center of the Guilt. He felt anonymous as everyone focused on collecting the crystals. The guards were also equally distracted by scuffles in the crowds.

Andy took the stairs down and pushed against crowds racing to the higher floors to take advantage of the skybreak. He recalled travelling up in the cylinder lift and knew getting back down would take some time. He was grateful for the tumult.

When he felt like his knees might give out, Andy stopped on a random floor. He looked into the central plaza and considered the local shops and houses. Inside the windows of one shop he spotted a shape moving up from the floor through the ceiling.

Was that an elevator?

Andy saw a sign above the door, "Amrel's Guilt Lift."

Andy stepped inside and saw a brutox standing lazily by the elevator door. He pointed at a box. Unsure, Andy stepped aside as another couple came in. Andy watched them deposit two copper pieces; the brutox was also paying attention.

"Down please," the man said.

Andy fished out his bag and found a copper bit. He showed it to the brutox before tossing it in the box.

"Down," Andy said.

The brutox pulled a heavy lever. They waited silently, until a car came to rest in one of the banks. A goblin opened the door for them.

"Where to?" he asked.

"The base," the woman said.

"Me too," Andy replied to the goblin's glance.

Once the elevator rumbled into motion, Andy was surprised to hear the other passengers talking.

"That was the worst skybreak I've seen in years," the man said.

"And they'll be fighting for hours up there. We were lucky to get in and out so quickly," she replied.

"Did you find any etherium, young man?" the woman asked Andy.

Andy shrugged. "Maybe a little," he said, honestly.

"Oh, you need to be more careful," the woman

said, suddenly looking about in her purse for something.

Andy spotted a cloth full of purple crystal bits, though she produced a small, dark carrot.

"No thanks," Andy said. "I'm trying something new."

They both stepped away from him and stared.

"They'll kill you. You can't leave the Guilt like that. Even the base of the pillar is unsafe."

Andy nodded and accepted the carrot, though he stared at it for a long while, not sure what to do. He didn't know where to go, though he did recall Ziesqe telling him to keep an eye out for hidden writing. Ziesqe had betrayed him, but it seemed like his only option. Andy sighed and pocketed the carrot. The woman noticed this.

"Marcus, I heard that someone was waving around an Argument. It happened close to the Cogito, up near the top." She spoke to Marcus, but her eyes remained locked on Andy.

Andy sighed. "What are you going to do with those crystals?" He asked, hoping to change the subject, but they only redoubled their glares. If they could have backed away any further, they would have.

Andy stood in silence.

I escaped Caspian, but that's not what was supposed to happen. Ziesqe knew what was up there. He wanted me to take the Cogito. He knew that Caspian would steal my body. He planned on it. But why would he want to release Caspian? Ziesqe wants Degoskirke safe, so he can rule. He must believe that Caspian wouldn't destroy the city. Maybe he doesn't realize that the Cogito keeps it safe—or maybe he does. Maybe he wants a catastrophe like the pure water drying up so he can step in and save the day. He also wanted me to run around and wave the Argument, to scare people into believing him.

Andy looked over at the couple, who tried to blend into the elevator wall.

But what do I do now? Ziesqe doesn't expect me to come back.

Finally, the elevator stopped. The goblin opened the door and the couple ran off as soon as they could.

Andy exited the lift and noted the plazas were much wider, further down the pillar.

He saw a welcoming tavern, but turned away, back to the gated entrance to the Guilt. Humans and ychorites were rushing. There were murmurs about the skybreak and several people asked Andy if he had any etherium to sell. Andy shook his head and pushed through the crowd. The guards were too busy to cast more than a glance his way.

Andy came to a fork in the road and turned left on a whim.

I haven't heard Caspian's voice in my head for a while. I don't feel his presence like I did up there. Maybe the skybreak distracted him.

Andy walked randomly, favoring downhill turns over others. The more he thought, the worse he felt.

The renewed chorus of debate he heard passing through the plazas gradually caught his attention. He stopped to watch a man, wearing something akin to a military dress uniform, paired with shining black armor, argue with a Braid.

"This monarchist forgets the thousands of years where humanity flagged under the failed notion that any one man or woman was possessed of the innate right of rulership. How could any reasonable person, bearing even the simplest historical education, posit such a repeatedly failed system as the basis for our government?"

Andy breathed a sigh of relief as the argument washed over him. People in the audience cheered and booed. Andy saw other braids and uniformed participants bellowing complaint and cheer from the audience. One of the uniformed men noticed Andy and came to stand by him.

"You are the bravest man I have ever seen, and yet, you are just a boy," the armored man said, in an almost scientific manner.

"Why is that?"

"Those clothes—if the guards knew what they were, it would be a death sentence. Don't let an Exegesuit priest see you," the man concluded in a tone implying Andy already knew this. The man gave him an affirmative nod and clapped him on the shoulder before turning back to the debate.

I don't know why, but I like it here.

The black uniformed man stepped forward on the stage and almost scowled at the audience before speaking, "This simple democrat has taken the first step on the road to the Overman. He has been blinded by the success that this step has afforded and would shut your eyes and ears to the nature of the next step. The monarchs and emperors of the past were much as any one of us today, occasionally great, mostly mediocre, and often disastrous. Very rarely was there an enlightened ruler: A Pericles, Aurelius, or an Augustus, whose overflowing virtue would last longer than their bodies. With such example, how can we not see that, much like the Greek school argues, there is an ideal ruler. We know that such a thing is possible, but where is the endeavor to find this near perfect ruler? They are rare, certainly, and the past systems that sought to discover them were flawed. Democracy is indeed an improvement on those systems, it can keep out the very worst, but it also keeps out the brilliant, the catalysts for change, and those who, by turn of fate, could be the very best. We are inured to our mediocrity! An ideal ruler, and more importantly, the system to attain that ruler, should be the basis for our great experiment."

"Experiment? You would hazard all with tyranny from within, while we have spent centuries enduring that from without. You hunt for impossible ideals and expect too much virtue from mere flesh! You would tinker with the delicate framework that keeps this city great!"

"Great? Walk a thousand yards Pacward and see the sunken wreck of the first Odeon, or the swimming pool that has overflown the Second Globe. Hallmarks of our city's birth and height, sunken, like the supposed and decayed, greatness of our city! Yes, indeed the Overman is ideal! And yes, we are mortal, but do we not strive for the ideal in all things? Is not democracy an ideal balance of bearable unhappiness for all? Can we not step beyond? Inside, we are demoralized, afraid on all sides, yet, even within you, o braid of the past, lies the seed of fearlessness. The urge to cast away the trappings of a tradition that has run its course, and to seek that new philosophy!"

"Vague and bombastic!" the braid replied.

Cheers and boos rang through the plaza.

I have no idea what's going on, but I love it.

"The great sun will rise and herald the dawn of a new mankind!" a man next to Andy cheered.

"We're not all men, you know," an ychorite complained.

Andy laughed as the debate grew heated. He didn't want to leave.

Moments later, he felt a tug on his sleeve. A boy stood staring at him. The boy had a gray-green tinge to his skin. His eyes were golden. He wore a plain tunic and pants, though his expression seemed more mature in its analysis of Andy.

"You should come with me," the boy said, gesturing to the crowd.

Andy saw a group of guards questioning people on the fringes.

"You don't have to tell me twice," Andy said.

Once they left the noisy plaza, the boy regarded him again. "You don't seem like the Voice."

"I'm not, kid, I'm a failure. I refused to take the Cogito."

"The songs don't mention anything like that."

"You should have seen Caspian's face. He wasn't

pleased, and then the cracking lights and fields of crystals."

"Ah!" the boy said, "Skybreak. I've never seen one, but I heard one today. The battle was magnificent."

"Yeah, it was too loud for me—say, where are we going?"

"To a street over in the mer quarter. I hope you don't mind a little water."

"No problem, I could use a bath—but why are you taking me there? Is someone going to come out and try to kill me? Because I have this," Andy said, brazenly producing the Argument.

The boy's eyes went wide. "Put that away! Do you want the Exegesuits to chase us and tear apart the quarter?"

Andy did as he was asked.

"Thank you. And no, this is no trap," the boy said.

"Could you explain a little more than that?"

"It might sound strange."

Andy stopped in his tracks. The boy noticed, staring at him questioningly.

"Strange? It might sound strange?" Andy sputtered. He looked around in every direction. "Kid, strange is a word that no longer exists," Andy felt the urge to break out into laughter but spared the boy's dignity.

"Indeed," the boy said, unsure if he should continue, "Don't repeat this to anyone, either."

Andy nodded.

"A great number of people from all the races

have been awaiting your return. In the mer district, the faith is still strong. I, from all the others in my year, have been chosen to look for you. I must help you find one of your old houses. If you are really the Voice, you will know which is yours."

"I see, another test."

The boy grinned.

Minutes later, they came to a place where the water lapped up into the street. Around the corner they saw a field of structures sinking away into the murk. Andy shook his head at the sight.

"This way," the boy said, tugging Andy's arm.

They climbed over rubble and occasionally waded through waist-deep water. Andy noticed the boy moved faster in the water. He saw movement in the buildings, and spied teal faces looking down on them.

Another mer child rushed out into the street from her home.

"No, Beryl, go home! This is my job!" the boy yelled, but the girl refused to listen.

"It was my job last season!" she complained and grabbed Andy's other arm.

A few minutes later, at least a dozen other children had joined them, much to the original boy's dismay.

They finally stopped and looked up a short street that terminated in a circle of tall houses.

"It's almost like a street on the surface," Andy muttered.

The children would not travel far up the street, but instead, waited and watched.

At their prompting, Andy walked up the street, his eyes moving from house to house. He heard the murmurings of the children fade as he went.

Unsure of what he was looking for Andy stood in the circle, staring at the ring of houses around the street.

There! The Infiniteye!

He spotted a glowing Infiniteye painted above a door. He walked towards the house, and as he did, a cheer rang out from the children.

Andy approached the door cautiously. He reached out and touched the handle. It was cool brass. His frayed nerves expected a trap. He turned the knob and the door swung silently open. When no burst of flame or flying bolts appeared, Andy sighed and went inside.

He found splintered and water-damaged furniture strewn about the main room. Couches and upturned chairs on a table were also covered in sheets. Green bottles had rolled into a far corner and sat amid warped floor-boards.

Andy checked all the rooms on the first and second floor, but found them mostly bare. On his second time through the first floor, he spotted an almost imperceptible Infiniteye painted on a running board in a bedroom.

Andy pushed the bed aside and saw the faint outline of a trapdoor. However, he saw no way to open it.

Well, if I've learned anything...

Andy found the Argument and held it up to his eye.

The trap-door is locked.

Andy saw that the lock was connected to something outside the room. He followed the axle through the wall, it changed direction many times. Reaching its termination, Andy found himself standing outside the house.

The trapdoor linked with a pair of statues that stood in a small fountain near the front door. The statues were facing the walkway and each held a welcoming hand out to any visitors. Andy inspected the statues and saw they would pivot on their plinths. He turned them towards each other and felt a slight click. The statues seemed just as natural welcoming each other as they had guests. Not wanting to ponder over-long about what meaning there was in this, Andy went back inside and found that the trapdoor now sat just high enough for him to get a grip.

He opened the door and saw a ladder, though it was dark further down. The air was cooler as he descended. The silence and stillness of the black space made him nervous.

His foot touched off on solid ground. He felt it was about thirty feet down, though it wasn't flooded, as he expected. Andy produced a glow with the Argument.

The room was covered in glowing writing. He saw the Infiniteye painted a few dozen times on the walls and ceiling. Long paragraphs glowed here and there; some were in English. The room otherwise looked like a cozy barracks. Bunk-beds lined one wall, while couches crowded around a fireplace on another. Tables and chairs filled a corner, and maps and books were strewn about the table. A well-stocked wine rack sat nearby, and a few armor stands stood, still bearing clothes and armor not far removed from his own, though these were of a far higher quality, and adorned with devices and medallions he didn't recognize. There was also a banner, half fallen, still clinging to the wall. He held it up.

"*Occidentus Obscura!*" it read. *I thought that was the mouse organization. Maybe these Seers were a part of it too.*

Andy spotted a lever on the wall, near the ladder. He pulled it, and heard the trapdoor shut itself and lock tight.

I'm probably safe down here, for now at least.

Andy flung off his cloak and tossed it at an empty clothing rack before walking over to the table. There was a thick cloth laying on a round object in the middle of the table. Andy removed the cloth and saw a golden piece of Argument, less than half the size of his own, floating above a candlestick holder. Andy released the grip on his Argument. The expected darkness was replaced by a soft, golden glow from this Argument, which must have served as a remarkably expensive lantern.

Someone threw the cloth over it to get some sleep. How long has it been sitting here?

Free to use both hands, Andy looked through the maps and books. He felt himself becoming lightheaded at the glut of glowing letters. Almost everything present was written in Seer script, making it hard on Andy's eyes.

He found a book with an illustration of a hand grasping an Argument on the cover.

"Manual for the improvement of apprentice Seers in the area of martial utility, with critical tenets of the Silvereye." What a title.

Andy's jaw dropped as he flipped through the pages.

"The establishment and accretion of etherium armoring," "Tuning and honing one's blade to protect against catastrophic recoil," "Storing the Argument within, or, how to free one's hand."

Andy saw diagrams and illustrations of how to grasp the Argument, how to flex one's muscles, and further on in the book, how to focus the mind. These later illustrations featured elements of what he saw with the Silversight.

This is exactly what I need!

Andy pored through the book, occasionally stopping to stand and practice storing the Argument. After a moment of practice, he found the Argument would indeed float in his body, with no to be focused into a limb.

Now someone can search me and not find it. I wonder if it's safe to keep it within all the time. Ziesqe kept his on a chain—maybe he never learned this trick, or maybe the Counter works differently.

Andy skipped ahead to another chapter and practiced blade tuning.

I think I might know a little about this already.

He twisted his wrist and summoned the articulated blade, it seemed more solid than in its simplest form. With a tightened thrust the blade elongated to an absurd size.

"Damn!" Andy yelled, accidentally slicing through a bunk-bed on the other side of the room.

He turned the page and saw how to slacken the blade by bending the wrist back. He did so and was surprised when the blade fell limply to the floor, burning a trail along the ground.

Andy laughed like a maniac and turned the page again. He saw how to make a shield, and wanted to try it. He almost bent his arm in the right way, but the lank blade crackled and reeled into his arm, tearing a couch and part of the floor to explosive pieces in moments.

Andy ducked as the debris flew against the wall. *Maybe I shouldn't be practicing inside.*

Andy looked at the shield illustrations and saw that his wrist had started in the wrong position.

He had been too excited, and besides that, he was sleepy. He tried to keep reading, but once he realized how tired he was, he couldn't stop himself from yawning.

It's been a long day, but at least it ended well, minus the destroyed furniture.

Andy untied and then kicked off his annoying leather sandals, before climbing into a bunk.

"Top bunk!" he yelled to no one in particular.

The last thing he saw before closing his eyes was a shimmering Infiniteye staring down at him from the ceiling.

Chapter 4: The Free City

Letty gazed up at the collection of confused looking banners hanging from one tower and then to the plain surface of the other.

"I don't know much about the various Archatian houses, but they are on the left, while the secular Exegesuit priests stand on the right," Quill said to their confused faces.

"What the hell is any of that supposed to mean?" Dean asked.

"Look, the city has two governing arms, one is simple, while the other is completely insane, almost beyond words. The right-hand side are the Exegesuits. They call themselves—" Quill took a moment to get the name right in his mind, "The Anteschismarian Order of Exegesuits, or Exegesuits for short. They guard the city against Seers and ryle alike and collect a small fee from all commerce in and out of the city. They are the face of the city to the outside world, and they command the guards. Their doctrine is violently opposed to the Argument and the Counter. They deny that either exist and punish or censor any mention of them to ensure peace with the ryle lords that dominate the rest of Pansubprimus."

"Okay," Dean said, "that makes sense, politically, I mean. But the whole, denying things exist stance, I don't see why they would."

"They are the last free city in this part of the Netherscape, and it's not by accident," Staza replied.

"Okay, that's the Exegesuits, but what about

the other side, the one with all the banners?" Letty asked.

"That's the other half of the city, the Archatian system. The domestic governance. They are composed of dozens of large and small factions. Most of those factions are ideologically opposed to each other, but occasionally they get along. These factions govern the city at the same time as the Exegesuits, but they aren't supposed to deal with foreign matters like diplomacy and war. They are in constant competition with each other for popular approval, and control of the city, which is divided into administrative parcels."

"Really?" Dean asked. "That's ridiculous."

"You haven't heard the worst part. As one group is voted in, their collected laws are instituted in that parcel immediately. The Egalitarian Redistributionists, for instance, will rush their supporters into a parcel and overwhelm the plaza. They will blitz for control and, once they have it, will set about looting houses and businesses for everything they have. The locals might not be prepared, but once they figure out what's happening, the redistributionists will be shouted out and whatever rulership the locals prefer will return, though the looting will have been completely legal."

"It sounds like piracy," Emma said.

"There's no way that works," Dean sputtered, near to pulling out his hair.

"Well, they've agreed to starting and stopping points for the debating, so antics like that can only occur during decent hours," Staza replied.

"So, the crown above the banners moves as the local rulership changes?" Letty asked.

"Right, and whoever is in charge, when it's our turn to enter, gets to tax us," Staza said. "Pray for good luck."

"I've read that only a few factions tax pedestrian entrants like us. They are mostly interested in merchants who do business in the city," Quill said, not sounding too sure.

The line they were standing in was far shorter than the line of carts, but it was still a slow process, as everyone was searched and subjected to blank signs held by the Exegesuits.

"Letty," Emma whispered.

Letty turned her way.

"Your eyes; you need the carrots."

Letty felt suddenly afraid. "Is anyone staring?" Letty asked, unshouldering her pack.

Emma looked about at the people standing in line. Most were distracted by the performance going on at the gate and on the tower.

"Take them now," Emma whispered, "before we get up there."

Letty and Staza poked through their bags as innocuously as possible before finding the carrots. Letty passed them out and she and the Caspians gulped them down.

"Thanks, Em," Letty said.

"We can't forget—" Emma said, turning back to the gateway. "—but what do we do when we get in?" she asked.

"Find a portal," Letty said.

"It's not that easy. Pythia knows how to make portals, but almost no one else does. Even if we do find something, it will probably be expensive," Quill said. "We'll have to trade more of our possessions."

"Or," Staza butted in, "we get a little aggressive. I don't care to lose any more of our equipment."

"We have to be peaceful. Seers aren't welcome in the city as it is. We don't need any extra attention," Quill whispered.

A man atop the tower called out the word, "Braid!" and the crown changed location.

Letty heard the cart owners sigh in relief.

They approached a man in a long-braided wig, who smiled, and asked to see into their bags. "Just for anything illegal that is, no seizures here!" he said, with some venom for the pair of ychorites in red, carrying bags.

They placed their packs on a table, while the temple priests approached them each with their blank signs.

"Eyes here!" one snapped at Letty, insistently.

Letty stared.

I hope those carrots are working.

The priest went on to Emma.

A moment later, Letty felt a little nervous. One Braid whispered to a priest.

"Would you please come with us," the Braid said to Letty and their group.

Murmurings rose from the people behind.

"Contraband?" one merchant asked another.

"Did they fail the test?" another traveler asked.

Armored guards appeared, and they were escorted into the city.

How did they find us out?

Letty barely heard the excited cheering and raucous debating coming from a nearby stage.

What are they going to do to us? What did they find? None of us should have failed the test—was it me, did I fail? The priest didn't look like I did; he looked bored.

They were taken to a nearby strong house and sat at a wide table. The Braid waited with them as the priests left.

"What's the problem? If I may ask," Quill said.

"Oh, well, a few things possibly. But, please, I'm being rude. I am Phineas Aldridge, speaker for the Peace and Parley Party, also known as the Braids," Phineas said, with a slight bow and a small smile.

Letty introduced herself and her friends.

"Hmm, you don't sound like Elazene or Wrecklanders. But I thought I recognized your type a few moments ago." Letty shared a nervous look with Staza and Dean. "You're from Caspia, aren't you?"

Quill took a deep breath. "You've found us out, Phineas. We are children of Pythia, and we have traveled for so long in secrecy, the habit still sticks. This is our destination, and I apologize for not being more forthcoming at the gate."

"No, no, not at all," Phineas said, rushing to take a seat, before turning and opening the door, "Tea please!" he paused, and gave them an ingratiating smile. "A light lunch for six as well, and inform the emissary that he is needed for once!" Phineas waited at the door for a moment, and accepted a tray full of tea cups and a kettle. He returned to the table, and nervously poured for everyone.

He's suddenly so nervous. What does it matter if we're from Caspia?

"It's been quite some time, three decades perhaps, since we've received a Caspian envoy. I hope your Mistress is well; her words still carry weight in even the far corners."

Wait—he thinks we're an envoy—whatever that is.

"I hate to pry, and please, feel free to tell me to mind my business, but I simply must ask if your Mistress intends on visiting in person?"

Letty opened her mouth, but Quill was the first to reply. "That is a forward question, Phineas, and you esteem us too highly. She does not make us privy to more than she means to."

Phineas tilted his head in earnest thought.

"I'm not a diplomat, so please excuse my poor conduct. I'm only a simple arguer; I speak for the common man, and am not versed in the courtesies of statecraft. The Exegesuit emissary, a fine ychorite named Silius, will arrive any moment and greet you properly."

"Don't worry, Phineas, we are pleased to be in your city, the only other free place in our corner of the Netherscape," Staza said.

Phineas smiled and took a nervous sip from his teacup.

He's afraid that Pythia is following along after us. I wonder why that should frighten him.

"Could you answer a few questions for us,

Phineas, before our host arrives? You seem a forthright person," Quill said.

Phineas gave a quick nod and coughed as he put down his cup.

"We need the services of a portal master. How might we find those?" Quill asked.

Phineas leaned back in his chair. "Well, not a tall order is it?" he laughed nervously. "There is only one permit to create portals still outstanding in the city. It is held by the mer of the Sink. Their part of the city is rather damaged, and dangerous to navigate, even for veterans. Silius might be persuaded to arrange an escort for you, but word has it that there is a high cost associated with portal travel. If you need the portal to return to Caspia, we might be able to arrange another mode of travel. The Exegesuits stable a small fleet of ravagers, or perhaps a cutter can be hired." Phineas looked like he might continue rambling, but a noise at the door put a stop to it.

A brutox clad in heavy robes appeared and clicked twice.

"Ah, you're wanted," Phineas said, standing. "Oh, you should put on your state attire first, traveling clothes would go amiss, and those robes are—dated."

They were directed to changing rooms and told that they would be received on the steps of the great Secular before a large crowd.

"Letty! What do I wear?" Emma asked from another stall.

"Something nice! I have one dress, but no heels."

93

"All I have is a few of your skirts and jeans!"

"Make do Emma, they won't understand our clothes anyway."

Letty straightened her dress and gave her hair a good brushing.

This is ridiculous.

She met Emma and Staza, outside her stall. Emma fretted in Letty's skirt and long-sleeved sweater, while Staza looked pleased to be back in her Caspian outfit, which was more like armor than clothing.

Quill appeared in the door to the hall.

"Emma," he said.

Emma turned, surprised and approached.

"It's Dean—he wants to talk to you," Quill said.

Emma nodded and left without a word. Letty and Staza followed her to the hall.

"You can't go in there," Staza said, noting the other changing rooms weren't for women.

Emma scoffed and entered anyway.

"What's wrong with him?" Staza asked Quill.

Quill shrugged and the two stared at Letty, who edged closer to the door, until she heard the soft tones of Dean and Emma on the other side.

"—I'll just mess it up for all of us," Dean whispered.

"You're doing great—everyone thinks so—"

"No—she still thinks I'm useless."

Letty stared down at the tiled floor, knowing she had caused this.

"You saved us, Dean—you fought the ryle, and you negotiated with the Elazene—" Dean tried to

94

interrupt, "—no, listen; I know you'll do even more for us here. Now take my hand and come on."

Letty heard them approach and quickly backed away from the door, ashamed that she had been listening in.

Dean and Emma appeared, and Letty noticed their hands separate at the scrutiny of the others.

"I—I couldn't decide what to wear—and you know Emma is good about fashion advice," Dean said, his voice softening to a pathetic whisper as he finished.

Dean wore slacks and a navy button down, borrowed from Quill's pack, by way of Letty's father. Quill, however, was Staza's match in his own Caspian armor.

Feeling guilty and awkward, Letty determined to treat Dean with more respect. The Caspians were silent, and Letty couldn't think of anything appropriate to say. Though she wanted to put Dean at ease, she knew saying something now would only humiliate him.

They left the hall and followed the brutox, a lavender beetle, whose chitin gleamed green and red hues under the vinlight.

Letty checked on the Argument in her pocket
Luckily, they didn't search our bags too thoroughly.

They were accompanied by a dazzling honor guard of a few dozen sergeants, shining in their armor, bearing banners, impossibly tall swords, and even muskets.

"So much for sneaking in," Letty muttered to Quill.

"I know—I just panicked!" Quill replied.

"I'm not sure that this is a bad thing," Dean leaned in, almost eager to be of use, and whispered. "Nobody knows who we really are, and they are taking the envoy from Caspia story seriously."

"What if we're found out?" Emma asked.

Before they could continue worrying, the guardsmen started marching.

A human in robes marched up alongside them and presented Staza with a pole bearing a banner. The banner was topaz, and featured a slitted reptilian eye. "Would you care to bare your people's standard?"

"Of course," Staza said, taking the pole. She looked up at it. "It's not a bad copy."

They left the cloister of administrative buildings and entered the streets of the city. People booed and cheered. Debaters on the stages praised and denounced Caspia, and before long, there was a lengthy procession following along, or rushing ahead to the great Secular.

Quill and Staza stood taller and marched in time with the guardsmen. Even Emma and Dean were infected with excitement from the impromptu parade.

There is something about this place. I can't explain it. It almost reminds me of the Caspians; it's fiery and loud.

"Look!" Emma pointed at a dome which stood above the other buildings.

They rounded a corner and saw the rows of buildings give way to a massive plaza laid before wide and gentle steps which led to an equally wide and squat cathedral, the Secular.

Banners of many colors featured a human figure composed of orbs and lines. An orb sat at the head, heart, both hands, and both feet, the lines connecting every orb were also prominent. The figure held its right hand aloft, as if holding a sword, though its sword was in a scabbard at the waist.

Crowds had filled the plaza in anticipation, and they parted as the armed procession pushed through.

An ychorite in simple white robes stood near a podium watching them arrive. To his left stood five banners bearing the form and the orbs.

The guards marched them up the gentle stairs towards the right-hand side of the podium, where a flag stand stood waiting. Staza was directed to place her banner there. She did, to the sound of a cheering crowd.

The ychorite, whose feathers were powder blue, raised his hands for silence. "Degoskirke! The Archatians aren't the only ones who can bring a crowd! Give me diplomacy any day! Any day would be fine! Even once a year, please!"

The crowd enjoyed that, and Letty heard the guards chuckling.

I guess they don't get many diplomatic guests.

"We are pleased to host five disciples of the mighty Pythia, here from the fair city of Caspia!"

The crowd cheered again, and Quill and Staza took to waving, Emma followed suit, but Letty and Dean remained aloof.

"I suspect the finest tailors will want to

get a look at their wardrobe; I am told that it is extensive and exotic, with a great number of novel contrivances. Sadly though, we varied Exegesuits have our own strict uniforms. As much as I would love to get ahead of the fashions, it is white robes and lonely days for me, your sole, under-appreciated diplomat."

The response to that was varied. Some people laughed, but Letty also heard remorseful compliments. "Oh shut up, everyone loves you, Silius!" "Be grateful you're useful today!"

Silius raised a hand. "Indeed, and I am enjoying being useful a little too much. I can already sense the glowers coming off my peers, so, without further enjoyment of my civic service, I must call! Mind, Heart, Blood, Hands, and Feet, come forward. Most gratefully, the Sheathed Blade, may remain absent!"

As he finished, figures emerged from the crowds. The guards parted and let them through. Each approached and stood by their banner.

From the left, the first person was actually a mouse, but one of massive proportions, at least for a mouse. His fur was moss green on his left side, and rich red gold on the right. He wore a cream suit almost of a military cut, which was also well tailored for his proportions. He held himself with surprising grace and dignity, despite his appearance.

He must be three feet tall. How is that possible?

"Ventalus, foremost member of the Mind, we thank you for your presence." Silius said to the mouse, and then to the Caspians. "Ventalus, also known as the farspeaker, high orderer, and commander of the Sheathed Blade."

The guards gently, but brusquely, tapped their weapons on the ground.

Ventalus inclined his head at the gesture.

"I'm sure he'll have many questions for you," Silius said.

The second representative was hunched and covered in filthy, threadbare rags, their face obscured by a hood.

"As always, a faceless representative speaks for the order of the Heart," Silius said.

The hunched figure made no motion to recognize the announcement.

The third representative, a stalwart ychorite draped in fine black and red robes.

He's just like the ones at the city gates, only his clothes are much finer.

"Vegus, high priest of Blood, we thank you for joining us. Sadly, our guests do not arrive at the head of a mile-long caravan, but I'm sure you will find commercial news hiding somewhere in their minds."

Vegus scowled at Silius's forward comment.

"I'm just as pleased to see foreigners as any Degoskan. This might be a preamble to stronger relations; don't foul the waters, Silius," Vegus said lightheartedly, his voice surprisingly deep.

Some in the audience smiled and laughed, though the last two representatives were not as popular as Silius and Ventalus.

The fourth representative was a human female. She had an appraising eye, and wore the clothes of a fine craftsman. Her blue and white striped tunic was covered in pockets filled with countless precision tools.

"Belmani, one of only three high-artificers, is here today to speak for the Hands. I am certain that she is grateful to not be wearing her robes of state."

Belmani ignored that and addressed Letty and her friends. "Caspians! I have read and heard accounts of the marvelous works of engineering and architecture in your young city. I hope to entice you to come to our temple and sit with our initiates and draftsmen and tell us of your home. We will gladly show you anything you might like to see in return."

"Now, now, Belmani, everyone will get time with them," Silius responded with a chuckle.

Belmani didn't spare him a glance.

This might not be the best idea. It sounds like they'll be keeping an eye on us and wasting our time with events like this. We aren't here to make friends; we have a job to do.

As this realization dawned, Letty struggled to keep the scowl off her face. Dean saw this.

"I'm certain that we can learn more this way, don't be upset," Dean whispered to her.

The final representative was actually two people. A goblin on stilts stood near a bulky brutox, with the many eyes of a spider, and the massive and segmented body that might have once been a tarantula. Long, sharp looking hairs, that were more like blades, lay flat in fields along his crossed arms. He looked absurd in a simple robe, colored purple at the feet, and lightened into a blazing orange at the head and throat.

"I don't know if I should laugh or scream," Emma whispered.

"They don't make a broom big enough," Dean replied, shaking his head in disbelief.

"Oort, and his translator, join us from the esteemed faction of the Feet." Silius expertly took in a breath to cover a slight chuckle.

Others in the audience weren't so polite, but a glance from Oort, and the sound of his considerable muscles tensing was enough to preemptively silence any heckling.

Oort leaned in to his goblin and clicked a quick string of unintelligible sounds.

"Oort would like to extendy warm and filial greetings from the many such farmers, herds-people, and fisher-folk, of this, our finest city in the land."

Oort nodded at the goblin's message.

"There it is! The five factions of the Anteschismarian Order of Exegesuits have extended sincere greetings from our city of Degoskirke."

The audience cheered, but was then waved to silence by Silius, who gestured to the guests and spoke, "Would one of you please say a few words, and deliver your message? We are eager to hear."

Everyone looked to Letty.

"What the hell are you looking at me for? Quill, you get out there. Everyone knows you're the better speaker—but don't make any stupid promises!" Letty whispered angrily.

Quill coughed and played with the collar on his armored shirt. He looked pale.

"You've had large audiences before," Staza said, giving him a nudge.

Quill stepped forward and raised a hand to calm the confused grumbles from the audience.

"High Exegesuits and welcoming citizens of the free city, please excuse our hesitation. We did not come prepared for such a grand welcome! The words in my heart fall far short in their effort to thank you for this graciousness."

Letty relaxed and was grateful that she had ordered Quill to speak. His calm manner and careful words quickly won over the audience, though the high Exegesuits were all as attentive and cautious as they been at first.

"We come from a small city nestled against another shore, and have traveled across lands hostile to us all, sometimes in hiding, but always afraid. Today, when we passed through your gates, we let our sword arms rest," Quill finished, eying the banner and its Sheathed Blade.

"May they remain so," Silius added, solemnly.

The crowd murmured its agreement.

"We've come to you with no great proclamation, but only with an open palm and the fair hope that this meeting might spur friendship and cooperation between our two cities, who, though far apart, are filial in spirit, and are beset by the same plagues and foes."

A few of the Exegesuits whispered to one another.

Vegus, the robed ychorite, stepped forward. "Fair words, young Caspian. I hear the echo of your

Mistress, so blessed in magnetism, surrounding us today. Do I also sense her expedient thrift in the face of largess?"

Quill narrowed a brow.

The mouse, Ventalus, raised a hand. "Please, forgive my cutting to the meat of the issue, where my compatriot is so careful. What he wants to know is what gifts have you brought to exemplify this future friendship you so nobly aspire to?"

"Ah," Quill replied, looking down for a moment.

There was a grumble stirring in the crowd.

"Indeed, where abundance meets thrift there may be misunderstanding. Please, see us not as empty handed; our gifts were carefully chosen and are subtler than gaudy silks which would only slander friendship and exemplify bribery."

The grumble changed pitch and sharpened into an almost guilty denial coming from a thousand throats.

Quill approved of this response. "Instead, each one of us bears our gifts, inside, where, through the success or failure of our meetings they might blossom into wealth and knowledge, however they be taken." Quill gestured to Staza, "Staza, swift, and sure, is champion in Caspia, and will share her skills with any who might be her peer, I hope at least one such person lives in Degoskirke."

Staza liked what she heard and stood a little taller before casting a haughty and superior expression across the audience. Loud exhortations came up from bellowing warriors. Silius laughed, and even Ventalus seemed impressed.

"Dean, my new brother, is possessed of transcendent wit and tact, the likes of which have not been seen for centuries—"

Dean took Quill by the shoulder and whispered, "Are you trying to get me killed?"

Quill laughed it off. "See how eager he is!"

Some of the audience cheered, while others echoed the exhortations of the warriors.

"Emma, our youngest sister, is blessed with a sense for the finer things. She will keep your socialites on their toes and the dressmakers busy around the clock."

Letty saw Emma turn bright red. "I'm not a fashion designer!" she whispered angrily.

Quill was paying attention, though. He remembers them asking about our clothes, Emma is the best person for that job.

"Our leader, Letty, has visited the surface—" Quill paused as the murmurs turned into a roar.

Silius raised his hands to the audience, and spoke over them, "Truly? She has been to the surface?"

Quill nodded, before continuing, "She has, and will make herself available to the archivists and historians."

God damn it, Quill. I said no stupid promises.

Letty crossed her arms, trying not to look as angry as she felt.

Finally, the crowd silenced.

"And lastly, the least of us. I am Quill, and due to lack of any real competition, have been accorded a place as Caspia's poet. I will speak or recite at any salon which might want me," Quill finished, quickly, with an embarrassed look.

"Speak a little truer, young man, you are blessed with words," Silius replied.

Quill rubbed his neck nervously before finishing, "We are a city poor in luxuries, but rich in matters of mind and aesthetic. These are the treasures we offer, and I hope they are received in the spirit with which they are given."

Silius smiled. "You know how to touch our hearts, young Caspians. We welcome you!" Silius bellowed, stirring up another cheer.

They stood and waved for a long time before their escort approached and ushered them towards the Secular.

"What was that, Quill?" Letty snapped, as they left the crowds behind. "I said no stupid promises."

Quill shook his head in vexation. "I didn't know what else to do. They wanted gifts!"

Staza disagreed. "It was the right move. Without that quick thinking they might have supposed us spies from Pythia."

"That's probably true," Emma interjected, "and Quill got us off the hook, as far as gifts go. I can give fashion advice all day."

"Yeah, I have to debate with these people, who probably do it for a living," Dean complained. "But that was quick thinking. I didn't realize how well you speak."

Staza elbowed Quill. "He's shy about it."

"I'm sorry for all this, Letty; it will slow us down," Quill said.

"Maybe not," Dean replied. "We'll have access to the most powerful people in the city; they might be able to help us."

"Yeah, but then they'll know we aren't just here to be diplomatic," Letty replied.

"They don't believe that now," Dean replied.

"Why don't we just say that Andy is another Caspian, and we're also trying to find him? Say that we have two missions," Emma whispered.

Everyone stared at her in surprise.

"What? That bad?" she asked.

"No. That's exactly what we'll do," Letty said.

As they came closer, the tall doors of the cathedral were thrown open. Banners hung down over the fluted stone arches that towered ever so narrowly to their peak.

"This place is huge," Letty said.

"It's the largest structure in the city, unless you count the pillars," Belmani, the woman covered in tools, said to them, after sneaking up from behind. "With the crowd service out of the way, we can get down to business."

They were led through the massive Secular proper, down a side hall, and then off through several calm and mossy cloisters, before finally arriving in a spacious meeting room.

The Exegesuits walked to the far side of a table. Letty and her friends followed and stood by their chairs, not sure if it was polite to sit.

"Oh, look," Emma said to Letty, pointing at the person hunched over in their rags.

The faceless representative of Heart stood up

straight and disrobed. A moment later, there stood a woman, tall, trim, and utterly unlike the character she had been portraying moments ago. She took her hood off, and the newcomers were startled by her harsh beauty. Her skin was a soft shade of blue-green, and her pinkish eyes settled angrily on the newcomers. Under the robes, she wore simple cloth wrappings that did little to hide her physique.

"Onya, I didn't recognize you," Silius said to the woman.

"You are a blustering dilettante, Silius. Now call us to seats, and let's get on with this farce."

Silius coughed in embarrassment and was interrupted by Ventalus.

"Just a moment, please, Silius. We have to observe the forms; it's been so long. Deacon! The Blade please." Ventalus watched in annoyance as a younger man, in similar clothes, rushed up with an ornate sword laid across his hands. Its grip, guard, and scabbard shone with gold, ivory, and sparkling rubies. "Hold it up for me now; I'm only a builder."

"Yes, sir," the Deacon said, holding the sword up for all to see.

"The Blade is Sheathed. Let it remain so," Ventalus said firmly, and the Deacon placed the blade on the table.

"Ah, yes. To seats!" Silius said.

Everyone sat, and Onya immediately launched into a tirade. "Look, you snake spawn, we know what you're up to! That heathen woman will not interfere any further with our city!"

Letty's eyes nearly fell out of her head at the

sudden attack.

"Onya, please! Good form—" Ventalus raised a paw, but she ignored him.

"Good form is for theists! Haven't the Archatians taught you anything? Straight at the enemy, and overwhelm them with the force of argument! Now listen, we will spare your lives if you tell us every detail of Pythia's plan. How will she strike at the Cogito, now that we've captured you?"

"I—" Quill tried to speak.

"You what? Spit it out, boy!"

Letty stood up so quickly that her chair toppled. "We don't know what the hell you're talking about!"

Onya looked like she might leap over the table at Letty.

"More respect! On all sides, or I'll terminate this meeting," Silius commanded, suddenly quite stern.

"Do it, you parasite! I'll have them bleeding in the gutters before the hour is out!"

"You are expelled, Onya! May the Heart be ashamed of this behavior and strike you as a leader!" Silius yelled, pointing at the door.

Onya scoffed and grabbed her bundle of rags. "The sanctity of secularism is not debatable, not by any of you. Mind your tongues out there, there are listeners on every corner," Onya leveled the last command at the newcomers before turning and leaving.

Letty shared a nervous look with her friends.

Silius sighed and looked ashamed. "She is right on one point. Any talk of the God that failed, or the one who might not have, can be a death sentence in certain parts of the city. Those parts are anywhere the Heart has listeners."

Letty was silent, as was the room.

"I hate to echo Onya, but will you please tell us why you are really here?" Vegus finally asked, his polite tone a sharp contrast to the bloodthirsty accusations of a moment ago.

Letty looked at her friends and then to the Exegesuits.

"Ah, I had her pegged as the leader," Ventalus muttered.

"The speaker named her as leader, mouse, or weren't you listening?" Belmani asked.

Ventalus scowled at the woman.

Letty waited for the awkward exchange to end, before speaking. "We have lost one of our pupils. He is dear to us—"

"To Pythia, you mean," Vegus interrupted.

Letty's face sharpened. "Yes, to our Mistress as well. We know that he was captured by a certain ryle. We have come here in the hopes of learning more."

"And we'll need to use the portals," Emma said.

Letty glared at Emma so harshly that Emma nearly fell out of her seat.

"What? They're going to follow us around anyway," Emma complained.

Silius laughed. "She's right."

"Portals are expensive, young lady," Ventalus said, pulling on a whisker. "But, that's beside the point. The real question is: Do we arrest these potential saboteurs, or do we give the people what they were promised?"

"With yesterday's skybreak and all the unsubstantiated claims of a rogue Seer, I say we give the people something wholesome to replace the religious gossip. There is room for us all to gain here, as long as we keep an eye on them." Silius replied.

Oort, who had been silent, if not huge, rumbled a whispering series of clicks into his goblin's ears. "Right, so, is we to take it that there won't be any of the fun times and follies and such, mentioned at the official greetings?"

There was a sudden mumbling between the Exegesuits.

"Well, let's make a deal," Ventalus said. "If you Caspians agree to gift our city in the ways that were mentioned, we will provide you with food, lodging, proper attire, and a security detail—eh," Ventalus's ears flattened in consternation, "in case Onya follows through with her, particular brand of zeal. However, it cannot be thought that we would supply you with funds for something as blasphemous as portal creation."

"Will you agree to our terms?" Silius asked. "You must provide the gifts specified, and we will arrange a schedule of events and provide the services promised—"

Letty interrupted, "We need time to conduct our business as well."

"Yes, time for your business as well. But the caveat stands: If you are involved in any such—" Silius coughed nervously, "religious warfare, Onya and the Heart will not hesitate to exterminate you—

for the good of the city, of course."

Letty paused only for a moment, before agreeing.

"I am alarmed by these claims of a rogue Seer wielding the Argument and walking the streets naked, with his eyes out for everyone to see," Belmani said, and those around rankled at the words. "It has been more than a week with no verification, but your sudden appearance is suspicious. If there is any connection between that alleged Seer, and you, it will violate this agreement."

No one disagreed.

I wonder if that's Andy—It can't be though; he's been captured by Ziesqe. How could he be here?

Silius got to his feet. "Very good then! I'm looking forward to the dinner. All the socialites will want to see you! A few brutox queens might attend—careful Oort."

Oort clicked a long and suggestive click before lumbering to his feet. "Oort says there isn't a pherimony factory around what could make him forget his zeal to the AOE," Oort's goblin said dramatically, as Oort made his way to the door.

The high Exegesuits, save Ventalus and the diplomat Silius, left the room. A few deacons with parchment, ink, and quills, arrived.

"Can we hear of your tale?" Ventalus asked. "Please, do not be scant with the details; you come from far."

I better tell it. We can't have anyone slip up and accidentally let them know that three of us are from the surface, and I'll have to make up something about my supposed visit to the surface.

"We left Caspia about a week ago; it's been crazy on the road," Letty said, before telling about their trip to Sentinel's watch from Caspia.

"Why go by the faithful builders? They should be bad company," Silius asked.

"Well, they were, but we couldn't take any chances going pacwards from Caspia. The ryle who control the lands outside our city are hostile. We had to go a bit norwards to get around them," Quill chimed in.

Silius nodded. "Did you notice anything else when you were passing through the mouse country?" Silius asked, offhandedly.

Letty paused.

"What, like how their fortress was destroyed?" she asked sharply.

Ventalus nodded, his ears flattening. "Just a verifying question, dear; no need to get upset. It was for the best, in the end. Most of them retreated here. Hopefully they will forget their old follies and join us in the new era of cooperation. The Argument and Counter have been nothing but a blight to the Netherscape, and adherence to either will eventually wither away. They are failed designs."

So, the mice all came here? I wonder if Titus and Taptalles are with them? We should try to find out.

"Pardon me, Ventalus, sir," Emma interjected. "I was wondering why you look so different from the other mice that we've seen. You must be three feet tall."

Ventalus narrowed his brow sharply.

"Emma, that's a rude thing to mention," Quill said. "Please forgive us, it's just simple ignorance."

"No, that's fine," Ventalus replied, his whiskers still on end. "It's rather difficult to be taken seriously at barely a hands width of height. So, I used much of the wealth I had earned trading over the years in the Panforum to tinker with my own design."

Silius chuckled approvingly. "Some would call it vanity, but I've always found that a few improvements pay for themselves many times over, even if Onya and her type wouldn't approve."

Ventalus agreed, "Indeed, it isn't as noticeable on Silius here, but he is nearly as old as myself, well past a century, and he looks like an ychorite of only four decades. He is also hewn from stone, the robes obscure that, and don't think all that wit didn't receive a polish."

"More than a polish, Venty; I just reread some old speeches I wrote before my first Myr step. Whew! I was worse than a one Sici initiate!"

Ventalus laughed heartily, his whiskers twittering with mirth.

"What's a Myr step?" Letty asked.

Silius was still chuckling. "Nothing much, just the means to near-immortality and endless self-improvement! Though far more expensive than a portal, and not, strictly speaking, the most secular activity."

That might explain all the beautiful people walking around.

Ventalus finally calmed himself. "A healthy sense of humility, that's why I like you, Silly. No one else on the council has learned this simple truth: Life is better if you don't have a ten-foot pole—" Ventalus sputtered and burst out laughing.

"Now, now," Silius said. "Oort isn't as bad as the others. Let's get back to business here," and then ignoring Ventalus, and looking at Letty, he started rambling, "So you saw the ruins of Sentinel's Watch burning, yes, yes, one more page turned, another stone crumbles. You then traveled sur, sur-pac, through Vichy lands?"

Letty nodded.

"Stop me if you want to add anything. But then you met some Elazene?"

"Yes," Letty said, trying to get Silius to stop for a moment. "They're being hunted down by a cult!"

"The cult of Supthoi, out of Yyonvere," Quill added.

"Yes, they need help. Degoskirke is huge, bigger than I expected, and if we sent out word, they could come and hide here," Letty said.

Silius and Ventalus shared a wry look.

"Was that their idea?" Ventalus asked.

Surprised, Letty shook her head.

"I didn't think so. The Elazene have a love-hate relationship with their land," Ventalus said, looking at Silius like he was getting ready for another joke. "Not unlike us here, with the Archatians." He paused for a quick giggle. "This type of relationship is often bloody, but Elazene culture is tied to that land, like our city is sewn together with equal parts abstinence and debate."

Silius nodded, and the scribes happily scratched

away, recording the meeting.

"Why do you even raise the point, girl? I thought you were here about a lost pupil," Silius asked.

Letty frowned. "I didn't think helping the Elazene was possible, and then we ended up sitting with the most powerful people in the city. I figured I should at least ask. They were very good to us."

Her friends nodded in agreement.

Ventalus tugged on a whisker before speaking carefully, "Well, sad facts are what they are, and I hope you become inured to likelihoods; you may be facing a bleak one again. If you do not find your brother pupil, please do not let it sour all the positive rapport we have built here. Young, smiling, and skillful people like you will do a great good in the city. You might even calm the Archatians enough for the paint to dry between their various parcels."

Silius took a heavy breath. "May calm heads prevail—there is one last detail. You were seen entering the city with a blue mouse, my report suggests that he was a local."

Letty blinked. "Blue," she said, checking her shoulders, and then looking over at her friends. "I haven't seen him since we entered the city."

"He stays so quiet most of the time that I forget he's there," Dean said.

"I see," Ventalus said. "Check your purses and bags. Some of the locals aren't the most honest."

Letty wondered where the mouse had gone and if he had abandoned them.

Another robed deacon entered the room and

approached Silius with a piece of parchment.

"Ah, yes, your timetable."

Letty felt herself cringing as they poured over countless details of the schedule.

"Right!" Silius said, standing. "You'd better get dressed. You all have a very full dance card."

Chapter 5: Ithmene

Andy rolled under the covers, stretching and yawning, before opening his eyes. The Infiniteye shimmered softly on the ceiling. He felt like it was staring down at him. Andy sat up and felt uneasy about how comfortable he was.

I wish I could just stay. This place is like a Seer hideout. I could just live here and practice with that book. I might go down the street for supplies; I still have money.

Andy got up and walked around the room, paying attention to the writing on the wall.

"Ryle running the Greylapse, mind the arches." "The Usurper will be the end of us, unless we fight back!" "Killing ryle in public will damage our legitimacy." "Study first, so you don't die second." Another comment, next to the last, read: *"This is a silly saying!"* Andy looked to another wall. *"Don't forget to bring a builder! Many chapter houses are locked by mouseport!"* An arrow pointed to the floor under this last message.

Andy followed the arrow. It pointed to a bunk. Shifting the bunk and rolling up the carpet beneath, Andy spotted something.

Another trapdoor.

He tugged on the ring that attached to the trapdoor in the floor.

It stuck tight. Andy found his Argument and put on the Silversight.

The trap-door was attached to a mechanism that disappeared into the wall. There was a small, but deliberately carved mouse-hole in the wall.

Andy leaned in and saw tiny carved letters on

the arch above the hole. They were Latin.

Murum Portu.

Andy scowled.

Damn Latin. Well, it's mouse sized.

Andy heard a bell tinkling near the ladder that led down into the hideout. He leaped to his feet and involuntarily summoned the blade.

He saw a small bell hanging on the ceiling. A string ran up from the bell and then disappeared upward. Andy wondered if someone was at the door.

He grabbed the training manual before turning the lever that unlocked the way up. He climbed back into the house, summoned the glow, and was ready to call the blade as he moved towards the front door.

Who could it be? Those kids brought me here, but I bet everyone in their parcel knows about me now. Maybe word got out and the guards are onto me, or maybe it's Ziesqe, wondering about his plan.

He looked through the window and saw someone with long crimson hair walking away. Andy opened the door. A breakfast tray sat on the floor. Andy was touched and ashamed of his suspicion and then his rudeness in not answering the door. Not wanting to waste the food, and grateful that he wouldn't have to leave right away, Andy grabbed the tray, which smelled better by the second. He recognized toast and red butter. Though the tall pot of steaming soup featured one too many mussel shells and tentacles for his taste.

Andy took the tray to the sitting room. He idly noticed that it seemed a little different, cleaner and more organized than it had before. He sat down at a table by the window. Someone had been here and had taken the sheets off the furniture.

Andy ignored the changes and ate through the apple, toast, and flaky pastry before realizing that he was still hungry. Sighing, he grabbed the spoon and closed his eyes before taking a spoonful of the soup.

Seafood.

Andy cringed through a few bites and found himself surprised at the mild flavor. The texture was still a little sickly though. He averted his eyes as he ate and finished sooner than he expected. He had a taste of the tea and found it was more like a sweet coffee. Despite his reservations, breakfast was delicious. Putting his cup down, he resolved to thank whoever had left it.

Andy got to his feet and was confused about what to do with the tray. *I don't want to leave it outside. Oh well, they can come in and get it. I'll thank them then.*

Andy knew he should be nervous or cautious, but couldn't be bothered with either. His stomach full, he went to the back yard. It was enormous and overgrown. Whoever originally designed the yard aimed for a natural effect, with curving pathways, and a small pond near a bench, but the silver-barked trees and the red ferns had grown out of control and overwhelmed the yard.

Andy sat on the bench and pulled out the training manual.

> Novice bladesmen will find their untrained blades loose of form and occasionally fluttering or going out. This is due to a lack of honing.

Twist the wrist as in Ill:2. Execute the following exercise to the point of nerve fatigue, and no further. Continue in this way until you find that position where your blade is most solid and your grip becomes comfortable. That is your hone. Never fight a Counter equipped foe without finding your hone. The results are disastrous.

You might find the blade changing shape, color, length, or even going slack, if so, consider charging your Argument and returning to the illustrations. It is also likely that you are making extraneous movements as a result of poor dexterity. A slight misplacement of tension in the fingers, upper hand, or wrist, can all mean changes for your blade. These changes will be instrumental in further technique, but for now, you must master this first step.

It was all confusing, and he wished a teacher were on hand to explain. He paused and looked up from the manual.

Did I just wish for a teacher?

Andy shook his head, got to his feet, and tried the exercise.

I've made the blade change consistency before, but I don't think I've ever found the hone.

Andy tensed his fingers and moved them as it showed in the illustrations. The blade changed colors. It was now a striped, silver-copper color. Andy swung the blade a few times, feeling uncertain.

The blade popped and slackened into the pond. Steam shot up from the water, and he loosened his grip.

This'll take a while.

Andy practiced until he felt himself getting hungry again. He loosened his grip and looked around the yard. Several trees were now missing limbs, which littered the grass. Andy bent to pick up the branches he had accidentally sheared.

He piled them up near the back door and then heard a slight clicking as he dropped the last load of branches.

Andy's hand glowed, his tension almost autonomic. He stepped inside and saw his breakfast tray had been replaced. Andy rushed to the front door and stepped out into the street. He spotted red hair swaying in the distance. A few teal skinned children were playing down the street. They paused and looked up at him, one waved, but another pulled her hand down.

Andy sighed and waved back before going back inside to inspect the restocked tray. He tore through a pile of sandwiches and a tall pitcher of ice water.

Andy leaned back in his chair and looked out the window. Blossoming bushes swayed gently under a light wind. Their small leaves flickered and, for a moment, Andy felt like he was at home on a summer day. He looked down at his clothes.

I wish I had some jeans.

Andy took a deep breath and felt the urge to get back outside.

If I was at home, Dad would be yelling at me about homework, or Mom would be on me about taking out the trash and doing the dishes. I know I have to go outside and keep practicing, but it would be nice to have someone yell at me about it.

Andy laughed at himself and returned to the yard. He planted a few of the sliced branches into the ground to stand in as training dummies.

His blade was changing. After the hours of practice, it had continued adjusting color. It was now steel colored at the core and licked with a coppery flame. He ran across the yard, turned on a dime and sliced a path through the army of standing branches.

When he had reached the pond on the far side of the yard, he realized that his blade hadn't failed during the exercise.

I almost forgot about the grip altogether.

Andy smiled, confident that he had mastered the first step, and returned to the manual on the bench.

> Form II: A shield. It is requisite that the bladesman complete the Silversight preamble, before attempting to learn this form." Andy flipped through the book, until he found the Silversight section. "The blade might be the more alluring of the two primary schools of Argumentation, but even the most basic blade forms depend on a solid understanding of the Fyr, or communing with God. Which is the traditional way of referring to containing the Argument orb within oneself.
>
> A novice bladesman might find the blade a dependable weapon, as the Argument rests easily in his grasp. Further training will require the student to become comfortable with the Silversight, and then with a semi-permanent

state of Fyr, or the act of containing the Argument form within oneself indefinitely, before they learn how to shift the Argument from limb to limb, within themselves.

Andy flipped the page, convinced he already knew how to use the Silversight. He skipped forward to the Fyr.

Hold out the off-hand and tense the muscles leading from your face to your off-hand. This is an ineffective method for moving the Argument form through your body, but it will aid your training. Maintain Silversight, and follow the preceding instructions.

Andy assumed the Silversight and felt overwhelmed by the rush of noise coming from all around. It was far louder outside than indoors.

I've never used the Silversight outside like this. Maybe I shouldn't have skipped the last chapter.

Andy felt his head spinning and he stumbled inside to continue practicing. He focused and held out his arm.

I think I've accidentally done this once before.

He tensed his muscles and felt the sight leave his eyes. A pulsing warmth flowed down his arm and rested heavily in his off hand, which glowed.

Yes, I did this once before. But was it actually Caspian?

He looked back to the book in his other hand.

Practice moving the Argument essence from limb to Sight to limb.

After a few minutes of practice Andy had to

take a seat; he was dizzy. He flipped back to the shield section and studied the illustrations; he considered them simple enough.

A few hours later, Andy was swinging at branches while bearing a blade and a shield, but only for a few seconds at a time.

I can maintain the forms indefinitely if I just stand with them, but once I move and swing it's so much harder to keep the nerves flexed in the right way.

Andy set up a few more branches and tried to fight his way through them. His weapon and shield popped and sputtered out after a few swings. Andy reset and tried again. He continued training until he felt like it was going dark outside.

Looking up at the ceiling, Andy saw a tiny cluster of steel flashing between the other, more dominant colors.

Not sure what to make of that, he felt a rush of soreness from his complaining limbs. Yawning, he went inside, and was not surprised to find a tray of dinner waiting for him.

I wonder what they think about me. Why don't any of them come and ask what I'm doing? Speaking of that, what am I doing?

Andy felt the desperate need of a plan. What were his priorities, and why did this Seer manual feel so critical? He tried to think back to Ziesqe and his plan for the city, but he shivered with shame and anger every time he tried to consider Ziesqe. He found it easier to keep flipping through the first few chapters of the manual. He felt like Pythia in the Juncture, and considered staying in the mansion for a few years, hiding and training. If they kept on feeding him, he'd never have a reason to leave.

Andy looked at his plate and realized that he had eaten half of his dinner: a pair of black lobsters. Afterwards, he crawled down to the hideout and fell asleep under the watchful presence of the Infiniteye.

He opened his eyes at the sound of the tinkling bell. He had slept in.

Andy got to his feet, failed to dress, and rushed to the door, hoping to thank the red-haired person who had been bringing him food. He stepped out into the street in time to see the hair, tied back today, swaying over the shoulder of a feminine figure.

I still haven't even seen her face. She gets in and out of here so quickly, and I'm always distracted.

Even then, Andy had the urge to devour his breakfast and return to destroying the yard. After eating, he did just that, but shortly found himself stuck at the same problem. His blade and shield kept flickering out.

Andy returned to the manual and started at the beginning. He read the first few pages, which featured a basic training section:

> Argument cessation is often caused by poor dexterity or body control. Run through these stretches, these strength-building exercises, and the focusing methods detailed on the following page as a requisite precursor to a daily routine.

Andy did stretches and pushups, as well as sprints in the yard. After the precursor exercises, he found his sword and shield combo would last longer. The training made him realize where tension in his body cropped up, and how it was disrupting the form.

I've been getting ahead of myself, Andy thought. *I need better control of my nerves and muscles before I continue learning about the blade, but I can learn more about the Silversight.*

Andy read and found he needed basic mechanical components to practice more advanced forms of the Silversight. He recalled seeing components that matched the description down in the hideout.

Andy found a few clocks and small steam engines, but also noticed a collection of strange implements that almost looked like wrist and arm armor in one of the footlockers. Andy knew what they were. He had just read about pressure clothing, which, when worn over various parts of the body, helped with keeping the correct nerves engaged. They were worn to counteract weak form. Andy put on a pair of gloves and sleeves, found dials on the wrists, and set them to sword and shield before trying the form.

Hmm, I can feel the pressure, but is it helping?

Andy took a few swings, careful not to destroy anything. He was surprised when the blade and shield refused to flicker out. He dashed across the room and turned on a dime, swinging as he did so. It made a considerable difference.

These are great, but the manual specifically says not to use them, for fear of dependency, and that they aren't easy to manipulate in a high-stress situation. It's impossible to change them from blade and shield to any other form in a fight.

Andy took the sleeves off and put them on his bed, before continuing to look for a mechanism. He found a box, described in the manual as a puzzle cube, bearing three switches on one side and a crank on the other. Andy took the puzzle cube, a watch, a small engine, and several tools, upstairs with which to practice.

With the Silversight, the cube was almost too simple to master. The only issue came from the trick of its construction, which featured three inner walls that, according to the manual, were specifically made to challenge Seers using the Sight.

> The Silversight might seem a foolish tinkerer's tool to the uninitiated, and it is the uninitiated who fail as a result of their neglect. Do not be like so many others who only learn the most basic forms and then return to the blade. Silversight training may begin with the tedious dismantling of toys, but even a moderate amount of effort will allow a Seer to accurately see through simple structures and walls, into spaces beyond. Not to mention, Seer architecture remains secure through the use of this technique. Do not fail to be its master, or you might find yourself starving on the wrong side of a Juncture enigma.

Andy sighed. *I already know the truth of that,* he thought. *Thankfully Martin talked me through my first use of the Sight.*

> Experiencing the Silversight can be a frightening and daunting task for a novice. The masters, who pour their knowledge into this manual freely,

admit that they are unsure about the schematized form in which reality appears to the Sight. What are these lines and the words that compose the world? Why do voices seem to read off what you see, even when you don't want them to? The masters concur that these words and frames are representative of some truth inherent to their physical form. There is knowledge packed away in the framework of everything, but it might take a power akin only to God's to comprehend the fullness of that complexity. For the beginner, it is only essential to know that what you see is real. You will spend most of your effort with the Sight trying to ignore these voices, and focusing on simple connections. Resist the urge to chase macro connections or to understand the essence of another living being, say, a tree, or another person. Even skilled Seers have lost themselves in these attempts. Let it be reiterated: You can lose your mind if you give yourself over to the Silversight. The simplest way to avoid this is to not stay connected to the Sight for more than an hour at a time. If you find yourself far too focused on one single strand or wire, pull back immediately.

Andy pondered over the previous paragraph. *That's scary. I remember feeling comfortable with the Sight once, back with Pythia. I didn't realize this could happen. Luckily, she was there to pester me.* He continued reading:

There are wonders that only the most heroic Seers of history have discovered through their use of the Silversight. It is said that the power to understand true motivation, and even to be blessed with the ability to speak, like God, rests at the end of this dangerous and misunderstood path.

Andy spent the rest of the day alternating between the tedious act of disassembling delicate machines, exercising, and practicing his blade forms. He had hoped to see the girl who brought him his meals, but would only ever find the tray on the floor outside, or on the table.

He spent the day this way, and the next, and then he lost count.

I've been here for five—maybe six days. No, wait, I had lobsters again yesterday, that's a week now.

Andy felt he had mastered blade and shield, and he had done it without the pressure sleeves. Though his moment of triumph foundered when he slipped in a rut he had worn in the yard. He smacked onto the ground and heard a truncated laugh.

Andy looked up and saw a teal face with golden eyes staring at him through a window. His cheeks went instantly red. Andy and the girl froze, staring at each other. She was striking. Her lips parted, half laughing and half afraid. He felt the twisting within worsen, the longer he stared.

"Hey!" Andy finally yelled, slipping as he tried to stand.

Once he had gotten inside, she was gone, though lunch remained. Andy ate, and tried to return to training, but he felt suddenly nervous.

I bet she's watching me right now.

Andy shifted the Argument through his arms and into his eyes. He took apart the walls and looked as far as he could into the spaces beyond. In the process, he was surprised to see several mechanical components sewn throughout the walls of the house.

Andy tried to figure out what they were, or what they were connected to, but the whole thing was too complex for him to follow. Resolving to return to the problem with more experience, Andy continued his uneasy training, but felt himself formulating a plan for the next morning.

I've got the alarm clock working, and I have a good sense of when she comes with food; it's always about the same time. I'll just wake up early and catch her.

Pleased with his ingenuity, Andy spent the rest of the day training indoors, with the shades drawn, by the light of the spare Argument.

Andy moved ahead in the blade section, and quickly mastered the third form: blade and parrying dagger, finding it barely different from blade and shield.

Any weapon can be reproduced with the Argument, but for the weapon to sustain itself outside of your touch, or away from your body, is impossible to almost every Seer. Do not attempt to create a ranged weapon, of any sort, at this stage of training. Practice with recognizable forms, and you'll find that most melee weapons are possible. Good results have been had with a long blade, and spiked knuckles for the off-hand.

Form IV: Armor. The leap from masterfully reproducing weapons, to shielding one's whole body in the Argument is wide indeed. Practice your basic forms and exercises until absolute mastery, before attempting form IV.

Andy raised an eyebrow.

What's the worst that could happen?

He studied the illustrations and read the muscle instructions for a breast plate.

It's completely different. I have to tense my core muscles too. How am I going to do that and sustain a sword and shield? I'll be stretching the Argument from hand to hand and down into my chest!

Andy felt like kicking the table as he realized exactly how difficult it would be to make any further progress.

I might as well try. Just the armor for a start.

Andy repeatedly stopped and started, always to look back at the illustrations. Frustrated, he cobbled together a simple lectern by standing two chairs on each other and leaning his lunch tray on them at a tilt, so the book would lay open for easy reference.

Andy tensed his midsection and stood in a fighting stance. He felt the Argument struggle to leave his palms, and when it did fill his chest, the slightest flick of a finger seemed to reel it back.

Andy stood, practicing, for so long that he began to feel lightheaded.

Just a little more.

He looked down and saw a steel color shimmering over his chest in the shape of a mangled piece of armor.

His midsection moved slightly as his neck craned down to look, and the armor morphed with the movement. He tried to take a step and the armor disappeared with a slight pop.

Andy struggled for hours, stopping to drink and sit while going over the illustrations, which were becoming more complex, the further into the manual he went.

He looked at his repaired alarm clock and realized that it was almost time for bed.

Just one more go.

Andy stood and assumed his stance. He felt his muscles tense just the right way, and looked down to find himself wearing a completed breast plate.

He tried to maintain the feather balanced tension the book insisted on. He stepped. The armor flickered, but stayed. He carefully walked around the room.

I think I've got it. It's only one piece of armor, but it's a start!

Andy felt the urge to try for a helmet, or maybe even a blade as well.

He went out into the yard and practiced walking, and then running with the armor. He moved the Argument through all the forms he knew, and found a fluidity to the process. He felt the urge to try mixing the forms.

I saw Ziesqe with a full suit of Counter armor and a blade once. He even wore regular, metal armor beneath. I can't imagine how hard that must be.

Andy felt the urge to rush ahead, but his head was spinning, and his heart felt like it might burst.

Maybe I'll try tomorrow.

Andy took his equipment, and the alarm clock,

to bed. With his body tired and sore, he fell asleep almost instantly.

His alarm dinged.

"Tomorrow's not Monday," Andy mumbled, reaching for the clock and falling out of bed in the process.

"Damn clock. Why'd I leave it on the table?"

Andy suddenly remembered why.

The girl!

He dressed and tried to get a look at his face in a piece of polished metal, once part of a clock.

Damn, I need a haircut, and these clothes are the worst!

Andy heard noise at the door. He dropped the polished metal plate, climbed the ladder, and rushed to open the door. She had already laid the tray down and was walking away. She flinched at the sound of the door opening and sped up.

"Excuse me!" Andy said, following her.

She continued walking.

Andy ran out, passed her, and then stood in her path.

He opened his mouth, but found himself struck mute.

Her golden eyes flashed and her red lips curled in an uncertain smile. She clasped her arms in front of her, and the brass sea shells adorning her simple white dress rang with the movement. Her teal skin glistened under the vinlight. She tilted her head and let her long crimson hair fall across her face, as if she were hiding behind it.

Why can't I say anything?

Andy felt his throat tighten as he realized that he looked like a complete idiot.

Finally, she spoke, "You make immense progress with the Argument. I'm looking forward to seeing you fully garbed for battle. When you kill the ryle, my sisters and I will be there to sing your hymns. Please remember our loyalty in your moment of death and glory."

She smiled and walked past. Her hair brushed his arm as she went. Andy wanted to say something, but could barely keep himself from gawking.

She thinks I'm Caspian, but I told that kid what happened.

She smiled and waved before turning the corner and disappearing.

I didn't even ask her name.

Andy went back inside, feeling like a fool. He tried to choke through his breakfast.

She knows what I'm doing. Of course, she's been watching me.

The red in Andy's cheeks refused to relent for the next few hours, and he forced himself through his routine of calisthenics and strength building exercises.

He found himself constantly shifting to the Sight and looking through the walls and into the nearby houses. He could only see so far, and the process tired him faster than almost anything else, but he continued to do so.

It's probably a good habit to get into anyway—for security reasons.

Andy spent the next few days focused on

training his ability to mix the forms, to wield weapon and shield, while bearing a full suit of armor.

Occasionally he spied a female form through the walls of the house next door. She had been watching him from up there as well.

One afternoon, Andy took his lunch outside and leaned back on the bench as he ate. He took a deep breath before spotting movement through the window.

He remained calm and started eating as he shifted the Argument from his palm to his eyes. He cast them over the wall and saw her hiding near the window. She was peeking through the curtains at him. He saw that her muscles were shaking, as if she were afraid, or ready to run if he should look her way.

Andy blushed and looked away, realizing that clothes were also little impediment to his Sight.

Andy finished his lunch and passed a quick glance over the window.

She's still there.

He stood up and stretched, patting his stomach to show her he appreciated the food.

He stepped towards his last two dummies; Andy had long since trimmed the trees well back. He ran through his forms, the illustrations of the manual flashing into his mind as he executed the movements. He played with the blade and made it transform into a halberd, an axe, and even a crescent bladed saber.

He cast a glance at the window and saw she was

still there.

He went into the fourth form and covered his body in a suit of armor. He felt the urge to split the Argument and tighten his palms to create a pair of blades to go with the suit.

She would love it.

Andy walked through the yard at ease in the full suit, trying to fight off the urge to draw blades.

She said that she was looking forward to this.

He tightened just one palm, in compromise with himself, and felt his head instantly swim. The blade appeared. He heard a loud crack and felt empty before he hit the floor.

Andy was falling, but it was like falling through water. His skin tingled like he was being engulfed by a warm bath. The water tugged and he had the sense of pulling away from some shore. His thoughts lolled back and forth, rocking with the gentle surf. He smelled sea foam and vanilla and felt the spray splashing against his face. His head lolled to the side and his back sunk. His mind flashed with the sensation of the Silversight. He saw shapes cloaked in their schematized form. Water sparkled and filled his foggy thoughts. A voice echoed in his mind, reading off the infinite minuscule details that appeared in the place of water when he sunk beneath the surface.

Andy tried to pull himself up. The urge to take in a breath was suddenly overwhelming and he opened his eyes, heaving. He sat up, gulping for air, and feeling the sense of emptiness rushing back.

"It's okay; you should be fine," a soft voice said.

Andy felt a hand on his chest. His vision focused, and he saw the girl with the teal skin.

Andy struggled with two strong urges: embarrassment, and the need to discover the source of the strange emptiness. He flexed his left palm, but nothing. No light, and no sign of the blade appeared. He tried to stand, but she held him down.

The Argument isn't here! I must have lost it when I fell.

"I need the Argument!" Andy said, sounding more desperate than he expected. He pushed against the girl, trying to stand.

"Please, wait, just for a moment. I'll get it for you," she said, fear in her voice.

"Can you touch it?" Andy asked, still trying to sit up.

It looked like she wanted to force him back down to rest, but she was afraid.

"No," she admitted.

She's shaking. Why? I'm the one with a bump on my head.

"It's okay," Andy said, "I'll be fine without it, for a while at least. It just feels so urgent. My body is telling me I need it. I'm not used to that."

She calmed. "You've kept the Argument within for so long. It is said to be like being with God." She looked nervously over to the door, desperate to leave.

"Will you tell me your name?" Andy asked. "I want to thank you for all that you've done for me."

She paused and titled her head in thought. She avoided meeting his glance, but considered him, nonetheless.

She bit her lip and clasped her hands together. The sight of her slight and graceful movement made Andy feel a plunging pain in his stomach.

"My name is Ithmene," she whispered.

"What's the problem, Ithmene? You're acting strangely."

"Strange," she quipped. "You haven't been back home for so long, and I, of all the maidens, have to attend you. None of my teachers have ever even spoken to a true Seer, much less the Voice of God—"

Andy interrupted her, "I am not the Voice of God."

That shocked her to the point of silence. They stared at each other for a long moment, before she finally rushed to the door.

"Please! Please, don't leave me alone," Andy cried out, suddenly terrified. The crushing loneliness of the past days felt like a thousand hands grasping at every inch of his body. Seeing her leave was like being pulled under the earth by those hands and held tight until all memory of him disappeared.

She paused, with her hand at the door, and looked back at him. She was crying, and her face contorted, as if he had struck her.

Andy struggled to stand.

"I'm afraid," he whispered.

"I'm sorry," Ithmene said, wiping a tear away from her golden eyes.

Andy held a hand out for her.

She rushed to him and they embraced. He nearly stumbled back onto the couch.

Andy felt her arms wrap around him. He felt his mind melting at the touch of another person. His face flushed as if aflame. The mountain of fear that had built up inside was suddenly present. He felt his mouth open and the words were there, as if they had no choice.

"They put me in a cage," he whispered. A wave of grief wracked his body. "They chained me." Andy shuddered and clutched her. "They made me a killer, and I'll never forget." He heaved a gasp and felt Ithmene's fingernails bite into his back as she shook at the words. "Every person I've met wants me gone and replaced. People look at me and see someone else. There's a voice in my mind, the Usurper, and he wants to kill me."

Ithmene held him tightly, her own body tensing as she cried.

"I don't know what to do," he finished, breathing heavily and realizing the truth of his words.

They stood and cried on each other. Andy breathed in gasps, tasting the smell of sea and vanilla in her hair as he burrowed his face into the nape of her neck.

"What do you want me to do?" She asked.

He sensed something strange in her voice. He pulled away and, though she tried to hide it, he saw terror in her eyes. Andy immediately regretted what he had done.

"I'm sorry. I shouldn't have said all that to you. A few weeks ago, I was home, with my family, and now—"

"A few minutes ago, I was sure that you were the

reincarnation of Caspian."

Andy pulled away from her, realizing that his words, his admission had hurt her.

"I'm sorry. I don't know why I did that," Andy said, too ashamed to even blush.

She shook her head. "You didn't take the Cogito, but you wield the Argument. We are unsure of what to do. You matched so many of the songs. I've waited my whole life to see you," she said, biting her lip, and tearing a rent in her dark orange dress.

Andy felt his heart ache as the fabric ripped.

Why did I even open my mouth? I ruin everything.

"Stop," he said, reaching out to lay a hand on hers.

"What do you want from me?"

Andy was silent until he knew.

"Just stay with me for tonight. I'm sick of being alone."

She nodded, and they sat on the couch.

"You think that I'm something, something that you want me to be, but you don't understand what happened. Will you listen if I tell you? Maybe you can make some sense out of it."

She nodded. "I would like that."

Andy told his story, from the beginning at the gallery, to the moment he refused Caspian and escaped the Guilt.

She sat and listened, wide-eyed. Then she started singing, so softly at first, that Andy had to lean in:

Laughing God, o killing God, withheld,
our hope renew!
Hear the foe, now still, now low; loyal
voices, dying sighs!

Take the boy, your Cogito; stand amid
the faithful few, And fill our ears with
their cries!

Cisterns bulge with purple flesh—
yawning jaws on steel rasp.
Taste the Guilt of vacant hands, turned
to naught and withered will!

Silver eyes, now rouse our lands! They
fear those that dare to clasp,
Dare to seize, and dare to kill!
Decrying he the mantle, hiding, afraid
and alone.

Dare the boy to step aside, when the
ground is rent at noon?
Steel vinlight is spilt from on high!
Hordes will dream till all is done,
Till a blade is raised at noon.

Andy was silent, not knowing what to make of
the song.

"We thought that this foretelling was lapsed,
that it wouldn't ever mean anything," she said. "But
since you've arrived, it might become true. You
cannot step aside, when the time comes."

"Step aside?" Andy repeated.

"No one is sure," she said. "It might mean

accepting Caspian, or rejecting him, however you interpret those words."

"I rejected the Cogito, and I won't subject this city to him. He is a liar and a destroyer. I don't care how poetic you make it sound; he'll steal my body and get me killed. It'll be another pointless attempt to eliminate the ryle."

Ithmene reddened, humiliated.

"Am I wrong? Does he not fail, every time?"

After some thought, she shook her head. "I don't care if you aren't Caspian. The Voice of God chose Caspian, a mere Seer, more than five hundred years ago. Since then he has been reincarnating. Before that, any Seer could be blessed and ascend to be a Voice of God. If things have changed again, we can change with them. The mer are allied to the Argument, and not just its most famous champion. I am married to the Voice of God, and if that is not Caspian, it might be you."

Andy felt his breath quickening. Did he hear the word, "married?"

"I—I'm afraid to ask, but how do you know if I'm the Voice of God?"

"When Caspian was champion, he declared it loudly, but there were always clues in the foretelling. These songs and signs seemed to be among us, coming in on the lips of traders and in the song of birds. I just sang the song that predicted you. You spoke those exact words to me, 'I am so afraid,' you said. You rejected the mantle, and you live here in seclusion, while the word is slowly getting out."

She stood and took his hand, before leading him

to the yard.

"Look up," she said.

Andy did.

"There is the steel blossom. It grows larger every day and the secularist diviners are running out of ways to explain it away. The people in the city know; your old songs are being whispered in corners. Even the high Exegesuits have come out to deny your existence."

Andy didn't realize how much time had passed since he hid himself away.

"There is fighting in the sewers, but nobody does anything. There are guests from the snake city, and some confused people are saying that one of them is Caspian reborn. They only arrived a few days ago, but they are already the talk of Degoskirke."

I wonder if I know any of them. Maybe Quill's back from the surface. I saw him escape with Letty. Maybe it's Caston or Poll. They're military guys; this might be an expedition. I hate to think that I'm causing trouble for them.

Ithmene continued, "They match a few of the lines from specific foretellings. As a result, they are under watch. The city is on the brink of a riot."

Andy shook his head, still staring at the blossom. "People are expecting Caspian, aren't they?"

"It is in their blood. The stories we hear—" she paused and looked up, a smile growing across her face. "There was no greater time to be alive than when Caspian walked the scape. The sky lit up for months at a time with fields of silver lightning.

The forked bolts shot down and incinerated the ryle in their towers. Fires burned for weeks across the horizon. Flowers bloomed on the surface of every building. The sea water ran clear and tasted sweet." She laughed, "Two incarnations ago, he opened a portal in the sky, so everyone could watch as he destroyed city after ryle city. He mangled their God and its monstrosities. My grandparents laughed at the Exegesuit guard, tittering, and sewing cobbled sheets together and running them between the buildings, so people couldn't look up and see Caspian. Sadly, his adventures would only last for months, or a year at most. But, in that time, all creation would change. Landmarks and towns would spring up, new rivers would be born, and the Netherscape would re-parcel its pieces, or be further cloven. People believed that anything was possible. They all believed that this was the time, this time the ryle would be banished back to whatever hell spawned them. People loved his laughter and his handsome face. Just thinking about it gives me shivers—but, he did fail, every time."

Andy felt his stomach sink. His choices had stolen the hope of these people.

"There are a few Eldermer who downplay Caspian, in favor of the forms of the deep past. Before Caspian, the Seers and their orders were more permanent, and, according to these elders, more dignified. There were many thousands of them, wielding the Argument, and training, much like you do. They held kingdoms and protected their people. They were the heroes and politicians of the ancient world. They called Caspian the Usurper, because he somehow became Voice and reserved an overwhelming amount of the Argument for his undertakings. It's no coincidence that after thousands of years of warfare that the Seers, and their influence, faded almost completely after Caspian's second or third wave of incarnations. He always excused it by saying that the ryle had become too efficient at culling young Seers, and that a new method was needed. Many of those who followed the Argument left the faith. The mer always stayed true; they even redoubled their commitment. I am proof of that." She hung her head at the last, and sighed.

"Why are you proof of that?"

"I am married to you, of course. Or, to what you might be—I'm not sure. No one knew anything like this could happen." She paused at Andy's incredulous expression, "Let me explain: It was known that Caspian had a weakness for beautiful women. He wasn't shy about it, and a disguised ryle seductress once ended his life. Our branch of faith was devoted to giving him everything he needed to succeed. One of those goals was to find the most enchanting woman alive, and raise her to love him, so she could never kill him. The Eldermer gave the most beautiful girls the choice of taking your vows. We live for you. We memorize your sagas, sing your songs, sew clothes for you. Young men come from across the scape to try and tempt us away; we're that renowned," she said, clearly pained.

"Instead of Caspian, you end up sitting next to

145

me. I cried on you and crawled on the floor." Andy laughed.

"I thought you disapproved of me. I was going to get my replacement."

Andy laughed even harder.

"I'll only say this once, because it will ruin me to say it twice, but, you are painfully beautiful," Andy said, feeling like an idiot.

She laughed and twisted her hair, leaning back into the couch. Her face blushed, and she pulled a pillow over her eyes. Andy joined her in laughter and started to relax.

She's not so bad.

She finally put the pillow down and cocked her head at him. "Are you sure he's not—that sounds like something he'd say. He was a breaker of hearts."

Andy felt a twinge of doubt. He listened carefully to his thoughts, searching for signs of the Usurper.

Andy shivered, but was forced out of his thoughts as Ithmene put an arm around his waist and rested her head on his shoulder. He felt himself start to melt. A warm flush rose across his face, and he leaned back on the couch.

Worst, or best day of my life?

He grinned like a fool.

But what about Letty? Would she even care? She always hated me, until the end. She even slapped me when I came to get her. No, she punched me!

"What did that painting look like? The one you saw in the Juncture, the one with the long story written on it?"

"Oh," Andy sputtered, "It looked like a large page covered in glowing Seer script."

She reached out and brushed a hand across his face. "No, I mean, what did it look like underneath? You said you made an image—"

"Took a picture."

"Took a picture, then."

"Well," Andy tried to remember the details. "It was a modern piece. Shapes and alternating complimentary colors. It wasn't bad for something like that."

She yawned. Andy looked over at his alarm clock and realized that he should have been in bed hours ago.

"When you were telling your story, I remembered, there is something like that. We have the Greylapse near the Panforum. It's like the gallery you described. It has a painting similar to the one you saw in the Juncture. I saw it a few years ago. We can go in the morning. It would be good for you to get out."

Andy felt himself clench.

"What?" she said, sensing his response. "You don't want to be seen with me? I have other clothes, you know."

"Do ryle own the gallery?"

She chuckled. "It is said so, rather often, but how could anyone know?"

That's it. That's my plan. I go find the other ryle and warn them about Ziesqe. Maybe together we can stop his invasion. Ziesqe told me they were hesitant. Maybe I can convince them, let them know what he actually has planned.

147

They'll just think I'm Caspian, like everyone else! But maybe—they must know that the Cogito is still in place, that I haven't taken it. Maybe they'll work with me.

Andy sighed.

"What is it?"

"A ryle army is preparing to invade the city."

She shot up, her eyes wide.

"I think I might have a plan to save the city."

Shame it's such a terrible plan.

Chapter 6: Twice Truant

Letty rolled her eyes for the tenth time in under an hour. The float rocked gently as it took them down another grand avenue. People leaned out of their windows to wave and cheer. The guards, circling their float, were also tired of the fanfare; hafted weapons flagged against shoulders.

"Three days. I'm going to murder Quill. Three days of parades, parties, and wasted time. And not once could I get away. And these clothes! I'd rather be wearing the brutox armor," Letty whispered to Staza.

Letty pressed down on her puffy orange dress; it refused to flatten. The float creaked as they were pulled over a bump in the road. The brutons were goaded to pull gently, which took extra effort from their handlers. Other, more legitimate, road goers had piled up behind the float, and, thanks to the heavy guard presence, were only grumbling about the delay.

They came upon a plaza and the two debaters on stage, a woman wearing a red doublet, and a goblin carrying a mouse on his head, paused their lively back and forth to bow as the float trundled past.

We don't even get to listen to the debates.

Letty sat back in her ornate throne and slumped.

The deacon Silius had assigned to them on the first day tapped her on the shoulder. "Sit up straight, please! It's the least we can do."

"Why does anyone even care that we're from

Caspia? What does it matter?" Letty complained.

Quill and Staza paused their pained waving and looked over.

"Why do Emma and Dean get to do fun things, while we have to go on these parades?" Letty asked.

"Because you three are the most presentable, and also the most likely to cause trouble. Now perk up. The Daughters of the Secular Revolution are hosting a gala lunch and cultural dialogue for us. We should be there in half an hour."

Cultural dialogue! What does that even mean?

Letty slumped further in her throne and when the deacon came to nudge her, she stared daggers his way. He relented.

She took an agonized breath before sliding even further down her chair and watching the faces roll by.

Wow, look at her.

Letty sat up and stared at a young woman with teal skin and, what looked like golden eyes.

She's gorgeous.

The woman waved, and nudged a hooded figure who stood nearby. The figure lowered his hood.

No way—

Letty's eyes shot open as far as they could.

Andy!

She shook her head and pinched her cheeks. A moment later, they were gone.

That's it.

Letty stood and approached the float driver.

The deacon laid a hand on her shoulder. She stared at the hand and looked over to Quill and

Staza. "Hold onto something."

"Excuse me, young lady—" the deacon stammered.

Quill and Staza grinned, expectantly.

"I'm sorry, you've been very good to us, but this isn't what we agreed to," Letty said, before throwing the deacon off the float and into the crowd. She grabbed the lash from the driver, pushed him overboard, and then yelled at the brutons, "Heyah! Go, go!"

They looked back at her, unimpressed.

"Damn it!" Letty yelled, before Staza took the lash and cracked it angrily. The brutons took the hint and picked up their pace.

Quill yelled, nearly flying overboard at the burst of speed.

Staza laughed at the top of her lungs, and held on to her throne, which was luckily nailed down.

The guards scattered and people screamed as the brutons charged down the busy street.

"Get out of the way! Watch out! Oh, sorry!" Letty yelled at the passersby, the last of which took a mean tumble into a pile of vegetable refuse.

The open spaces of the Panforum loomed ahead.

We need to get off the float and duck down a side street.

Letty looked at her friends. "We're going to leap off in a moment; hopefully they'll keep chasing the float. Get ready to run."

"We'll break our legs!" Quill yelled.

Letty looked out for a way to avoid breaking bones.

"Like this!" Staza yelled. "Do what I do!"

Letty was only a little surprised when Staza leaped from the charging float and, with her right arm outstretched, grabbed onto a lamp post. Her arm tightened, and the forward momentum transformed into rotation. She spun down and around the post before stopping on the ground and then chasing after them.

"I don't think I can do that!" Letty yelled.

"Come on!" Quill replied, before following Staza's example. Though his dismount involved slamming into a surprised ychorite, who changed colors a dozen times in his trip to the floor. Quill spun about his post and came to a stop.

Letty took a deep breath and jumped. She grabbed a lamp post and swirled down exactly as Staza had. Her arm was instantly sore from the violent stretch, but otherwise she was unharmed, if not the focus of a few dozen surprised pedestrians.

Staza and Quill caught up to her, and they turned down the first alley they could find. There were no guards in sight, and the sounds of the rampaging brutons and the rogue float could still be heard minutes later.

"What's the plan, Letty?" Staza asked, as they paused for a moment in an enclosed trash area behind a tavern.

"That was—the plan," Letty said, catching her breath.

"Damn good plan," Quill replied. "The last few days have been hell. I'll take the trash over another inane party."

"Why'd you suddenly decide to do that?" Staza asked.

"I just—" she paused, remembering what she saw, "my guilty conscience is getting to me. I thought I saw Andy for a second back there. I just couldn't waste any more time," Letty said, glaring at the absurd orange dress they had her in.

"Of course, but what do we do now?" Quill asked, chafing in his high collared doublet.

They heard a noise and looked up at a goblin with a bag of garbage.

"No squatters in trash area please! Wait—you's the Caspiards, aint ya?" the goblin asked, suddenly excited.

"No, we aren't. We just look like them," Quill said.

"Ah, well, might you like to come inside the 'stablishment and take drinks with the mates. We—"

"They're over here!" A small voice called out.

They looked up and saw a few mice deftly bounding across the bricks of the buildings. Another mouse appeared from a window and raced across a clothesline.

"They're here! We found them!"

The goblin looked up at the noise. "Talky vermins, only drink thimble fulls."

"Thank God we found you," Blue's voice called out from on high. The familiar mouse climbed straight down the side of the building before alighting on the goblin. He didn't look right; his fur was painted white, and he wore a robe concealing his face.

"No God talk in my 'stablisment, damn red robes will put me outa businesses!"

Blue ignored the goblin. "We didn't know you were going to make a move. It took you long enough!"

"You could have warned us that this would happen!" Letty complained, confused by his appearance.

"How was I supposed to know you'd tell them that you were all from Caspia? The two cities have only hated each other for decades!"

"Fine," Letty said. "But why did you paint yourself?"

"It's my own business, girl! Don't mention it again," he insisted, casting glances at the humans.

There was a long and angry silence.

"So—drinks?" the goblin asked, gesturing to his rickety tavern. "Ten percentages off the thimble-brau, for the miceys!"

"To hell with your thimble-brau!" Blue snapped, before gesturing to his mice.

A pair of mice lowered a silver coin on a string in front of the goblin.

"Err, for your silence, sir," Blue said, in a grudging, apologetic way, before turning to Letty and the Caspians. "Let's go! We need to get you dressed properly."

"Thank God," Letty blurted out, as Blue climbed up her shoulder.

"This way. We can get you to a nearby safe house and have the clothes delivered there," he said, tugging on Letty's ear to get her to turn, like she was a giant horse.

Letty swatted him away. "Directions only, please," she sniped.

"Right, right, it's just rather dangerous for us at the moment—stop back up!"

Letty did as she was told and bumped into Quill and Staza. Blue gestured up to his mice, who were following along on the sides of the buildings.

Letty and her friends crouched behind a pile of crates as a single armored guardsman came into view. He was breathing heavily and looking down every alleyway. He turned towards their alley and stepped closer.

Letty grasped the Argument but doubted that she could hurt a human.

Blue saw what Letty was about to do and pointed out a team of mice as they climbed across a wall and descended to knock a trash can over behind the guardsman.

The guard turned about and rushed towards the noise.

"Now!" Blue whispered.

They rose and sneaked by, turning down another side lane, before rushing away.

Blue led them through Degoskirke, always favoring side streets and alleys, where they were available. However, they were forced onto a busy main street by a fallen building. Letty, distracted by the debates on a nearby stage, bumped into an ychorite carrying a basket of clean laundry.

"Excuse me," Letty said.

"You're fine—" the ychorite replied, only to

awkwardly pause, face to face with Letty.

Letty blinked and took a step back, surprised by the ychorite's sudden stare.

"Well step aside then!" Blue yelled from Letty's shoulder.

The ychorite dropped the basket of laundry and pushed violently through the crowd.

"What's his problem?" Quill asked.

Blue yanked on Letty's hair. "Ow!"

"Look at me, damn it!"

Letty turned her gaze to the mouse on her shoulder.

"Your damn eyes! They'll get us killed!"

Letty felt her stomach sink; she had been rolled out of bed by the diplomatic committee so early this morning, she forgot her carrot.

"Well don't just stand there! Get moving!" Blue demanded.

Letty nearly tripped over the fallen laundry. Pushing down the street, she looked over her shoulder and spotted a handful of people in torn, filthy robes investigating the fallen laundry and looking through the crowd.

Despite their clothing, Letty could see the healthy, strong forms of the bodies beneath, and she remembered Onya of the Heart, and her threats.

Commanded by Blue, she and the Caspians turned down a side street. Blue led them on a circuitous route, which finally terminated at a dingy coffee shop.

An old woman sat them in a corner at Blue's request. As they were arranging the rickety chairs,

Letty realized that the woman was blind. Letty took a deep breath and felt herself relax.

"What are we doing?" Staza whispered.

"Sitting silently and enjoying our coffee," Blue whispered, his ears flat and his brow furrowed to the point that no one dared utter another question.

Minutes later, a team of Blue's associate mice entered the shop wordlessly, scampering along the baseboards.

"I have seats for builders in the window boxes." The mice winced at being noticed. "Or I can set this up for you." The old woman paused, reached behind the counter, and produced a tray covered in mouse sized tables and chairs, all somehow affixed. "You can sit at the large table if you have business with my other guests, which I think you do, as you're headed right to them," the old woman said.

The lead mouse of the team gulped, but Blue spoke up from their table. "The tray will be fine, miss."

The old woman smiled and expertly moved their dishes, making room for the tray. She produced a miniature samovar and cabinet, and hung a tablecloth from underneath the tray, allowing the cloth to fall down to the floor.

The mice scurried up the cloth and found appropriately sized cups and plates within the miniature cabinet.

"I'm sorry I don't have someone your size available to serve you—I hope all the dishes are in good shape, my fingers are too foolish to sort them," she said sheepishly, bearing her hands which shook with a slight tremor. "I trust my guests to help keep them in order for me."

"I'm sure they are more than adequate, and you've made us most welcome," Blue said. "Some of the finest restaurants fail to keep settings for us—we are touched," Blue finished, his words earning him a beaming smile from the woman and curious glances from Letty and the Caspians, though he deflected these with a stiff, wagging finger, wordlessly insisting that his courtesy never be mentioned.

The old woman left their table as a pair of brutox entered the shop.

The team of mice had carried with them three of the needful carrots, though these were rather orange, as well as a few coins to pay for coffee and a plate of pastries.

Blue's mouse associates looked rough, with patches of missing fur and the occasional bite mark. Watching the team of coarse mice sitting and drinking their coffee from miniature cups nearly made Letty laugh.

"That could have gone much worse," Blue whispered, his eyes on the newly arrived brutox, who took a table at the far end of the shop. Blue ordered several mice to scout the nearby streets, and when they returned with no news, they paid and thanked the woman.

Blue angrily inspected Letty and the Caspians, making sure their eyes were in order, before leading them further onto the lane outside. "These orange carrots will have to do for now, but they won't protect you for more than a few hours," Blue said.

"We're used to the dark ones," Letty said.

"Well, there weren't any on hand—but we need to remember not to let them lapse—" Blue paused, glancing upward. "We're late!"

"For what?" Letty asked.

"Avera will chew my head off," Blue muttered, directing them down the lane.

"Who's that," Staza asked.

"An old friend," Blue muttered, between shouting clipped directions at them.

"Here, turn right, and head down there," Blue said, pointing at a set of stairs that descended beneath a building.

Letty took the stairs and slowed to look at another, far smaller, set of stairs carved into the wall of the stair well. The mice, who were not far behind, took the smaller set of stairs to a tiny port door that opened at the sound of their knocking.

They waited for a moment before Blue cursed and leaped off Letty's shoulder. He went through the mouse door, and they heard shrill arguing coming from the other side.

Letty tried the regular sized door's handle, but it was locked tight.

A moment later, there was a loud click and the door popped open.

They stood in astonishment and looked in on dozens of mouse sized floors that filled the space on the other side of the door. It was a tiny, or, in mouse sizes, huge, multistoried restaurant and bar.

"It's like looking at a model building, sliced in

half. Look at all the levels and the little tables and stairs," Quill said.

The mice were rapidly clearing the furniture. A few looked up at the awestruck humans and grumbled about their lunches being ruined. Once the furniture was gone, they pulled on chains connected to the floors. The floors split apart at the center and wound up, like rolling carpets, making vertical room for the humans to enter.

"Clear twenty cubic feet for them—I don't know, somewhere in the back! Yes, they're late—but who's surprised by the tall and slows! And get the band back on, we have customers here!" A pink and red mouse, standing next to Blue, yelled at the working teams.

Letty, Staza, and Quill entered carefully.

"Close the door, please!" the pink mouse yelled at the humans. "It takes fifty mice to do what one of you can, so spare us the trouble!"

"Of course," Quill said, closing the heavy metal door.

The mouse floors were unwound and laid back out as they passed, effectively locking them in. Mice replaced their furniture, returned to their drinks and dancing, and generally did all this while eying the humans.

"You should know better! Showing up late, but with them in tow, I can't blame you!" the pink mouse said to Blue, who gestured widely to the humans.

"Letty, Staza, Quill, this is Avera, proprietress of the Thungile Alehouse," Blue said, from a floor at about human eye level.

"Alehouse!" Avera repeated. "Did you hear that everyone? The daft paint-mouse says we're an alehouse again!"

"So, what is it now? Besides a tasteless, cavernous, monstrosity?" Blue asked, clutching his robe tight and looking over his shoulder nervously.

"We're a proper parcel now, with full representation in the Archatian registry. Thungile pocket-parcel, this is! See the plaza on the tenth level!" She pointed.

Letty looked, and saw, way in the distance, on the tenth level, a mouse sized stage, occupied by a pair of arguers dressed up as a Braid and a Greek.

"This way we avoid any wild law changes and the looting that brings," she concluded.

"Nice to meet you," Letty said, before immediately shrinking back under a field of annoyed looks.

"Now, now! No need to bring the rafters down, dearie!"

Letty rankled. *I wasn't even loud, but I guess this is their place.*

"Quick now, make a path to the sewer! Let's get this back in order as soon as possible," Avera commanded.

The mice continued pulling up the floors and opening a path to allow the humans to travel further inside their little city.

"What are you looking at? You go off for years to live like a mercenary, and then you come back looking like a fool, and you expect a smiling face?

How could you still be that stupid after so long?" Avera chided Blue, who was staring expectantly.

"Well, she can't be that mad; she's helping us after all," Quill whispered.

"I heard that, you gangly human! Don't think I won't take a bite out of your ear!" Avera snapped, and Blue laughed.

As they slowly moved through Thungile, Letty listened in on the mice.

"And there's some rogue Seer in town causing trouble, or at least that's the rumor, nothing has happened in a while," one mouse said to another, who looked aghast.

"I can't believe it! I leave for a few weeks to our family farm in the Wreck, and the sky breaks, and people think Caspian is back. What the hell happened to the Secular Right?" the other responded.

Letty turned her ear to another conversation.

"The fighting in the sewers hasn't affected our distributorship as much as the competition's. We've been lucky as regards the advancement of the city wall around Third Gate. They just built a new segment over a few tenements. They sealed off the holes, but the pipes still go through. We've transitioned all of our commerce to this point, and completely cut out the sewers. The best part is, my wife doesn't hate how I smell anymore!"

Letty chuckled as silently as possible, but was still met with flattened ears and twinging whiskers.

"So, the old mice—you know the ones from Sentinel's Watch—they still won't frequent any of the native establishments in the city. They turn their noses up when we go by and consider us traitors! We didn't lose the damned ancient city!"

Letty sighed, remembering Titus and Taptalles.

"Delivery, from above!" a mouse called out.

Letty looked up and saw a pulley system of cords and clips wired to hang just underneath the ceiling. She spotted a rolled-up blouse being pulled along.

"There's the target! And hurry up, this convoy is blocking up the delivery ports!" the mouse called out to the team who was working the rope system.

They unhooked the blouse and it fell unceremoniously onto Letty's head. The blouse was followed by a blue skirt, socks, a pair of flats, and then clothes for the Caspians. The clothes were of simple, but local cut.

"Damned humans, can't get away from them. Even in Thungile they're clogging the roads," a mouse complained, looking up from his table at the massive interlopers.

They finally cleared a path to the sewer entrance, which was fortified and covered in hundreds of mouse-sized locking mechanisms.

They don't want anything coming up through there.

"So," Letty whispered. "What's the plan, Blue? Do you know where we can find a portal?"

A few hundred mice shushed Letty.

"We'll discuss the plan in a minute, but you had better put those new clothes on, you don't want to be changing down in the sewers."

"Not happening," Letty said, Staza and Quill

nodded in agreement.

"Oh hell. Everyone look away from the humans!" Avera snapped, loudly.

Letty heard a loud crack. It was the thousands of mice turning their chairs, tables, and faces away from them all at once.

They are weirdly organized.

There was silence, save one mouse, some sort of radical, still on the stage. "We will not be told where to look! This is systemic humanism, a failing trait of our species since it's tragic—" the railing mouse was sidelined by his opponent, and the two struggled on the floor.

Letty sighed.

Well, my dress is huge. I can use it like a tent and get dressed underneath.

Letty and Staza had no trouble putting their clothes on under their dresses, and then pulling the large dresses off. Quill, on the other hand, looked away from the girls, but shook his head and refused to change.

"Don't say I didn't warn you," Blue quipped. "Well, it's more for the girls anyway, your only problem will be getting filthy or standing out in a crowd."

With the embarrassing show finally over, the hatch was opened, and they climbed slick and grimy rungs to the sewer beneath.

"I'm glad we changed; those stupid heels and that baggy dress would have been hell on these rungs," Staza said.

At the bottom, Letty produced a glow with her

Argument.

The sewer was more cramped than she expected, and they all had to hunch. They listened as the latch was replaced and secured.

"Well, Avera will be glad to see us gone, the old bird. But look, you shouldn't mention the plan in public, and, mouse company or no, you should be more careful about what you say, and when you say it," Blue chided, climbing up Letty's shoulder. "You, dark haired girl, I'm talking to you!"

"Yes, I'm sorry. I'll be more careful." Letty replied, holding her nose shut and scowling.

"Get used to it! If you hadn't gone on a diplomatic holiday we wouldn't be in this literal mess!"

Everyone shrunk under Blue's glare. Quill folded his arms guiltily.

"We are headed to the Sink, or the crystal shore, depending on who you ask. It's that way, get moving," Blue chided, and Letty started walking. "The Sink is the domain of the mer. They are the last robust, religious hold-outs in the city."

"Why do you say domain? Are they independent?" Staza asked.

"No. They pay their due to the Exegesuits, but they do not tolerate the Archatian system in their parcels. Say the braids try to come in and debate in the Sink, they will find the plaza empty. If the Redvolutionists try anything—well, they drown as quickly as anyone else."

"So, they violently keep the debates and law changes out of their area?" Letty asked.

"Yes. Think of them as a niche and simply distinct from everyone else. They are part of the city, an old part as well, older than the secular church. We are going to their streets. We must come appropriately. That means respect and courtesy. I trust you three more than the other two surfacers, but still, mind yourselves. The mer are a formal people."

"Is it far?" Quill asked, cringing at the smell.

"We have a quick stop first, and if all goes well, we won't have to return to the sewer for the second part of our journey."

"What's the stop?" Staza asked.

"We need to go see Dean, and quickly, before he's placed under tighter custody."

"Good idea," Letty said.

"Well, the best part, you haven't heard yet. My fellows have been keeping an eye on Emma and Dean. Dean has been succeeding in the debates, but the fool boy doesn't realize that the Sici he wins are worth quite a bit. He has the money we need to secure the mer portals."

Letty started laughing.

"What?" Staza asked. "Why is that funny?"

"If Dean and Emma turn out to not be as useless as I said they were—" Letty grinned painfully. "I'll have to apologize like I've never apologized before. Blue, how much money? Exactly how wealthy is Dean right now?"

"Extravagantly," Blue replied.

"And we're going to rob him," Letty concluded, before breaking out in more tragic laughter. "The poor guy!"

Quill and Staza became infected, but moments later they had blue tugging on their ears.

"Ow!"

"Be quiet, you idiots!" He spoke in a cross between a yell and a whisper. "There are gangs down here! And a war is being fought not too far away."

"What's this about a war?" Staza whispered.

"A surge of compelled brutox have been making incursions into the sewers. They are called compelled when they are led by ryle or queens. These look to be ryle led, considering the numbers. They are blocking commerce and continue fighting under the great walls and into the city proper. The builders, who know all the territorial gangs, believe that the invading force is inching towards the cisterns."

"Why? Is anyone trying to stop them?"

"None of the gangs have the strength to oppose them. I've heard from smugglers that they've seen ravagers in the sewers too."

Letty shivered at the thought.

"A ravager can bend its legs further than you would expect, but it would still jam the whole sewer! And you would have nowhere to go as it chased you down. But I don't think one could fit in this sewer," Quill said.

"Right, only the warriors fight in the service sewers like these, the larger tunnels, however," Blue anxiously plucked out a whisker, "They are certainly after the cisterns. Those are the only way ravagers might slip silently into the city."

"Well, besides the gangs, is anyone doing anything about it?" Letty whispered.

"Of course they are! But Degoskans are strange, they argue about everything. The church will deny it until there are ryle waving purple blades and ravagers in the streets. The Archatians can't agree on what to do. The only groups that are working together, oddly enough, are the street gangs, the builders, the goblins, and the brutox queens."

"Queens—what are they doing?" Letty asked, remembering her suit of plate armor.

"The queens, who escaped the ryle for Degoskirke, have the ability to control most brutox through the use of scent, or something of the sort; it's all very mysterious. They have laws against the queens compelling more than one hundred brutox a piece, to keep them from forming small armies in the city. So, working together with the cobbled defenders, the queens are keeping the invaders from advancing any further into the city. The enemy commanders seem to understand the danger and have fortified their positions. They rely on the ravagers, and, oddly, on ychoron fighters to hold back the local repulsion—"

Staza reached out a hand and silenced Blue. Letty stopped and waited for Staza, who crouched low and reached for a dagger that wasn't there.

Letty released her grip on the orb. They were shrouded in darkness.

Heavy footsteps splashed in the sewers nearby. The sound echoed off the walls. Letty felt Staza grab her arm.

"Be ready," she leaned in and whispered in Letty's ear.

The heavy footsteps paused, there was the sound of metal scraping on stone, and then silence. They all held their breaths.

How close is it? The sound in here is misleading.

Finally, the heavy steps faded, echoing into the distance.

"What was that?" Quill whispered.

No one answered, and they continued moving, silently at first, and then faster, as if whatever had made those noises might be right behind.

"Turn here. Left, no, the second left! Stay out of the main sewer, we don't want any company," Blue said.

They saw light pouring in from the drains above. They had entered a room built around a large pipe that led straight down. In the spaces around the pipe, a few brutox had built themselves a little shelter. Threadbare mats lined the floor, and creaking shelves held belongings on the far wall.

One of the brutox jumped up at the sudden sight of them and readied a shoddy dagger.

Letty moved to fight, but Blue tugged on her ear. "Wait," he whispered, and then spoke loudly for the brutox, "Please, we mean no harm. May we ascend through here?"

The group of brutox had a quick, click-filled huddle, and then, apparently, decided to let them pass.

"Thank you," Letty said, before climbing up another set of metal rungs.

She pushed against the sewer grate and moved it aside before climbing out. Another group of brutox were sat there, staring.

"Pardon us," Blue said, politely.

Looking around, Letty realized that they weren't in the nicest part of the city anymore. The buildings here were shabby, crumbling, and in need of fresh paint or plaster. The roads were jammed with shanties, toppled carts, and piles of ruined or burnt out ornamental furniture.

Blue directed them towards the sounds of cheering and hissing, but they avoided the main streets, and found themselves climbing over piles of debris and through destroyed buildings, suffering collapsed roofs. Those tumbled roofs were full of soil and half-grown plants.

Black and red streamers linked several buildings, though these were often in tatters. Letty noticed a preponderance of brutox in the area.

"They come here, with the mien of a lord and would dare to tell you, people of People's Parcel, that you have made a mistake! This stranger from a strange land, where they worship a woman and hold to her as a supreme ruler. This lotus eater! Opium smoker! Monarchist slave! Dares to come to the freest part of the freest city to tell you how to live!"

The crowd exploded in outrage.

Letty peeked around the corner of the alley and spotted Dean, surrounded by guards, who were trying to shield him from the rotted foodstuffs presently giving the People's Parcel's Plaza a new coat of paint.

"People's people! Hold your mulch till the encore, please!" Dean's awkward voice called out. "Will you judge before hearing me?"

The crowd grumbled.

The sign says this is Redvolutionist territory. I hope Dean knows what he's doing.

Blue sighed. "It doesn't look like this is going to end anytime soon, and he's already surrounded by guards."

Dean continued as the grumbling settled. "You are noble in intention, even my mangled eyes can see that. But, I'm telling you, this could be a much better part of town."

The people booed.

"Judge us not by our dust and ragged clothes! Thus stricken are the zealous foes of the elite! These are badges of the Revolution!" the man in red and black bellowed.

Dean held up his hands for silence. "I see that! But the issue is, I've been going through your local laws," he tapped the absurdly massive book that hung from a pair of chains behind the stage. "I see that you still technically have an agreement with the Free Green Goblins of the Wreck. I've learned that they are a garbage service."

The crowd grumbled, and Dean's opponent wasn't sure where he was leading.

"Yes, it is worth grumbling about. People of People's Plaza, you've been robbed!"

The crowd exploded. Violence erupted for an awful few seconds, but Dean, surprisingly, looked confident behind his thick wall of guards.

"You have been robbed, by this man!" Dean pointed at his opponent.

"Slander!"

"You pay taxes in excess of seventy five percent! It's driven three dozen, so-called, traitor businesses out of the parcel, and another five dozen businesses have collapsed altogether, but the remaining companies have been parcelized. That means the Redvolutionists own them, and they keep good records; so, they know exactly how much money is being made."

"Look! The noble auditor, he's come to bewitch and befuddle you good people with charlatan's tricks. He intends to use his elite education—"

Elite education—hah!

"—to confuse and agitate you against your own party!"

"It is actually very simple. You have squeezed an amazing amount of wealth and capital out of this parcel. But where is the trash service? You could pay for it a hundred times over, every month, with what you make, even after devastating the community!"

The crowd was silent for a change, as if in some dissociative fugue.

"Garbage! He complains about garbage! People starve in the streets and the Redvolutionist cause chooses to feed the starving! And if the roads aren't up to your pedigreed specifications, you may be damned, because we hold ourselves to higher than superficial standards!" the Redvolutionist concluded, tugging nervously at his collar.

Parts of the crowd cheered, while others still

grumbled, arguments broke out between a few spectators.

Blue leaned in to Letty's ear. "I'm going to try something. Do not move from this spot, or it will take me three days to get you free again," Blue complained, before leaping off her shoulder and scurrying straight up a two-story building.

Letty spotted the mouse climbing a cable over to the plaza, right as Dean calmed the crowd.

"Yes, food is far more important than trash removal." The crowd grumbled again. "But I'm glad he brought up food. I see that in the Redvolutionist addendum, subsection: Wholesale Independence—"

"I'll give him this," Dean's opponent interrupted, "he is devoted to reading our founding documents."

"Well, this is an addendum, and was added on later, but I'd like to point out that your policy of self-determination, as nice as it might sound, is responsible for the vast majority of the structural collapses," and with more emphasis, "also known as destroyed homes and buildings, in this parcel! This lawful document demands tiny patches of farmland on the roof of every building!"

"No, no! The record clearly shows that the past rulers of this parcel, elitist monarch sympathizers to the very last one of them, built these structures as cheaply and shoddily as possible, in their attempt to further defraud their tenants!"

"Are you seriously telling me that these buildings should have been built to sustain all that soil? Look at that one over there!" Dean pointed across the plaza at the ruined building Letty and the Caspians were hiding behind. "It's fallen down, and all that soil caused it." The Redvolutionist tried to interrupt, but Dean continued. "I understand city farming can be a good idea… when the prices of food are high! But, prices of food from the Wreck are low, especially compared to the costs you sustained buying supplies, soil, fertilizer, and equipment, as well as the damages! You could have spent a fraction of the cost on actual food!"

"Those farmers—they're enemies of the people!"

"Farmers? Enemies of the people? They sound like they are the people! And if you had allowed the parcel to buy the cheap food, they could have spent their time on more productive pursuits, instead of farming in the middle of a city! And we wouldn't be swimming in garbage, broken buildings, and promises that were so flawed to begin with, that it's a joke you're still standing here!"

A segment of the crowd cheered for Dean, while several uniformed people looked ready to start more violence. Letty wasn't sure if they were angrier with Dean or their representative.

The referee mice in the stands called the debate for Dean, who was immediately awarded two Sici from his foe. Dean gave the stage to a Braid, who immediately extolled the virtues of a free market, despite the mob, which attacked their representative. Letty was impressed, and she thought Dean might make a respectable politician one day. The Caspians both wore approving looks.

A moment later, Blue landed on Letty's shoulder. He bore three large silver coins on his back, which he gave to Letty. "Turn left at the fork. We need to find a money changer and get on to the Sink."

"So, that's how government works here." Quill said, a little astonished.

Blue rolled his eyes. "You wouldn't believe the range of crazy ideas, religions, backwards philosophies, and people claiming to speak for the Secular God. You name it, and it's probably governed a portion of this city at one time or another. As insane as it might seem to someone who worships a snake, the standing parties have been whittled into near perfection over the centuries. Though people get lazy in places like the People's Plaza, and certain factions simply expect no one to challenge them in the heart of their territory. I expect you'd find corruption in the Braid home squares, not like this, but it exists."

Staza and Quill scowled at Blue. He didn't care. *They don't really worship Pythia, do they?*

The conversation died down as they followed Blue's directions.

"There we go, a silver corner," Blue said, pointing at stands and shops all market related.

Letty spotted accountants, banks, actuaries, church and guild offices, as well as money changers.

Blue directed them past a pair of hawking goblins, and to a tiny stand nailed to the awning post of another, human-sized stand. The tiny stand was run by a small team of suited mice, who were

175

pouring over ledgers.

"Brothers!" Blue called.

The mice looked up, unimpressed.

"No loans," one said.

"Nay! Letty, produce the coins. Three Sici stamped by the Archatian mint. One is even collectible, look the figure is facing the wrong way."

The lead moneymouse waved the other mice back to work, straightened his shirt, and stood up to inspect the coins which were quite large in his paws.

The moneymouse hummed and hawed for a moment, before looking up at Blue. "How much do you want for them?"

"What they are worth. They are Sici, after all."

"Well, they are, and they aren't—"

Blue sputtered. "You damned bazaar mouse! Pay the bloody rate and take your five percent! Don't think to bandy with me like you would some bumpkin!"

The moneymouse shrunk under Blue's ceaseless barrage. "Yes—" he finally said, checking a nearby book for the values.

Blue hopped onto the shop front and swiped the book to have a look.

The moneymouse glanced at his neighbor, a sarcastic looking ychorite, who was trying not to laugh at the absolute thrashing the moneymouse had just taken.

"Yes, thirty-eight seculons, and a dozen ludma. Thank you, I'll have this back before tomorrow," the moneymouse said flatly, to his neighbor, who he was apparently in business with.

Letty accepted the bag from the ychorite and counted the coins, before nodding to Blue.

"I hate to ask where you got those Sici," the ychorite said.

Blue gave him a glare and motioned Letty away.

"Blue, did Dean know you took those coins? I watched you climb onto him, but I don't think he noticed," Letty said.

"No, I swiped them from his pocket, right before he got the two new ones. The small riot distracted everyone, despite how predictable it was," Blue concluded.

"Hmm, so when are we going to get Dean and Emma? I also have all my stuff locked up in the Secular. All our gear is there—"

"One thing at a time, girl. We're going to learn about Andy first. We'll pay one of my contacts to bring out all of our things, and the less useful surfacers, at the right moment. Then we'll escape the city, possibly through a portal, with our things, our surfacers, and we'll be ready to hunt down Andy."

Letty whistled approvingly.

"Well done, Blue. I didn't realize you had such a knack for strategy," Quill said.

"Well, a decade on campaign with a bunch of brain-dead points—it was become a strategist, or be eaten by brutox. I do miss them sometimes."

"Maybe we'll find your friends, too," Staza said, "they know Andy, they might want to join up with us."

"Join up?" Blue scoffed. "What are you going to do after we find Andy? Go back to your viper's pit, that's what."

"No," Staza snapped. "We're—"

Letty turned and saw Staza and Quill looking at her intently. "What is it?"

"You're a Seer, Letty."

Letty was silent.

"It's just that real Seers—" Staza started, not sure how to say what she meant.

Letty turned down an empty alley, stopped walking, and rounded on her friends. "We don't have time for this."

Staza looked hurt, and Quill seemed unsure.

Blue spoke up. "You're all children anyway. The old Seer's calling—" he shook his head and ruffled his whiskers, "It made sense a thousand years ago, but not anymore. The ryle are a fact of life. Crusading to free the surface and the Netherscape was a romantic dream, fit only for the suicidal," Blue said, with a note of certainty in his voice. "There is no shame in accepting that fact. I was a soldier for ten years, and I never felt like a coward knowing that I was at odds with my species' first purpose. The same is true for you. You were meant to be killers, but you don't have to be."

Letty didn't like the sound of that. She felt the urge to argue, but simply turned away and started back down the alley.

"You three might want to have a few of those carrots, if we can find some; your eyes are starting to show," Blue added, as they continued, downhill, towards a tall, black dome.

Letty ignored this suggestion and stopped as

they approached a flooded intersection. The water lapped up against an embankment made mostly of fallen structures dragged to serve as a makeshift shore. Algae and shore plants cropped up in the debris.

"But the dome is further out. It must be flooded," Letty said.

"Part of it is, as I recall. I hope you don't mind getting a little wet. The shore water isn't the same as the sea tar," Blue said, tugging at his whiskers, and looking for the right way.

"Sea tar?" Letty asked.

"Did you see the shore at Caspia? It looks like tar, and the things that live in it—" Quill trailed off.

"The roof way! That's what they call it. Letty, climb up on that building," Blue said.

They climbed up the side of a collapsed and half-sunken house. Letty looked out onto the flooded streets. Bridges connected several buildings, roof to roof.

They traveled towards the dome, but minutes later, they were intercepted by teal-skinned men, clad in black armor and bearing barbed spears. The men had appeared all around them, some dripped with water, while others fell upon them from cracks between the buildings.

"Friends, let me be the first to welcome you to the domain of the mer," the leader, wearing a red velvet scarf under his helmet, but over his breast plate, said with a slight flourish. "How may we help you?"

Blue cleared his throat to make sure that they

noticed him. "Fair soldiers of the crystal shore, we seek to conduct business at the Sunken Temple," Blue said, sounding unsure of himself.

The soldiers shared a look.

"Though we may look destitute next to these flooded wrecks, I can assure you, friends, that the cost of any such business is to be weighed in gold," the lead guard spoke firmly.

"Of course," was Blue's response.

Satisfied, the guards escorted the party towards the dark dome. Further into the Sink, they saw barges and small poled craft. Children swam in the waters, and people waved at them from windows and the flooded streets.

"They're friendly here," Staza said, waving to the children.

"Because they love you, Seeress," a guard said.

"What?" Letty replied, surprised.

"Your blood is remembered by my people. History is still alive here. That faith is being rewarded as well. We are expecting a new Voice of God to bring righteous change to our city."

"And we expect it quite soon," another replied.

"I told you, you need more of those carrots," Blue whispered in Letty's ear.

The guard laughed, "Fair builder, the sight of you is fondly reminiscent of my favorite stories. Seeing you sat upon a Seer's shoulder, fulfilling your duty, lifts my spirit. We have always had faith in your kind. Secular life never suited you."

Blue scoffed and folded his arms, though the torrent of complaints Letty expected never came.

They approached the stairs of the dome, which emerged from the water and climbed another dozen feet before terminating at a broad, flagstone paved foundation supporting the great dome.

The entrance was heavily guarded, and their escort bid them, "please wait a moment," as he went inside.

Letty looked around from her high place on the temple steps. She saw boats and swimmers approach and climb the steps. The guards became more attentive, but did not stop the mer as they neared Letty and the Caspians. The locals crowded around. Whispers picked up, and Letty heard the word, "Voice," "Seers," and "Argument?" on a number of tongues.

Letty studied the structure and saw damage to the pediment. It looked like pieces of the building had been torn away.

"The name of this building was once written there. It is now lost," Blue said to Letty, following her gaze. "It is now the Sunken Temple."

The lead guard reappeared, followed by six women, each as striking as the girl Letty had seen on the avenue earlier that day. They wore extravagant and ornate gowns, though each was light of color, and featured decorations from the sea in construction or decoration. Letty saw shells, mesh nets, sea weed, scales, and even layers of fine bones.

They almost remind of the clothes the Caspians wear, only less like armor and more for decoration.

The lead guard gestured towards them. "High consort, these are the visitors. They even have a builder guiding them."

Letty felt Blue shuffle uncomfortably on her shoulder.

"We sense the Argument. Are we wrong?" the lead consort, a tall woman of trim, yet still pronouncedly feminine form, asked.

Letty looked at Staza and Quill. Neither seemed sure.

Oh, well. What's the harm?

Letty held out her hand and presented the Argument.

They didn't seem pleased by the sight.

"Do you wield it?" the high consort asked.

Letty sighed, and grasped the orb tightly. The blade appeared.

The crowd gasped and then cheered. Several guards took off their helmets and dropped their weapons.

The consorts all responded differently. Some seemed angry, while others behaved like those in the crowd. The high consort let loose a shriek at the sight of so much awe and rushed inside.

Another spoke, "So, it's true. There is more than one committed Seer, and this one is a female at that. Does this mean the reign of the Usurper, is over? Will we return to the old days?"

The remaining consorts seemed unsure.

Letty released the blade and spoke, "What do you mean by committed Seer? All three of us are Seers."

The consorts laughed.

"No, no," a consort, wearing a violet gown,

replied. "There are still countless thousands with the Seer blood, but you would find not one of them who could grasp that orb—or maybe not, perhaps things are changing. Is reason coming back? Either way, any person with violet eyes merely has the chance to start down the path of a true Seer. For quite some time, Caspian has been the only committed Seer in all of Pansubprimus, and that is only because he took the bodies of newly committed Seers and spent them for his purposes."

Letty turned and offered the orb to her friends. They stared at it for a long moment, but neither tried to take it.

"I don't want to know," Quill said, and Staza nodded in agreement.

"But we have delayed you for too long. Our champion says you have business here," one of the women said.

"We need a portal to a place called Zentule," Quill said. "It is a ryle palace, somewhere in Euboia."

"Simple enough. Though you are led by a true Seer, we still need to levy our toll."

Letty held up a bag of coins.

The consorts gestured that they should come in.

The crowd waved and cheered as they went into the temple.

The halls were dim, being lit by boxes filled with something that glowed in soft green shades. The chambers were mystical in the flickering light, with waves of mist and the scent of flowers wafting through the dark, and Letty wondered if she should be afraid.

They came out into a massive rotunda. The dome raced high above, and an intricate network of golden filaments lined the walls and dome in a pattern reminiscent of a circuit board, or a labyrinth.

"Wow," Letty whispered, craning her neck to look up.

Thousands of branches of the gold filament terminated in a wide golden circle in the center of the room. Five pillars stood around that circle, and, further back, up a slight set of stairs that led to a stage, stood a tall box.

"Go around to the pillars, one at a time, and place a seculon in each hub," a consort directed Letty, who did so, accompanied by her friends.

"This is like nothing I've ever seen," Quill whispered, his eyes still wide.

Letty approached the first pillar. It was enveloped by a nexus of golden wires that all terminated around a slot that would accept the coin. She pressed a coin into the slot on each pillar.

"And the sixth coin into the box, please. We need to eat too," one of the consorts said with a laugh.

"So, they don't actually do anything?" Staza whispered. "They just make money off this old contraption—"

Letty scoffed, but did as she was told.

"Now, very carefully, toss one last coin into the circle. Be careful to aim for the center. As you throw the coin, say the name of your destination. Speak clearly; bungling this can be expensive."

The consorts and the guards stepped back. The

guards also leveled their weapons, as if expecting a threat.

Letty felt nervous as she produced one more gold seculon and aimed for the center of the circle.

"There's a girl," Blue said cautiously.

Letty flipped the coin and said, "Zentule!"

The coin was stuck by light from the five pillars and it exploded in a spray of liquid gold across the circle. The complex filaments pulsed with blinding light, and there flashed a portal.

"Whew!" Blue yelled, through the sudden shock of wind coming from the flat, glittering, disk.

On the other side stood tall, thick jungle. A sprawling, yet deceptively low series of slate structures stood in the distance.

"How long will the portal stay open?" Letty yelled, through the wind.

The consort in blue approached and spoke in her ear. "It will stay open for a day, unless you pay another gold seculon and we can stoke it for a second. Come, I'll show you through."

She gestured to the guards, who rushed through the portal, and then waved for Letty to follow. Letty handed the woman another coin, just to be safe.

Letty took a deep breath and shared glances with her friends.

They stepped through. The consort and a pair of guards followed.

The other side was humid and filled with the cacophonous cries of jungle birds and millions of insects.

"Here," the consort said, producing two devices

that looked like sea-stars. She handed one to Letty. "Control the portal this way." She laid her sea-star against the portal and twisted it. The portal shrunk if twisted one way and grew the other. "We keep it closed tight, for our safety, and, with the sea-star, you can open it up when you want to come back through. Just, whatever you do, do not lose the sea-star!" she concluded, stepping back through with her guards, and tightening the portal to about the size of a coin.

"Service with a smile," Blue said sarcastically.

They all turned and looked up at the rugged palace in the distance. The sky above was shot through with forked light.

"Scary place," Letty said, leading the way.

Chapter 7: Greylapse

Ithmene took another bite of her ice cream. "Thank you for lunch. It's been a while since someone else cooked," she said.

Andy eyed her bowl and she pushed it towards him. He tried a spoon full. It tasted faintly of licorice.

"Of course," Andy said, distracted by the flavor. "And thank you for so many meals—I like seafood now. This was the least I could do. Could I maybe pay you—for all that work you did cooking, I mean?"

Ithmene gave him a stern glance.

"Right, it's just, you've done so much for me—" Andy trailed off, feeling embarrassed and remembering the night before. He had cried.

Ithmene took another bite before pushing her dish away.

He felt the glances of other diners.

They know she's a temple maiden. They're wondering what she's doing with me.

"We're causing a fuss," she said. "Let's get to the Greylapse."

Andy paid the bill before following Ithmene to the door.

Before exiting, she turned and produced a carrot.

Andy scowled.

"I can't—if I take it, I won't be able to recognize—" he paused and leaned closer. "I won't be able to see them."

Ithmene sighed and closed her fingers around

the carrot.

"Just stay behind me and keep your eyes down," she whispered.

Stepping outside, the sounds of the street and nearby debate filled the air. As they walked, Andy sensed something else; an uncertain murmur seemed to follow them. He saw a child point to the sky, at the steel blossom, and then exclaim, only to be silenced by her parents.

Even the debates had lost their usual red-hot verve as speakers occasionally turned their glances skywards. The blossom, unlike the cyclic colors of the city, sat stationary, growing with the days. Even the mice in their gutters and the goblins in their rickety hovels arranged chairs to gaze upward. Others trundled carts full of food or jars of pure water at a clip through the streets.

"Doesn't it infect you, Andy?"

"What do you mean?"

"Can't you hear them? Even the children know something is coming. They are expecting Caspian. Cataclysm is in the air."

"I'm not taking the Cogito. The city will not be destroyed," Andy replied, as if in denial of her observations. Though he knew she was right. The city had a sixth sense, and was readying itself for a storm.

"You may not take the Cogito, but there will be change nonetheless."

They walked in silence for a while, the nervous anticipation washing over them until Ithmene turned to him and asked, "Do you plan on stopping the ryle?"

"Not with force; it's not possible."

Ithmene rolled her eyes. "Instead of allying with the other ryle," she practically spat the word, ryle, "why not win the people to your side? More are ready to support you than you'd expect. Ryle tyranny is real, and the people living here know it. They see it, always just beyond the gates, waiting to get in. Come back to the Temple, we'll spread the word, and allies you've never met will come to fight with you."

"So, you're a strategist now, Ithmene?" Andy asked.

"I have developed many talents in my time. All to serve you."

Andy stopped walking and looked at her. "We're not married."

"Who knows what we are? Everything is changing. We can do whatever we want. You have the power of God in your hands and our enemies cower at your coming. They are even more afraid, because you aren't acting like Caspian. He'd never wait this long."

Andy felt the weight of her words.

"Anything. We can do anything," she repeated, sensing the affect she had.

Andy had the urge to agree, to do whatever she wanted to keep the smile on her face.

"What's your plan?" he asked.

"Take off those robes and wear this," she said, producing a silver face mask from her purse.

"Does that belong to Caspian?"

"No. It is our gift to the next speaker, and that

is you. Forget Caspian. People who know the songs, will know this."

"Why are you so confident in me? I'm just a—I was crying on you last night," Andy said, looking away.

"You can do what no one else could. They call Caspian the Usurper because he stole the Argument from the Seers. None could resist as he took their bodies and used them for his ends. You resisted him. Somehow you did it. Maybe you were too young, or the snake woman, in trying to prematurely summon Caspian, made you aware and distrusting. Whatever happened, you are the sign of change. You won't have Caspian's centuries of experience, but you will have me."

"So, dress up like the Seers of old, wear a silver mask, and what? Attack ryle in the streets?"

"Yes. Kill them in the streets. Force the Exegesuits to reckon with you. Take your case to the high court and walk them down into the sewers to see the attacking army. They will have no choice but to support you."

Andy recalled the graffiti in the hideout. Despite his progress, he knew himself to be no match for Ziesqe; his recent practice against tree branches underlined that.

"You can save the city, regain everyone's support, and demolish the secular church. They will raise you to a new station. We can call you Consul, or Majesty, whatever you like, and maybe—if you choose, I can be your wife."

Andy grimaced as memories of Pythia came

back to him.

This is too much like Caspian. It will never work. The Exegesuits will execute me, why does she think they would listen? They have guns that can shoot through my armor. Even if I did beat them, the ryle would kill me. And, if despite it all, I somehow won, what business do I have being king?

Andy held out the mask as he looked into Ithmene's lovely face.

He finally shook his head. "I won't do it."

Instead of bursting out with anger, or pouting, or even turning and walking away, she simply took the mask, replacing it in her bag.

"Are you upset?" Andy asked.

"Of course I am, but I stand beside you. Do not look so surprised," she said, moving on.

Andy scowled under his hood, puzzled by her response.

"There it is," she said. "The Greylapse: finest gallery and museum in Degoskirke. It can take days to see everything, but we'll find the painting wings. I want to show you something specific."

Andy recalled the piece she mentioned last night.

"Do you still plan on meeting with the owner?"

Andy nodded.

"You plan to turn the ryle's greed against Ziesqe?"

Andy nodded again.

She was silent, and they stood facing the building for a long time.

"If I was better trained, or knew the city, or had some kind of power, I would agree to some of your plan. But as it stands, I know the ryle want to keep their status. They will not care to be subservient to Ziesqe. They will be better able to resist him and get the wheels moving to stop the invasion. As it stands, I can't fight them. I don't have the power you think. I have to hide my face in public."

Ithmene seemed stung by Andy's analysis. "And what if Ziesqe has already made arrangements with the ryle here? What if they would prefer to see the city topple? What if they stand to gain more in the change, than they do with the status quo? What if they turn on you, inside their home, with their guards?"

"Then I'll have to fight, and you might get your way by accident."

Andy hadn't noticed, but during his conversation with Ithmene, a patrol of armored Exegesuit guards had been moving up the lane towards them.

"Stand aside!" one bellowed.

Andy moved, but he wasn't fast enough and was shoved aside. His foot caught on a flagstone and he fell to his knees. A pair of the guards laughed, and a sudden burst of anger forced Andy to his feet in a flash.

"Careful now, pup!" one said, grabbing his robe and pulling Andy closer. "Wouldn't want to lose any teeth, now would we?"

"Decent people make way for the guard," another added.

Outraged, Andy struggled to behave cowardly. He kept his eyes on the floor, though his humiliation in front of Ithmene felt deadly serious. Thoughts of grasping the marble filled his mind.

"Gentlemen, please," Ithmene said.

The sound of her voice caught their attention.

"Was he bothering you, miss?" one asked.

"My boy is often too attentive—he mustn't have heard you coming," Ithmene mused, her voice a shade more melodious than Andy was used to.

The guard holding his robe released him, and even took a moment to straighten it out.

Andy heard the guards muttering about how Ithmene must be a temple maiden.

"Is it true that you can retire—if, uh—say the right one was to come along?" a guard asked.

"He would have to be very right," Ithmene said, her voice luscious.

All but one guard was trained solely on Ithmene. This final guard grimaced at Andy. He approached and nocked Andy's hood off. "Look at me, boy!" the guard insisted.

"The right one, must be gentle," Ithmene insisted, laying a hand on the intrusive guard's arm.

The intrusive guard slapped Ithmene's hand away, eliciting sounds of shock from his fellows. Ithmene gasped, filling the sound with notes of pain and displeasure.

"Bilton!" one of the guards cried, taking hold of the intrusive guard. "Get back on patrol!"

"Show some respect!" another insisted.

The enchanted guards shoved Bilton further down the lane, but still looked attached to Ithmene. Andy felt his hand reach into a pocket and grasp the

Argument.

Ithmene saw this and tapped him gently on the shoulder. "A gentle touch," Ithmene said, "and courtesy will win my favor."

The guards nodded. "Gentle—" "Proper manners, of course," they muttered.

"Come and see me in precisely three days' time, at the temple. When you arrive, ask for Olessa."

The guards nodded, still not taking the hint.

"Be prompt—and if I see any of your faces before that exact moment, I will never speak to any of you again!"

The guards gasped and practically vanished in their rush to get away.

"Will I be that stupid—when I get older?" Andy asked.

Ithmene laughed and pinched his cheek. "You're older than you think," she said, before leading him across the street and to their destination. "Poor Olessa," Ithmene said, chuckling, "and she looks quite like me, too."

Andy wanted to join in the mirth, but was stuck by the size of the museum ahead.

Approaching the doors to the Greylapse, Andy was stopped by attendants. A hulking pair of brutox checked him for weapons, but ignored Ithmene.

"As you have seen, being a maiden has some advantages," she said, as they entered.

Past the door, Andy looked up and felt his jaw drop. The foyer was dominated by a painting that covered the entire opposite wall. It featured a massive table surrounded by hundreds of people from many races. Some were robed like Exegesuits, while others wore strange uniforms and bore weapons. Even a curious, velvety, walking lizard stood by the table. A human and an ychorite clasped forearms over a prominent document, which read:

> Charter of the twin cities of Neichenheim and Middeskirke, henceforth known as Degoskirke. All ychorons will, from now until eternity, be free ychorites when under the protection of Degoskirke and its peoples. Members of the brutox matriarchy will be welcome in Degoskirke forever more, and will never be, by force or coercion, made to serve against their will. The Anteschismarian Order of Exegesuits will be empowered to keep the peace between the two Voices and their servants, both foreign and domestic. The Archatian clans will be charged with the day to day governorship of Degoskirke, which is to be divided into administrative parcels as approved by their citizenry. This founding document serves as seal of union and requires that any addition or amendment be heard in Quoratota and unanimously agreed upon by a representative from the five most prominent Archatian houses and the five branches of the Anteschismarian Order.

The Exegesuits started as peacekeepers. Now they rule the city. This mentions the two Voices. That must be Argument and the Counter. At some point we were allowed in the city, but now we're outlawed.

Andy stood and stared for so long that a docent, a uniformed ychorite, came by. "Do you need any assistance?"

"No thank you; it's his first time here," Ithmene answered with a smile, while reaching for her purse. She handed the docent a silver coin. "Our gift."

The docent nodded. "I'll make sure the guards know to let you by. Thank you and enjoy your visit."

A floor-plan on the wall showed three wings, all branching off from the entry way. Andy read the signs: "Pac-wing: Degoskirke, its peoples and their history. Lantic-wing: Secularist masters - plastic arts, furniture. Sur-wing: Old Greylapse, the voices of madness, and the armory."

Let me guess which one we want.

Ithmene led him to the sur-wing.

Andy lowered his eyes and let her lead the way past the guards. The few visitors were outnumbered by the brutox guards.

In the next chamber, Andy pulled back his hood and took in the sight of Seer work. The room was like a forest full of deer, if a forest were made of metal trees weighed down by enameled leaves fringed in gold wire. Everywhere he looked, Andy saw the hidden switches and levers built into the hundreds of mechanical trees and the herd of deer, which occasionally picked up their ears and blinked their ebony eyes.

Andy felt his heart tense at the sight. Light glittered off every surface, and the leaves seemed to sway in an unseen wind. Lighter stones stood in for rays of light that cascaded down the walls and across the floor. Carefully inlaid tiles were placed so delicately as to resemble an actual forest floor.

I don't need the Silversight to see this was made by

Seers. I'd like to look though. This room is complex. It might hide something.

Andy felt Ithmene take his hand and pull. Reluctantly, he let her take him away.

Andy moved with her through the wondrous forest and into a wide room full of display cases featuring arms and armor. One wall was devoted to the battle armor of the Exegesuit guards. The suits were lined up by generation, showing their development. He wondered why they still wore armor if they bore guns.

Andy saw a wall lined with ragged ribbons. The ribbons were of many colors and sizes, and they all featured Latin script.

Felicitas, Recipro, Bellum, Causa Sui, Armoria.

Andy wanted to read the placards because the ribbons seemed important, but Ithmene pulled him further into the gallery.

Andy had to keep from laughing as he gave in to Ithmene.

Not too long ago I hated being in a place like this, and now I want to be here, but I'm being dragged around by the best-looking girl in the city.

He rolled his eyes, wondering how it came to this.

"Here it is," Ithmene said, stopping in the next room.

Andy scanned the room and only saw a single guard at the far end. He pulled back his hood and took a look. He knew that a painting was there, but all he saw was a tall rectangle the color of glittering quicksilver.

It's a solid canvas full of writing. It might be the Englishman again. I wonder what the painting looks like to her eyes.

"What does it look like to you, Ithmene?"

"A sphere cut in half. The top half is exploded out into hundreds of pieces, though, if they were all pushed back together, they would form the complete sphere."

"The colors?"

"Many colors, but they aren't jarring. They are all complimentary."

Andy wondered if the guards would be upset if he took a closer look. He leaned in, but couldn't start at the top, the painting was too tall. After reading for a moment, he realized that the painting was covered with the same message, written repeatedly, to fill the canvas. The artist must have known that his painting would glow like a beacon to a Seer.

"Stare not too long, Seer! There are eyes in this place—hopefully still the Greylapse—and they are watching. Stop now and read the placard!"

Andy did so. The guard looked up at them. A moment later, Andy returned to the canvas.

"Beneath the Greylapse rotunda lies a Seer chapter-house. Though this place is no longer a safe haven, it can be accessed from the Intersticine tunnels beneath the city. You are close to family, but do not attempt to gain entry here! It is watched at all times! Ryle own this institution. Do not let them see your eyes. Find a friendly builder, you will know them by their demeanor. Ask them the way to the Intersticine; they will help you. Step away from the canvas."

The rotunda?

"Where can we find the rotunda?" Andy asked.

"It's in another wing, with the local art," Ithmene answered, surprised at the question.

"Let's walk," Andy said, letting her lead the way.

Keeping an eye out, Andy looked carefully at every doorway, and even eyed the other visitors. If the place was ryle owned, why wasn't he seeing their inky traps?

"What did you see?" Ithmene asked.

"It was a message about this place and another Seer chapter-house. It might be the Englishman; the base painting is the same style, but the message didn't sound like him. Maybe he saw this painting first and took the idea."

Ithmene nodded. "I'm glad I could be of use."

They walked through a wide hall, filled with oil portraits of famous Exegesuits and then entered the rotunda. The space reminded him of the dining hall in Caspia.

The rotunda was multi-tiered, with paintings hung in a circle on the wall of each sunken level, until the final circle, which featured a tall golden artifact that Andy didn't recognize. The artifact was covered in arches, buttresses, and opaque glass panels, making it appear as a segment of a cathedral, bent into a circle. A glow pulsed from within its ornate windows.

"What is that thing?" Andy asked, quietly, aware this area was full of visitors.

"The reliquary," Ithmene said. "Properly speaking, it should be in the age of madness wing, but I suspect that they don't know how to move it."

Andy inclined his head and slowly approached, pausing on other descending circles to admire various paintings. He noticed that none of the other works in the rotunda glowed.

Finally, Andy neared the reliquary. He looked for guards; none were paying him any attention. He let the Argument rush into his eyes. With the Sight, he saw that the reliquary was stocked with hundreds of pieces of Argument. It was almost too obvious that segments of buttress would twist, opening connected panels and revealing pieces of Argument. He also saw that the reliquary was hinged in such a way that it would split open. Andy looked towards the base and saw the frame of a narrow cylindrical elevator tucked away inside.

That must be the way to the chapterhouse.

Andy heard footsteps nearby and he pushed the Argument from his sight and back down into his body. A few museum-goers walked past.

Facing away from the reliquary, and confident that no one was watching, Andy twisted a piece of buttress. He heard a soft click, turned, and saw a piece of argument wrapped in a chain necklace sitting behind an opened window. Andy snatched the Argument and the window snapped shut.

Andy palmed the chained Argument into his robe pocket.

He saw that people were leaving the room and felt suddenly nervous.

"Andy," Ithmene called to him.

Guards started filling the hall.

Andy looked at the reliquary, suddenly

desperate. His eyes flashed with the Sight, and he tried to trace the way inside.

There are switches behind the paintings—some combination opens the reliquary. I'll never get them right in time.

"There's nothing for you here," a cold voice said. "The Seers down there are long dead."

Andy turned and saw Ziesqe, who was flanked by Kal and another, unfamiliar ryle.

"Why haven't you taken the Cogito? This wasn't the plan," Ziesqe said, his voice calm.

He thinks I'm Caspian.

"I see you've found your wife, and a lovely one she is, but this time wasting is unlike you."

Andy stepped forward and the ryle flinched.

Purple blades appeared and Ziesqe and Kal flexed their muscles in familiar ways, coating their bodies in purple armor. The other ryle couldn't hone his blade, and it crackled weakly.

Andy noticed that the warriors around the room were mostly ychorons, and not the guards he had seen in the gallery. They leveled crossbows and listened for command.

"No, this isn't like you at all—Lysander? Is that you in there?" Ziesqe asked.

"I'll cooperate if you allow me to walk her outside," Andy said.

Ziesqe grinned. "It is you! No wonder."

Kal's eyes shone violent and sparkling purple. She gazed his way for a long moment. "It isn't the boy. If it is, he's changed."

Andy realized she might be seeing the

Argument he had hidden inside.

"Caspian was always a fool for women. I know how to cut through this," Ziesqe said, reaching down and holding up a cloth covered cage. "I came prepared to meet either," Ziesqe said, pulling away the cloth.

Titus?

Andy knew the mouse, who looked up and recognized him.

Titus called out, "Lysander! Don't listen—"

"Silence, vermin!" the nameless ryle snapped.

"Lysander has a soft spot for this mouse. Where Caspian had a soft spot for women," Ziesqe explained to the others. "Just watch." Ziesqe shook the cage.

Andy nearly lunged.

The warriors panicked, and a few loose bolts flew past Andy's head.

"Hold!" Kal commanded, though she had raised her blade.

"Now, now, Lysander, it is you, after all."

Andy was silent.

"We can still save the city from invasion. You can still help them, even if you aren't Caspian. Throw down your Argument and come with me. Our arrangement will still stand. Once the city is under my command, we will release you and your friends. Everyone you care about will live," Ziesqe implored.

Andy looked around the room. He saw Ithmene's desperate eyes. He could even see the broken expression on Titus's face.

I can't fight them. I might escape if I ran, but they

would die. What good would it do if I did escape? There aren't any Seers to help me. I can't even walk in the street without hiding my face. If I can keep my friends alive and the city safe from destruction... It's a gamble; Ziesqe is a liar, but nothing I do will make a difference. If I acted alone, I would only make things worse.

Andy held up his palm.

The warriors tensed.

But...

Andy reached into his robe.

I don't have to give them my Argument. I have this spare.

Andy held out the new Argument from its chain.

But will they know that I'm holding so much back? Kal has her Sight on me.

Andy let go of the chain. The Argument clattered on the ground.

The guards rushed forward and took Andy and Ithmene into their custody.

The nameless ryle relaxed, and even Ziesqe lowered his blade.

Kal however, stared at him with her Sight. "He still isn't safe."

Ziesqe scoffed. "Of course he isn't, and he never will be. He speaks with the Voice of the Dead God, even if he isn't Caspian. Shackle him and bind his hands with the old gauntlets."

"You should cut his fingers off," Kal said.

Ithmene cried and struggled as the guards grabbed her, but Andy accepted chains, yet again. He felt metal gloves being slipped over his hands. They were made to keep his fingers splayed and incapable of making a fist. He couldn't call the blade with them attached.

Andy's head was covered with a sack, and he was thrown onto the floor of a passenger cart. The feet of a dozen sitting guards occasionally gave him a kick. After a bouncy ride through the loud city streets, he heard a large door open. The sounds of the city became muffled, and he knew they were indoors somewhere. He was carried from the cart and finally sat on a throne, while the sounds of saws and hammering echoed through the space.

The next few hours were a flurry of activity, none of which he could see.

"Good! He looks brilliant! Do we have his proper uniform? No, the one with the armor, you idiot!" A voice shot orders from nearby.

Finally, the bag was pulled from Andy's head, and he saw the large chamber. It looked like a garage full of carts, and it smelled like a barn. That impression, however, was offset by all the equipment and activity. Ychorons and a few brutox were busy decorating several carts. They appeared to be parade floats.

Andy spotted Kal on the far side of the room, near a table covered with papers. Other ryle tarried, but she kept her glowing, purple Sight on Andy.

She's been watching me this whole time.

Andy was pulled to his feet and brusquely dressed in the outfit that Pythia had once put him in. They even strapped on the blackened pieces of plate armor, which made sitting on the throne painful.

Ziesqe appeared from a side door, batting away several attendants. He looked stately in white and gold regalia. "I want to speak to him."

Kal kept her eyes on Andy, but spoke to Ziesqe, "He's there. We're almost ready."

"Do you still believe it isn't the boy?" Ziesqe asked.

"I do not know."

Ziesqe tugged on one of his tentacles for a moment, before climbing onto Andy's cart.

"Lysander. Let us speak before these imminent events. You know to play the part; you have already done an admirable job of stirring the populace, but your behavior makes me nervous. When we go into the city, either keep your mouth shut, or act as Caspian."

Andy was silent.

"Why didn't you do as you were told? It would have made things simpler. How have you spent your time recently?"

Andy shook his head.

"I see."

Ziesqe was silent for a while.

"I apologize for the chains and the restraints on your hands. I'm told they are quite painful. Sadly, they are necessary. Kal and I both sense the Argument about you. It is likely that Caspian still lingers in your thoughts, though his failure to control you is an unknown element. In the past, he has always been consistent."

Andy nodded. "That was your plan. To let him

loose. He thought it was."

Ziesqe smiled. "Indeed."

Andy sighed, looking at the chains and then down onto the brutox working nearby, he recognized the shape of a large metal cage being assembled.

Ziesqe almost grinned. "So, you did speak with him. I will lay my cards on the table, Andy. I always want to be honest with you."

Andy rolled his eyes.

Ziesqe continued. "Caspian and I had a tentative agreement. He promised to leave the ruins of this city to me and my rebellious allies, if we would help him inhabit your body. It seemed to us that his intent was to attack the City in the Sea, the seat of the Maelstrom. Of course, he would fail, but it would keep the Maelstrom off our backs for long enough to cement an untouchable position here."

Did he believe that Caspian would let him live? This was the flaw in his plan. This was why he sent me up the Guilt alone, so he could hide if Caspian tried to seek him out. I bet he even counted on it. But after failing to find him, Ziesqe probably reasoned that Caspian would leave to attack the Maelstrom.

Ziesqe paused and scanned Andy's face.

"My plan is in tatters. I am forced to rush. Though this path does have its benefits. With the Cogito still in place, the city will fare better. It is a tradeoff and the better one for you, Lysander, because your body won't be destroyed in pointless suicide."

"You sent me to the Cogito knowing that it

would lead to my death," Andy said. "You tried to give me the Casque, hoping for the same thing. It was the same plan, with different means."

"Right, either the Casque or the Cogito, or any of a number of Caspian's old possessions might make him manifest. There is even a chance that it could happen spontaneously. This isn't a science. I'm playing with fire here, Lysander. That's why I warn you against any rash measures in the coming hours. Rules will change. Many of the changes will be unpleasant for you. For instance, I will return you to your cage."

Andy tensed, the Argument pulsing within.

Kal approached Ziesqe and tried to pull him away from Andy.

"This is too dangerous," Kal said, but Ziesqe raised a hand to silence her, and continued.

"If you endure the cage and the chains again, if you comply with our little charade, I will see that our old agreement is fulfilled. Do not think that you have no choice. You do. You will likely be allowed to speak when we stand before the High Exegesuits. If you destroy my illusion, you will force invasion." Ziesqe looked over to Kal. "Are we prepared for that possibility?"

Kal nodded. "The cisterns are captured; we could storm the city at any minute. Waiting is ill advised, as Viqx, in her impetuosity, might signal the attack on a whim. She absolutely will attack in two days, if we aren't successful before."

Ziesqe looked back to Andy. "That is a guarantee, in case something should happen to us.

If Viqx does not receive word, she will attack. Make peace with your conscience. We are leaving shortly. If you cannot comply, let me know before we leave."

Andy rattled his chains for their attention. "What have you done with Titus and Ithmene?"

"Their fates, and indeed the fates of their kin, are bound to yours. To be plain, I am saying that if you dissatisfy me, I will murder every one of Caspian's wives, starting with the fair girl in the other room. I will torch every known nest of vermin and then hold your friend's cage under the water for you to see, and that's just to start. Keep me happy, and be grateful that I am making such grim promises, they make it easy for you when the moment comes. No need to tax your mind or suffer pride," Ziesqe said, turning away.

Chapter 8: Friend of my Friend

Letty, Staza, and Quill pushed against the massive stone door. It swung open with less resistance than they expected, particularly considering its size.

"Be careful," Letty said, making her fist glow as they stepped inside.

"This is a stupid plan," Blue whispered. "Coming into a ryle palace."

"The place is abandoned. There was no one outside and no one guarding the door. Did you just want to sit in a shrub and stare at the doors?" Quill asked.

"Of course not, but we should at least wear disguises, or sneak around the back, or something! This is too brash!"

"I don't want to waste the time, and how would we disguise ourselves as ryle anyway?" Letty trailed off as they entered the main hall.

A long dark pool of water ran down the center of the yawning, resonant hall. The roughhewn walls and low benches made the place feel like it was coming down on them.

"I don't like it," Staza said. "Living here would make me go insane."

"Ryle did this, and that was probably their intention," Quill added.

"It's to keep the servants subliminally awestruck," Blue replied.

"But why the indoor pool?" Letty asked. "Do they have parties?"

No one answered.

They walked down the lengthy hall, leaning into empty and ransacked rooms.

"They left in a hurry," Staza whispered, standing in an empty dining hall.

"But where did they go?" Letty asked. "If we can figure that out, we know where they've taken Andy."

Blue nodded. "I'd like to agree, but it looks like Ziesqe was on the run. Why would he abandon a place like this?"

Letty was about to speak but heard a tapping noise coming from the main hall.

They leaned out the door and saw a pair of flapping skulls and a few dozen slithers.

"What are those?" Letty whispered.

The flapping skulls looked like small ryle heads with large bat wings for ears.

The two heads snapped and chattered at each other before glancing at the door Letty was hiding behind.

"They see me."

A moment later, the flapping heads and their attendant slithers charged off down a side passage.

"What were those things?" Staza asked.

Everyone looked at Blue, who simply shrugged. "I've heard stories of ryle spawn," he said, unsure.

They listened for a moment longer, before moving on. They went from room to room, eying the dark water as ripples on the surface hinted at something beneath.

"More flapping heads?" Quill asked.

No one ventured a guess, but they avoided the water nonetheless.

They took stairs down, and then up, and then down again, but they always found new rooms to search.

"This place is massive and like a maze," Letty complained, kicking over another empty footlocker.

Minutes later, they found themselves staring at a dead end. Preparing to turn back and find another way, Staza gasped and grabbed Letty, pulling her away from a narrow pool. A tentacle floated from the water, holding a small leather pouch.

"Our money!" Letty cried, producing the blade and swiping for the tentacle.

She split the tentacle from its stump and, in so doing, cut the pouch, spilling the coins into the water.

"Damn!" Letty yelled, releasing the blade and lunging for the water. She was held back by the Caspians.

"Let it go," Staza said.

"We don't know what else is in there," Quill added.

"That was a lot of money," Blue whispered, and then endured the heavy glances of the Caspians.

Furious, Letty stomped all the way back to one of the larger side halls. They were more than surprised to see a few dozen flapping heads and a couple hundred slithers. The creatures sat still on the walls and even hung upside-down from the ceilings as if the act were simple; a few of these even held onto their attendant flapping heads. The swarm of little beasts edged closer, as if probing the humans.

Letty produced the blade, and the Caspians drew daggers they had lifted from an abandoned barracks minutes ago.

"What do you want?" Letty yelled. "We've already been robbed!"

The noise and show of strength gave the creatures pause. Though, slowly, they continued to come closer.

"I don't think we can beat them, Letty," Staza whispered.

Letty swung her sword wide, hoping to scatter the beasts. The air crackled with its energy, but the monsters only flinched, they did not retreat.

"I think you're right," Letty replied.

"Run?" Quill asked.

"Run." Letty said, releasing the blade and turning.

They raced to the nearest stairwell and found themselves forced to go down.

"Shouldn't we be going up? The way out was further up!" Quill yelled.

"I didn't see another way!" Letty replied, as Blue held onto her blouse with all four limbs.

They turned a corner and Letty tumbled over a small, green bundle of spindly limbs.

"They's attacking behind!" the creature yelled.

Letty kicked it away, and was surprised to see a hallway full of heavily armed goblins.

Letty rolled to her feet and produced the blade.

"They aints the flappers or the slitherers!"

Another goblin smacked the first. "They's humans! And lookety that blade! It shineys like—"

A third goblin, taller, and covered in ramshackle armor, slapped the second goblin and approached Letty.

"The Teeth!" Blue warbled, astonished.

Teeth?

The goblins saw him, but didn't recognize the white mouse.

"Forgives us, please. Not time, fighting flappers."

"Right!" Letty said. "There are more coming from behind!"

The lead goblin, with three tin stripes and chevrons bolted to his pauldron, gestured to his warriors, who rushed up besides the Caspians and took defensive positions against the stairwell.

"Dey's comin from both sides! We need Takka!"

The goblins groaned, while Takka cheered.

"Which flankey, Mastery Surgeon?" Takka asked, unraveling countless strings on his armor.

"Help humans!" The Mastery Surgeon demanded.

A moment later, the swarm of slithers poured out of the stairwell. They clung to the ceiling and then dropped onto the fighters.

Letty swung at them as they came down and the Caspians found their daggers next to useless against the lithe foes. They resorted to snatching them and throwing them at the wall or stomping on them. Letty cried out as one bit her ear, but Blue leaped into it, and the two fell, tumbling to the ground.

Takka, with his strings finally loosened. Rang up a cacophony of chiming. The slithers shrieked and exploded at the noise.

Letty watched in stunned silence as Takka cut a swathe through the mob of little beasts. Finally, a pair of flapping heads, also shrieking, but not disintegrating, dove onto Takka.

Staza grabbed one flapper by its wing and used it as a club to knock the second from the goblin's face.

The rest of the flappers joined the fray.

Letty nearly lost her focus when she saw Takka swinging two of the heads, one from each hand, and spinning as he stumbled towards the now broken enemy.

"And don't comes back!" Takka yelled, hurling the heads up the stairs.

Letty realized the goblins were still fighting behind her. She turned and saw a figure, seemingly made from jolting electricity, zapping the enemy heads.

Takka yelled and ran past Letty and the Caspians to join the battle on the other end of the hall. The goblins cringed and made way for the stumbling riot of noise.

Chimes ripped off Takka's harness as he tumbled into the sea of slithers.

Between Takka, the goblin's javelins, and the figure electrocuting the heads, the enemy on this front broke in moments.

The goblins had to carry Takka away from the carnage, an act they seemed familiar with, but Letty was more interested in the figure, which took the shape of an ychorite covered in orange feathers. He looked their way.

"Who are our friends, Clang?" the ychorite asked.

"It's me, you idiots! Forget the paint!" Blue spat at them, having just recently re-assumed his perch on Letty's shoulder.

A few goblins instinctively rolled their eyes at the sound of that voice.

"Blue!" the ychorite yelled.

"Damn right! I didn't find the boy, but I found his friends. A far cry better than you, skulking around ryle holds. What are you doing here?"

"Blue, would you introduce us to Andy's friends? I see one wields the Argument."

Letty grimaced, and released her grip on the blade.

Blue nearly launched into another tirade, but glares from Letty and the Caspians stopped him cold. "Well—right. Ahem. These two are Caspians, Quill, and Staza, warriors both."

"Indeed," Martin said to Staza, "I didn't get the idea to go after the heads until I saw her swinging one around."

"Ahem," Blue interrupted, "and this is Letty, one of three surfacers who have come to find Andy."

Martin shared a glance with Clang. "Andy has quite the collection of allies. I propose that we pool our efforts. How does two hundred goblins and a spare ychorite sound? Could we be of some use?" Martin asked.

Letty cracked a smile. "Of course. It would be great to work together. What were you doing in the battle? You were almost invisible, and it looked like you were electrocuting those flapping things."

Martin inclined his head politely. His feathers flickered, and a moment later he was invisible. He snapped a pair of phantom claws and jolts of light sparked there, illuminating the outline of his arm.

"Most of my kind never learn these tricks, the slaves that they are. Slavishness keeps one infantile, undeveloped even. Training takes time and costs etherium, two things Degoskan ychorites have little of. Most have no idea we can do this. The downside is that I must consume etherium at a far greater rate."

"Interesting," Quill replied. "What color etherium do you consume?"

"Gray, neutral, or the mix as it is known in some places. Fairly pricey, but managing a mercenary corps has its advantages."

Clang grunted. "Having the Martin has its advantages."

The goblins banged their weapons together in wordless approval.

A moment later, Letty noticed a few goblin ears perk up, then Blue's did as well.

"What is it?" Letty asked.

Blue looked to Clang, who inclined his head towards one of the side passages. "Something down there calls."

Clang clicked and gestured to his goblins, who moved without a word. Martin advanced towards the sound and disappeared as he went. A group of six goblins approached the humans, encircled them, and then motioned them to the rear of the battle group. They were next to a pair of stretcher goblins who had to carry Takka, while a medical goblin saw to his wounds, which didn't look serious.

He's stuck all over with those little tridents the slithers had, poor thing.

"He blasts the slithers with his chimes. It's a new weapon, that harness. It's quite effective, but not without its hazards," Blue whispered into Letty's ear.

Letty and the Caspians followed along.

"Very useful, these goblins, a real fighting force," Blue continued.

They heard a moaning cry. "—I'm here—" its voice echoed through the halls.

They turned down a narrow stairwell and found themselves in a dungeon.

"Here!" Martin called, from far ahead.

Clicks fired back and forth and the goblins came out of their tense crouches. They were gestured forward. Letty and the Caspians pushed through the goblins and approached a cell that held an ychoron, who was trying to bargain with Martin.

"Listen, I'm not letting you out of here until you tell us why the palace was abandoned," Martin insisted.

"I'm starving, please. I've been here for days," the ychoron begged from his hands and knees, sounding parched and weak.

Martin sighed and nodded towards Clang. A moment later, a small bag appeared. Martin inspected its contents and tossed the bag into the cell.

"Mix?" the ychoron said, displeased at the contents.

"You're lucky to get anything," Martin sneered.

The ychoron plunged his hand into the bag and a crisp whining followed. It reminded Letty of the sound a certain type of candy made when wet. The sound droned out into the cells beyond for a few moments, and, as it did, the ychoron's black feathers perked up and lightened to a deep blue.

"What's your name?" Martin asked.

"Llanyly," the ychoron replied. "And you?"

"Martin. Would you please tell us where everyone has gone?"

"Martin? This is no ychoron name."

Martin took an annoyed breath and looked over to Clang. "It's my own name, Llanyly. Of course, I am an ychorite."

"I see," Llanyly replied, embarrassed. "I didn't realize."

Something's going on here. They both seem ashamed.

Letty saw that the Caspians had also noticed.

"Would you please tell us where everyone went?"

Llanyly's feathers shuddered. "I am no traitor."

Martin lunged forward and slammed the bars. "They left you to die!" and then to Clang, "Find the key! When I get inside, I'll strangle this cowardly creature."

Llanyly balked at the sudden fury.

"You have until they find that key to convince me that you aren't a humiliation to our race. You must have done something to land yourself in here."

Llanyly shook. "I spoke out—"

"Against what?"

"The Master. He was confused—and blasphemous—"

Martin shook his head while Clang and the goblins searched for the keys.

"Who was your Master?" Martin asked.

"Lord Zyzqe Ziesqe, The Just, Tamer of Nightmares, and Master of Zentule."

The Just?

"What was his blasphemy?"

"He claimed that the Voice of the Dead God spoke again, through a boy."

Letty's eyes widened.

"Who was this boy?" She asked, pushing ahead of Martin.

"A surfacer, pulled in during action around the snake pit. I believe the name was Lysander."

"That's him!" Letty cried, looking back to her friends.

Quill and Staza both nodded.

"He was in these halls," Martin continued.

Llanyly nodded.

"Now, as to your fate. You have already spoken out against your Master. Free thinking, loose talk, this punishment, these are all signs that you have the spirit of an ychorite," Martin spoke, and Clang approached, handing him a ring of keys. "Thank you, Clang. Listen closely, Llanyly. Tell us where they went and all you know of your Master's plans, and I will open this cage and embrace you as a brother.

If you cannot do this, I will end the misery of a creature separated from its owner."

Llanyly kept his eyes on the ground. He shook with fear and backed against the rear of his cell.

"Please—" he begged.

A voice, sharp and concise, echoed throughout the prison, "Well done, friends, but it is time to step aside."

Letty drew the blade and turned. Something shaped like a human was standing among them. It had two long rents running down its face and under its scaled armor. On the left of the rents, its body was covered in black feathers, like a raven's. On the right, it was covered in patchy, matted fur. In the center, however, it wore the scales of a massive snake. One eye was beady and black, also like a raven, and the other was green, speckled with flecks of copper.

The creature's sudden appearance startled everyone, and several goblins stumbled over each other to get away, while others had to be restrained from throwing their javelins.

It held a hairy claw out for Martin to step aside. "Please, excuse my sudden interruption. You were doing very well, Martin, but Llanyly has shut himself up, and is resigned to execution now. If you had kept the chattering children away—" the creature paused and looked at Letty. Its eyes shone with surprise. The air between the creature and Letty's blade sparked and hissed.

The room was silent.

"Well now. You aren't Caspian. Would you

loosen that weapon for a moment? We will both benefit from my speaking to Llanyly here."

I'm not Caspian?

Letty stepped back and released the blade. She saw that Quill and Staza were also astonished at the statement.

The creature inclined his terrible head in thanks before turning to the caged ychoron.

"Now there, who do you expect I am?" the creature asked.

Llanyly shook his head.

"Who did your Master fear most?"

Llanyly balked. "I have never seen a beast such as yourself, but I suspect you are a servant of the Maelstrom, sent to find my Master."

The creature sputtered a laugh.

"Even Puktifa didn't quite understand who I was, but a mere servant hits the nail. Good. The moment Ziesqe dreaded has come, and he made it come. So, tell us, where did he go with his household? And, keep in mind, I already have a strong idea of the answer."

Llanyly looked down into his opened palms. "They first mounted an expedition to Hyadoth. I was imprisoned shortly after. I suspect Ziesqe wanted me to let my guard down after he left. My infraction upset him. Sadly, I wasn't executed, but left to rot and starve. The expedition did not return, or so the whispers told me. For a number of days, the footsteps echoing to my cell grew much louder, as if great activity was afoot, and then, nothing at all. I believe the Master has instituted his final plan.

221

I expect you will find his forces hiding around the city of Degoskirke, and you might find him, and whatever allies he could intimidate into defying the Maelstrom, scheming to conquer the city from within—"

"He plans on conquering Degoskirke?" Letty gasped. "Would he have taken Lysander with him?"

The creature turned an intrigued eye to Letty.

Llanyly scowled. "The boy—he is the reason I'm here now."

"Answer the question," the creature commanded.

"Yes. Whether Ziesqe believes the boy is the reincarnation of Caspian, or not, doesn't matter. He will use him as a tool to cause chaos in the free city."

The creature took in a deep breath. "Yes. But, what about you, Llanyly? You have betrayed your Master. You have aided our ancient enemy," he gestured to Letty. "What punishment is fit for you?"

"No, he did the right thing. We're letting him go." Letty said, reaching for the keys.

Martin grabbed her by the hand, desperation bent his eyes and his face split with dread.

He's terrified.

Letty looked to the creature, who smiled politely her way.

"Fair Seeress, only a third of myself has any experience with your kind, so please, forgive my crudeness. Would you indulge me? What would you do with this creature, Llanyly?"

Letty paused, struck by fear. The creature's eyes were upon her.

"I—I would let him go."

"Ah, piquant." The creature turned a cruel eye to Llanyly. "He may walk these abandoned halls for the rest of his life, never brave enough to venture the Nightmare outside, but caught eternally in the memory of the purpose he had scorned. He will be a free soul, given reign to preside over this edifice of ambition, of dreams, ashamedly purposeless and ever without hope. You are cruel, dear Seeress. It is the perfect punishment." The creature reached out and touched the cell door, which melted away into an inky cloud.

Llanyly heard the words, and despite the cell door disappearing, simply crumbled to his hands and knees in silence.

"You may call me Chimerax," the creature said. "May that name be a signifier for as short a time as possible."

Chimerax lunged for Letty at lightning speed. His hand grasped her throat and his eyes blazed with purple light. He stared heavily into her eyes.

The goblins attacked and even Staza delivered a biting stab, but every attack was deflected by the sudden shimmering of purple armor. Martin lunged and grasped Chimerax's throat, only to be jolted on contact. The air cracked and Martin fell to the floor. Goblins rushed to pull his shivering body away.

Letty stood, terrified, as the beast's whisper broke through her sudden fear and need to retreat.

"Caspian is trying to find a way into the boy, but he has also moved your arms. There he is now."

Letty's hand tensed and the blade appeared. It

cracked against the purple armor but refused to do more.

"Caspian is desperate to reincarnate, but you are too far removed for him to do more than influence your thoughts or move your arm. I suppose that means he is having no luck with the boy, then. Perhaps the boy is dead already; Caspian could never hold onto a body for long."

Letty shivered, and the air hissed with the sound of her blade colliding with the creature's armor. Purple and silver crystals formed along the floor, ceiling, and on the bars of the cells.

"Hmm, Pythia had her way with the boy. She made an agreement with him, signed a contract even. I expect she attempted to bring back her lover as quickly as possible and bungled it. But none of this matters to you if the boy is already dead."

"Let me go!" Letty cried releasing the blade, raising her fist, and summoning it again.

Letty's arm twisted, and her fingers articulated on their own. The blade appeared, but narrower and reddish. Chimerax saw it coming, but could barely flinch before it crashed into his face. A purple helmet appeared, but her blade pierced it and Chimerax cried out, letting her go, before stumbling into the wall.

"Go, now!" Clang ordered, pushing the humans and Martin towards the stairs.

Clang gestured, and his goblins formed an orderly retreat, throwing javelins and firing arrows as they went. Chimerax's body undulated and expanded. Letty looked back and saw a dragon's head spewing burning purple letters at a pair of flagging goblins. The goblins fell to the floor, their bodies shrunken and discolored. Letty tried to see, but she was pulled up the stairs.

"Run!" Martin commanded.

They escaped the stairwell and followed Clang.

"Did you come by portal?" Martin called out over the loud clanking of the rushing goblins.

"Yes, but it's outside the palace!" Staza replied.

"Too far!" Clang replied, suddenly changing direction and running for another stairwell. "We go to fighting pit!"

Letty looked back and saw the stream of goblins, but out of a shadow emerged a scorpion's tail, preceding an impossible body. She felt as if the claws were still about her throat.

Oh, God.

Letty nearly stumbled.

"Watch outs, girly!" An underfoot goblin yelled at her.

Stop looking back!

Letty ran after Clang until they suddenly left the great hall and the bright, flashing sky was all around.

"We're outside!" Staza yelled in surprise.

"Our portal, there!" Clang yelled to the humans, pointing at a rectangular arena.

They ran down into the arena and towards a small floating orb.

A piercing noise, like that of three creatures roaring at once broke out over the arena.

Letty summoned the blade and looked up to

see the monstrous shape cast its shadow. It had three heads. Letty saw a raven's beak, the muzzle of a jackal, and the scaled hide and hollow eyes of a dragon. It alighted on the stands and stared down at them as Clang struggled to get the sea-star into position on the portal. Finally, Staza slapped the sea-star out of Clang's hand and tried to open the portal herself.

Letty held up her blade, as if to keep the monster at bay.

Smoky letters drifted down out of the dragon's mouth. The smoke settled over the stone benches of the stands and corroded them into gravel.

Staza got the portal to twist open, and everyone piled through.

"Letty, come on! before it attacks!" Quill yelled.

Letty kept her blade leveled as she backed away. The corroded gravel sprouted thick strands of orange and black lichen.

The crow cawed at her. "We will take Caspian to Maelstrom, no matter what body he owns. Keep him from your friend, if you can," the crow said.

Confused and afraid, Letty turned and leaped through the portal. She turned and looked back through to the arena and noticed that Chimerax had a growing look of mischief on its crow and jackal faces. The beast lumbered towards the portal.

"Close it!" A voice cried out.

Letty saw a mer guard running towards the portal with one of the sea star keys.

Chimerax's scorpion tail shot towards the portal and burst through to their side.

Goblins and humans ducked and dived, slamming into walls, one another, and the floor to avoid the sting. The mer guard finally twisted the portal shut slicing the stinger, and ten feet of tail, clean off.

The tail writhed on the floor for a long moment, before finally turning to inky ash.

"Good lord!" the guard exclaimed. "This is the worst posting in the entire Sink."

"Silence!" A temple maiden called out, pushing through the crowded hallway. "Somebody get these goblins out of here! And you, humans! Give me your key, we need to shut your portal immediately! Especially if that monster is trying to get through."

The sea-star was produced and handed over. Letty took the reprieve and tried to get her bearings; she was surprised by the confines of the hall.

"Where are we?" Letty asked. "This isn't the temple, is it?"

"We're down in the catacombs. This is where we keep the portals after they are summoned," the maiden said.

Staza gave her a quarrelsome look.

"We can't just leave them up in the temple. What if another customer should appear? Besides, there are some portals that have been open for years; this is where we keep them."

"I thought they would go out after a day or two," Blue replied, venom in his voice.

The guard laughed. "That's simply what they say to get a little extra out of you. Who knows how long the portals might last?"

The maiden gave the guard a scornful glance and then cast that same expression over her hallway, which was now teeming with goblins.

"An old and profound institution of fidelity and dignity," she mumbled, raising an eyebrow.

Martin approached Letty. "Let us go into town. We have captured a large basement beneath an abandoned building, near the pillars. We need to rest and consider our newfound knowledge."

"I don't know," Letty replied. "If Andy is in the city, it could be that he was the Seer causing the problems everyone was talking about."

The maiden scoffed. "You mean the Caspian that wasn't? Young lad, handsome, if poorly behaved."

Letty glared. "You know where Andy is? Did you know this whole time?"

The maiden stepped back, realizing the hundreds of beings surrounding her had paid dearly to find a boy she knew was in the city.

"I didn't realize you were looking for him! We don't ask questions of our clients!" she replied, stuttering. "And, even if I did, we wouldn't give him up to you."

"Give him up to us," Quill scoffed. "We're here to save him from the ryle!"

"He's been captured by a ryle who wants to conquer the city," Blue explained.

The maiden crossed her arms. "That's strange. He walked into our parcel unaided and alone. A child recognized his signs and welcomed him. He was no one's prisoner."

"How?" Letty whispered, astonished. She couldn't believe it. "So, he's been freed? Or maybe he escaped. Oh, God. Did I actually see him? Was that really him on the streets earlier today?"

"How long ago?" Martin asked the maiden. "Where is he now?"

"Ten days—" the maiden said uncertainly, before facing a guard.

"Going on two weeks now," he corrected, "Word has it that he's been training. Nobody knows if he really is Caspian. The signs are there, but he acts strangely."

"Take us!" Letty stammered at the guard, who looked to the maiden for approval.

"I shouldn't allow it, but these are unique circumstances. Just send another fighter in to take your post," the maiden concluded, grateful the conversation was over, and desperate to get the mob out of her temple.

They stumbled up the narrow stairs and were led through a few tight halls before they finally broke out into the day.

"Martin, how did you know Andy was at Zentule?" Quill asked, as they were going up another set of stairs.

"Probably the same way you did. I knew Ziesqe had him, and, in ychoron circles, it isn't hard to find out where a lordly ryle has his palace. To be honest, we expected to suffer heavy losses even scouting the damn place. I am thankful that instead of them, we found you," Martin mused.

"What about that monster?" Letty asked. "You

understood what it was."

Martin shivered. "It was a creation of the Maelstrom; a beast made to fulfill a purpose or answer some question."

Letty remembered the monster's claws on her throat and felt bumps rise up her spine. "What was it after?"

"It mentioned Caspian," Quill said.

"Everyone here thinks that Andy is Caspian," Staza added.

"Pythia did too," Letty replied.

Blue pulled on a whisker. "If Caspian is trying to manifest through Andy, he will need Andy to take possession of one of his artifacts, or become so weak as to allow Caspian in."

"How do we stop this?" Letty asked.

The maiden, who was silently listening, interrupted. "Stop this? The boy belongs to Caspian, who is the Voice of God and the only hope for salvation. If only Ithmene can convince him of that."

"What!" Letty cried. "You're trying to make it happen?"

Blue pulled on her ear. "Careful now, we need friends here."

The maiden ignored Letty.

"Blue's right," Staza said, "we need to find Andy; the rest is speculation."

She's right, but who is this, Ithmene, and what has she been saying to him?

Letty was silent as the maiden departed and the mer guardsman led them over the rooftop roads and on a jagged path through the sink, to the drier fringes.

"Just up this street here," the guardsman said.

A group of mer children were playing nearby. They spotted the strangers, and rushed for cover behind the bushes, while braver ones approached.

"How is the Voice?" the guardsman asked the children.

"He's not here now. They went into town," the child said, gawking at the army of goblins. "Besides, I don't think he is the Voice anyway."

"What?" the guard blustered. "She took him into town! What for?"

The child stepped back and shrugged.

Letty felt desperate. She looked from face to face for an answer. "So he's not here," she finally said, keeping her fury in check. "Which direction did they go?"

The child shuffled uncomfortably. "They went towards the Panforum, but I don't know where to exactly."

"What's in the Panforum?" Letty asked.

"Too many things for us to search," Martin said, before considering Clang. "Let's leave a couple of goblins here, in case he comes back. We should also break into groups. We'll head to the Panforum and keep an eye out. Maybe if we ask around someone will know something. He was with a temple maiden, after all."

"What's so special about that?" Letty asked.

"They are famous for being the most beautiful women in the scape," Blue replied absentmindedly.

Letty raised a brow. "I see." She was nearly

seeing red.

"Come on now, and break up this goblin mob. We'll meet back at the basement every few hours," Martin commanded, moving the group back down the street.

Letty walked along in a rage, ready to attack anyone who so much as spoke to her. She unclenched her fists and followed along behind Staza and Quill, noticing that the goblins had dispersed.

They walked past a plaza and a Redvolutionist yelled at them in passing. "Are you for the repealing of all property law?"

"Oh, shut up!" Letty screamed at the woman on stage.

Everyone went silent, and the crowd parted as Letty fumed her way through. Even Staza and Quill cringed and passed through awkwardly.

Ithmene—what a stupid name. Trying to make Andy think he's someone else, just like Pythia did to me.

Letty remembered the striking woman who she saw next to Andy earlier that day. She remembered the lovely dress Ithmene had been wearing.

I'll rip that dress off and strangle her with it—

Letty bumped into Staza, who had stopped short.

"What is it now?" Letty snapped.

"Don't look," Staza said, grabbing Letty by her arms.

Quill's face twisted with too much emotion. He helped Staza restrain her.

"What!" Letty burst out instinctively struggling.

"What is it?"

"We're too late," Martin said.

Letty pushed against her friends and finally saw the cause.

Andy?

Her throat tightened as she saw Andy, chained and in a steel cage, being carted through the Panforum.

Letty shrieked and tore at her friends.

The crowds had been cheering, but she didn't know what for, and now she saw.

They have him!

Guards surrounded the procession, and an ychorite stood on the cart calling out to the crowd, "Caspian, the Usurper, has been captured! He will be seen by the Exegesuits in an hour! Head to the Secular to witness his execution! The Cogito is protected, and Degoskirke is saved!"

Letty reached for her argument, but her friends restrained her.

"Let me go! I'm going to kill them!" Letty cried.

Andy's eyes met hers and she stopped struggling.

He sees me.

Andy looked away as his cart split the crowd.

Chapter 9: Extraction

The Seeress, Letty, had broken down. Though restrained, she still refused to leave the growing procession that followed Andy's prison cart. Martin knew he needed to take charge.

"Clang, send some boys out to collect our searchers; let them know we've found Andy, and to regroup on us," Martin whispered. "Also, bring those carrots for the Seers, their eyes are starting to show."

Clang nodded. "Will do. But the Teeth is many, we scare guards for certain."

Martin shook his head. "Have them assemble in smaller groups nearby, in case we need them."

Clang grunted. "Good thought, Martin, and the girl? The wailing gives us up, no?"

Martin considered the crowds and the guards, noticing several other crying followers. "The Exegesuits aren't stupid; they won't start arresting these people, even if they are crying for Caspian."

"Two other surfacers," Clang mumbled. "What to do for them?"

Martin blinked, his face thoughtful. "This is the perfect cover. Every eye in the city will be on the Secular steps. I'll take a walk into the cathedral and find the other surfacers."

Blue leaped from shoulder to shoulder before speaking to Martin. "Could you bring the baggage as well? We have minoe, weapons, and more equipment. We might need it. Also, Clang, scare up some robes with hoods, we need to cover up the humans. Everyone may be distracted right now, but someone might recognize them in the crowd."

Martin raised a brow. "You don't ask the impossible, do you?"

Clang whispered orders to a pair of goblins, who rushed off through the mass of bodies.

Likely to separate people from their clothes, Martin thought.

Blue's ears flattened in thought. "The humans will be useless until this shock wears off. I understand why they are upset, but we expected to find him as a prisoner."

"Truths change and the heart rages," Clang said, casting a pained eye to the humans. "She has a shiny blade; if all the Teeth come, can we not strike?"

Martin grimaced. "Look at all the mercenaries and guards. They are ready for a response from the crowd. Even with her blade, we would take too many losses. We cannot fight a battle in the open."

Clang took a deep breath and looked to his eager goblins, waving his hand to the ground. The goblins were disappointed, but not surprised.

Martin followed the cart for a long while, keeping an eye on Letty and the Caspians.

I woke up today not even knowing about them. They seem like a liability, but, if they want to help us recuse Andy, we should continue working together.

Martin scowled at their violet eyes.

Seers, all. They have no idea how valuable they are to the ryle, or how dangerous it is for them in this city.

Finally, a squirrelly goblin pushed his way through their group, carrying a bundle of human-sized robes.

Martin motioned the humans off to an alley and kept an eye on the entrance while they put on the robes. Staza had to help Letty, who was still shocked.

"Perhaps I could arrange an escort for you to our safe-house. I'll keep an eye on Andy and have you informed of any developments," Martin said, cautiously.

Letty refused with an angry face that quickly filled with tears. "No. I'll be quiet, but I'm not leaving."

Quill and Staza looked to be of the same mind.

"Fine, let's get back out there."

Martin led the way through the crowd, back to Clang and the Teeth. They continued after the slow-moving procession, through the city, and all the way to the Secular, where the banners were already out and the High Exegesuits were standing by. A few hundred Exegesuit guards lined the steps. Their halberds gleamed and each wore a rugged cudgel at their waist. Lines of guards armed with wheel-locks stood behind the halberdiers.

We cannot stand a fight here.

Martin looked down at Clang, who clearly thought the same.

There are so many armored warriors. They haven't even spared the wheel-locks. The Exegesuits are taking this seriously.

Silius, the ychorite diplomat, had the podium and held out an open hand to silence the crowd.

The procession of mercenaries that accompanied Andy's cart parted to reveal a man dressed in the fine clothes of an affluent merchant.

His gait—he walks with purpose. That one's in charge of this group, but there's something else.

"Ziesqe," Letty spat.

Martin took a second look.

Those eyes of hers. They see more than mine. And, yes, he moves like a ryle.

Silius's voice flowed and calmed the crowd. "Fair merchant, word has reached this hallowed place of an achievement most unprecedented. Whispers speak of the opium dealer, the Usurper, the so-called Voice of God. More than that, his supposed signs are everywhere." Silius paused as people craned their necks to take in the blossom of steel, casting light, from so far above. "The Anteschismarian Order of Exegesuits has never denied the existence of this criminal, but has always been on guard to keep the people of our great city free from his failed influence. That said, it is also possible that signs have been misread. Merchant, we will take this prisoner into our custody and perform the observation, now, and on these steps."

The merchant bowed and gestured openly to the cage.

A dozen Exegesuit guards handed off their weapons and approached the cart. The mercenaries ran poles through loops beneath the cage. The guards grasped these poles and hoisted the cage off the cart. They carried Andy, in his barred litter, up the steps.

Martin cast a glance at Letty, clutched tight by her Caspian allies, short cries escaping her throat. He looked around the crowd, hoping that no one

237

else noticed, but to Martin's surprise, instead of suspicious glances, he was met with weeping faces.

I thought this city was secular.

A pair of priests held scrolls for Andy. Even from so far away, Martin saw Andy's eyes flash silver for a moment.

The crowd gasped.

Silius raised his hand again. "Calm, now. Any Seer will show the same. We will now test whether he has aligned with the false-Argument."

Another priest produced a rod and chain connected to a compartment containing a piece of Counter. The priest cautiously approached Andy and fed the canister through the cage bars. A flash of silver and purple shocked the audience. A loud crack broke out and a few people screamed. The priest struggled to free the canister from the cage.

A wave of grumbling and whispering broke out.

"Friends! That test only shows that he is indeed committed. This is likely our rogue Seer from not long ago. This is an achievement, but it is not proof of Caspian, as he has never allowed himself to be captured, at least not in the long history of our city."

Angry and confused shouts filled the air.

The merchant, high on his cart held out his hands to speak. "High Exegesuits! Face the boy and ask him! He will admit what no one in all the Netherscape would dare!"

The crowd exploded, and dozens of people charged the stage, whether to attack or free Andy, Martin couldn't tell. Fighting broke out, and cudgels rung out over flesh, but the violence did not scatter the crowd.

Silius held out a hand and Ventalus, the mouse, called the guard officers to him. Violence drowned the proceeding until the crowd finally calmed.

Silius walked over to the cage and asked, in his resounding voice, "Seer, are you Caspian?"

Andy looked up. "Yes, I am!" he called.

"Why?" Letty screamed.

Fighting again erupted across the plaza. Martin saw Letty raise a glowing fist while Staza and Quill struggled to tear the piece of Argument away from her.

"Clang, get them out of here, now!" Martin yelled over the din.

Clang and his goblins leaped into action and quickly subdued Letty.

"Blue, go with them, and keep the peace," Martin insisted.

"No! I must see what happens," Blue replied, tearing at his whiskers.

Martin looked back and saw that Letty wasn't the only person being carried away. He looked down and realized that his feathers were mottled and changing from orange to red and yellow in places.

He took a breath and tried to focus.

"There!" The merchant called out, over the crowd, his voice resonant. "Caspian, delivered! The zealot is responsible for more than you know! Dear friends of mine, respectable merchants of this city, for decades each, have been systematically murdered by his hand during the time of his supposed silence. Not to contradict this austere company, but he is indeed acting as Caspian!"

"Brave merchant, may we have your name, and the names of those he has slain?" Silius asked loudly.

The merchant recounted a list of a dozen names, many of which were familiar with the people.

"But, you have withheld your own name," Silius stated. "And, it must be admitted, that Caspian has never had a taste for common murder; he kills in a louder way."

"Ah, straight to the point. Degoskirke, you are well served by this diplomat, he sees through to the heart. I will now make a most painful admittance, but I shall do so unreservedly, for now is indeed the time to strike through to the heart!" the merchant spoke passionately, but the audience was confused.

Silius crossed his arms, an uncharacteristic response from the diplomat. "What is this painful admittance?" he asked.

"Produce a vial of that torturers tincture, the mixture that is said to reveal shape," the merchant said.

Silius stared silently for a long while. Ventalus gave orders to his officers, who relayed them, and moments later, the merchant's mercenaries were facing off against the Exegesuit guards.

"What are you afraid of, Silius?" the merchant bellowed, standing straight as steel despite the encirclement.

Silius shook his head and looked to the High Exegesuit of the Heart, who produced a vial. A guard took the vial and pushed his way through the crowd to the cart.

"I can't believe it," Blue whispered into his ear. "Ziesqe is going to expose himself."

"What? That would be suicide!" Martin replied.

"No, not after delivering Caspian," Blue said.

The crowd jabbered confusedly. A few, here and there, called out what was obvious to Blue.

The merchant held up the vial, unstoppered it, and drank the contents.

Many in the crowd gasped, and Martin had to rub his eyes before he would believe it. A ryle, purple skin shining and eyes glowing red, stood on the cart. The audience was silent.

"How free is the Free City if one such as I, a patriot, must hide my flesh in its streets?"

Silius shook his head and retorted angrily. "You do not—hide your flesh—as you put it. Your kind is all but invisible to almost everyone! You appear falsely as a matter of nature!"

"Is it nature that bars me from the city I love?"

Silius looked for the right words, but Ziesqe barreled over him.

"I have done Degoskirke the greatest service. My compatriots, respected merchants all, are dead at Caspian's hands, and I have decided to show you who has done this service! Now, facing pain of certain execution, I, with my last words, demand that you vote to repeal this ban on ryle from now to eternity! Vote now!"

The crowd clamored in anger and confusion. People attacked the cart. The Exegesuit guards, not knowing what to do, pushed the attackers back.

Martin felt someone nudge him sharply, though he was distracted by the disbelief on Silius's face.

"Brother, take this coin and shout for Caspian's vanquisher; he has saved the city!" another ychorite said, holding out a handful of coins.

Infuriated, Martin threw a heavy punch and knocked the ychorite into unconsciousness.

"He has plants in the crowd," Martin said to Clang, who was trying to keep his goblins from killing the ychorite.

"Get the Teeth out there and subdue, by all force short of mortal violence, every one of the provocateurs," Martin commanded.

Clang nodded and rushed off with his goblins.

Two hundred goblins should be able to counter this.

Martin turned back to Ziesqe, who was staring squarely at him.

Martin felt his heart sink.

"What is it to be? Will this unjust embarrassment of law finally be struck down? Or will I mount the gallows a martyr?" Ziesqe called out.

I should get inside the Secular, but I must see what happens. What is decided here will shape everything.

Martin felt the urge to run deeper into the crowd and vanish, but he stood his ground and watched the Exegesuits with desperation. Occasionally a pained cry would ring out and he would see a pair of goblins bludgeoning a provocateur.

The Exegesuits argued with each other and it

became clear that the vote was tied.

"The vote is stalled!" Silius announced triumphantly. "Bribery and hollow spectacles will not win today! Mind, Heart, and I stand against Feet, Hands, and Blood. The motion fails!"

"Hold!" Ziesqe cried raising a hand to the Exegesuits. The rancor in Ziesqe's voice was enough to silence the audience and get the attention of the guards. "Produce another flask of your tincture! Hand that flask to your diplomat!"

Silius nearly lunged off the stage.

"You brought this on yourself! The people have a right to know!" Ziesqe spat.

The audience became increasingly aware of the insinuation.

"Take it, Silius; shut his filthy mouth!" voices called out.

Silius let his head hang as a vial was handed to him.

Ventalus was clenching his tail and waving the guards away from their diplomat.

"With Silius out of the way, he'll win his vote. He will probably move to have Andy executed as quickly as possible," Blue said.

"What?" Martin spat, taking Blue on his palm to look at him.

"That isn't Caspian. Andy won't hold up to Exegesuit questioning. For some reason, he's playing along with Ziesqe's plan, but eventually it will fall apart. Ziesqe must know that."

They paused and looked back up to Silius. He had downed the flask. Moments later, a coppery skinned, musclebound ryle stood in his place.

The crowd grew silent.

"Silius, you are stripped of your station!" the speaker of The Heart called out.

Ventalus failed to keep his guards in check as they subdued Silius.

"Don't hurt him!" Ventalus commanded.

"The vote!" Ziesqe cried. "Silius is guilty of high treason and his vote is forfeit!"

No one on the stage disagreed.

"Forgive Silius, fair people; he may have committed treason in lying about what he is, but he has served the city as well as any of the now dead merchants! Let us hope to see him back in his old position, after the ban is repealed!" Ziesqe called.

Silius cried out in fury and struggled against the guards, his strength pulling nearly a dozen off their feet.

There was more activity on the steps, and Andy's cage was carried into the Secular; the audience was too distracted to notice.

They are taking him inside. It's my time to move.

Blue raised a hand to Martin, sensing his eagerness. "He isn't done."

Ziesqe raised a hand to Andy's fleeing cage. He waited for a long moment as the doors closed and the cage disappeared. "Where are you carting the Usurper off to? Is he going to avoid a punishment?"

Martin spotted another provocateur trying to bribe people nearby.

Martin tapped the man on his shoulder and struck him across the jaw. He bent down and took the man's bag of coins and threw them to the crowd.

"Caspian must be executed this very day! His continued existence puts the whole city at risk! He will slip those chains and try to take the Cogito the first chance he gets!" Ziesqe called out. "Vote!"

Martin saw a surge of new figures rushing through the crowd to the stage. The guards responded, pulling the Exegesuits away from the danger and forming lines to protect them.

Military cries rang out across the plaza and many in the crowd panicked and ran as the guards leveled their real weapons for a fight.

"It's the Archatians!" a voice yelled to the crowd.

"It must be speakers and supplicants from a dozen schools," Blue said.

"Cease this tyranny!" An old braid, almost drowning in Sici, cried out in a crisp voice. "The Anteschismarians may change protocol regarding foreign matters, but domestic policy is the domain of both houses!"

"This is it!" Martin looked at Blue, who said, "I need to get on that stage!"

Blue climbed to Martin's shoulder and held on has he pushed his way, sometimes aggressively, through the crowd and toward the mob of Archatians who held one half of the stage.

A pair of supplicant Greeks spotted him and moved to keep him back.

"Listen! You must convince your masters to dispute the right to execute the boy!" Martin pleaded.

"Must we?" one of the Greeks sneered.

Blue shouted over the crowd, "That ryle is no local merchant! He never mentioned his name, because he is Ziesqe, ruler of Zentule, and he is commanding the force in the sewers! He is using this scheme to demoralize and divide us! He will conquer the city! If it comes to violence, the boy is our only chance to fight back!"

"Take your faith in the Dead God and shove—"

"Wait, he might have something," the second Greek said, interrupting, "the ryle never said his name. It should be an easy hinge for a debate. Why would he omit something that basic, unless it were a weakness, and a fake name would be too easily seen through by the people of the city?"

"Okay, ychorite, hold on," the first Greek said, turning toward the group of Archatians.

A moment later they returned with a senior Greek, whose long patrician's robes were weighed down with Sici.

"These lads say there is fair debate here. Do you have any proof that this ryle is leading the supposed force in the sewers?"

"No," Martin admitted, "just go down there, you'll find ravagers."

The Greek scoffed. "No, we need something substantial, challenging his name and asserting the ryle ban as a domestic issue would be enough to call for a Quoratota."

The Greeks perked up at that, and even other Archatians heard the words and paid attention.

"What's that?" Martin asked Blue.

"A great debate where several schools of house Archatian, and every branch of the Exegesuits decide an issue for the city."

That would be perfect, it would give me enough time to save Andy!

"But we need more," the senior Greek said.

"This merchant, when still appearing as a human, was in the company of the initiative to restrict queen activity," a braid said. "It passed, and now every brutox queen is required by law to spend half of the day in their walled parcel. He was with the backers, I'd swear it!"

A few others nodded in agreement.

"Right!" Blue yelled, his mind working at lightning speed. "He spearheaded that motion because the queens are the only thing keeping his largely brutox army from invading."

"Is that enough?" one of the younger Greeks asked the senior.

"It'll have to be. If you speak truth and we catch this before it unfolds, you two will be heroes," the senior said to Blue and Martin.

Martin calmed his breathing as the senior Greek barged onto the stage, howling. "What dreadful words of encroaching tyranny drop on my ears! The cloaked song of this mockingbird has made fools of you! Listen deeper and hear the low peal of a war trumpet from beyond the horizon! Convenience beyond measure and nefarious showmanship have carried you away from reason, people and potentates of Degoskirke! This creature has too keen a taste for the flagrant murder of our law! See how he cuts a swathe, from one to the next, with the grace of a practiced dancer, or indeed, the careful hewing of a headsman, happily at work on the unwary! Can even one of you tell me this creature's name?"

"That was the right man!" Blue yelled, his whiskers twitching with excitement. "This is exactly what Ziesqe wanted to avoid!"

Right. Ziesqe needs to avoid a protracted debate. His moral veneer will fall apart. He's crafty though, he still might find a way to slip through. The only problem is, none of this stops his attack.

Martin held Blue to his face and whispered. "I'm going in for the surfacers. I don't think I'll be able to free Andy, but I'll try. We'll have to hope that we can figure something out before Ziesqe attacks."

Blue's ears flattened. "I've just had an awful thought. Do you suppose the attack might only arrive in the case of failure here?"

Martin cringed. "If so, I'll go down as a villain, and you for helping me."

Blue scoffed and leaped off Martin's hand, aiming for an open shoulder in the crowd.

Martin ducked into the mass and felt his feathers tense as he shifted into invisibility. He hoped no one would notice in all the excitement.

Martin weaved through the crowd. He headed towards the cathedral, avoiding the guards. He stood by a side entrance and waited for a group of guardsmen to pass through, before following. He inched past a sentry, who suddenly stood from his stool to approach one of the entering guards.

Martin held his breath as the men exchanged worried words about the proceedings. He waited until they spoke of the prisoners.

"We've got him in the reliquary. A Blood is seeing to him now."

What will they do with Andy if they discover he isn't Caspian? It will ruin Ziesqe's plan, but will it be too late by then? They will almost certainly execute the boy for wielding the Argument. The Archatians don't have a leg to stand on in that department, and we can't count on them anyway. They would face punishment for defending him. Even the Greeks, as keen to argue as Blue said, will not commit suicide for him.

Martin tried to push the torrent of thoughts to the back of his mind and focus on the problem at hand.

He walked through cloisters, peeking through windows and listening to idle chatter. Most of it was about Caspian, but he needed to learn where the surfacers were being held.

He found his way into a chapel and listened to the whispers of the many deacons and representatives of the branches. Desperate scheming and last-minute deals were being struck.

He sneaked close to a nervous pair of whisperers.

"The sword will be out, mind you. Ventalus will bring war before the Archatians rebel against policy. That's the pact."

"The boy is the problem. The Drawn Blade is a foregone conclusion, but the people will not take kindly to the boy being executed. He's too young and has no substantive crimes to his name—"

"He wields the argument!"

"Posh! Many won't consider it enough. Despite sentiment, the AOE will have no choice but to try for execution against the boy, and the Archatians will rouse the rabble because they are being left out of a policy decision. To add to it, he was brought in by a scheming ryle, who now tries to change our laws after making himself the hero. The least he could do was wait a year. This much change, so quickly, will tear the city apart."

"Right, therefore the Quoratota."

"Do you think having a huge debate will clear anything up? It will only aggravate everyone involved! Have you ever walked through a plaza? Nothing is ever solved."

Martin threw his voice. "What about the Caspians?"

The two were silent for a moment. "Who was that? Marcus of the Hands, asking about the Caspians?"

"He's right though. This smacks of that snake. I bet she groomed this Caspian to behave differently. Her venom is on every ear—her prophetic verse whispered in dark corners."

"What if he's in league with the ryle? What if this is all a show to distract us? You've heard the stories about fighting in the sewers."

"I don't know—there are too many pieces. Why send her students? It only shows her involvement and gets our attention up. I don't think they are directly connected."

"But a few of them slipped their leads this morning. We only have two of the five now."

"This morning?"

"Yes! Isn't that a coincidence?"

"Is it the popular two we still have?"

"Yes. They are still quartered in the visitor's wing, when they should be behind bars."

Martin rolled his invisible eyes at how obvious the answer was.

The visitor's wing.

He quietly left the whisperers to their fearful gossiping.

After finding a floor map painted on a wall in the main foyer, Martin had finally made his way to the visitor's wing. He saw a guard sitting idly at the end of the hall.

It looks like there is no way out, save past this guard. There are three turns and two doors from here to the general safety of a small plaza outside. It shouldn't be too much hassle to get them free.

Martin slipped past the guard, careful of his breathing, and checked room after room before finally finding a young boy and girl sitting on a couch next to each other. Both looked distressed.

"We never should have come—" the boy mumbled.

Martin stepped inside and closed the door. They both looked up.

He released the tension on his feathers.

The girl screamed.

"No, no! I'm here to rescue you! Please be quiet."

Martin heard footsteps coming up the hall.

The boy and girl gave him apologetic looks and almost showered him with questions, but Martin raised a hand for silence. He tensed his feathers again and disappeared.

"Amazing," the girl said, right as the door burst open.

"What's the fuss in here?" The guard asked, stepping inside and looking around. "You two are the good ones; don't go changing that now."

Martin clasped his hands around the guard's neck and jolted him into unconsciousness.

The children reared in fright, but they stayed quiet.

Martin slowly lowered the guard to the floor, careful not to clatter his armor.

Reappearing, he spoke, "Get your things, we are leaving immediately."

"Who are—" the girl started.

"No time for questions—I'm with Letty. We know where Lysander is."

The two had gotten to their feet, but they stopped in shock.

"Where is he?" Dean sputtered.

"Somewhere in this building; now hurry!"

They piled as many bags onto their shoulders as they could, yet there was still more.

"What the hell did you bring? Supplies for a siege?" Martin asked.

"These arrived for us a few hours ago," Emma said, pointing at the large bundle. "The Elazene have repaired our suits and delivered them."

"We didn't get to talk to them, but the guards let

us keep the suits."

"Suits?" Martin said, confused.

"Brutox plates, made into armor," Dean replied.

"Ah, Elazene armor. Well, we can't leave it," Martin said, lifting the bundle over his shoulder and moving towards the door. "God be with us."

In calmer times, Elazene arriving with gifts would have been a source of gossip for weeks.

They approached the first turn and ignored the sounds of racing footsteps at Martin's order. They went through the door and noticed an empty stool. Turning the corner, they went unnoticed by a dozen guards, fresh from the riots outside, huffing and puffing in their armor. Martin and the surfacers slipped through the second door with a score of other Secular staff. They finally thanked a guard who politely held the exit open for a stream of Exegesuits rushing out. Martin, Dean, and Emma filed in with the people and went unseen.

Martin felt his feathers flexing in fear. He knew his color wasn't solid, but he was too frightened to control it. He counted the seconds as they walked away from the door, waiting for a shout.

None came.

"Carrying the cargo legitimized us," Dean said, noticing Martin's surprise.

They slipped into the crowd.

"Why all this junk?" a heavy voice asked.

Martin nearly jumped. He saw Clang and a few dozen goblins, all in good spirits after their tussles in the crowds.

"Here," Martin said, dropping the bundle on a

253

few goblins. "These belong to our new allies; do not lose them. Surfacers, this is Clang: Mastery Surgeon of the Broken Teeth."

Dean and Emma were nonplussed.

"They are a goblin mercenary band. You don't know it yet, but our two groups are working together," Martin said, looking back at the Secular.

"We'll mind humans. Are you set for another sneak?" Clang asked.

"Indeed, another sneak," Martin said, turning. "Take them to the others!"

Clang waved Martin's concern away.

"Find Blue! He's with the Archatians in the plaza!" Martin shivered at all the unknowns. He felt his feathers tense, telling him they were suffering from fatigue.

He slipped into an alcove near a shop front and disappeared before heading back towards the Secular.

They're holding Andy in the reliquary.

Chapter 10: Final Moves

Andy's head lay against the gauntlets that covered his hands. A small part of himself wanted to inspect the room they had put him in, but all he could think about was seeing Letty again.

Though he had no reason to believe, the look on her face said it all. She had come to save him. He knew this should have been a joyous meeting, that he should feel relief, or something, anything positive, but all he felt was guilt.

She's in the city and that was Staza and Quill with her. They saw everything.

Andy felt the urge to cry but nothing would come.

I wish she'd never seen me like this. I wish they thought I was dead and never came.

Andy heard the door open. He looked up and had to narrow his eyes. The room was painted in gold leaf and the furniture glittered in the light from dozens of lamps. He looked for the source of the noise but saw nothing.

"Just checking in on me? I'm not going anywhere," Andy said. "Is it dinner time? My old warden used to give me treats for good behavior."

He tried to laugh but only felt numb.

A moment later, he heard the door open again.

"I haven't gone anywhere!" Andy yelled, brushing his face against his shoulder.

A figure in the red robes of The Blood approached Andy's cage and stood in silence.

"No dinner? Maybe some questions or torture?"

"Who are you?" the figure asked.

Andy scoffed. "Loosen these chains a bit and I'll show you."

"Why didn't you take the Cogito?"

Andy rattled his chains. "You could never understand the Voice of God."

Andy heard a low, scraping laugh. It was familiar.

The figure pulled back its hood. Andy recognized Ziesqe. "Very good, Lysander. I see that you are keeping to our arrangement."

Andy was silent.

"I've brought you a gift, since you've done so well," Ziesqe said, producing a cage.

"Titus!" Andy cried, pulling against his chains.

The mouse was hunched and withered.

Ziesqe unlocked the cage and motioned for Titus to hop out. The mouse refused to move.

"Despondent?" Ziesqe asked, reaching in and grabbing the mouse. "Your friend here does a great thing. Please, noble builder, take your place at his side, and aid him." Ziesqe implored, reaching through the bars of the cage and placing Titus on Andy's shoulder.

"Titus, I'm sorry," Andy said.

"A cage and the chains," Ziesqe mused. "Excessive for anyone but you, and that old barbarian."

"How is Thrag? And Ithmene?" Andy asked.

"Thrag's body will never die, though his mind will always be broken. He is enchained as well, not far from your young bride. She will be released tomorrow, no matter the outcome. Thrag, however, will be taken by ravager and then by cutter to another scape altogether, before I release him on some old friends."

"What do you mean, 'No matter the outcome?'"

Ziesqe gave Andy an appraising glance. "Right to the point, I see. I was hoping to have some words with you, maybe learn what you have been up to. Ithmene hasn't been talkative on the subject."

Andy tensed.

"I haven't hurt her, though my curiosity can overstep bounds, it hasn't yet. But, since you were in such a rush, I'll get to the crux. Those manic Archatians forced this. There will be a farce tomorrow—a massive debate and then a vote. Step by misstep, we must dance to the summit, despite all turns of fate and fortune. I intend to defeat the Archatians handily, as regards the ryle ban, but on the second matter, that of your execution—" Ziesqe paused.

Andy stayed silent, but Titus leaped to his feet.

"Stay your venom, mouse; I keep to a deal you know nothing about. I will press for execution. It must be done, so the rag-bound inquisitors of The Heart never get their hands on you. Be grateful they are only questioning you now and not applying the screw. The Exegesuits want you looking presentable tomorrow."

"Andy!" Titus pleaded. "Tell me execution wasn't part of this!"

"It is only a farce, dear mouse." Ziesqe leaned in and whispered. "None of the Archatians will argue strongly against execution for fear of The Heart. You must suffer that sentence, as long as you continue to act the part. I have already purchased the loyalty of the city executioner. To the audience, it will appear to be a genuine death, but you will be secreted away, back to your home on the surface."

"Of course, he's lying!" Titus spat. "How could he fake a public execution?"

Andy took a heavy breath.

"You aren't obliged to do any of this, you know," Ziesqe said, to Titus's surprise. "This mouse might find a way to release you from your chains. You might speak tomorrow and throw my work into chaos. You have other friends in the city; they might also succeed. But keep in mind—tomorrow at noon, the invasion will begin."

Andy looked up at Ziesqe.

"Yes. The only way it will stop is if Viqx walks into the city unhindered, to greet me at the gate. If I am debating endlessly by the time noon strikes, the attack will commence. If you have trained with the blade, as I expect you have, you might kill me, you might kill the other ryle, but you will not kill us all. You do not have the ability to stop the invasion. If Caspian still whispers into your ear and you give over to him, who knows what might happen?"

Andy considered this.

"You can take the night to think it over, but I already have. Almost every path before you leads to ruin and death. Only one will bring you home. Do as I have said; perhaps you might even enjoy the tears and fanfare, knowing the world will be a better place after Caspian is defeated in the eyes of these people. They might finally move on."

Andy spotted a shifting in the air behind Ziesqe. A sudden burst of sparks flared and there were a pair of hands wrapped around Ziesqe's neck.

"Martin!" Andy cried out.

Ziesqe bent and twisted away from Martin's grasp, a sheen of purple armor appearing over his body. Andy saw the nerves and muscles articulating in Ziesqe's arm as he spun about.

"No!" Andy screamed, pulling against his chains and hopelessly trying to clench his own fist.

The purple blade flashed into Martin's stomach for only a moment before Ziesqe released it.

Martin crumbled to the floor, his feathers immediately becoming visible. Andy grasped against the gauntlets as hard as he could, trying to make a fist, but only a faint glow appeared about his hands.

Guards rushed into the room.

"Clear this up, please," Ziesqe said.

The guards complied without hesitation.

Andy screamed at the sight of his friend on the floor.

Ziesqe stood while the guards removed Martin. After they left, he reached through the cage and grabbed Andy by his scalp, pulling him up to the bars. Titus bit down on the clawed hand, but Ziesqe didn't flinch.

"You have come far and done so well; we're almost there. And remember," he said, moving aside and forcing Andy to watch Martin being pulled through the doors, "this image of someone near to you, bleeding across the floor. Let no more of your friends die, Lysander."

Chapter 11: Accredited

Letty rubbed her raw eyes and everything from the day before returned.

Andy.

She rolled over and felt the panic bloom.

I can't cry, they're going to kill him. I have to do something.

Letty sat up and crawled out of her bag. It looked like she was in a basement. She was surprised to see their luggage sitting in a pile nearby.

She scanned the room and saw tattered, white banners painted with broken teeth. On the floor, she spotted Emma and Dean, lying not far from the Caspians. She didn't recall them returning, or even getting inside her own sleeping bag.

Letty didn't dare sort through her memories of the day before; she was ashamed of how she behaved. The image of Andy in the cage tried to creep back into her thoughts, but she shook her head and stepped carefully over the goblins and her friends to the door. A few beady eyes looked up at her.

She climbed the steps and found herself in an abandoned tavern. Clang was sleeping in a chair by a large dining table, and Blue snored sharply in a teacup, sat by a large makeshift map on that table. Clang stirred as Letty approached.

"Up, I see. Are you tame?" Clang asked.

"Yes. I'm tame now," Letty replied.

"Good," Blue said, stretching and wincing at a pain in his back. "Your Argument is on the counter."

Letty approached the bar and saw a burlap sack. She reached in and found the Argument. Touching the orb made her realize how empty she had felt. The Argument was soothing, and she felt her determination sharpen.

"Today isn't going to be easy," Blue said.

Clang nodded. "We fear. Martin rescued surfacers, but is not returning from cathedral. Captured—maybe worse."

Blue shook his head. "We barely spoke before he went and disappeared."

"Was he trying to rescue Andy as well?" Letty asked.

Blue nodded. "It was a stupid notion. There was no way to get that boy out of there. He must certainly be under heavy guard."

Not wanting to wallow any further, Letty approached the table and considered their map. "What have you planned?"

Blue huffed and swiped pieces off the map. "It's just as stupid! There is no way we can fight our way to Andy and then escape the city! Even with your blade!"

"The sewers!" Clang retorted.

"Are full of the enemy! There is no way!"

"The Martin would know where to find victory," Clang muttered.

Letty looked at the map, and saw the word: Panforum, scrawled across the top. It featured a massive open-air theater. She looked at their notes, scrawled on a few pages nearby.

"What's this?" Letty asked. "Quoratota. What

does that mean?"

"It's the chance," Clang said.

Blue sighed. "The Archatians have challenged the Exegesuits. I don't understand the rules; it goes back to the pact and the union. Laws this big can't just be changed by one part of the city—both sides must have a say, and that is the Quoratota. They are going to decide whether to repeal the ryle ban and—" Blue paused.

"Tell her," Clang said.

"What? Tell me what?"

Blue shrank away and hid his face behind a bent ear. "They are also deciding if Caspian—Andy, is to be executed."

Letty stared; she felt the urge to scream but bit down on her cheeks. Clang and Blue leaned away, as if expecting a storm.

I need to stay calm. This won't help.

Letty felt the Argument. It was warm and reassuring. She stared at it for a long moment before speaking, "What are we going to do?"

Clang and Blue shared a look. "The Greeks and the Braids are going to fight the repealing, but I couldn't convince them that the invasion was a credible threat; it has relented over the last week. We expect that Ziesqe's forces have only pressed in as far as he needs. Considering this, the Archatians are not compelled to save Andy. They are afraid of the Exegesuits and have only promised to move that his execution be softened to life imprisonment, for strategic purposes."

Clang shook his head. "We prepared sneak-attack on stage in case words fail."

"We prepared nothing! There is no—" Blue broke off, tired of arguing.

Letty looked at the map.

"Who gets to speak, on the stage I mean?"

"I've already thought of that, and no, only accredited speakers of house Archatian may take the stage."

Letty considered Dean. "Can we get Dean accredited? Can we get him on the stage to argue for Andy?"

Blue's ears perked up, but his eyes remained tentatively narrow, "How many Sici has he earned? We need ten of the damn coins, in hand, to have him accredited!"

Letty shrugged and cringed all at once, remembering the Sici they traded in for currency the day before.

Clang hopped from his chair. "I'll wake them!" he said, heading to the basement.

Loud and groggy complaining rose from up the stairs. Minutes later, Dean, followed by the Caspians entered the tavern.

"Where's Emma?" Letty asked.

"She just rolled over when Clang prodded her," Staza said.

"Dean, how many of those Sici coins do you have?" Letty asked.

"Why?" Dean asked, rummaging through his pockets.

Letty explained the situation.

"And you stole some from me?" Dean blustered,

counting the coins in his hand.

"We didn't know it would come to this!" Blue replied.

"Eight! I have eight coins!"

"We need ten," Blue muttered.

Everyone winced.

"I would have had—"

"Shut it!" Letty interrupted. "We don't have time for whining." She caught a few askance looks, "Myself included. I'm ashamed of how I behaved yesterday, and it won't happen again. But we need to move. Let's get into the streets and get Dean on a stage somewhere. I'm sure he can earn a few more before the Quoratota starts at noon."

Dean guffawed, unbelieving.

"Good plan," Blue muttered, climbing up Letty's shoulder.

"I'll join in too," Quill said, snatching a Sici, "but I need at least one of these to start, or no one will argue with me."

Everyone looked to Letty for confirmation.

"Fine, it's a better use of your time," Letty said.

"The Teeth might find a few loose purses, eh Clang?" Blue asked.

Clang grunted, catching Blue's meaning. "More than a few," Clang grumbled, strapping on a knife.

"Yes, we might be able to convert regular coin back into Sici, if we need to." Letty had a sudden doubt. She turned and faced Blue and Clang. "Why are you helping us?" she asked, plainly.

Blue's whiskers twitched wildly at the insinuation. "Why are you helping us, Miss?"

Clang raised a hand. "Andy saved us from quick death, when most refuse us even speech. We return favors."

Letty nodded and looked over at Blue. "The boy is worth saving," he said angrily. Letty and the Caspians all leaned in with speculative looks on their faces. "I've been with you for how long, and now you're suspicious?"

"It just occurred to me," Letty said, a little embarrassed.

"Martin said something, when we learned of Andy's capture. He said the Teeth will never make it as mercenaries, that we needed someone just to follow if we were ever going to matter. You have to understand, an ychorite feels like he has no purpose without a master, a goblin feels like he has no place in the scape, and a builder like me knows that his people have failed. We decided to find Andy, hoping the search would give us purpose," Blue said, crossing his thin arms.

"I'm sorry for doubting you," Letty said, turning to the door.

"What about Emma?" Staza asked.

"It's Dean and Quill who are the better speakers. Emma can join us when she's ready," Letty said.

They crammed a few hard biscuits into their mouths and prepared to hit the streets.

Blue called out to everyone, "If you get separated, ask for directions to the Brazen Filibuster! This is our meeting point, and goblins will be here, should you need them!"

Dean showed Letty the parcel of Elazene armor.

Letty was about to ask everyone to wait until Blue gave her a shake of his head.

"You can't just go around town in that, it will upset the brutox," Blue said.

Letty ruffled at this, thinking, *I'd like the armor in case of violence, but I see his point. We're going out to win debates; the armor will make us look bad.*

"Fine," she replied, "but we'll keep our armor in our packs, in case of attack."

Blue conceded to that, and, bulky packs ready, they piled out of the door into the busy city.

Dean mumbled, "The plan is for me to debate on stage, in front of the whole city, when I know nothing about the law."

"It isn't what you say," Quill retorted.

Dean nodded, trying to control his trembling hands. "It's how you say it."

The first parcel they found was dominated by a man in a dark suit of armor speaking to a crowd, not against an opponent.

"The Overman is merely a word we use to describe the striving for higher potential. It is the terrible potential, within the few, to forcefully shed our city's false pretenses, herd instincts, and embarrassing scraping to outmoded institutions. The Overman is a calling to change, so when the strike comes from without, we are stronger within! Yes, change is terrifying, but we must take that terror by the horns and become the thunder! We must strike, or ere long our people will become wholly alloyed with the status quo, with the paltry and suicidal status quo!"

"This should be easy," Dean said approaching the stage and showing his coins to an attendant.

Quill spotted a pair of young upstarts loitering and looking for a fight.

"Go, and be witty! Banter is the key; never let up, never get bogged down! It's better to scoff and start anew if you can't respond to an insult," Blue advised, as Quill approached the toughs.

"You there! Parley today?" Quill started, awkward and aggressive.

"Staza," Letty said, "support Quill!"

Staza grinned at the toughs and sauntered over as a small crowd formed.

Okay, so Staza and Quill are debating nearby, Dean is on the stage, and Clang and his goblins are robbing people. Letty had an uncomfortable feeling. *I don't like it, but we have no choice.*

Dean clambered onto the stage and his foe analyzed him from head to toe.

That man thinks little of Dean.

Dean cleared his throat and raised a hand. "What this man is saying is so vague and without purpose that I am surprised they even let him on the stage!"

There was laughter at that. The mice in the stands took note.

"The debate is on!" Blue cheered.

The man in armor grinned at the jibe, and then turned his glance onto the audience. "Laugh, do you? You would make light of the specter that haunts every citizen of this city?" The man gestured out to the crowd. "Every person knows that certain words and ideas have been falsely imbued with threat, taboo, and extreme punishment. The institution that would ban a thing, also supports that thing by lending it mystique. This is foolish. You mock me out of caution, but I bet dearly," he held up a Sici, "that you would not speak such dangerous words here, on this stage."

The crowd buzzed with fearful anticipation. They behaved as if Dean had just fallen into a trap. Dean simply looked confused.

"What? Do you mean about the Argument and Counter?" Dean asked.

The crowd gasped, and several people immediately turned from the stage, as if they hadn't been listening.

The man grimaced and tossed Dean the Sici.

"Yes!" Letty cried. She refused to shrink at the dozens of glances that came her way.

"You are bold, young man, or perhaps, quite ignorant. If the former, I hope to endear you to our own bold philosophy. We are Pioneers in an age of decadence! And what we seek is daring, fearless people like you to wield the hammer of reason against the past, which clings like a cancer to our sinking berg!"

The rancor in the Pioneer's voice won several cheers.

"Again, is it just me, or is this guy speaking like a magician? Mystical language and obscure goals serve nobody. The people of," Dean paused to look at the sign hanging over the stage, "the people of Berrickvard deserve fact-based legislation, not pointless philosophizing! How will you govern? How will you deal with the other Archatians? Do the Pioneers have a single parcel to their name? Why are you wasting everyone's time?"

The crowd cheered for Dean.

The Pioneer raised his hand to speak, but the audience had decided for Dean, and, moments later the mice in the box concurred.

The Pioneer gladly handed over a second Sici as he leaned in to speak to Dean. "We do have answers to all those questions, but I see that I have a lot to learn about my presentation. My offer still stands, come and find us near the Warrens. With practice, a speaker like you could help break apart the old factions." The Pioneer bowed to his foe and left the stage.

Dean looked for another speaker to rise. He even glanced over to where Quill was having his debate, but none of the toughs dared approach the stage.

Letty turned to Quill who was approaching her with a red face. "Twice a breech is just short!" he blustered. "How the hell does that count as wit?"

Staza patted him on the shoulder. "Stick to poetry and speeches; debate is another animal," she said.

"Did you lose that Sici?" Blue yelled.

Quill's face flushed, his eyes fixed on a particular flagstone.

"Damn! And Dean just made us two more!"

Dean descended the stage and waved to someone in the crowd.

Emma was there, escorted by a pair of goblins and rubbing her tired eyes. "What's going on?"

"We need one more." Letty said, ignoring her friend.

"Or money to convert!" Blue snapped, standing tall on his hind legs and looking for goblins in the crowd.

"Money?" Emma asked, taking her backpack off.

Everyone stood in silence as she rooted through her things.

"Is this enough?" she asked, hefting a bag.

She held it open for Blue to inspect.

Blue's eyes widened. "You have all this! Why didn't you tell us?" he demanded.

Emma leaned away from the loud mouse. "No one asked," she replied.

"How did you get this, Em?" Letty asked.

Emma glanced at the women in the crowd. "There's a pair," she said.

Letty looked and saw a pair of women wearing something akin to denim pants.

"I don't get it," Letty said.

"While you got to go on parade, they had me working with local designers. Apparently, the economy is suffering because lack of confidence or something, and outside innovation is needed to stimulate something—" Emma trailed off. "Either way, they loved my ideas."

Letty gawked in amazement. "They wanted you to design pants?"

"Well look, that's the third pair I've seen this morning," Staza said, pointing at a local woman, who seemed to appreciate the attention the new fashion was affording her.

Blue waved a coin angrily. "We don't have time for this! We need to find a money changer!"

Emma gave Letty the bag and they raced through the crowd, Blue calling directions as they went.

"You, goblins! Get to Clang and call off the operation! Have all the Teeth meet us in the Panforum, concealed Teeth only!" Blue ordered.

"Yes, mousy Sir!" the goblins said, before disappearing into the crowd.

Concealed Teeth? Maybe he means disguises?

Letty huffed under the weight of her pack and nearly crashed into a dozen surprised pedestrians. Blue's backseat driving only made it worse.

"Turn at that inn. No, the other inn!" he cried.

They approached a familiar stand that featured a smaller, mouse-sized money changer's stand nailed to one of its posts.

"No refunds or returns!" the mouse sitting in the smaller stand said firmly, recognizing them.

"Hold up the bag," Blue ordered.

Letty did.

"Sici! One of them! Now!" Blue insisted.

The accounting mice didn't like the tone in his voice and were overwhelmed by the size of Letty's group.

The accounting mice quickly borrowed one Sici from their neighbor. "That will be fifteen seculons and ten ludma, please."

"Bloody hell!" Blue spat. "Pay the thief ten!"

The ychorite at the neighboring stand started laughing.

"Twelve, at least!" the accountant begged.

"Fine, eleven it is." Blue commanded.

Letty opened the bag and quickly counted out the coins on the small stand.

"I thought you weren't a haggling bazaar mouse," the accountant said to Blue, remembering their past meeting.

"I'm not. I'm cheap and in a rush!"

The ychorite laughed even harder at that, and Letty had to push it all out of her head as she finished counting out coins.

"There!" Letty said, snatching the Sici. "Which way?" she yelled at Blue, who almost tugged on her ear to drive her.

"Left, no! Down the avenue and then left! Yes, this way!" Blue said as Letty turned.

They raced off again, slamming into people and apologizing as they went.

"We need to go to the Archatian office in the Warrens. We can get Dean accredited there!"

"I'm going to be dead before we get there—if we keep running!" Dean wheezed. "This city is huge!"

Letty struggled through the next few blocks, thinking about how close they were to saving Andy.

She suppressed a growl, shoving past a pair of brutox blocking the path.

Letty came to a rail and looked down onto a cluster of rectangular open spaces filled with tables and chairs.

"Which way?" she gasped.

"The large building in the center of the Warrens," Blue said, pointing.

Letty turned down a set of stairs and led the way, wiping sweat off her brow.

"Why did I insist that we carry our armor?" she muttered between breaths.

There was a line outside the window at the larger building.

"Initiates looking for acceptance in one of the larger factions," Blue said.

"We aren't waiting in line," Letty insisted.

Letty walked past all the petitioners and held up her bag of gold. "A coin for every one of you to step aside!"

They stood and stared. "Why?" one asked, almost haughtily.

Letty felt the urge to reach for her Argument.

Quill grabbed her arm. "Wait," he pleaded. "Friends! We go to almost certain death! We intend to take the stage at the Quoratota and defend Caspian against the Exegesuits!"

Jaws dropped and a few people within earshot turned and left, afraid of such dangerous speech.

The line dissolved almost immediately, and few took their promised coins. A random pair of the petitioners approached.

"God be with you," one said.

"In beauty there is truth. Today, I learned there is also fearlessness," the second said to Letty.

Emma and Staza scoffed while Dean and Quill whistled and laughed. The forward young man turned and left.

Letty, a little red in the face, approached the window and grabbed Dean.

"He has his ten Sici and needs to be accredited, immediately."

The man looked at Dean, the pile of Sici, Blue, and then Letty.

"Fill out this form, please," he said. "There will be a service fee of two silver ludma; union membership rates apply where applicable."

Letty tossed the man the coins and snatched the small slip. She read it over and saw that it asked what faction Dean would be joining.

"He's independent, not with a faction; does that matter?" Letty asked, filling in the form.

"Well, usually it wouldn't, but I overheard you. He can't speak at the Quoratota unless one of the invited factions puts him on the stage."

Letty stared at Blue, who tugged on a whisker.

"Is he that good?" the man asked. "He looks a little young, under-seasoned. I'd recommend one of the academies. He looks like he favors the Greek."

Dean raised an eyebrow in annoyance, but everyone ignored the man and stared at Blue.

"I made the acquaintance of one of the ranking Greeks; he spoke yesterday at the cathedral. He might be persuaded to let us on the stage. Keep that bag handy," Blue said to Letty.

The man handed Dean his chest-board. "Here is your complimentary badge of status. Feel free to clip your Sici here, or, whenever you join a faction, trade it in for the appropriate uniform."

The man barely finished before the chest-board

was snatched up and the vexing group raced off for the Panforum.

Chapter 12: Together Before the End

The litter bearers bore Andy into the plaza. Titus sat on his shoulder. The Exegesuits argued for almost an hour about the mouse, but no one dared put a hand in the cage to remove him.

Andy took a heavy breath and prepared for screaming or crying, as he had heard yesterday, but the presence of Titus on his shoulder struck the crowd rather differently. The faces were still as the litter and hundreds of armored guardsmen marched through the city. The clamor of the plazas also dimmed to unnatural muteness as they passed.

People from every faction removed their hats and watched the cage; whispers rose about the mouse who was unchained and on that shoulder willingly.

Andy struggled to turn in his seat. The chains restrained him, but he caught a glance of the long procession following behind. Among the crowd he saw clubs in hands and impromptu armor, likely borrowed from the border painters he had seen on his first day, glinting under robes. He even saw cyclostones trailing along somberly in the sky, their propellers barely turning.

"They come to support Caspian," Titus said, earning a scornful glance from an already nervous guard.

"Armed with clubs and wearing pots," a guard sergeant, clad in gilded armor, replied. "Do not stir them any further. We do not want to hurt the people—certainly not over you."

Andy let his head sag. He stared down at his encased hands, remembering the sleepless night he had, arguing with Titus about resisting Ziesqe. The mouse had surrendered a few hours before dawn.

But he refuses to leave me.

The street opened to the wide expanse of the Panforum. Hundreds of stalls had been cleared from the massive stage. Andy spotted the Exegesuits and Ziesqe surrounded by guards on one side of the stage. Opposite them, stood a large and chaotic group.

"The Archatians are already arguing among themselves," one guard said. "This shouldn't take long."

Andy spotted small stands built to hold the mouse vote keepers, just like in the parcel plazas. The people in the audience were also sharing or readying strips of cloth of various colors. Andy recalled those as well.

As they carried his cage up the stairs onto the stage, Andy saw what the Archatians were arguing about. Letty and her friends were there.

Dean! And, is that Emma? What are they doing here?

Andy tried to rub his eyes with his gauntlets, but the chains stopped short, and his movement startled the guards.

The Archatians ceased their quarreling when the cage appeared.

They all stared. Letty had been speaking, but she stopped short and watched, wide-eyed, as Andy's cage was lowered.

Andy turned away, feeling his stomach twist.

They came back for me. Even Dean and Emma. Dean is a coward, and Emma hates me. But they came.

The guards set Andy's cage down in the center of the stage.

He heard Letty struggling with a guard sergeant. "Let me see him!" she yelled.

I have to tell them to leave. I can't stand that they'll see the execution, but I have to let the Exegesuits sentence Caspian to die.

No, you don't.

Andy tensed at the voice.

Leave me, Caspian! You caused this!

Andy pulled against the chains and gritted his teeth. The guards stepped back and raised their weapons.

The sergeant interpreted Andy's moves as a desire to see Letty and ordered his men to let her through.

"No! Keep that girl back!" Ziesqe shouted from the Exegesuit side. Ventalus, who had looked resistant to Ziesqe the day before, now commanded his guards to keep Letty away from the cage.

Andy barely noticed as he listened for another sign of Caspian.

Silius's replacement, a tall woman with a booming voice walked to the center of the stage.

"People of Degoskirke, the Quoratota is called and assembled! Two issues await the leaders of your city. The first is that of the ryle ban. Will it be repealed, or will it stand? The second issue is that of Caspian and his punishment. The five branches of the Anteschismarian Order of Exegesuits each

279

cast a vote. The five chief Archatian factions also cast a vote. Those factions are: The Peace and Parlay Party—"

People in the crowd held up blue stripes of cloth and shouted, "Braid!"

Opponents laughed and called them, "The bored to pieces party!"

The announcer continued over the noise, "The Greek Idealists!"

"Idle-Greeks!" a detractor shouted.

Several robe-wearing Greek Idealists shuffled at the outburst.

"The Egalitarian Redistributionists!"

The crowd was peppered with cheers and boos. Calls of, "Red-baggers!" were heard most of all.

"The Redvolutionists!"

The crowd outright raged at the name. "Murder the people party!" was a common reply.

How are they so powerful, then? Everyone hates them.

"Finally," the announcer said, a little unnerved by the vitriol. "Chosen by toss up, we have The Pioneers!"

Andy recognized a few trim young men wearing blackened suits of armor. The audience was indifferent.

"The ten votes lie with the representative of each faction, as chosen by that faction. Any person accredited and empowered may speak for the Archatians, as any person approved by the Exegesuits may speak for them. The audience may address their need for representation, as always, to the Archatian side of the stage. The Exegesuits will vote with a mind to the charter and founding documents of Degoskirke."

The crowd grumbled.

"It has always been so," she replied.

Andy heard sneers coming from the Archatians.

"We are opening the stage up to the speakers. Ventalus, will you speak?" she asked, looking at the large mouse.

Ventalus shook his head and gestured to the Archatians.

"Fine!" a Redvolutionist said, stepping forward. "The honeyed words and sublime achievements of one, Ziesqe, not even a known parasite of these streets, but a sceptered lord and slave master from afar, have had their moment! Yes, indeed! He is more than just another exploitative merchant; he rules over hordes of serfs as if they were cattle! Who stands in his company? Other merchants with their eyes set as high! The Exegesuits stand beside him! What does that say for them!"

Andy gawked at the lightning words. The Redvolutionist moved across the stage in a frenzy, his eyes flashing with hate.

The crowd cheered and surged, and the guards pressed forward to calm them.

Andy heard the word, "treason," already coming from the Exegesuit side.

A representative of The Heart pulled back their hood to reveal teal skin and brilliant golden eyes. She raised a hand to the Redvolutionist. "I will forgive your heresy just once! If I hear another outburst like that, I'll have you hanging by your neck over the city gates!"

The audience was mostly stifled by her answer, though a few, outraged at the threat of violence booed and beat their chests furiously.

The Redvolutionist turned back to his peers and gave them a nod. "My body will hang as a constant reminder of your institution's fail—"

The mer woman snapped her fingers and a pair of guards lunged at the man, capturing him and shutting him up at once.

A few pockets of fighting broke out between sympathizers and guards, but they were put down quickly. This surprised no one.

"Are they really going to hang him?" Andy asked, again alarming his guards.

"Probably not," Titus said, "I bet they'll tan his hide and throw him back onto the streets after everything is over. They don't want a martyr."

A venerable looking braid in a long coat and white wig took the stage.

"What we need is more respect, all around," he said firmly.

A few people mock yawned, while many agreed.

"The point of this Quoratota isn't to further divide the city—though somebody will always take a stab—we are here to make informed decisions for the wellbeing of Degoskirke."

Vegus, the ychorite representing The Blood stepped forward. "Indeed, and nothing would benefit this city more than the repealing of this, once necessary, but now outmoded law. The ryle fight each other; they do not threaten us. Opening

trade and relations with them will help put
Degoskirke on a stronger footing in the diplomatic
arena of Pansubprimus. Our only other ally has
been the embarrassing city of Caspia, and we know
what treachery crawls from there," he finished
sarcastically.

An aide approached Vegus, whispered, and
pointed over to Letty and her friends.

Vegus laughed. "I see! Our envoys have
appeared! We thought you had been abducted.
But it is worse: You involve yourselves with these
troubles!"

The woman who spoke for The Heart stepped
forward again. "Remember my warning? I knew
that you were sent here to aid Caspian! The viper's
old lover."

Vegus nodded. "All that time, pomp, and money,
wasted on infiltrators, and here they are! Of course,
they plan to interfere with our autonomy!"

Dean stepped forward. "We are still here as
friends—"

"Does this criminal speak for Archatia? Why
are they not in chains?" Vegus demanded, looking to
Ventalus.

The senior Greek stepped forward. "He speaks
with our permission; he will not be denied!"

Ventalus did not order their arrest, despite
protest from his peers and Ziesqe.

Dean continued, "You kept us hostage for three
days, when you knew we had business in the City.
It cannot be held against us that we escaped. Also,
there is a foreigner trying to change your laws. He is

standing on your side of the stage, not ours. And, to you, Heart lady, I say that this is not Caspian at all!"

The crowd gasped and Ziesqe stepped forward. Andy met Ziesqe's eyes.

He was right, my friends are screwing this up. I have to stop this, now!

"No!" Andy yelled. "I am Caspian!"

The Heart priestess rolled her eyes and smiled at the crowd. "He admits it still!" she cried.

Andy spotted Blue whispering into Dean's ears. "He left the Cogito!" Dean yelled "He hasn't taken it for himself. I'm told that Caspian would not have done this! This young man allowed himself to be captured! If he is Caspian, and so forthcoming, ask him to walk you through basic history of the Netherscape! You will find him completely ignorant, where Caspian would know everything. Ask him to perform any feat of Caspian's. He will fail, because he is a surface boy being used as a prop by that ryle!" Dean concluded pointing at Ziesqe.

The announcer interrupted. "We are to discuss the ryle ban, not Caspian's legitimacy!" she insisted.

The crowd disagreed, loudly.

Vegus opened his mouth to speak but was booed so soundly that he shrunk back.

Damn it, Dean. Why'd you have to be home-schooled? This will blow up in our faces.

"Letty!" Andy yelled, shaking his chains. "Let me see her!" he snapped at the guards.

Letty saw this and pushed her way through, the guards were too distracted with the crowd and failed to keep her away. Though once she was at his side, those who noticed, relented in removing her.

"What? What's wrong? Why do you keep saying that you're Caspian? You aren't, I know it's you!" she insisted.

"The city is going to be attacked! At noon! If Ziesqe doesn't get his way, his armies invade. They're in the sewers, all around. I know it's true, I saw them weeks ago! I even heard them planning the invasion. The only way to keep it from happening is for the laws to change and for me to be executed."

Letty's knees gave way. She stumbled and clutched the bars.

One guard found this suspicious and tried to grab her.

"Stay back!" Andy yelled pulling his chains taught. His gauntlets glowed, as he tried to make a fist despite them.

The guard saw this and stepped back.

Andy turned and saw Ithmene, standing next to Ziesqe. She was afraid and staring his way.

"Letty, you don't understand," he whispered, leaning close to the bars. "They won't actually kill me; it'll just be for show. Then we'll get to go home."

Letty reached through the cage and slapped him across the face. "What happened to you! How can you believe it! Of course he'll kill you! It's getting rid of evidence. He'll do the same to the rest of us too, because we know too much! Why don't you understand this?" Letty raved and cried. She held a hand up to his face and touched where she had just slapped him. "What did they do to you?"

"She's right," Titus said, from his shoulder.
Andy tensed.

They're both right.

"What do you want me to do? No matter what I say, this city will be ruled by the ryle! No matter if I fight or die, we cannot win against what he has!" Andy cried out, breaking down. "I deserve these chains! I'm just a boy! I don't know what to do! I don't know where I am, and seeing my friends from inside this cage—I can't!" Andy heaved and gasped, his eyes streaming and his face flushed. He slammed the gauntlets against the cage.

Exhausted, he slumped forward against the bars. He wiped tears on his sleeve and noticed how silent it was.

Every eye was staring. The debating had ceased and those on the stage had stepped aside. The audience was still, and the only sounds were the banners against their poles and then Ithmene weeping into her palms.

Andy knew he should feel more ashamed than he ever had, but instead, there was something else. There was relief.

Ziesqe stepped through the Exegesuits. The motion was jarring, as if the whole world, except he, was frozen in place. "You did your best, Lysander."

He's going to attack! Now, Lysander! You have to act now!

Images of the brutox queens flashed before his mind. He saw flames and the crumbling towers of Hyadoth. The faces of his friends screaming in agony seized his heart; he heard their terror and

286

gasped. He saw Letty, staring at him through the bars and he knew what to do.

Andy heaved in a breath and faced Letty. "Go to the parcel where they keep the brutox queens! You have to free them!"

Letty instantly turned and rushed to the Caspians, grabbing them and Clang before racing off through the confused crowd.

Ziesqe approached the cage. "You've just sent them to their deaths."

"What is the meaning of this?" the senior Greek, yelled.

Ziesqe flung his robes off to reveal a full suit of crimson plated armor. Andy saw his wrist articulate and the purple blade appeared.

Ziesqe sliced the Greek in two, right as several other purple blades appeared. The guards lunged, but Ziesqe merely swung and lopped their halberds to pieces. The sight made them retreat.

Cries rang out, but the guards seemed paralyzed.

Andy saw a pair of ychorons had daggers on Ventalus. They had his mouth shut, though he struggled.

Finally, a few muskets were trained on Ziesqe.

"Ah!" He yelled. "Shoot me and he dics!" he said, pointing at Ventalus. He then looked at Andy. "This could have been a simple matter! There were three paths. Now there are two!" Ziesqe declared slicing Andy's cage apart.

Andy tensed, expecting to meet his end.

Ziesqe won't kill you. He is stalling.

What? Why—

"Unlock the prisoner. Let us test whether he truly is Caspian!"

Because he still wants me! He wants me to take the Cogito and fight—

Ziesqe paused and looked up, shuddering.

Andy did likewise.

What the hell is that?

An abomination flew high above the stage on crow's wings. It trailed a scorpion's tail and looked to bear three heads.

Ziesqe tensed at the sight. When no guard appeared to unlock Andy, Ziesqe swiftly and expertly sliced his restraints apart, piece by piece.

Andy stood and felt the chains and gauntlets falling from his body.

He sensed Caspian looking through his eyes and flexing in his arms and legs.

I've almost given over to him. I can't let him take me!

Ziesqe turned and walked to his retinue, holding a hand out expectantly. A ryle produced a windowed container. Inside was a small piece of Argument.

He doesn't know that I've hidden more, far more, inside.

The ryle bearing the container approached the broken cage.

Andy felt a grin breaking out on his face. He heaved in a huge breath and looked up at the steel blossom. It stretched and grew across the cavern ceiling as his lungs filled.

Now!

Nerve by nerve, he tensed the muscles in his body; he felt the Argument within surge through his limbs. Andy stepped towards one of Ziesqe's ryle, tightened his fist, and impaled him on the blade as it appeared. His victim expected anything but this. Andy loosened his grip and moved towards Ziesqe, who still had his back turned. The ryle with the container could not believe what he saw.

The crowd exploded and Ziesqe's retinue tried to call out warnings as Andy advanced.

With a smug look across his face, Ziesqe turned on his heel, gesturing widely, and then he saw Andy, far closer than he expected.

Andy tensed his off hand and threw a punch. Ziesqe's face went from amused to shocked as a parrying dagger appeared on Andy's fist.

Andy recognized the motions in Ziesqe's exposed musculature; the tendons in his neck tensed.

Is he faster?

Andy's dagger cracked against something rigid. Ziesqe rolled off his feet and down the stairs. Thick streams of black blood stained the stage.

Andy saw a glowing purple helmet, but beneath its hollow shimmer, Ziesqe suffered the loss of a tentacle, which writhed on the floor.

Press the attack!

Andy gave in to the command and leaped into the air raising his hands and summoning the blade to match the dagger. He fell onto Ziesqe, who was too shocked to fight back.

Andy hammered against his armor. Bursts

of lightning shot out into the air as the glowing Argument struck the Counter. Andy felt the thunder of thousands of voices cheering him on.

He released his primary blade and grabbed Ziesqe's arm, twisting it out of position. Ziesqe flinched and could no longer maintain his weapon. With his enemy disarmed, Andy brought his dagger down against Ziesqe's helm over and over, until it flickered out.

Andy felt a sharp kick to his groin.

He cried out, losing focus.

Ziesqe grabbed Andy by the throat and twisted him to the floor. Ziesqe tried to summon his blade but Andy grabbed his wrist and twisted it back.

Ziesqe growled and cracked his helmet against the bridge of Andy's nose.

Call the armor!

Andy felt his muscles obeying Caspian all on their own. The Argument bent inside and he glittered with silver armor.

"Caspian! Come out to see us! Everyone wants to meet you!" Ziesqe howled. "Does this body need more convincing?"

Ziesqe held up his right arm and twisted his fingers in a way Andy didn't recognize.

A war-pick. He'll try to pierce your armor! You must overpower him!

Ziesqe swung the pick into Andy's shoulder. Andy screamed at the blow. The weapon stuck and the noise of the Argument and the Counter touching for too long was deafening. A hissing pop underscored the bursts that sounded like gunshots.

Andy saw purple and silver frost growing on the stone floor nearby.

Ziesqe twisted the pick and Andy's armor shattered.

Fight!

The pick raised again. Andy tried to lift his arms, but the pain was too great; he felt paralyzed.

Instead of death, Andy spotted Titus leaping and latching onto Ziesqe's unprotected neck and climbing under his helm.

Ziesqe tried to swat him away, but cried out as Titus bit down on his wounded face.

Andy felt his arm wrack with spasms and an axe appeared. He screamed out against the pain, reared back, and struck Ziesqe across the chest.

Ziesqe toppled and Titus tumbled to the floor, singed, smoking, and missing most of his whiskers, but still alive. Titus pointed at Ziesqe and growled angrily, "Focus, Lysander!"

Andy growled as he gained his footing. He reached out and batted Ziesqe's feeble blade away before grabbing the ryle by his throat and clamping down hard.

A shrill scream filled his ears. Andy's eyes shot up in time to see Kal hurtling through the air. She tackled him. Their armor sparked and cracked as they tumbled away.

Andy rolled to his feet to find Ziesqe's retinue had rescued him. Kal broke off and ran to Ziesqe's side. She held a flask.

Andy pulled himself to his feet again, the pain making his vision blur.

The crowd booed and, in its outrage, broke through the barrier of guards before attacking Ziesqe and his retinue with nothing but clubs and their hands. Andy cringed as they were cut down, but he was focused on something else.

He lumbered towards the ychorons who held Ventalus prisoner.

They yelled at him to stay back.

Andy raised his blade and screamed. They flinched, some stumbling as they backed up the stairs, but they were all too distracted to see the city guardsmen closing in from behind.

Andy watched as the guardsmen slaughtered the ychorons. Once freed, and de-gagged, Ventalus cried out. "Guards! Level arms!" The guards with wheel-locks raised their weapons against Ziesqe's retinue and Andy as well. "Aim!"

Andy raised up his hands. "Don't kill him yet! An attack is coming! It's coming from the sewers! If you take him hostage, we might stop it!"

Ventalus paused as the Archatians and the other Exegesuits rushed him from all sides. An argument broke out.

Titus limped up to Andy, and, too weak to climb, Andy helped him up.

"You might have done it, Lysander! There's no coming back from this."

Clang and Ithmene pushed through the guards and rushed to Andy. Ithmene snatched the vial out of Clang's hands and opened it.

"Letty?" Andy asked.

"Not back, has half my force," Clang said.

Ask the mer where she was kept!

Andy flinched, but obeyed. "Ithmene, where did Ziesqe keep you prisoner?"

Ithmene described a counting house as she tended Andy's wounds. Andy remembered the building from her description. "He has another man chained up there, as well as many caged mice."

Andy and Titus both perked up at the news.

"Clang, take the rest of your force and assault that building. Free everyone inside."

Andy had never seen Clang smile before. The sight was a little unsettling, especially as Clang didn't respond, he simply turned and piled through the guards towards his goblins.

"Titus, you had better go with him. He looks bloodthirsty."

Titus's face betrayed his desire to argue, but he obeyed.

Andy looked up at the sky.

It's almost noon.

"We don't have much time!" Andy called after his friends.

Chapter 13: The Queens

"But how do I get in?" Letty snapped at Blue.

The bodies of dead guardsmen made her nervous as she tried to slice through a pile of burning refuse. The pile was barring the single entrance into the queen's parcel.

"Can't you cut a way through? Or maybe, try climbing!"

Letty loosened her grip on the blade before looking up at the walls.

"I can't climb that! They're far too high. But I need to get inside!"

"Wait!" Blue yelled. "The map, the sewer map!"

Letty barely remembered the map she had found so long ago at the sphinx library.

"Get the map!" Blue demanded.

Letty found it in a pocket of her pack.

Blue snatched it and had a look. Letty felt the urge to don her armor, realizing that something foul had happened.

I hope the queens are okay on the other side. Someone doesn't want them loose; Andy had the right idea.

"Wait here!" Blue insisted, bounding up the side of a building.

"I can't wait!" Letty yelled.

The goblins struggled to put out the fire until a local told them where the closest well was.

"This is better than doing nothing," Letty said, as the goblins appeared from around the corner with buckets. "But it will still take too long, and they might be dying on the other side!"

Blue reappeared with a handful of local mice. "The intersticines! Those are the Seer tunnels! They have an exit in the queen's parcel and we have a map!"

"How do we get to the tunnels?"

Blue leaped up to her shoulder with a pair of unfamiliar mice.

"Lanticward, my Lady," one said, pointing back the way she had come.

"I'll try to get the gate open from the other side," Letty yelled to the goblins. "Keep working here!"

"Yes, Mistress!" the goblins answered.

"Don't call me that!" Letty cried, racing around the corner.

They directed her to an alley and then she waited as the mice crawled through a small mouse port.

She put her ear against the wall and listened to them inside.

"Just a second!" Blue said, clearly exerting himself. "This thing hasn't been oiled in ages—come on, keep turning!"

What are they doing in there?

Letty stepped away and saw a circular recess appear on the stone wall. The stone unfolded in slow pulses, linked to the noises of exertion coming from the mice.

Blue poked his head out from the mouse port. "Is there a door handle? Are we getting anywhere?" he asked.

"I don't know what this is," Letty said, staring at something that looked like a plunging lever.

Blue bounded up to her shoulder for a look.

"That's it lads, you can stop!" Blue said. The other mice appeared, clearly exhausted. "Produce a glow and try pulling on that lever."

Letty felt a little suspicious, but there was no time for doubt.

Alright, here goes.

She summoned the glow and grabbed the handle, expecting a trap to catch her hand or worse.

Nothing happened.

She pulled the lever, which took both hands and a fair amount of force, before the frame of a door appeared, loosely in the stone.

"That's it!" Blue cheered.

Letty pulled the door open, and, glowing hand ready, stepped inside. The door snapped shut behind them, leaving the other mice stuck on the outside. There were stairs leading down to a wide, clean tunnel. Signs glowed on the walls; they were directions, but the names were all unfamiliar.

"I don't know which way. Left or right, Blue?" Letty asked, staring at the names.

Blue pondered. "I was right, these weren't sewers, these are the intersticine tunnels. The Seers of old used them to travel the city in secret."

"Which way?"

"Hold on, girl! These are old names. Things change."

Letty produced the map and held it up for him.

"Ah, that helps!" Blue said, pointing down the left-hand tunnel. "That way!"

Letty felt safe running through the mostly clean

tunnels at a jog and only slowed for turns and signs on the walls.

She spotted an armored door and a bastion built not far ahead.

"Is that it?" Letty asked.

"No. I expect that's a secret way into a Seer chapter-house. It might hold countless useful artifacts, but we have no time. I suspect we're under the Greylapse," Blue muttered.

Letty grimaced as she came closer and saw bones and ragged suits of armor scattered on the bastions and barricades. Stone blocks on the low walls and several armor elements looked like they had been rent cleanly in two.

"They were fighting with the Argument down here."

"Come on, don't slow down," Blue whispered, his voice somber.

Letty continued down the hall.

"There, turn up those stairs."

Letty did. She found another lever, pulled it, and the door popped. However, this door was far harder to open. Letty pushed with all her might and heard a strange, crispy cracking coming from the other side.

"Something's blocking us," she said.

"Slice through the gap, you might clear it," Blue reasoned.

Letty summoned the blade and found it would not cut the door.

I've seen that before.

She slid the blade through the gap and slowly cut her way through whatever was holding the door shut.

With a final kick, she forced the door open.

She stepped out into the queen's parcel and was astonished at the alien nature of the buildings all around. They reminded her of towering insect hives.

She shuddered at the sight.

"Ah, they'd sealed over the door," Blue said, looking at the building behind them.

Letty turned and saw he was right. Whatever organic material they used to the build these structures had been pasted over the stone buildings underneath. Letty looked up and saw that the hive spire tapered in width up to an unbelievable height.

"The core of this is a regular building, but further up, it's all insect," Blue said.

Letty heard the sounds of violence nearby and rooted for her armored suit in the pack.

"I'd better get ready," she said. "Go and scout for a second."

Blue nodded and disappeared around the corner as she put the suit of brutox armor on over her clothes.

"Thank God for this," she muttered before pocketing the map of the Seer tunnels.

She peeked around a corner and saw three ychorons, wielding rapiers, trying to encircle a lithe brutox queen. Letty felt the pistol in her pocket.

Five bullets left.

She tightened her fist around the Argument and summoned her blade.

"Leave her alone!" Letty cried, racing out from behind the cover.

The ychorons were startled. Letty cut through them and their steel weapons like they were paper.

Letty was shocked at how easily she killed all three.

The queen stared at her. The insect face, inhuman beyond question, still expressed something like surprise.

Letty lifted the visor on her helm. The queen backed away, and Letty realized that her suit was the problem.

"I was with the Elazene, and I've come to get you out of here." Letty paused. "Which way to the gate?"

The queen, a ruddy ant-looking creature raised her claws and looked like she might strike.

"Careful, Letty!" Blue said, reappearing.

"I'm on her side!" Letty said, raising her blade to keep the queen at bay.

"You're wearing her people!" he insisted.

"Of course! What's wrong with me?"

The queen lunged, and Letty stepped aside.

What did Ahmet say—that day he gave us the armor?

Letty dodged another attack.

"If I bear you as mantle—" Letty said, trying to remember the rest.

The queen stopped.

"If I bear you as mantle, will you bear me as— progeny?" she asked, unsure if those were the right words.

The queen inclined her head. The violence ceased, as if it never was.

"They know the Elazene," Blue whispered. "They go back a long way."

The queen led Letty through the strange buildings and around the oddly winding streets. Letty raced towards any fighting she saw and struck down ychorons where she could, but she dared not stop for long.

I must get the goblins through the gate, if we're to stand a chance at saving the queens. They could split up and cover much more of this parcel than I alone.

The roadway descended into a tunnel beneath towering, bulbous structures that looked like termite mounds. On the other side of the tunnel Letty saw the parcel wall.

"Damn!" she grunted.

The gates were guarded by a dozen ychorons and an unfamiliar ryle.

Letty took a breath and readied herself to charge.

I need to get through that gate!

The queen reached out and grasped Letty by the arm. She shook her head, and then put on an abashed expression. Letty watched as the queen gestured with her hands.

"You think I should try to surprise—no, you think I should trick them?" Letty whispered.

Letty looked down at her armor.

"They'll think I'm one of you; it won't work."

The queen tapped Letty's helmet, indicating that she should take it off.

"That might go over. They will probably be confused by a human in brutox armor."

Letty felt a smirk tugging at her cheeks. She pulled off her helmet and rushed out towards the gate.

"Quick, open the gate, I need to get back to Ziesqe!"

The ryle and the ychorons responded as expected. They were astonished at the sight of her.

"Wha—who are you?" the ryle blustered.

"Do you think Ziesqe lets just anyone know his plans? Open the gate damn it! We have a problem!"

That flustered the ryle, "No—well, it's barricaded on the other side, wait! What problem?"

"What's your name? I want to know who is being executed tomorrow."

The ryle scoffed. "I report to Viqx, not to Ziesqe, let's get that clear."

This isn't working.

Letty slid her helmet back on before nonchalantly summoning the blade. She swung through a handful of unsuspecting ychorons. She had aimed for the ryle, but he dodged backwards at the sight of the blade, falling into the debris.

Letty readied a strike, but the remaining ychorons had raised their weapons. Daggers and rapiers were coming at her.

How can they not know what happens to steel when it touches the Argument?

Letty deflected blows and watched the looks of surprise flare up as weapons fell into pieces.

A recently disarmed ychoron dropped his useless dagger and lunged at Letty while she was distracted with another. Letty felt his blows come down heavily on her armor.

A moment later, she felt a second and a third

grab her tightly. She struggled free and sliced one, but the other two still held on.

"Get a hold of her blade arm! Hold it steady," the ryle croaked, getting off the floor.

Letty saw him summon his weak blade, but then she heard fast footsteps.

The ryle looked up, surprised. The queen was charging.

Letty lunged towards the gate, slamming one ychoron into the gate and losing the other. She wrenched her arm free and sliced through the bar that held the gate closed.

Letty turned and saw the ryle charging toward the queen who had drawn him into a feint. But the ryle, heedless of Letty pressed the chase and rushed after the queen.

Letty stepped forward to slice the ryle from behind, but she felt a tugging on her feet and fell to the floor.

"No!" she cried, kicking the ychoron who had grabbed her squarely in the face. She dashed to her feet in time to see the queen crumble to the ryle's blade.

A loud creaking from behind threatened to draw her attention, but she stayed focused on the ryle and charged. He was facing the wrong way, turned, lost his balance and failed to raise his blade to counter Letty's blow.

Letty felt a deep sting at the sight of the queen crumbling to blackened ash. She put it from her mind and turned to see a hundred goblins pushing through the gates.

"Takka!" Blue yelled. "Get the bones ready, sound the alarm if you find anything. What took you so long!" he asked.

Letty, was in no mood for his attitude, though she didn't protest when he climbed to her shoulder.

"Search the parcel, rout the ychorons, and save the queens! Assemble in the plaza at the center!" Blue commanded.

The goblins bellowed shrill cries and stormed down the winding streets. Letty ran to the sounds of violence and found the ychorons retreating or being overwhelmed by goblins.

These ychorons aren't very good soldiers, but the ryle can't use brutox here.

A long train of queens and their few remaining brutox followed Letty and her group of goblins as Blue led them closer to the plaza.

A loud scream echoed around the curving structures. Letty wasn't sure which way to turn. They heard the loud chattering of Takka's chimes go off.

"Which way?" Letty asked.

Blue's ears tensed at the sound. He craned his neck this way and that, but was still confused

One queen, a slate gray spider, approached and pointed down a twisting path between the hive buildings.

Letty took off at a run, she had to duck slightly as the path turned into another tunnel.

On the other side, they saw a pack of goblins evading a giant ryle woman. Her skin was red, and she screamed as her dragonfly wings flexed and flapped in bursts, pushing her towards another goblin.

She watched as the ryle skewered the goblin on her blade.

Letty almost attacked but wondered if she could possibly win.

The ryle moved with a fury and the goblins barely evaded, climbing up destroyed buildings, and shrinking down into wreckage.

The ryle I killed at the gate called her Viqx. He behaved like she was an equal to Ziesqe.

Letty felt the urge to run, but it was too late. Viqx spotted her and the gang of queens trailing behind.

"Kill every queen you find!" she called out to her ychorons.

She thinks I'm one of them! I've got the helmet on!

The goblins rushed forward and parted like waves around a jagged rock. Each tried to menace Viqx, but none would chance coming within reach. Their javelins and arrows barely scratched her thick flesh. Letty felt her heart sink at the sight.

She doesn't even need armor.

Letty whispered to Blue. "Get the goblins to pile on from above when I distract her."

Blue nodded and leaped from her shoulder towards the goblins.

Letty stood still as Viqx lumbered towards her, ignoring the goblins.

Viqx looked amused as Letty refused to retreat. She raised her meaty arm.

Letty ducked under the blow and lunged upward tightening her fist at just the right moment.

The blade ripped into the ryle.

The goblins cheered.

Instead of falling to the ground, Viqx roared, backhanding Letty with a powerful fist.

She tumbled across the wreckage, her helmet flying off. Letty moaned and rolled to her feet, barely aware of the goblins helping her up.

"How is she still alive? I caught her in the chest!"

Viqx stared for a moment, realization working in her awful face.

"A Seeress, all for me," she growled, ignoring the queens and rounding on Letty.

A dozen goblins leaped from the taller buildings, screaming as they flew. They landed on the giant ryle, stabbing and chopping as they did.

Viqx shrugged off the wounds and then tensed her muscles in a strange way. The blade vanished, but her body was suddenly covered by shining and translucent purple armor.

The goblins shrieked and flew off, singed and jolted by the armor.

She can't do a blade and the armor. It's one or the other!

Letty picked herself up and swung at Viqx. The ryle let the blow bounce off her armor before swiping at Letty.

Letty dodged the attack, but quickly realized that she was massively underpowered.

She isn't unarmed; she could kill me barehanded.

Blue barked orders at the goblins. They readied their javelins and short bows. Occasionally Viqx would swipe at one, forcing him to break off or dive for cover, but she couldn't press an attack for fear of exposing a side to Letty.

How can I get her to lose the armor?

Viqx roared and lunged towards Letty who dived and rolled under the ryle's massive legs. Without looking, Letty rolled to her feet and took off running.

"You can't escape, Seeress!"

"Pursue!" Blue ordered, riding a goblin's head and holding onto his ears.

Letty turned at random down the winding streets. The eyes of the queens lifted to the noise from various round windows and doors. Letty descended into a tunnel but heard a sudden, sharp buzzing sound, like that of a one-ton honeybee.

She's flying over the building to catch me on the other side.

Letty paused, looking around the tunnel at the doors to the buildings. She tried one and found it locked.

"Come out, girl, I won't bite," Viqx said, bending and pulling herself into the cramped tunnel.

Letty tried to keep herself from shrieking in fear at the sight.

Think! Think!

Letty used her blade to slice a way through the righthand tunnel wall. She rushed through the breach and found herself inside a wide, empty chamber. It had once been a normal building with rectangular rooms and long halls, but some regular masonry had been destroyed or replaced by smooth, curving insect walls.

Letty realized the interior was large enough for Viqx to stand.

Keep moving!

She ran to one of the curving walls and cut a square into it before kicking the square chunk out to the other side. She looked through and saw the space on the other side was the same.

"I see you!"

Letty flinched and saw Viqx ripping the wall apart and pulling herself into the building. The roof buckled and dust trickled down.

Bring the building down!

Letty leaped through the hole she had just cut and ran around the perimeter of the room, slicing chunks out of the walls.

Wait! What if it falls on me?!

Cringing, Letty turned and sliced a way through another wall. There was only earth on the other side.

Right, I went down a tunnel and then inside this building. I'm one floor down.

Letty heard a blade rip through the wall behind her.

With fear gripping, Letty dashed through the closest door and ran down a hall, looking through each door for stairs.

"The more you run, the worse it's going to be!" Viqx yelled, from not far behind.

Letty ignored the doors to her sides and raced for the end of the hall. She heard a heavy buzzing coming from behind but dared not look. At the end of the hall she saw stairs leading up. She took them two at a time. The buzz was deafening and suddenly on top of her.

She felt a claw grasp her leg and pull her back down the stairs. Letty struck with her blade but another claw intercepted her arm. Both claws wrenched, cracking her plated armor and tearing her skin. Letty cried out. Viqx raked her claws across Letty's face.

"Is there anything sweeter than destroying beauty?" Viqx whispered.

Letty drew her pistol. Viqx raised a brow but recognized the threat too late. Letty focused through the pain and her trembling, and knew that she couldn't miss. She pulled the trigger.

Viqx released an unearthly rasping cry.

Letty struggled free. Viqx had been shocked by the wound, but was not killed.

Letty grasped the banister and pulled herself to her feet. She struggled so ferociously backward up the stairs that she couldn't keep traction and ended up on her hands and knees.

Viqx growled in fury and Letty heard her moving again.

She isn't dead! How isn't she dead?

Letty raised the pistol and fired it until every round was spent.

Viqx only screamed. She refused to die.

What do I do?

Viqx pulled her trembling body up with the strength of her arms. She drove her claws into the walls and climbed up the stairs after Letty.

Oh, God!

Letty gasped and crawled up the stairs, dropping her spent pistol, before finally willing herself to stand. She felt something wet running down her face. She looked down onto her breastplate and saw blood twisting across its smooth surface. Shaking and nearly falling on every step, she finally reached the top. Her cheek felt like it was on fire. Heaving in breaths, she swung her blade at the walls of the stairwell, tearing them into pieces and collapsing them down the well. She went through the room, limping and swinging at the walls and beams. When the building finally creaked and shifted, she turned to the door. Letty looked back and saw the pile of debris in the well; it was still moving.

She stumbled outside. The goblins spotted her and raised the alarm. They had scores of queens in tow.

"Stay away!" she yelled at them, dragging her blade through the entire length of the building.

She swung and swung, but the building only splintered and creaked. She cried out and kicked at one of the corners before the whole thing collapsed.

Letty screamed at the top of her lungs and finally crumbed to her knees, before clutching her bleeding face.

Somewhere in the distance, a bell tolled noon.

Chapter 14: Noon

"Send your guards to the sewers! There are ravagers and brutox, in the thousands! They will attack at noon! These few ryle aren't even the beginning! You have to listen to me, Ventalus!"

The mouse rubbed at a bloody spot on his throat. Andy hadn't seen him take the wound, but assumed it happened when the guards subdued his captors.

Ventalus, surrounded by grumbling Exegesuits, was mortified by what he saw, but was still unready to listen to Andy, despite his rescue. Andy looked down onto his blade and knew they must dislike seeing it.

They would prefer the ryle and I just kill each other and be done with it. Well, that won't be the end.

Andy refused to release his blade and looked back at Ziesqe's crumpled body, which was still receiving treatment from Kal.

Ventalus listened to the complaints against Andy, while people screamed at the guards to shoot the ryle, while others cried that Andy and his friends be killed.

"He flaunts the sacred law in front of our eyes!" an Exegesuit complained. "We cannot send the guards on a fool's chase in the sewers! It is clearly a trick to leave us exposed! They are acting, and still in league with each other!"

"Guards! Fire on the boy!" An Exegesuit ordered.

The guards looked to Ventalus to repeat the

order.

Ventalus was silent.

Andy noticed a robed figure fidgeting nearby. The figure wasn't heatedly yelling and screaming, like everyone else, which made him stand out.

Andy let the Argument flow into his eyes, granting him the Sight. The rush of noise sent his head spinning, but he saw beneath the figure's robe. It was an ychoron, bearing a hidden dagger mounted on a piston. The device was strapped to his wrist and he was approaching Ventalus, crouched and ready to strike.

The crowd gasped at Andy's shining eyes.

"Heresy!" one yelled, the sound coming to Andy as if through a thick mist.

Andy raised a hand. "Assassin!"

The ychoron flinched at the word but, after a moment of hesitation, lunged for Ventalus, the pneumatic blade shooting out from his sleeve. He was too late. The guards had taken the threat seriously and subdued him by weight of numbers.

"The ryle are trying to kill you, Ventalus!" An Archatian yelled from across the stage. "How many times must the boy save you? Listen to him! Don't be a fool!"

Andy was about to speak when a bloodied guardsman pushed his way through the crowd and approached the stage. He was limping and his sword had been broken. All he held was a hilt and half a foot of blade.

"They are attacking the brutox parcel! Ryle heretics and a force of mercenaries!"

"This is his plan!" Andy roared. "His army is almost all brutox! He's trying to kill the queens, because they are the only thing that can stop him!"

Ventalus stepped forward, his whiskers in one hand and his ears tense in thought. The Exegesuits continued pestering him, but he raised a palm for silence.

"Commander!" Ventalus said to a guardsman in gilded armor. "Get a company to the brutox parcel, and have half of your men take up positions around the cisterns!"

"Aye, sir!"

A sudden bustling attracted Andy's attention. He turned and saw the Archatians had just settled something and were splitting up and heading in different directions at a run.

"Well done, Lysander!" Ziesqe said, back on his feet and looking fresh, despite the wound on his face. "You've forced this city down the last and most violent path. Like a coward, you attacked me from behind. Actions define us, and for all this, I will—" Ziesqe paused at a sudden screech from above.

Andy looked up and saw the beast circling above. Its roar was an unsettling mix of bird, dog, and what he expected a dragon might sound like.

People looked for the sound but could not see it.

"What's making that noise?" Ithmene approached and asked.

"I don't know," Andy answered, feeling his spine tingle.

Andy realized that Ziesqe and the other ryle could see the beast, where almost no one else could.

"Guards!" Ventalus snapped at Ziesqe's tirade, "Arrest those ryle!"

Ziesqe shook his head and raised his blade as the guards surrounded him. "It's too late, tall mouse."

The bells tolled out noon.

"What does that mean! He's surrounded! Aren't we safe now?" Ithmene asked.

Andy shook his head.

The ground rumbled, and a hollow sound of scraping filled the air. Andy saw the buildings all around begin to shake. Birds panicked and flew from their nests in droves and a low roar rose from the crowd. Some ran for cover while others avoided the buildings and filled the plaza, hemmed in on all sides by creaking structures.

Letty, did you free the queens?

A bursting sound rang out and a heavy metal grate exploded out from a nearby manhole. The street surrounding the manhole crumbled and burst outward. A loud shriek filled the air.

"Ravager!" Andy cried, pointing to the creature's head as its massive jaws cleared a way.

"Take aim!" a sergeant cried.

The ravager, having freed its head, erupted from the ground at speed. A few dozen pale manti leaped from its back, into the crowd.

"Fire!"

Wheel-locks all around fired, belching flames and smoke.

The closest ravager cried out and faltered, collapsing onto a building that abutted the plaza.

A cheer rose from the guards, who were instantly reloading their weapons. The cheer stifled as a second and then a third ravager spilled out from the ground. Andy saw the massive frames of other, larger ravagers, rising from the ground across the plaza. The dozens of invading brutox became hundreds. They surrounded Ziesqe who eyed the force of guards.

He's going to focus all his strength against the leadership. You must protect them!

Andy saw fighting break out between the guards and the rushing manti.

He's right.

Andy released his blade, tensed the muscles along his trunk and down his limbs, he felt the Argument flow and manifest as his suit of armor. Andy knew that he couldn't wield the blade and armor, but as he thought this, his arm bent to one side, keeping the tensed nerves of his shoulder from affecting those lower. He took a breath and grasped. His honed blade appeared, its shape defined to such a degree that Andy thought he was holding an actual rapier.

"What good will it do you, Lysander?" Ziesqe spat, raising his own blade and armor. "Surrender, and we'll take a pleasant walk up the Guilt!"

"Guards! Fire at the ryle! He's their leader!" Andy cried out.

Ziesqe seemed unafraid.

A pair of wheel-locks burst and Andy saw the Counter armor shimmer as the bullets bounced off.

"Wha—" Andy looked at the guards, "the

Etherium tipped bullets! Use them!"

A guard shook his head and Ziesqe laughed. "Each of us only had one loaded. There was never meant to be a battle!"

Andy crouched and turned his side to his foe. His parrying dagger rose on its own. He found himself flanked by the guardsmen and their field of lowered halberds.

Andy charged into the enemy, killing two manti before turning towards one of Ziesqe's lieutenants. Ziesqe gestured, and the lesser ryle pushed through the line towards Andy, while he stood aside with Kal. "Take him alive, hew off his hands if needs be!"

Don't let his posture fool you! Ziesqe will wait until you become entangled with his underlings before striking! Fight with the halberdiers at your side!

Andy resisted the urge to press forward. The ryle looked disappointed as Andy waited for the slow-moving wall of guardsmen to reinforce his flanks.

"What are you afraid of?" a ryle spat, waving his blade and slicing the top off a halberd. "Should we kill your friends first?"

Ziesqe raised a claw. "Charge them!" he cried. The brutox suddenly fell onto the guardsmen. The manti focused on getting their scythe-like limbs around the halberd hafts to split the weapons, forcing the guards to resort to their broadswords.

Andy felt his anger rising as he saw the guardsmen being cut down, but he kept to his place and only struck at the enemy when they came within range.

"Push! Funnel them to our core!" the guard commander ordered.

The halberdiers strengthened their attack by pushing their flanks forward and trying to funnel the enemy towards Andy, who defeated them with ease.

"Muskets inside!" a sergeant commanded.

Andy's peripheral vision caught more guards weaving into the fighting formation. They were armed with the wheel-locks.

"Free fire! Advance to envelop their center!" the commander bellowed.

"Get our champion to their command! He'll cut off the snake's head!" a sergeant cheered in response.

Andy sliced through another mantis and saw that Ziesqe and his lieutenants were getting closer.

Andy stepped out of the line and surprised a ryle by batting away his feeble blade and striking with his parrying dagger. The others were waiting for this and pulled away from fighting the guards to move in on Andy from three sides.

Get back!

Andy broke off his attack and stepped back until he saw the field of halberds again at his side.

You are nothing without support! Don't let success swell your head! If they surround you, it's all over! You cannot fight more than two ryle, even with the armor. A single misstep could mean a missing limb!

Andy growled his dissatisfaction for Caspian's

advice. Seconds later, he heard a shriek and the sounds of snapping jaws.

Ravagers.

Several beasts had demolished the buildings protecting the formation's flanks and had since formed up to strike from those sides.

"Shiltrom on the banner! Fall back to the guild-house!" the commander bellowed.

"Damn!" A guard spat, "we almost had them!"

"The sides can take it, just push a little further!" another guard yelled.

"Silence! Make a circle, damn it! Pull in the sides! They will slaughter us at the flanks if we don't!" a sergeant commanded.

Andy saw the guards surround the High Exegesuits inside a circle of halberdiers with their banners at the center. A guardsman tried to pull Andy back with the formation, but was shocked by his armor. Andy barely noticed. All he could think about was the ryle.

Ziesqe will get away!

Two of the ryle saw Andy hesitate and suddenly pressed the attack, cutting him off from the guards.

Andy let their blows bounce off his plates. Sparks and flashes burst when blade met armor. One let his guard down to lunge, and Andy deflected him with a riposte before finishing him with his parrying dagger. He faced the other. The ryle knew he had no chance, neither he nor his late partner could coat themselves in armor. Andy intimidated him into releasing his blade.

"Throw down your orb!" Andy demanded.

The ryle moved to obey, but took his time about it.

Behind you!

Andy turned in time to see a ravager's massive jaws bearing down on him. He had stayed too long from the circle.

The creature shrieked and snapped as it overran him.

Andy rolled into the snap and ended up beneath its jaws and hundreds of piston-like limbs. He morphed his parrying dagger into another long blade and swiped at the passing legs. He sundered many, but several struck him in passing, beating him breathless, despite his armor.

The ryle who had surrendered raced to Ziesqe and his growing circle of newly arrived brutox warriors. Many were gesturing wildly with their weapons as if asking for permission to attack, but Ziesqe held them back.

The ravager had wheeled around and dipped one half of its body, to give the many dozen brutox armed with crossbows and flame spitting lances a good look at Andy.

Andy fell to his knee and raised his off-hand, morphing the blade into a shield. A torrent of bolts and gouts of flame glanced off his shield and armor.

This isn't going to work! How can I fight it?

Andy heard a shriek and turned too late to see a second ravager bearing down from behind.

He tried to stand but felt himself lifting off the ground. He cried out as a pair of chitinous jaws clamped onto his breastplate. A crack split the air as the ravager's massive jaws crushed down. His feet kicked against empty air; the ground was far below and he heard the agonized shouts of the guards. His vision darkened and then he heard a loud snap. His etherium armor had failed beneath the weight of jaw, but the ravager was burned by the Argument. The beast cried out and he felt himself being flung a great distance before scraping across the ground. The sounds of ravagers shrieking and guns firing seemed to fog and mix in with the shouts of the guardsmen and the ringing of steel.

"Grab him!" A human voice echoed in his ears.

"They're coming!" another voice yelled, an instant before crying out in pain.

Andy felt his body being dragged. He felt hands pulling him into a crowd. Belt and baldric buckles sparkled in the light of spitting flames as his eyes opened. He saw muscled legs tense against the slam of beasts larger than a thousand men. The ravagers circled the halberdiers, dipping their flanks to let their crews fire, and then raising again to shield the reloading crew from wheel-locks returning fire.

Andy's eyes tried to count the forms, but they spun and melded into each other. Their shrieks, splitting his ears. Their snapping maws rattled the ground and shook his bones.

Another volley of bolts whistled through the air. He heard the sounds of metal splitting and saw shafts puncture the shining plate all around.

"This is suicide!" A guard screamed, his voice like a child's, drowned in the raging surf.

Andy's head lolled as he struggled to rise. He

saw streams of blood spreading out beneath the guards and pooling between the polished flagstones. He saw their boots slip and their greaves clatter and stain with blood as they buckled to the ground. A banner caught fire from a strafing lance. Its bearer hefted it like a spear and impaled a passing ravager, to no effect.

A sudden crash overwhelmed all the other noise. Andy lifted his head. A blue ravager, somehow even larger than the others, had just side-swiped the nearby guild-house, tearing down a portion of the structure.

"There's nowhere to go!" "The doors are caved in!" guards yelled.

"Stand your ground!" the commander bellowed, several bolts piercing his gilded armor.

Another ravager made a sharp turn towards the circle of guards and snapped its jaws as it collided. Brutox leaped from the back of the ravager which pulled away moments later, embedded with halberds and crying in agony.

These brutox were a kind Andy had never seen before. He barely recognized them as locust-like before he was dropped to the ground, as his bearers drew their broadswords. Other guards were forced to abandon their halberds and resort to daggers and fists as the locusts slammed into them. Andy struggled to stand on the bloody ground. His body shot with pain but, grasping at the armor of the men next to him, he pulled himself to his feet amid the crush. He tried to draw the blade but the pain and press from all around made articulating the right muscles impossible.

A locust leaped off the back of a guardsman, its huge wings buzzing thunderously, before crashing into Andy. Its many claws and blades stabbing as it snapped its mandibles.

"Caspian!" Andy screamed in terror.

Andy's off-hand shook and flexed painfully. The blade burst into the locust, but it jolted wildly and was lacking hone.

Andy felt his heart nearly explode in his chest. Guardsmen were crumbling to the floor all around.

I'm going to die here.

Andy felt a hand grasping his arm. He looked and saw a guard with a broken wheel-lock. His armor was split apart and singed from the flames. He was staring at Andy with glassy eyes.

"I always believed!" the man yelled, before letting go.

The sight broke his heart.

I can't do this.

Never had he felt the urge to give his body over to Caspian so strongly, but Caspian did not take him. Andy sank and slipped in the blood.

When he was certain of death, a mountainous roar broke out over the fighting.

Thrag!

Andy wiped his tears and felt a surge of hope. It was Caspian's hope filling him.

The fighting slackened and even the ravagers slowed to a halt as the roar filled the air, resounding with the force of a hurricane.

The barbarian was riding atop three cyclostones

that had been chained together.

He leaped and crashed onto the pilot of one of the ravagers, ripping the antennae from the brutox and hurling him into the confused crew behind. Thrag growled and piloted the beast at full force into another. The two ravagers shrieked wildly before violently spilling their crews across the sky. Thrag leaped from the crashing beast onto another.

The guardsmen cheered at the sight.

A trilling flight of missiles filled the air. The sound was foreign, and Andy looked for the source.

"The mer!" a guardsman called.

A few hundred of the mer fighters had spilled out into the plaza from a side street. They wore their distinctive black armor and bore recurved bows, spears, shields and sabers at their sides. They were standing in the path of the circling ravagers. He saw Ithmene with them.

"I need to get to them!" Andy yelled.

A pair of guards heard this. "Yes, sir!" one replied, shouldering his blade and grabbing Andy by the arm.

They struggled towards the edge of the fighting.

Andy saw Thrag rolling to the ground nearby, a slack brutox in each hand.

"Thrag!" Andy yelled.

Thrag paused, turned and raced to the sound of his name.

"Caspian!" Thrag cried. "Raise your voice and conduct the slaughter! I know not what nation or people these be!"

"We're in Degoskirke! Don't worry about that,

just—"

"Strange, the word is foreign to my ears, but this place has the look of ages about it! I should know it!"

He lost his mind before this city was founded.

Andy felt a pang of remorse.

"Thrag!" Andy repeated, trying to get through to the man. "Get me to those mer!"

"Ah!" Thrag saw Ithmene. "Always the ladies!" he said, grabbing Andy from the guards and bounding over the broken bodies of the ravagers.

The mer raised their weapons as Thrag lumbered towards them.

"Hold!" Andy yelled. "We're friends." Then to Thrag. "Stand me up, please."

Thrag tried to help Andy stand under his own power, but he still needed to lean against a broken wall to keep upright.

"Oh, no!" Ithmene cried, pushing through the mer fighters. "I just healed you! What happened?" Andy opened his mouth, but she continued, "This is the last minoe we have here! You must be careful; you can still die!" she said rushing to Andy with the vial.

"Hold on!" Andy said, raising a hand to her. "Who is in charge here?"

A mer with a red scarf stepped forward. "We have spoken before, your Eminence."

Andy nearly rolled his eyes at the title. "Get your force off the plaza it's too open—"

A ravager careened over the fallen bodies of its

fellows to attack the group of mer.

Thrag turned and bellowed, rushing towards the towering monstrosity.

The ravager snapped its jaws, the sound broke out like a thunderclap, before it dipped towards Thrag at full speed.

"What's he doing? He'll be ripped apart!" a mer cried out.

Thrag roared and caught the massive jaws. The ground shook at the collision. The shock of the sudden impact traveled down the length of the ravager, launching its crew high into the air. Andy saw every muscle in Thrag's body ripple, like waves over still water, as they opposed the impact. His feet tore into the flagstones and he screamed with a fury before the ravager finally lost its forward momentum.

Thrag twisted his body, bending the ravager in one direction, before snapping back the other way. The twist rippled down the ravager's torso. Its spindly legs shot out from underneath, ripping the flagstones apart, as it came tumbling to the ground from front to back.

The crew had spilled out and the mer charged, massacring them in moments. The remaining ravagers pulled back to discern the situation.

"Did the barbarian just wrestle that thing to the ground?" a mer asked, his eyes wide.

"Thrag!" Andy yelled in triumph.

The sudden change in fortune was not lost on the guard commander who ordered his men to break formation and head for the cover of the buildings.

Ithmene peeled the metal armor off Andy before applying the minoe. The armor came apart in pieces. Andy bit his cheeks as the minoe worked on his wounds.

"Too much in so short a time will sting."

Andy grabbed the mer commander by the scarf. "Don't fight them in the open. Aim for the pilots! We'll drive them from the plaza and give the Exegesuits a chance to escape!"

The commander nodded, a surprised look on his face. "Of course," he said before leading his archers. They advanced and used the fallen bodies of the ravagers as cover from which to fire at the others.

"There's a lad!" Thrag bellowed, cracking the ravager he had just wrestled to the ground over the snout with his bare hands.

"Never forget your old master!" Thrag said, laughing.

"Thrag! Can you pilot that ravager without crashing it?" Andy asked, still wincing.

Thrag responded by pressing on the ravager's head, forcing the creature to right itself, and then hopping aboard. "Hurry!" Thrag yelled, an eager note in his voice.

Andy moved towards the ravager but Ithmene grabbed him. "Are you insane?"

"We can get to the queens with the ravager! Maybe we can end the invasion," Andy said, pulling away.

Andy felt the strength returning to his body, though he was still limping. He regretted the loss of his armor, but was glad Ziesqe put it on him in the first place.

Andy climbed up the ravager and, before he was over the side, Thrag had snapped the antennae thrice, commanding the beast to rise and then turn about.

Andy tumbled into the hull, got to his feet, and scanned the city. He saw dozens of other ravagers tearing through the city, bringing fire and destruction where they went. He imagined how many more were beyond his sight.

"See my little gibla, so green and savage in the pell-mell!" Thrag said, enthused and pointing at a large group of goblins.

Gibla? He must mean goblins. Wait—that's Letty with them!

"Get over there, Thrag!" Andy commanded.

Thrag pulled on the antennae and they shot across the plaza. Thrag hooted and deftly slammed their ravager into another, surprising the other creature and tipping it over.

"I said don't crash us!" Andy howled, holding onto a convenient rope bolted into the ravager's hide.

Andy saw that Letty was covered in blood, and she moved with a limp too. A horde of oddly lithe brutox were huddled behind her. While her group of goblins was being attacked by strafing ravagers, mercenary ychorons, and even a few ryle.

"She needs help!"

Andy tensed his body and summoned up two short, armor piercing blades and his full suit of armor. He felt lightheaded as Thrag commanded the ravager to the ground.

"Reinforcements!" an ychoron called out.

"Not quite," Andy whispered. His eyes met Ziesqe's.

"Turn about! They're attacking from the rear!" Ziesqe called. Thrag leaped from the ravager and slammed into the wall of ychorons, snapping limbs as he went. Andy mounted the ravager's head and hurled himself at the last of Ziesqe's servant ryle.

Andy's armor cracked against the ryle's. The ryle wasn't prepared for sudden grappling and his knees gave out as Andy collided with him. They rolled to the floor.

"Andy!" It was Letty's voice.

"Attack!" a shrill mouse ordered.

"Broken Teeth!" the goblins cried, as they charged the confused enemy line.

Andy rolled with the ryle, stabbing at his armor before finally finding a gap under the arms and piercing. His foe crumpled and released a small purple orb.

Andy felt the weak stabs of the surrounding ychorons deflecting off his armor, but he knew that Ziesqe was seconds away. He struggled to his feet, waving his blade wildly to scatter his foe and was then surprised to see Titus bounding through the combatants to rapidly climb up his shining armor.

It doesn't hurt him.

"Lysander! How goes the battle?"

"It could be worse!" Andy replied, slicing through ychorons and looking for Ziesqe.

"Have you seen? All of Sentinel's Watch is

here!" Titus said, proudly, pointing up. "And me, with my whiskers singed off! What a scandal!"

Andy laughed and looked up. He saw scores of cyclostones flying over the battle.

A flight of bolts smacked against his armor. Several goblins fell to the floor. Circling ravagers dipped and continued with their volleys.

"The ravagers are trying to keep the brutox away from the queens by fighting from a distance! The queens can't help us this way!" Titus said.

Andy suddenly felt his mind click.

"Get those cyclostones down here and carry the queens, like they carried Thrag! Let them jump down onto the ravagers and capture their crews, one ravager at a time!"

Titus's eyes went wide at the plan and he was bounding away and up the side of a tall building before Andy had even finished.

Andy struck down another ychoron before he realized there were no standing enemies left.

Where is Ziesqe?

Letty ran up to him and pulled him back behind the goblin shield wall. "What's wrong with you! Get back here!"

"I've got armor—" Andy paused, suddenly aware of her wound. "Your face! What happened?"

"Forget my face! What are we going to do? We can't get the queens to help!"

"Titus has a plan!" Andy said, looking up and trying to spot the mouse.

The ravager he and Thrag had captured suddenly lifted.

What? But Thrag is right here.

Andy forced the Argument into Sight and peered through the ravager, whose lattice form looked nothing like any other creature he had seen. He pushed the peculiarity from his mind and saw through the beast to the pilot.

"Ziesqe and Kal! They're getting away!"

Andy was about to call an attack but a second, screening ravager cut too close to their line and fired a volley, forcing them to defend. Thrag rushed out, despite the flying bolts, and raised a fist, while bellowing a challenge.

The ravager broke off and turned away.

The goblins cheered but Andy clenched his teeth at the retreating ravagers.

"Who is that guy?" Letty asked raising a sarcastic eyebrow at Thrag.

"Long story," Andy said, watching a chain fall from the sky.

"Thrag! Reel them in!" Andy ordered.

Thrag laughed and grasped the chain, slowly pulling it in. Many dozens of the cyclostones had been chained together in clusters. Titus and other mice climbed down the chain to get a look at Andy and Letty, both bearing blades.

"Get the queens aboard the stones!" Titus ordered.

"Goblins, go two to a queen and protect them as they work!" Clang added.

Andy saw Quill and Staza appear from behind the queens.

"Where are Emma and Dean?" Andy asked.

"Back in the goblin's basement. They should be safe there," Blue spoke from Letty's shoulder.

Andy realized that Blue and Titus had never been introduced. They shared a still glance, from one shoulder to the other.

Maybe another time.

Andy ignored the mice and watched the progress at the chain and the procession of queens and goblins climbing up the stones.

"That's all we can take!" Taptalles said, hanging from the chain. "Lysander, is that you?" the mouse squeaked.

"There's no time, Tap, get them up!" Titus yelled.

Andy heard footsteps approaching. Thrag stood by Andy's side as dozens of various Archatians wielding swords and improvised-weapons appeared. A mer sergeant, with two fighters at his sides, also approached. Finally, a heavily beaten guard lieutenant joined.

"Where are we needed?" A frazzled braid asked.

"The buildings surrounding the plaza are now clear, but the ravagers have left the area, they are attacking other parts of the city!" The mer reported.

"Brutox warriors are rising out of the sewers all across town!" the guard lieutenant added.

"We have a plan," Andy said. "With the help of the mice we'll strike at the ravagers from above and quickly get the queens to where they are needed."

Letty spoke, gesturing at the remaining queens, "Protect these queens and try to head the brutox off in the sewers. They won't be able to escape or resist."

"Yes," Andy said, "the unarmored Archatians would be good in the sewers, there shouldn't be much fighting. They just need to keep the queens safe while they convert the brutox. Keep an eye out for any ychorons; they aren't affected. Most all the ryle should be dead. I will hunt down the last two, and make sure this never happens again."

"We're going to hunt down the last two," Letty corrected him.

"The blood is strong!" Titus announced, raising his mouse paw.

Blue looked both upset and moved by what was happening.

A man in black armor among the Archatians echoed the sentiment. "The blood is strong!" he roared.

Many of the others appeared afraid, though a few repeated the incantation.

"What of the mer?" the sergeant asked. "Where should we focus our forces?"

"And the guards!" the lieutenant added.

Andy thought for a moment.

"You can never chase the ravagers down, but maybe you can be in the right places to attack them. Keep to the roofs around the widest streets. Stay out of the open, or you'll suffer a repeat of what happened in the plaza."

The guard lieutenant nodded bitterly.

"Be aware of any captured ravagers with queens, they are friendly," Andy said decisively, before turning to the sound of an approaching ravager. "Thrag! Could you capture some transportation for us?"

Thrag let out a loud laugh and slapped Andy on the back, nearly sending him flying, before racing towards the beast.

The ravager lowered on its own. A familiar goblin had the pilot by the throat.

"Clang!" Blue yelled.

"We're going to hunt down the leaders. If you need more direction, find Ventalus; he's an actual commander," Andy said to the various representatives before climbing up the ravager with Letty, Thrag, and the Caspians.

"Hey! Wait for us!" Dean's voice called out.

"Hide somewhere!" Andy yelled.

"Let them come along," Letty said, "they've been fighting already. Look, they even have their armor on."

Andy shook his head no.

"Dean and Emma have saved all of us, whether you know it or not!" Letty insisted. "They even fought ryle."

Andy considered his fellow surfacers and then sighed. "I'm sorry, I didn't realize—and why not join us? Giant insect is the safest way to travel, right? Come on guys!"

Surprised and smiling, Dean and Emma scrambled aboard with several goblins.

Letty rolled her eyes at Andy, and he stopped, to look at her for the first time.

What happened?

It looked like she had been through hell.

"Letty, what—" Andy cut off, realizing that her

armor had been destroyed. He tried not to stare at her bloody face. "Has this been healed?"

"Yes. The goblins took care of it, and I still look better than you," she said with a pained laugh, "Don't worry about me; focus on Ziesqe."

"Right," Andy slowly replied, as Thrag took charge of the ravager.

"Who let the insane man pilot?" Quill asked. "Do any of you have the first clue of who that is?"

Andy chuckled. "Thrag and I go way back now."

"Really?" Staza scoffed.

"Yeah, and don't anger him. He'll kill everything; I've seen him do it." Andy said, half-joking, and holding on to a cloth tether as the ravager picked up speed through the streets.

"From whence calls the slaughter?" Thrag yelled, the wind in his hair.

"Of course, we have no idea where we're going," Andy muttered.

He pulled himself to his feet and looked out onto the city. He pushed the Argument into his Sight and nearly fell over at the noise and torrent of information.

Letty grabbed him by the shoulder to keep him upright.

"Is that the Sight?" she asked.

"Yes. It's bad," he said, trying to focus. "I'm trying to spot Ziesqe. He's with another ryle: Kal. She doesn't look like much, but she's powerful," Andy said, nearly stumbling again. "I can't look for long—" he added, before coming out of the sight. "It's too much."

Thrag growled and they saw an enemy ravager pulling alongside.

"Down!" Andy yelled as a hail of bolts flew their way. He heard Thrag take a few heavy steps.

Andy looked up and saw Thrag leap off their ravager and attack the enemy's.

"Thrag! Get back here and pilot!" Andy yelled, but Thrag was entrenched in the fighting.

"Is that them?" Emma asked, pointing up at a pillar.

"Who!" Andy snapped, still staring exasperatedly at Thrag.

"The ryle," she replied sharply.

Almost everyone in earshot gave her a slanted glance.

Andy raised his eyes to where she gestured.

He saw a ravager climbing up the base of the Guilt.

"They can do that?" Dean sputtered.

"Does anybody else know how to pilot this thing?" Andy yelled.

Clang and a few goblins came forward with their captured brutox. "This the pilot, Andy, sir," Clang said.

Andy considered the brutox for a moment.

He's still loyal to Ziesqe. Don't let him pilot or he'll crash the ravager and kill you all.

You're right.

Andy shook his head at Clang, who understood, before staring at the antennae.

Damn it.

"Everybody, find something to hold on to!"

Andy called out, before sitting in the pilot's place and grabbing the antennae.

"Andy, what are you doing?" Letty yelled.

"We can't let that brutox drive; he'll kill us," Andy said, tugging on the antennae.

The ravager picked up speed and Letty stumbled as she rushed to his side. "You don't know what you're doing."

"I don't, but Caspian does," Andy replied, softly.

"What?" Letty asked, confused.

"He speaks to me—"

"You're hearing voices!" Letty said, pointedly.

"He's already saved my life. I know I can't trust him, but—"

Letty was silent and stayed by his side.

"Look, there they go!" Dean called out, pointing to a few cyclostones parked over a motionless ravager. Andy craned his head for a quick look.

I hope that's happening all over the city and in the sewers.

Distracted, Andy didn't notice his ravager veering to the right.

"Pay attention!" Letty said, grabbing Andy's arm.

Andy realigned the beast.

"Pay attention," Andy repeated, before turning to Letty. "Please look out over the city and tell me what you see."

Letty grasped a nearby tether, bolted into the ravager's thick shell. She stood and looked across the city.

"Those flying stones are all over the place.

Most of the ravagers are stopped, but some are still running around—there's fire."

"It looks like we're winning," Dean said.

"But what about Ziesqe?" Quill asked. "What is he trying to do?"

"He's going to do something to the Cogito. He knows the pillar will come down if it's removed," Andy replied.

The Guilt loomed over them as they approached.

"How are we going to get up there?" Letty asked nervously.

"We're going up!" Andy yelled.

"Wait!" Titus barked. "He wants you to follow him! Don't you see?"

Andy pulled back on the antennae and stopped the ravager.

"You don't think I know that?" Andy asked. "I have to kill Ziesqe or this never ends! We can never go home again. The city will never be safe, if he's still alive."

"He's trapped up there!" Blue snapped. "If that's what he wants, don't give it to him!"

Andy pulled back on the antennae three times and the ravager lowered to the ground.

"What should I do? Let the guards go up there to be slaughtered. Maybe the mer? No. There is no one else! Everyone who is afraid to climb the tower, get off now! I'm taking this ravager up there!"

Andy stood and looked back at his friends. None made a move to leave, though their faces betrayed reasonable fear. Dean especially looked on the verge of a stroke.

"Well then, everybody hold on to something!" Andy said, commanding the ravager to stand and then move towards the Guilt.

For a moment, the creature didn't know what to do when confronted with the pillar, but then it bent back its forward quarters and latched on with its limbs.

"It's like a roller-coaster, only without the safety measures," Letty said.

Emma had the same idea and yelled, "I've never been on this ride!"

Dean laughed manically. "I don't really want to live, you know, so this only makes sense! I mean, my parents are going to kill me anyway—if I ever get back home! So this is only getting ahead of things!"

"Shut up and hold on!" Blue said, all four of his limbs clamped onto Letty's shoulder.

The ravager sped as its body finished the transition to the pillar. Andy's knuckles went white from grasping the tether with one hand.

They ran spirals around the Guilt, kicking up masonry as they went. Andy spotted Ziesqe's trail of damaged walls and kept it in sight.

The next few minutes passed at an agonizing pace. Andy refused to look over his shoulder, but based on their speed, and how close the ceiling had become, he knew they were more than halfway there.

A sudden flurry of caws, barks, and roaring nearly made Andy flinch and tug on the antennae.

"What was that?" he yelled to his friends.

"It's an abomination!" Titus replied, from his shoulder.

Andy took a second to look.

It's the monster I saw flying over the city. What is it after?

The abomination flew alongside them. Andy chanced another look and saw that the three heads were staring at him, cleverness and contemplation apparent in their eyes.

"What is everyone looking at?" Emma yelled. "I don't see it!"

"Neither do I," Dean added.

"Do we try to fight it?" Letty asked, standing and summoning the blade.

The abomination made a curious grumbling at the sight.

"No. I don't think we have a chance. Let's not provoke it," Andy said.

Letty slowly released her blade but refused to take her eyes away.

"There's the other ravager!" Blue called out.

Andy saw the creature, clinging onto the side of the pillar, mere feet from the glowing ceiling, which now shone like steel as far as he could see.

Andy slowed their ravager to a halt alongside the other. The two beasts regarded each other with a snap of their mandibles, but nothing more exuberant. Their ravager inclined its head towards the ring balcony.

"This balcony surrounds the pit that contains the Cogito," Andy said.

He climbed up onto the ravager's hull and

summoned the blade before jumping over the rail and onto the floor.

Andy tensed his body and pulled the Argument from limb to limb. The armor appeared. The motions now felt second nature.

"Neat trick," Letty said, landing beside him, her own blade drawn. "Can you teach me?"

Andy gave her a quick smirk but kept his guard up.

They stepped forward and allowed the others to climb over.

Clang gestured, and the goblins formed groups and advanced around the circle.

Andy shook his head, realizing that they would find nothing.

"They're down in the pit," he whispered.

Andy stepped towards the steel bars that encircled the pit and contained the Cogito. He looked down.

"You've made it," Ziesqe said. "It's time, Lysander. You should have done this when I asked and spared the city such destruction."

"The city is saved, Ziesqe. It's over."

Ziesqe snorted a derisive laugh. "I stand this close to so much death, to crippling destruction, and you consider the city saved?"

Vague threats, but no attack.

Jolting arcs of silver and purple light flashed between the ryle and the Cogito. Andy could see winces of pain on their faces.

"What can you do, Ziesqe? All that's left is to try and fool me with another empty threat. I know this is a trick."

Ziesqe remained silent.

"Do you know what I think?" Andy asked, eying his friends. "If you so much as touch the Cogito, it will incinerate you."

Ziesqe grimaced painfully. "If you have seen through me so, why come here at all?"

"To kill you."

Andy saw Dean and Emma give him a strange look, while the Caspians nodded approvingly. Letty's face was like stone.

Ziesqe shook his head and spread his hands. "What happened to the child I entered the city with? Where has he gone? You aren't Caspian, and yet, you aren't the boy."

Andy stepped through the open grate and started down the circular steps. He raised his hand and held the blade towards Ziesqe. Silver light arced between Andy's weapon, armor, and the Cogito. He felt wind suddenly coursing through the pit.

"Surrender!" Kal commanded, drawing her own blade.

Ziesqe tried to summon his armor, but thick arcs of silver light cut across him. He stumbled against the wall, heaving and losing his armor and blade.

Kal struggled to keep her blade steady as blasts from the Cogito buffeted her.

Letty took the top of the stairs and was ready to follow Andy down.

Andy reached the pit and approached Ziesqe and Kal. They backed away to the wall, both struggling and writhing with pain.

"It's time," Andy said, within striking distance.

"I will surrender if you touch the Cogito!" Ziesqe said, raising a shaking claw.

Andy sighed, releasing his blade and armor.

"Andy! What are you doing?" Letty called out. "Don't!"

Andy smiled and laid his open palm against the Cogito.

Every pair of eyes looked on in horror.

Nothing happened.

Andy's eyes stuck to the Cogito. Finally, he realized that the sound of rushing water had ceased. Everything was silent and still.

"It doesn't belong to me," Andy said, feeling it to be true.

"There's a lad."

Andy turned and saw everyone frozen in place. Caspian moved among them. He smiled and gestured out of the pit. Andy followed, a mix of emotion and uncertainty kept him in awed muteness.

There was other movement. Long shadows ran from the pillars in a circular motion.

"Their champion circles us," Caspian said. "I can see his purpose." Caspian's eyes shone silver and the air pulsed.

The beast roared in fury, as if sensing this.

"Will it attack?" Andy asked.

Caspian shook his head. "A part of that beast is mine. It knows courtesy, and will keep its distance, at least for now. If I should step among the living—"

The two neared the rail and looked out over the city.

Andy felt afraid to ask, but had to. "Why didn't you take me? I felt it. It was so close back there in the plaza, and again, here at the Cogito."

Caspian sighed. "At first, I thought it simple exigency, resisting Ziesqe's plan. He wanted this circling beast to attack and take us, which it will only do, if we become one. I cannot control you completely, and we would fail to resist its assault."

Andy nodded, looking out on the circling monster. "But that wasn't why?"

Caspian shook his head. "Not at all." He laid a hand on Andy's shoulder.

Andy felt the touch, but not in the way he had expected. There was no pressure, no touch to speak of, but there was a warmth.

"I hated you," Caspian said.

Andy blinked; past fear or dread, he felt pain, but not for himself.

"The things I have seen, Lysander—and yet, I feel I must apologize for the intrusion I now admit."

Andy felt his jaw drop. He expected almost anything from Caspian, but not this.

"Close your damned mouth," Caspian ordered, before chuckling. "My shameful act: I watched as you sat with my beauty."

"Ithmene," Andy whispered.

Caspian nodded. "I watched as you discovered yourself in the words that spilled. Past my will to scoff at you, to imagine myself in your place, to disparage your smallness, I felt every piece of your passion and agony. In the moment of your own pleading admission, when you clutched that girl, and I felt your heart burst, I remembered. When you cried on her, a girl I would know for a night, and you sat with her, warm and trembling, lost in the unknown and smiling despite it, I remembered."

Andy bit his cheeks to keep his composure.

"I could speak to you of the time when I was a man with another name. I could show you my glories. But no, I will speak to you of a lesson, taught to me by a dead man, two centuries on."

Andy scowled.

"Indeed, you should make a face. As should I. The lesson has been painted across the scape, plain to all, save these hollow eyes. I had perspective once, and it lent me greatness. I lost it, and now I clutch at its tail, fearful it may slip free this very moment."

Caspian was silent. His silvered eyes tensed and his brow furrowed, hinting at what storms spun in the mind of the immortal.

"I knew a man who said, 'I am the instrument of providence. She will use me as long as I accomplish her design, then she will break me, like a glass.'" Caspian took a deep breath. "I heard those words so long ago, yet they ring in my ears these past hundred hours."

Andy's eyes widened at the agony in Caspian's face.

"For a time, I was the instrument of providence. I did not know that she had broken me. I could not see what she had done to me. I did not have the dignity to die. Where did my time go, Lysander?

What songs may still be sung up there, beneath the sun? Does the sky still burnish? Do birds sing in the still before dawn?"

Andy nodded.

"I stood by the Aegean and the birds once called me to a dawn. The fall of Thea's hair about my face and the shining pins within begged me back to rest, but that morning, I left. She still sets a place for me, in a home I have never seen."

Andy saw a glint in Caspian's eye and a silver tear dripped onto the stone rail.

"I am broken, and my people are broken. Dreams of violence replaced our hope of full and free life. They accepted their chains and my promised blood kept those chains from chafing. I killed the last of the Occidentus and Orientis Obscura, the last human Seers of those ancient orders. I flung their bodies at the ryle. I killed millions. I mutilated their species." Caspian paused and clenched his fist. "The songs in my breast are now only thunder. The love for what goodness still clings to this sunken pit, is now only disgust. My gift to our people: a dread vision, rivers of blood. I lost myself; what was me, is spoilt."

The beast roared, its three throats bellowing over the city.

"And they love me for it."

Andy stood in silence, afraid that a single word of his would be a stain on the moment.

"Thrag used to sing once," Caspian finally said.

Andy couldn't imagine it.

"Look at him now."

An image in the sky appeared. They watched Thrag chasing down the last of the brutox before finally turning on the remaining shambles of the city guard.

Andy gasped. "We need to stop him!"

Caspian snapped his fingers and Thrag fell to the ground.

"Back to a cage, old friend," he said bitterly.

Andy raised a hand to comfort the man, but felt nothing there.

"Can I face myself? Can I admit what it took you to show me?"

They stood in silence as Caspian considered his next words.

"There is still much that is weak in me, Lysander," he paused, as if his next words were the most important. "I will step aside and let you live your life."

Something in Caspian's face made Andy believe him.

"Now, be a good lad and get back down in that pit. Ziesqe still thinks his forces have control of the city. That beast circling the Guilt will walk among you; show it no aggression. Is that clear?"

"Yes—wait, I have questions! Caspian, don't go yet!"

Caspian chuckled. "You will only be young once, Lysander. You will suffer these questions where you must, and you will endeavor to answer them where you can. I will not take that from you. There is violence where truth meets self, when a rare mind is purified in the struggle for understanding,

understanding it may never find. Yet, the thousand folds of self resent unwelcome or unearned enlightenment, no matter how hard it is hammered, and its shape is lost before the morn. You may stand on the shoulders of giants, but I will not let the apathy of such richness infect you. This is my one charge on your life, so hold it dear: You will hunt every piece of knowledge. You will hunger for truth and value it, like I once did. Inside that forge, the spirit within, you will transmute knowledge, and maybe, years from now, you will learn what I never could."

Andy wanted more, what, he couldn't say, but this felt wrong.

"I will leave you with this, Lysander: Whatever hells you may tread, remember my words. It wasn't the blade, Sight, or riches that defeated me, but that which I lost, which I may never know again, still alive and swirling, undefined, within you. You turned hate in the heart of an immortal to love. When you go naked into the cold scapes, you will always be armed."

Andy was astonished. Caspian gestured to the pit. Despite his need to know more, Andy accepted Caspian's request and went down to lay his hand against the Cogito. He felt calm and warm as the sound of flowing water filled his ears.

"The Usurper has failed," Ziesqe whispered.

"No, he hasn't," Andy said, removing his hand. "I want you to look out onto the city," he ordered, gesturing to the stairs. "Drop your Counter."

Ziesqe and Kal shared a look before holding out

their claws and manifesting their pieces of Counter. Both orbs sparked violently as the ryle dropped them and turned to the stairs. Andy looked back and watched the purple orbs shatter and burst. A dark cloud stained the side of the pit, but it evaporated. Moments later, the wall was stainless.

The Caspians and the goblins stepped aside for the ryle.

Andy led them to the edge of the ring.

Andy looked down on the rising columns of smoke.

If I'm going to do it, I should do it now, while I still feel hate.

Andy rounded on Ziesqe, ready to strike, but saw his shaking, bloody form leaning on the rail, as if he couldn't stand unaided.

Andy clenched his fist and opened his mouth. "What will happen to your lands and palaces?"

"They will be carved up and fought over for decades. Zentule will descend back into the jungle."

They were quiet for a moment. The people and goblins all around stood breathless, waiting for the final strike, but hearing only calm conversation, they became confused.

"Do you remember what you said to me?" Andy asked. "You told me about the genius, the fool, and the thousand steps."

Ziesqe nodded, his eyes tense with uncertainty.

"I was ready to give myself to Caspian. Once I recoiled in hate, and the second time he wouldn't take me. Have I fallen from the mountain?"

Ziesqe smiled, twisting his arm almost

imperceptibly. Andy recognized the motion. Instead of anger or fear, he felt grateful.

He's going to strike. He hid some Counter away in his body.

"Lysander, you have failed to see that the mountain has grown beneath your feet and lifted you to a height greater than Caspian's," Ziesqe finished, summoning his blade. "He would have failed."

Andy took a breath and turned, raising his blade to block Ziesqe's attack. His friends gasped, and Letty raised her own blade to Kal, ready for anything.

"I'm glad that you fought to the end," Andy said, grabbing Ziesqe's wrist while holding his foe's shaking figure in a protracted parry, "I couldn't bear to execute you."

"Still a boy then. You had better lose those trappings before the next ryle finds you, but what am I saying? I've always tried to make things easy for you, Lysander," Ziesqe said, at peace with what was about to happen.

A piercing roar filled the air and the fighters broke off to back away from the rail.

The abomination latched onto the Guilt and its dragon maw bit an intervening pillar. The pillar vanished into a cloud of black and blue smoke. The creature pulled its muscled bulk into the high-ceilinged ring. The ground beneath its mismatched paws smoldered and blackened before flaking and giving way to orange and black lichens.

Ziesqe gasped in panic, while Kal's eyes welled

up.

Andy was surprised when Ziesqe lunged at him with his meager blade. "Kill me!" he insisted.

The abomination roared, and its scorpion stinger shot out, flinging Ziesqe to the ground.

Andy's friends scrambled to get away. Emma and Dean had to be dragged in their blindness. The abomination kept its six eyes on the ryle.

The dragon head opened its smoking jaws and snapped them shut around Ziesqe. It released him in a flash and then snapped at Kal. The two ryle fell to their knees, crawling away, while black and blue smoke leaked from their wounds.

Their bodies slowly changed.

"Oh, God!" Andy's jaw dropped as he looked down on a pair of crying children.

"They're human," Letty whispered.

"The will of the Maelstrom carries to every corner of the Netherscape," a voice intoned.

Andy nearly drew his blade in fright as the massive abomination had been replaced with something nearly human. It stared down at the children.

"Neither Ascendant to the True God, nor Seer of the False, you shall live humble lives. The greatness of what could have been will ever clutch at your throats," the abomination said, before looking up at Andy and Letty.

"The Voice of the False God, the Dead God, floats in the air. I see his whisperings in your ears, his mark upon your hands, but you are not Caspian."

"Who are you?" Andy asked.

"We are the Right Hand, Chimerax, raised toward violent ends. Though your deaths have not yet been writ law, beware, Seers. If you ever let Caspian usurp your body," he paused, his glance moving from Andy to Letty and back again, "you will see us again."

Chimerax turned towards the railing. "Don't think of this as a victory. If this city was meant to fall, it would have. Your lives will not change because of today. You will never know peace."

Without a second glance, Chimerax morphed back into his monstrous form and leaped from the side of the Guilt, taking wing and banking towards the sea and the midnight spires far beyond.

Chapter 15: Going Home

Andy, Letty, and their allies stared across the horizon. The first to break the silence was none of their company, but a mouse on a cyclostone.

"Lysander," the mouse said, cautiously, "is there victory?"

Andy could only stare.

"There is," Titus answered.

Andy turned to Ziesqe and Kal, clutching each other in agony. He heard Titus and Blue speaking with the mouse from the cyclostone about the once powerful ryle.

"You'll have to take them," Andy said to the mouse. "If anyone in the city learns who they are—"

"Is it safe?" Letty asked.

They turned to Titus and Blue.

"It's the only thing to do," Titus said.

Blue was scornful, though he finally nodded. They took their old foes to the balcony and left them in the care of the mice.

The ravagers, tired of clinging to the Guilt, found their own way down. Andy didn't mind this, as he preferred to descend on foot. He went to give the Cogito one last glance, before noticing something in the pit. He gestured for his friends to wait as he descended and found the banner, bearing the name, Cogito, buried beneath coins. He freed it and, after cleaning it as well as he could, he draped the banner over the great orb's frame.

"Alright, let's go," Andy said.

As they descended, they met scores of curious

faces. Andy and his friends were alive; this was proof of something, but none dared to ask more. At the base of the Guilt, they found cheering people and the high Exegesuits, along with the chief Archatians. The battle had long since been won and the sewers made secure.

The leaders of Degoskirke asked that the events be recounted. Everyone looked to Andy, who told the story, though he kept what Caspian had said to him private. The potentates insisted that they be feasted in the great Secular or at the chapter houses of Archatia, but Andy refused and instead asked Blue to recommend a tavern. The Exegesuits looked scorned, but none raised complaint. Andy told them they would be leaving that night.

The Exegesuits wouldn't hear of it, and the Archatians, filthy from their fighting in the sewers, booed, but Andy, Letty, and their friends insisted. Some in the audience commented that leaving now was only prudent, despite the general complaint.

They readied their packs and Andy realized that he had no decent clothes to ascend in. A goblin was sent to buy a pair of pants, that Emma had helped design, from a local shop, and Quill gave Andy his wardrobe, borrowed from Letty's father.

Andy and Letty begged Quill and Staza to return to the surface with them, but the two balked. Quill cited a need to return home and prepare for the territorial wars that would crop up in Ziesqe's absence. Staza was quiet on the issue.

"Maybe we can claim some territory; we do have advanced knowledge," Quill said, considering the prospect.

Thrag was nowhere to be found, though a broken cage and battered guardsmen pointed down a trail of wreckage. The guards claimed that they would search after enough of their numbers had recovered from the battle.

Andy demanded that the statue the Archatians had planned to build in his honor instead be built in Thrag's likeness.

"The guy wrestled a ravager to the ground! You should have seen it!" he declared.

Clang and the Broken Teeth lamented the loss of their late mentor, Martin. Though his body had not been found, a quick, goblin-styled service was put on by the city, in the tavern to which Blue led them.

The establishment was called the Nooked et Alcoven. The tavern, like the city of Degoskirke, was a ramshackle and exuberant place, filled with conversation and host to talkative mice and silent brutox. Even goblins had tables in their corner of the place. Though all present turned silent at the entry of Andy and his friends. The owner, a woman named Miranda, promised to clear the place and serve the heroes of Degoskirke for free.

"Of course not!" Andy snapped. "I want to hear conversation."

Andy had the sense that Miranda was bright eyed and thoughtful, and that the Alcoven was rich with wonder, though he saw or felt none of this.

The Teeth had a private section of the tavern roped off for Martin's memorial, though, when

Andy approached, Clang refused him entry. The private section was empty, and the Teeth stood around, looking out of place, and eying their commander.

"There will be no memorial," Clang insisted. "Not until the Martin is found."

A few Teeth were sharing stories of Martin, yet, at a scowl from Clang, they ceased.

"There will be no tears," Clang insisted. "You must enjoy victory—or they might become confused."

Andy wasn't certain what Clang meant, but then he realized that he was referring to the people of the city.

Andy followed Miranda in silence, and they were directed to a table on a balcony above a stage, where a thousand-mouse symphony played bawdy music for ychorite tumblers and young arguers.

An ychorite, accompanied by a pair of young men and a silent mantis, approached Andy's table.

"Fair sir, I had sought drinks with thee, weeks hence," the ychorite said.

Andy looked up and recognized Mascutio, from his first day in the city.

"I'm sorry—" Andy started.

"I won't hear it," Mascutio insisted, and then he saw the state of the table. Sad looks filled faces and something in Andy scared him. "Please, forgive me. I didn't realize—If you come again, mayhap we will trade words once more, though your friend here frightens even me," Mascutio said, nodding to Dean. "I saw him on stage."

Dean smiled, and Andy laughed sadly.

"He frightens me as well. If I return," Andy said, taking Mascutio's hand, "I'll get you and your friends that drink."

Mascutio nodded gracefully and left them in peace.

Letty, Dean, and Emma struck up a conversation about the day's events, if only to keep Andy from his despondency.

Their dinner, featuring a large rack of lamb, was protracted, with city officials discovering their location, and news continuing to find its way to them during the evening.

Word of Martin's sacrifice spread, and the Exegesuits pledged to have a second statue commissioned to honor him. He had died in what people were calling the Coup of False Confidence.

When Taptalles heard that rebellious, ex-Vychy mice had built a new Occidentalis city near Steustace, he found several other mice ready to unhitch their cyclostones and fly there immediately.

When asked by Letty to join them on the surface, Titus was ambivalent, but Blue asked, "Why? Aren't you just planning on living a slave's life? I'll be with the other mice, heading for the new settlement."

Titus hesitated. "He makes a fair point. If we can regroup and capture Sentinel's Watch again, I might be able to return to my duty: safeguarding young Seers from the ryle."

Andy perked up enough to look hurt. "When was the last time you actually saved one?"

"Before you? Well, it's been a while."

"Why won't you stay with us?" Letty asked, as hurt as Andy.

"If you gave up the slave's life, we would take our places on your shoulders. If you ever grow tired of the surface, you know where to find us," Blue said, looking to Titus for confirmation.

"Titus?" Andy asked.

Titus looked away.

"Well, how's that for a goodbye," Andy spat, shouldering one of Letty's bags and leaving the tavern. "We're meeting the Caspians at the Sunken temple; they're seeing us off."

Andy apologized to Miranda for not being able to pay and he saw distress in her eyes as he refused to listen to her entreaty to stay and have dessert, nor spend the night.

Emma, Dean, and Letty joined him in the street.

A mer fighter stood by to walk them to the temple. "Your Eminence," the fighter said, bowing his head before turning to lead the way.

A few minutes later, they were confronted by Blue and Titus again.

"May we accompany you to the portal, at least?" Titus asked.

Andy crossed his arms. He could tell they were upset, and it wasn't easy for them to watch their humans leave.

"Come on, they don't want us here," Blue said, grabbing Titus.

"No! See us to the portal, please," Letty said.

Andy released his arms and nodded. The mice

took their places.

They passed through a raucous plaza, half-filled with the broken carcass of a ravager, but the debates had resumed, despite the destruction.

A man in a black suit of armor spoke with a rousing voice, "From whence does our failure to see a foe arise? That failure is borne from within, from our lack of purpose! If we lack meaning and drive, how can we ever know who are friends and who are enemies? We will ever stumble off a path we do not know to follow! Today has exemplified this truth and enshrined it in rotting husks! The dead have died doubly, for we now know who our true friends are, while they suffered before the mirror held by death. Only in their final moments did they grasp, bleeding, and afraid, to something greater. And that tragedy is our crime! Let us never again brook such a plague of cowardly apathy! Let us never again allow it to fester in the closed halls! Let us never again allow our children to face death without ever having faced themselves! For too long has this city been home to the emancipated, who look and despise the slaves without, never realizing that their lives, unyoked, grew even less fruit than those pressed. Is that all we are? The people who escaped the ryle?"

The crowd cried out, "No!"

"What does this man promise?" an older, Egalitarian Redistributionist asked the crowd. "He packages more war and violence as if it were nourishment. Tell me, young man, will pride feed the people? What can you promise besides adversity? Why should the people hand the ship of state to you, who would steer us into conflicts across the scape? When you ask if we are the people who have escaped the ryle, I say, yes! Let's keep it way!"

"Fair guardian of the impoverished and leveler of men, I say to you that your people have been starving for so long, that your sense for it has atrophied. Food is plentiful, housing is cheap, jobs are there, but the font of meaning is parched. The distraction of this stage is all that keeps their minds sharp and away from the crushing truth that their lives carry no meaning! We are purposeless!"

This shocked the audience.

"For shame! You would call our city purposeless?"

"Indeed, it is time to abandon our holy purposelessness and find meaning! People of Degoskirke, search your souls and know the torch of truth burns within! That fire will rekindle the spirits of our flagging city and she will rise from the sea, stronger, and braver than ever before! I will not speak the name of our long-neglected mantle, for it is still too dangerous a thing," The man paused, his attention caught on something in the audience. "Look! Beneficence has produced my underscore: The champions of Degoskirke stand at our sides still!"

The crowd turned and saw them.

Andy raised a hand. "Please, don't stop for us; we're here to listen," he called out.

They stood for a while and listened to the debates. A sense of danger and terrible possibility had filled the air as the speakers struggled to find new definition after their tragedy. Andy watched the Pioneers win their first parcel before turning and moving on.

I don't want to leave.

They continued along the streets before turning and bumping into a group of children with paint rollers, wearing buckets for helmets and pans for armor.

"Have you ever seen this?" Andy asked his friends.

Letty shook her head.

"The neighboring parcels compete with each other over the borders. They paint the lines on the streets and around the buildings, but it's almost like a hockey game."

"Does it ever end?" Dean asked.

"No, it doesn't," Andy replied. He wanted to stay and watch the wild children, more than that, he wanted to strap on a helmet, fight, and then nurse a bloody nose. He turned and led his group towards the mer.

They traveled over rooftops, the dome of the Sunken Temple growing as they approached.

"This is quite odd," the mer said, looking down the side of the building to a seaweed filled street below. "The tide isn't out. What's going on here?"

Letty looked over the side and saw people astonished at the now dry street.

They approached the temple and were confronted by crowds standing on a plaza that had once been under water.

The mer fighters kept order and the people

cheered as their champions came into sight.

They were ushered through the crowd, but they spotted Staza and Quill on the other side of the fighters.

"Let them through!" Letty insisted.

The fighters complied.

Quill spoke, "We just wanted to see you off; we have a long way home. Apparently Caspia survived Ziesqe's attack. It should be safe for us to return. We'll stay a few more nights before heading out."

Staza brushed a tear away. "We'll miss you. I'd tell you to come back and visit, but I'm not as confident as Quill about what we'll find back home."

"Hold on," Letty said, rooting through her bag. She pulled out a handful of gold coins. "If you can't stay in Caspia, come back to the surface—use the portal here. I mean it; we could be a family," Letty said, grasping Staza's hand and giving her the last of the gold, save the coins she needed for the portal.

Staza accepted the coins with a smile. Quill nodded sadly. Andy reached out and hugged them both. Soon everyone was embracing and saying their goodbyes.

Andy looked out onto the plaza, still overgrown with seaweed and barnacles.

Strange.

He had the urge to walk out to the center.

"Letty, guys, wait for a second," he said, pushing his way into the crowd.

"Don't get captured again! I'm not coming back for you a second time!" Dean yelled.

The people parted as Andy moved through

them. He got his bearing and felt he had made it to the center of the plaza.

This is the kind of thing you better not get wrong.

Andy held out his palm and forced most of the Argument he had kept inside to appear. An orb manifested in a blink. It was far larger than Andy had expected, about half the size of the Cogito.

He placed the orb on the ground.

I hope this helps them.

Andy returned to his friends.

"So, you're just going to leave your Argument here? What if you need it?" Letty asked.

"I'm keeping some for myself, and you?"

Letty held out her piece of Argument. "This is the one you gave me. I still have it. Maybe one day you can show me how you keep it inside, that looks useful."

"Sure," Andy said, waving to the sad and smiling faces alike, before turning up the stairs to the Temple.

At the top of the stairs, they were confronted by Ithmene and a dozen other mer beauties.

Ithmene looked hurt. "The flood retreats, and the city is saved. Caspian is now remembered only as the Usurper, but you leave us."

Andy pushed past her.

"Will you at least tell us your name, your full name?"

Letty smirked. "He's Lysander Vanavarre."

Andy rounded on her, an annoyed look on his face.

"What?" Letty replied.

"They think they're married to me—or Caspian, or maybe just the Voice of God," Andy said.

Letty's eyes widened.

Ithmene replied angrily, "We aren't perfect, but we only want to see the ryle defeated—"

"Just leave—go live your lives," Andy interrupted.

"You have no idea! Living only for ourselves was what made Degoskirke fail. We will be here, ready to aid you with the quest you spurn. Whether you return in this life or the next, whether you waste away your days as a slave on the surface, we will be here, praying that your heart grows strong again."

Andy looked away resentfully, feeling his resolve to leave shrink further still.

"You know why we do this, boy?" an older maiden asked.

Andy didn't reply.

"We do it because we can't raise the Argument ourselves," she said calmly, before stepping aside.

Andy, Letty, Emma, and Dean entered the temple. The maidens waited a time before following.

Andy felt movement on his shoulder and realized that Titus was still with him. He looked and saw that Blue was still with Letty.

Sometimes I forget they are there.

They entered a large rotunda, reminiscent of the domed eating hall in Caspia.

Andy watched as five gold coins were placed inside five pillars that encircled a round stage. Letty gave a sixth to a maiden and held out the seventh before tossing it into the circle. "Marble Hill Park!"

she said, as the coin burst into a spray of gold.

A portal appeared.

Andy held out a hand for Titus.

"This is it," Titus said.

"You know where to find us," Blue added, bounding away. He stopped and looked over his shoulder, his ears folding.

Titus moved more slowly.

Andy looked back into the temple and saw Ithmene wiping her face. She met his eyes and turned away.

Andy felt hands on his shoulder.

Letty turned him around. He saw through the portal and recognized the skyline of the city through the trees of the park. It was nighttime there.

"Do you want to stay?" Letty asked.

"Don't you?" Andy replied.

Dean and Emma stood in silence. Andy could see they were afraid of what might happen.

"I'm tired, Andy. I want to sleep in my own bed and see my parents again."

He nodded, remembering the moment he found her in Caspia.

"Right," Andy said conclusively, taking her hand and walking with her through the portal.

Once through to the other side, Emma and Dean celebrated. Dean fell to his knees and ran his hands through the grass. "We made it!" he yelled.

"I'm going to get a milkshake!" Emma screamed.

Letty laughed. "That sounds like a good idea. We

should probably grab one before going home."

Andy took a deep breath and tasted the diesel in the air and the sea not far away. He heard the motors of ten thousand cars humming in the distance and a train grinding on its rails. The blinking lights of a commercial flight trailed across the starry sky.

Dean got to his feet, teary eyed, wiped his knees and then spoke, "For a second there, Andy, I thought you were going to stay."

"Me too," Emma added.

Andy shook his head, still not sure how he felt.

"Come on, let's get that shake before we go home. I'm sure we'll have plenty of time to regret our decisions, when we see our parents," Letty said.

Andy followed along, but then looked back, trying to see the portal.

There's nothing. It's gone.

His stomach sank, and he felt his heart breaking, but Letty was there. She grasped his hand. "You know the way back," she whispered.

Andy took a deep breath and followed along silently. The lights of cars and buses filled his vision, the smiling faces of the city and their raucous laughter swelling over the sidewalks.

"It's Friday, Letty!" Emma said, turning on her cell. "We missed the whole week!" she exclaimed, enthused for the weekend.

"More than just one week, Em," Dean added, looking at his own cell.

"Oh, God, just put the phones away," Letty insisted. "Here's the place."

They stood in a line filled with people roughly

their age. Andy watched his friends smile like he had never seen before.

Emma and Dean chatted, but it all felt hazy. Letty stared at him, and he stared back.

She feels it, too.

They ordered their shakes and decided to have burgers as well.

The smell of cooking onions and grilling meat mixed with the bubbly pop and crisp sweetness of the soda fountain. Andy took a sip and nearly cried. He saw Letty look his way, their receipt in her hand.

They took their trays of food to the patio and were lucky to find a seat that faced the street.

Letty spoke with Emma and Dean, but she glanced over at Andy, who was silent throughout the meal. Andy stared at the passing vehicles and the groups of pedestrians.

All different.

"Andy!" Dean repeated, throwing a French fry his way. "What are you going to tell your parents?"

Andy laughed and leaned back on the bench. "I'll let them decide what happened."

"That won't work. Our parents will talk, and they'll know we're lying if we don't get our stories straight."

"Why not just tell the truth?" Andy asked.

Everyone stared like he was insane.

"Okay, fine. What's your plan?" he asked.

Dean shook his head. "I don't have one."

Letty put her shake down. "Look, they already know about the people found at the optometrist's office. Let's just pretend that we got caught up with it. We'll say the bad guys found out that we were investigating. They will believe Andy and I were there, and since you two are our friends," Letty said, gesturing to Emma and Dean, "it won't be hard to believe that you got caught up in it too."

"So, we were investigating for over two weeks?" Dean asked.

"Well, then we got captured, but we just escaped tonight."

"I'm not sure, Letty," Emma said. "Who captured us, and where were we this whole time? Also, how did you get that scar? I'm sure Andy is covered in scratches too."

"And the worst part is," Andy interrupted, surprising everyone. "When they pick our story apart, we might find ourselves looking at ryle again. They'll know about Ziesqe, since he owned the place, and then they'll figure out what happened. Even if they don't, our eyes will give us away."

That thing—Chimerax—was right.

"Wait, why don't we just say that we were afraid and ran away?" Emma asked.

"Let's just say that we were living in abandoned apartments, or an empty warehouse," Dean added.

"We have to pick one and stick with it," Letty started. "There is an empty unit in my building. We'll say we broke in there and stayed. If they ask us why, we'll say because we were afraid after the abductions; we thought people were coming for us since three of us went to that optometrist."

Dean shivered, remembering he had gone to the same optometrist.

"But why did we come back?" Dean asked.

"We got hungry, ran out of money, and felt like we would be safe now," Emma said.

Letty nodded. "That's it."

Andy tapped his drink on the table. "Yeah, that's as good as it gets."

Letty took a deep, sad breath before standing and taking her tray to the trash can. "Let's go."

Since Emma's place was the closest, they walked her home first.

"We wouldn't have made it without you Em," Letty said, hugging her friend.

"I just fired an arrow and designed some pants—"

"Stop," Letty interrupted, "without that money, we wouldn't have been able to get Dean on stage—and that arrow saved my life."

Emma blushed before giving each of her friends a hug. She headed towards her home and looked back at her friends before knocking on the door. Andy, Letty, and Dean hid around the corner, watching.

"Emma!" a woman's voice came from the door. "Where—! Wha—get in here this instant!"

She was pulled inside, and the door slammed behind her.

Letty laughed and then caught herself. "It's not funny—that'll be me in a minute."

Letty and Andy turned on Dean. "Which way to your house?"

"Aw, come on," he said plaintively, before sighing and turning to cross the street. "It's not far, fifteen minutes maybe."

They walked in silence for a while. The traffic was still heavy.

"Don't take this the wrong way, Dean, but I'm still amazed that you came," Andy said.

"Preaching to the choir, pal. I'll never understand it," Dean said, his eyes wide with remembrance. "I threw up over the side of a cart," he laughed, "I saw a girl chase a sphinx through the woods. I fought a giant centipede," Dean cackled manically, "you remember that?"

"Yes," Letty said, "I thought you wouldn't fight, but you did."

"I wasn't there for that," Andy said.

"No, that was when we were with the Elazene," Letty replied.

"You'll have to tell me some time," Andy said.

"You shot that ryle," Dean said twisting his face at the memory, "One shot and he fell. The purple blade didn't do him any good," Dean finished, trying to laugh. He suddenly stopped short and looked up at a tall building. "Damn."

"You live here?" Letty asked. "This complex is beautiful."

"Don't spread it around," Dean replied, turning to them.

"Thank you again, Dean," Letty said.

"Kill me, they're going to kill me, but, somehow, I'm not that afraid," Dean muttered.

"Why? You already graduated high school, you just took off for a few days," Andy said.

"What? You already graduated?" Letty blurted.

Dean rolled his eyes. "Great, now everyone will know. I was planning on fitting in at some point, and now they'll all think I'm crazy for going voluntarily—and that's not the issue, Andy, my parents killing me has nothing to do with missing school!"

Andy laughed as Dean yammered. "See you on Monday," Andy said.

"You don't know that!" Dean yelled, walking up to the glass doors.

"I'm not sure where we are," Andy said, looking at a street sign.

"I know. We're closer to my place than yours," Letty replied, leading the way.

"How do you know my place?"

Letty looked away and wrung her hands. "I might have visited your parents while you were gone."

"How were they?" Andy asked, cringing at the thought of his dad talking to her.

I bet he told stories about me.

"They weren't doing so well, but they'll be happy now."

Andy was silent.

"Why did you come after me?" Letty suddenly asked. "I was never nice to you. I was cruel even. I kept trying to figure out why. It still drives me crazy."

They stood at a crosswalk.

Andy stared at the red light before answering, "I don't know really. Maybe it was that day at the museum. We chased Titus, and I forgot who I was for a moment. At Ropt's office, we spoke. Then I knew you weren't a bad person." He paused, remembering, "I broke in there and found your things. I knew they had you. I just—"

Letty took his hand.

He bit down on his cheeks. "I wasn't going to let you disappear."

He glanced and saw her wipe away a tear.

She pushed him away. "Don't look."

He laughed. "Sorry. What about you though, why did you come back for me?"

Letty rolled her eyes. "Oh God, isn't it obvious?"

Andy looked at her confusedly.

"I just act like a bitch, Andy. I really hate it." She looked away, "You were the only person to make me see that," she said, taking his hand again and grasping it tightly.

Andy felt her stop and tug on his arm. "What—oh, we're here," he said, stopping short.

He looked up at the building to keep from meeting her stare.

She saw this and grinned. "Come here," she said, grabbing him with both hands before kissing him firmly on the lips.

Andy's head swam and he staggered, but she only grabbed tighter. He let his hand brush across her cheek, feeling the scars there.

She finally let him go and raced to the door, red-faced.

She stopped to look back at him for a moment.
What the hell just happened?
She smiled before turning and going inside.

I think she just kissed me.

Andy stood in silence for a long while. People passed him on the sidewalk, before he tilted his head to the sky and screamed, "Yes!" He roared like Thrag and leaped into the air. "Yes!" He turned, high-fived a stranger, and ran the whole way home, laughing at the top of his lungs.

He stopped in front of his home and wiped his teary face before reaching out and grabbing the doorknob. He stood there for a terrible moment before finally opening the door. He stepped inside and saw his parents sitting around the table.

"Why isn't this door locked?" Andy asked.

They looked up at him in shock. It was only then that he realized, his mother's eyes were just like his.

Dear Reader:

If you stuck it out this far—and I hope you did—I'd like to thank you. It felt like finishing a marathon when I closed the last paragraph of this book's final chapter, but I ran it a few more times for edits and rewrites, to create the best possible experience for my readers.

As for Andy, Letty, and their growing party of allies: Degoskirke remains free, the Builders have a new city to found, the ryle are in retreat and the Maelstrom is reeling, affording some much-needed rest for our heroes. They're finally back home and safe, but for how long?

If you enjoyed the adventure, please leave a review on the Amazon page. Your kind words will encourage new readers to give the series a shot.

The following pages contain an excerpt from Andy and Letty's next adventure: *A Night on the Serpentine*. Andy and his mother have fled to the West Coast, while Letty has been using her new skills to save Seer children. And while our heroes thought the worst was behind them, new trouble is brewing in ryle territory, putting pressure on the Maelstrom to find a solution. The Caspian crisis might be a precipitating event and, in typical ryle fashion, they begin their hunt for anyone connected to the failed coup that transpired in Degoskirke.

The fourth installment in *The Netherscape Chronicles*

will be released shortly, and more books are coming, too. First, I'll have to make a confession: Secretly, I moonlight as a sci-fi writer. I'm putting the finishing touches on the first installments in a series about a young biologist who finds her purpose among a strange people on the planet Martia (Mars, to the rest of us). I'm arranging a world filled with wild landscapes forged by the limitless potential of biology (giant mushrooms feature prominently). Beneath the mushroom caps, a clash of cultures is brewing. Civilizations separated by centuries of isolation are meeting. And the time is right for a secret society to emerge from the wilderness, to reclaim their birthright and lay hands on the reins of our collective futures. If this description intrigues, I'll invite you to read a chapter from book one in the Verdantsteel series, *An Impostor above Martia.*

Excerpt from *Night on the Serpentine - Tales from the Netherscape, Book IV*

A demon, with flesh of silver and ivory, flitted through the air above the foredeck. Its steps, at once a dance, then a hunt, finally became a violent surge, its fangs gnashing at empty air. The demon tumbled with the gait of a hound and scales of a serpent; it snapped with the maw of a sea monster and bore a mantle of tentacles, dangerously familiar. The demon turned and dived.

Ilfaeos, petty warlord of the Tulsh tibial waterways, curled his lip in anticipation. The demon collided with the flesh of his arm and burned away. Ilfaeos was still, despite the pain, though members of his crew: ryle, brutox and senitole alike, recoiled at the sight of the tumbling demons.

Clenching his fist, Ilfaeos summoned his blade. The falling demons crisped as the purple flame carved through them. He considered letting his crew suffer burns for their cowardice. When the demonfall subsided, he released his Counter and scowled until order was restored on the deck of his xebec. His first mate ordered the oars lowered and, moments later, they were underway.

Ilfaeos leaned against the taffrail and watched the oars emerging from below deck. The lake's surface swirled with faint glints of silver. Hands reached out from the deck below and cupped the water.

"Akhes!" he called. "Come here!"

The wide-eyed senitole, busy keeping accounts

of the ship's cargo, dropped his ledger and raced towards the captain.

"Aye, sir?"

"Look: it's as I said," Ilfaeos pointed to the galley slaves.

"The water," Akhes grumbled, his face bright with swift thought. "The slaves say the water is sweet. What pain can this cause you, my captain?"

"They will sicken," Ilfaeos insisted. "There will be no more of this. Have the whips ready in case of another demonfall. Is that clear?"

Akhes bowed, his comically pointed anole face wild with blinking eyes and jittery lips.

Ilfaeos watched as his first mate retrieved the fallen ledger, only to tuck it away between a pair of his velvety, banding-scales. The creature could create fleshy pockets, hidden away from sight, which was a considerable aid in a smuggler's life.

As they neared Aka Tulsh, his proud mansion-fortress, Ilfaeos kept a curious eye on his senitole. Akhes flicked his tongue and stood still, as if lost in thought. They were coming into dock, and Akhes was flaunting his duty. He should have been barking orders and preparing the ship to tie off.

"Spy a juicy fly?" Ilfaeos inquired, approaching his first mate.

"Captain, look," Akhes whispered.

Ilfaeos followed the senitole's bug-eyed stare and was struck by the sight of unwelcome banners staked into the grounds of his lake-bound island.

Akhes clicked his tongue and burst into action. "Rudder, pull to starboard! Quick on the oars, get us deep onto the lake!"

"Stay those orders!" Ilfaeos countered.

The crew surged into action, but the galley slaves weren't sure which orders to follow. Were the oars wanted out, in the water, or retracted, back into the hull. Afraid of the lash, the slaves scrambled in both directions, clacking their oars together.

Ilfaeos gritted his teeth, his tentacles twisting irritably as he glowered at the banners. Upon them he spied the emblems of the Maelstrom and its chief servants. There, on his dock, stood a robed Lixovore, scowling at his apparently retreating vessel.

"Oh, hell—" Ilfaeos started, raising a hand to Akhes. "No, my friend. We're not running." Then to the crew, "Make ready to dock!"

Eager to obey their captain, but afraid of what waited ashore, the crew froze and stared. The oars clacked again, several falling into the water.

"Master, please," Akhes started. "If they're coming for you, we can get word out—I'll slip overboard and swim to the warehouse—I can have most of the fleet at the mouth of Tulsh-cage before nightfall—"

Ilfaeos raised a hand to silence his friend.

"Master, no! We would be out of their reach past the cage! It's not that far up the river!"

Ilfaeos clenched and summoned his blade. With his free hand, he grasped his senitole by the throat. "Silence, you fool!" Ilfaeos leaned in and whispered. "If I call your name, run for the water."

Akhes gulped and nodded.

"You're not going to like this," Ilfaeos said,

before calling for a length of rope. "Just play along." Akhes trembled as he was tied and bound by the crew.

Minutes later, Ilfaeos' xebec, Her Blood, put into dock. The Lixovore and her armed attendants stood by. Glares of disgust marred several faces, though the Lixovore was still, her eyes busily analyzing the captain.

Stepping onto the dock, Ilfaeos was trailed by his brutox and Akhes, now bound by ropes.

"Mistress, I am humbled before the Lix. How may this simple warrior serve one such as you?" Ilfaeos asked.

"I know little of the nautical profession, but my sergeants tell me that you nearly turned your ship about, to flee at the sight of us. Is this true?" the Lixovore asked, her green skin gleaming under the purple glow of a piece of Counter, hanging from golden chains above her breast.

"My senitole," he replied, gesturing to the bound Akhes, "has too healthy a fear of armed ryle in my home. I informed him that you," he gestured towards the Lixovore and her attendants, "are quite welcome."

"Indeed," she said. "Then why is he bound?"

Ilfaeos took a heavy breath. "He is bound, for making me look like a fool. He ordered that retreat, against my wishes."

The Lixovore brightened at such an admittance. She approached the senitole and stroked the quivering velvet fur that lined his scales.

"You have made your master into a fool," she

said, tapping his considerable snout. "I think your master should have you skinned and turned into a purse," she said, looking back to Ilfaeos, her eyes dangerous.

Ilfaeos grimaced almost imperceptibly, before drawing his dirk. Akhes scrambled backward, scattering the brutox crew behind.

"Akhes!" Ilfaeos cried.

The senitole gasped and slipped his bonds before bounding towards the water. Brutox hands slipped on velvety scales, and Akhes was lost in moments.

"Twice a fool," the Lixovore said.

"Indeed," Ilfaeos muttered, watching the water. He sheathed his dagger and turned to his troublesome guests with a sharp smile. "Now then, I can offer sweet meats to you and your protectors—maybe drinks—or perhaps you want to cart off a few trunks of silk?"

"Do not insult bearers of the Lix, pirate," the Lixovore said, almost dolefully. "All we want is you," she added, handing him a sealed summons.

*　　*　　*

Demons of silver and ivory flesh flitted through the air above the mountainous corpse, Qavonzir. Their steps, at once a dance, then a hunt, finally became a violent surge, with fangs gnashing at empty air. The demons tumbled with the gait of hounds and scales of serpents; they snapped with the maws of sea monsters and each bore a mantle of tentacles, dangerously familiar. The demons turned and dived.

Teleka sat, near lifelessly still, as the flitting demons singed her arms and face. She smiled through the pain knowing that, soon, all this would end.

She was contemplative in her final hours as a simple ryle, a Limtzae priestess, and First Claw of Qavonzir. She sat in a stone-garden. The mountainous corpse of, Qavonzir, her saint, stretched out for several miles. She felt safe, here in the gardens of her rectory, though the demonfall underscored her need to forego the typical ryle ascendance. She had chosen to give herself to Qavonzir, who had, in ages far past, returned from the realm beyond to serve the Maelstrom again in this mortal plane.

Teleka heard the cries of initiates swarming the gardens. Their meager blades flashed back and forth, sweeping wildly at the demons, all in hopes of preserving the garden and the ground beneath, the flesh of Qavonzir. She grinned as they leaped and slashed, scorching the demons.

"Qavonzir, take my blade!" they cried.

As the demonfall ceased, Teleka approached the initiates. They released their blades as she approached and assumed the stance of submission: hands at their sides, heads bowed.

"Why do you raise blades in such violence?" Teleka asked.

The initiates squirmed at the unexpected quiz.

"The demons, they burn the garden—and the flesh of Qavonzir," one hazarded.

Teleka nodded knowingly. "They do stain and

sting, where they flit. But, Initiate, know you not Qavonzir?" She paused, to let them sit in painful silence. "A torrent of demons, greater than the sea above, could fall for a thousand years, and what sting would they have?"

The initiates were dumbfounded.

"You and I, indeed all ryle, would burn and melt away, but Qavonzir and his brother saints would still protect Szareyath. They will endure." She paused, giving them another moment. "With that in mind, what good does your own flitting?"

Another initiate rose to the challenge. "These demons are products of—" careful not to name the Dead God, the initiate stuttered, "—they are our enemies and, no matter how small, they must meet a blade."

Murmurs of agreement rippled through the cluster of initiates, though one, a younger female, lifted her head. "I agree that they are small, and our attention is better placed elsewhere, but why let them burn you?" she asked.

Teleka appreciated her curiosity, recognizing the rare gift. Gesturing to the other initiates, she spoke, "Very well. With such vigor, resume your swatting—"

The initiates turned to leave.

"You," Teleka said, meeting the eyes of the younger female. "With me."

Teleka led the initiate to a promontory on the brow of Qavonzir. She gestured toward the other saints across the city. "You asked why I let the demons touch me," she started. "When you look out, through the clouds, and spy the Five, what do they embody?"

The initiate's gaze swept across the broad expanse of Szareyath. The form and character of their capitol was shaped from and borne of the bodies of the five saints, dead ascendants so massive, their standing bodies would pierce the sea-sky ten times over.

The initiate's tentacles twisted around each other, as her eyes worked with uncomfortable thought. "They embody sacrifice, even beyond death."

Teleka inclined her head. "What pain can come to you or me? What trials will we face, and how small beneath Qavonzir, whose bones harbor rivers and lakes, whose ribs bear terraces, heavy with our bounty? What pain is this?" she asked, holding out her arm to show the burn a demon had made.

The initiate nodded, her eyes brimming.

"May ten thousand demons engulf me, that I may truly know pain—that this pain might better help me serve," Teleka gritted her teeth and turned.

The initiate grasped her hand to prevent her from leaving. "Thank you, and may Qavonzir be with you through your trial."

"My trial?"

"You go to your Synchrony, in the Amygdalion—am I wrong?"

Teleka sighed with relief. "Never a trial, dear. My life builds to this moment. Please, smile for me."

The initiate released Teleka's hand and smiled, her tentacles flexed faintly and the skin on her cheeks furrowed. The rare, ryle smile. Touched by the gesture, Teleka left the comfort of her garden. Alone, wearing the last of her possessions, she neared the Amygdalion, the temple of Qavonzir, seated deep within his skull. Past the stone doors and beneath glittering glass, waves of smoldering incense soothed her limbs. The leveled intonations, the rising melody of a thousand throats throughout the labyrinthine Amygdalion called to her. They were singing for her.

As she descended towards the Cortelion expanse, those she had known since her days as a Fifth Claw appeared beside her. Hands clasped hers, and words of praise and recognition, so alien upon ryle lips, dared to be uttered only under the protection of such an auspicious day.

At the gates of Cortelo, the point of no return within the Amygdalion, she was surprised to see a collection of misplaced ryle. These intruders stood in her holy place, bereft of humility, not wearing the robes of Qavonzir. Chief among these ryle, she spied a Lixovore and her bodyguard. The sight of Maelstrom servants sent a chill up her spine. She wasn't alone, and, painfully, the exuberant voices of her peers fell into silence.

Scowling openly, Teleka's day of Synchrony was ruined.

The Lixovore glowered in turn and Teleka's peers melted away, leaving her alone in the vast Cortelion. The Lixovore approached.

"The Limtzae of Qavonzir, the ever-faithful, are at your service," Teleka offered.

"What words," the Lixovore started, her eyes glancing around the yawning temple. "Service to the True God—" the Lixovore paused and scowled, her eyes seething over a coral statue of Qavonzir striking down a Seer.

Teleka scoffed. "What service we do the saints is done again—"

"—done again, a thousand times to the Maelstrom," the Lixovore concluded, handing Teleka her summons.

*   *   *

Demons of silver and ivory flesh coursed through the drooping boughs of the mangroves. Their steps, at once a dance, then a hunt, finally became a violent surge, with fangs gnashing at empty air. The demons tumbled with the gait of hounds and scales of serpents; they snapped with the maws of sea monsters and each bore a mantle of tentacles, dangerously familiar. The demons turned and dived.

"To the shroud!" Sethoro cried, leaping from his pallet and racing over the wooden catwalks of their hidden village. "Demonfall! Quick, to The Jackal!"

Dozens of the faithful appeared from their huts, many barely dressed. Ryle leaped down ladders, splashing into the tepid waters of their marsh. Hands searched the mirk for their cobbled tarpaulin.

The demons fell, racing hungrily for exposed flesh, eliciting cries from the faithful, but Sethoro's heart ached when the body of the mighty Jackal stirred.

"It's in pain!" another called.

Sethoro found one corner of the tarpaulin and pulled it free from the swamp. Others joined him, freeing more and more from the mirk. Soon they were clambering over the giant body of Seth's faithful Jackal.

The demons whipped up in a cyclone above before diving in sheets, reminding Sethoro of hailstorms he had seen, deep in his past. His arms and legs, barely wrapped in rags, stung furiously. Others cried out and fell, slipping into the water.

"They're burning the shroud!" a voice cried.

"It serves!" Sethoro replied, "May flesh be as faithful!"

Goaded by his words, many of the fallen ryle found their strength and spread their bodies over the holes in the shroud. Sethoro and the others groaned with effort and agony as they pulled, trying to cover the Jackal.

Finally reaching the far side of its body, Sethoro released the tarpaulin and clambered through the murk towards the Jackal's snout. Though the creature was shrouded, and relieved of the demonfall, it still needed to breathe.

"Blades, damn it!" he called to the ryle clustered around the snout.

Only one or two others had pieces of Counter to wield, and most resorted to flinging their bodies at the falling demons.

Reaching within, Sethoro found his Counter and summoned a honed blade. He twisted his wrist and the blade crackled and lengthened before going slack.

"To the water!" he cried, and the others fell into the swamp.

He whipped the lank blade in zealous fury; the air hummed with the sound of scorching demons, and severed boughs splashed to the water. Moments later, the air was clear.

Gasping, Sethoro released his blade. The massive snout of Seth's Jackal heaved in a grateful breath.

"He will rise," a voice intoned.

Sethoro took in the sight of the ragged faithful. Their bodies were scorched. Some would not recover. He considered heading to the fringes of Szareyath and trading some of his Counter for healing salve, and bolts of fabric to repair the shroud.

"May Seth know his faithful," another spoke.

"Seth speaks through his champion," said Jeka, his second in command, before taking Sethoro's arm and raising it in triumph.

The others cheered, but all Sethoro could see was the bloom. White and silver flowers budded and opened on the mangroves. He knew the water beneath tasted sweet, but he would never put it to his lips.

"The Dead God sees; the Dead God knows that what we do is just, and he mocks us with pain," Sethoro scoffed, and several in his audience echoed his indignant scoffing.

Gazing at the massive body of the Jackal,

now less than half-dead, Sethoro wondered if the insanity of their expedition could even be measured. Could the beast, alive or dead, possibly lead them to their fallen deity?

Never airing these doubts, Sethoro helped those who could still walk haul the wounded to mats and places of repose in their cobbled tree-village.

Jeka stroked the pallid brow of a delirious ryle and looked up at him. "We pay a high price," she said, leaving her own doubt unspoken.

Sethoro nodded, feeling responsible for their suffering. He missed his bed, and the comfortable stone walls and ceilings of the hidden temple to Seth which was once their home. The marshlands they had once roamed seemed a simple inconvenience, next to these damned swamps.

He and Jeka left the hut and walked in silence around the perimeter of their nameless village.

"Seth will reward us for our sacrifice," Jeka whispered, her voice a balm for his pain.

"Our sacrifices..." he started, wishing to air his doubt, but thought better of it. He knew that resurrecting the Jackal might do nothing, or worse, the Jackal might actually lead them to the body of the ancient deity. He expected to find the bones of a mighty ascended ryle, thousands of years dead. And if they did find the mountainous bones, what wealth was left to him would never resurrect a body that size.

"The True God needs us, needs this sacrifice," Jeka said.

"Though the path was made for giants, and

here we rot, small creatures of the muck—" Sethoro whispered, his attention drifting to a swirl in the swamp below.

A shape lurked behind a gnarled mangrove.

Drawing in breath, Sethoro tensed his body. Jeka saw this, but, ignorant as to why, she recoiled in fear. Clad in purple armor and wielding his blade, Sethoro leaped from the elevated walkway and dashed behind the mangrove.

Frightened, a muddy brutox tripped over the submerged roots.

Sethoro gave chase, and Jeka raced to catch up.

The brutox was a spider, swift to bound, but unsteady in this swamp. Sethoro's pace, while slower, was sure-footed and constant.

"Cease your folly, brutox—I will have you!" Sethoro shouted.

Finally, the brutox tumbled after a dangerous leap and found itself caught in the muck beneath.

Sethoro approached with a leveled blade. Jeka caught up and stopped at his side, pointing a dirk of her own at the strange brutox.

The brutox ceased its desperate retreat and stared at them. Sethoro considered the arachnid, wondering why it came so far. Just shy of asking, he heard a dreadful sound. Something moved nearby. Another sound, as of metal scraping a leather scabbard came from the left, and Sethoro knew he had been a fool to give such violent chase.

"How do ryle live in this?" a voice spat.

Jeka gasped, and Sethoro raised his blade against the latest threat.

A ryle, wearing stained robes girded up to her thighs, stood nearby. Armed and armored bodyguards, each more appalled than the last, appeared from behind the mangroves, while others rose from the swamp. Bowstrings tensed, while javelins were raised, all pointed at Sethoro.

"A ryle may endure any hardship in service," Sethoro replied, knowing this ryle was a Lixovore.

The Lixovore drew her brow in pious superiority.

"What hardships will you endure, you, font of heathenry?" the Lixovore asked, handing a scroll to one of her brutox.

The brutox approached cautiously, wary of Sethoro's blade, and offered him the scroll.

Jeka raised a hand and took the scroll before sheathing her dirk, allowing Sethoro to maintain his defense. She snapped the seal and read, "Heathen champion, self-named Sethoro, you are ordered to appear before the Szareyath Maelstrom—" the words caught in her throat.

"How long do I have?" he asked.

"You must report immediately," the Lixovore said. "Now, surrender your Counter to me."

"There are thousands of heathens like us!" Jeka cried, "Why would you soil your robes to come so far and deprive us of our—"

"Jeka, enough," Sethoro ordered, releasing his blade and armor.

"No!" Jeka insisted.

Sethoro rounded on her. He leaned in and whispered, "You must lead them now." Taking her hand, he forced most of his Counter into his palm. This, he rested in hers. "If I survive, I will return to you."

She tried to beg, but he was resolute. "Seth is of utmost importance; no one else can aid the True God."

"Dead ryle—no matter how aspirant to Godhood—are corpses for a reason," the Lixovore declared, taking a step forward and gesturing with her clawed hand for the Counter.

Sethoro produced a small orb and laid it in her palm.

"Cute," she said, ignoring the falsehood.

Her eyes flashed purple and rested on Jeka. "I will let your pack of heathens retain that Counter, if you promise to offer me no resistance," she said.

Sethoro inclined his head. "Thank you," he replied.

Hours later, he sat on the worn deck of a barge. The jungles trailed past as the polestox navigated them upriver, towards the Maelstrom, and his fate.

Excerpt from *Impostor Above Martia*

"There are men at the door—in the foyer now. They're Primarchy men, and they're here for you," the headmistress said, clutching Addy's shoulders and dragging her across the barrack hall.

Addy, still yawning and wondering if this wasn't a bad dream, followed in her nightclothes. Perhaps she had fallen into another prank set up by her sisters. But, as the mists of sleep fled, she felt biting cold in her toes on the stone floor and she heard the all-too-real throaty wheeze coming from the headmistress. She was awake, and this was no prank.

"What do these men want with you?" the headmistress asked, at once hushed and exasperated, before snapping her fingers at a pair of bleary-eyed assistants, who scurried over.

Addy blinked and rubbed her eyes. What she saw must have been wrong. The headmistress was never disheveled, and there was never a quaver in her voice, but here she was, shivering in fright and indignation as she whispered with her assistants.

A crash echoed down the hall from the foyer.

Hurried voices leaked through the hall door, which sat ajar. The glow of streetlights poured in through the windows, while skylights framed a jagged slice of the moon above.

"What do these men want with you?" she repeated.

"I don't know," Addy whispered. "Do I have to leave—I'm not dressed and it's cold; can I just go back to my bunk to grab my things?"

The assistants circled around her.

Her headmistress's wrinkled jowls dropped in decision. "The girl will need her clothes, but try not to wake the others—we don't want endless gossip disrupting tomorrow's lessons! And it will be endless!" Then to Addy, "is there anything else you'll need?"

The question was shocking; how could she know what the headmistress didn't. Addy found herself nearly speechless; she tried to turn the question around on the headmistress, but it was too late. The guards at the foyer had stepped aside and let the strangers in. Two men in crisp, black suits seemed to glide soundlessly towards them. The men cast their eyes about the hall; they inspected the headmistress, her assistants, and finally, let their glances fall on Addy.

"Addy Pershing," one said, now within arm's reach.

Addy recoiled. "Just let me get my things—I need my notes. There's homework I can do, and I need someone to check my experiment for bio—"

"Will you let us get her things?" her headmistress pleaded.

"Just clothes, no devices of any sort."

Eager to escape, the assistants ran to obey. Their absence, and the pause that followed, left the room painful and still.

One of the men produced a data-slate and inspected an old image, a yearbook photo of Addy.

"My hair's longer," Addy said, eyeing the

picture.

She had been fifteen then, and her awkward, gangly limbs and shocking red hair were tamed, still, and dignified in the barrack yearbook photo. She had even smiled.

The assistants returned with her clothes and a few toiletries. Addy retreated to a nearby washroom to change, though the gang of adults stood outside the door, awfully silent. Addy didn't know why she thought of them as adults and herself as a child; she was eighteen now.

Looking in the mirror, her hair was a mess, but her house uniform was in order. She sacrificed a few moments to tame her hair, but gave up when someone knocked on the door.

Addy stepped out, frightened and still disheveled. Seeing the state of her student, her ward, the headmistress stepped in front of the men, trying to bar their way.

"But why must she go with you? Any questions can be answered here and now—with our full cooperation," the headmistress almost begged the men, who were poised to grab Addy and carry her out of the building.

They refused to answer and gestured down the hall, towards the foyer.

Shuddering, Addy followed.

"But—what are we to tell House Pershing when they come looking for their daughter?! What does this mean for us as an academy? How can people trust us with their children if the Primarchy can simply abduct them?!"

Her questions were met with silence. The House guards stood aside as one set of double doors, and then a second, opened and shut, their click, a sound of dreadful finality.

Addy stood alone, outside in cold pre-dawn, clutching at her shoulders. The doors were closed, but they might as well have not existed.

A smooth, black sedan rumbled softly in the driveway. The car seemed to float, like liquid night, an unwelcome visitor to her mundane world. It was an intruder, here to gobble her up, to drag her from the safety and solace of her studies. Addy wanted to scoff; none of her sisters would notice her missing. She glanced at the license plate, recognizing the tags of L.A. Primarchy: two crossed palms above a golden bell, ringed with crests representing the subsidiary houses. The men coaxed her into the backseat. She sank into the over-plush interior.

A slim cell raised to his ear, one captor said, "Package C-17 is in custody. We are en route to the motorcade."

But why? What did I do?

She was forced deeper into the soft leather as the driver accelerated. The sedan sped down their driveway; she barely spotted the blockhouse and the guards, supposedly there to protect the students. Yet, here she was, being spirited away, and there they stood, saluting the Primarchy vehicle as it raced off, across the university campus.

The roads were deserted, and the sedan refused to stop for red lights. Addy's heart raced as the car decelerated before a red light, the driver looking left, then right, before racing through an intersection.

The world seemed to be dreaming, unaware of the crime being committed, of rules being trampled in these indecent hours.

They approached the central quad of Academy Fourteen. The older buildings, with their brick facades, seemed cloaked in mist as the sleek Primarchy cars assembled. A large, armored bus loomed ominously in the driveway. It was flanked by soldiers, armored in suits of black carapace, and bearing flechette rifles.

Addy was escorted from the car toward the bus. Her footsteps echoed in the still mist, attracting the focus of dozens. Eyes, and the blank stares of helmets, followed her across the street.

A woman with dark, curled hair stood sharp and crisp, despite the circumstance and hour, with her slate ready. Approaching this woman, her captor said, "C-17—Pershing."

"Our first guest," she replied, with an earnest smile.

"My name is Lynette," she said, though Addy's eyes locked to a pin on the woman's lapel, marking her as a senior member of L.A. Primarchy. Lynette coughed politely, attracting Addy's attention. "Yes, I'm a member of the L.A. Primarchy Board of External Affairs. We need you, and several of your peers, to come with us to Central—how exciting for you. We have questions and tests—nothing severe."

Addy breathed a sigh of relief. "Oh, that's good—will I be able to get back to classes today? I have an important project, and I can't leave it to my classmates—they'll ruin it."

Lynette consulted her data-slate, and waved Addy's escort away, leaving them alone. As Lynette tapped at her slate, Addy noticed more cars and other students arriving. All were in various states of dress and equally disheveled.

"Why so keen to get back to class?" Lynette asked.

Addy's glance drifted down to her shoes; she wasn't sure how to answer.

"I'm looking at your social games scores."

"Social games are a joke." Addy nearly barked at the woman.

Lynette's eyes widened and a smile pulled at the corners of her mouth.

"Why are we even talking about this?" She felt slightly insulted by Lynette's apparent disbelief. Addy crossed her arms and continued, "look at my human capitol scores."

Lynette nodded. "A respectable grade."

"I'm not popular in my barracks—but I work well in class and, look at all of my core subjects—ninety percent at least, across the spectrum."

"Why aren't you popular in your barracks?" Lynette asked.

Perplexed beyond reason, Addy let her arms hang defeated, at her side. As she did so, she noticed other students had lined up behind her. One young man, wearing the uniform of another small, specialty house, House Lederer, watched attentively, while the others fussed with their uniforms, belts, and shoes.

"Addy?" Lynette said, tapping her slate impatiently.

Addy took a deep breath and answered, "I'm unpopular because my bunkmate overheard a message sent by my father. She learned that my parents were on Four."

"*Were* on Four," Lynette repeated.

Addy furrowed her brow. "That can't be what this about—no, that's so pointless."

Lynette crossed her arms expectantly.

"My mother died on Four—I don't know how, and my father still works there, though I haven't heard from him in years," she whispered harshly, not wanting the others to hear.

Lynette tapped sharply at her data-slate. "I'm sorry to bring up painful matters," she said, before stepping aside and gesturing to the bus.

"This can't be about them—what does it matter?"

Lynette was silent. A guard stepped forward.

Addy scoffed and pushed past the guard. She mounted the steps to the bus and idled, looking back at the growing line. She stood and listened as the next student was asked the same questions.

Lynette gestured at a nearby guard. "We need a few more investigators; look at this line." The guard nodded, keying his communicator, which was recessed in a seam between his helmet and the fabric lining his throat. "Get them out of their cars," she added, "I don't care if it's cold."

Addy clutched the rail on the bus and hid much of herself behind the door. She wanted to keep listening.

"Miss," an armed guard patrolling near the bus caught her attention. He gestured inside.

Addy wanted to argue, but the blank visor brooked no disobedience. She boarded the bus. The benches were separated by thick, clear panes. The guard followed and waited for her to sit.

He leaned in and produced a metallic tie.

"What?" Addy recoiled at his closeness.

"Just relax," he ordered, his voice slightly inhuman, through the speaker in his helm.

He took her left hand and secured it to a bar, recessed between the two seats. The restraint was tight, and she yelped. She wanted to ask him to loosen it, but was too afraid to speak.

The guard left, and she looked out the window. New inspectors were processing their own lines of students. The Lederer student was arguing with Lynette. Addy used her free right hand to fiddle with the window, and found it would slide forward a few inches, enough to hear the conversation.

"—can't abduct students from their academies."

"It isn't abduction; it is emergency detention—"

"But notice must be given."

"Not in the case of an emergency," Lynette retorted. "It's plain in the L.A. Primarchy charter— the same charter that every subsidiary house signed. You'll find the same provisions in all Primarchies, across the planet."

"But what's the emergency? Should we just take your word for it?" Lederer demanded.

Lynette shook her head. "This is what I get for

being lenient," she said to the other investigator, who only grunted, not looking away from his data-slate.

Lynette nodded at a nearby guard. Though no order was given, the guard gave Lederer a quick shove towards the bus. For a moment, Addy expected Lederer to put up a fight, but he thought better of it. He came aboard and was walked to her bench.

She met his glance and noticed his cheeks were red. He was shaking, but seemingly not with cold.

He's full of adrenaline.

Lederer sat and accepted the restraint.

Now that he was so close, Addy looked sidelong at him, considering his pins and uniform. Eager to break the silence, Addy said what came to mind.

"I saw you in the line—House Lederer?"

He narrowed his eyes. "You recognize my devices," he asked, running a finger over the sails and compass that made up his House insignia.

"I study house morphology—for fun, really."

He eyed her, doubtfully.

"Well, there's a Lederer in my neighboring barracks."

"That explains it. I guess talking about our houses is a good way to pass the time," he said uncertain and eager to put humiliation behind him. "And you—" he leaned in and glanced at the pins on Addy's collar.

She felt her cheeks go warm and realized she was blushing.

"Pershing?" he asked.

Addy nodded, and awkwardly tried to shake his hand. His right and her left hand were restrained between the seats. Forced to shake his left hand, she laughed awkwardly, but he didn't seem bothered. More than that, he now appeared calm.

"My name's Nate—well, Nathaniel, but I prefer Nate."

"I'm Addy," she said, not sure how to follow up the introduction. "Do you get into a lot of trouble?" she asked, regretting the question immediately. He looked perplexed, "It's just that you seem so relaxed now—look at me, I'm shaking," she said, raising her free hand.

He laughed, raising his own, which still had a slight tremor. "I'm jittery too. All this is a little exciting."

Confused, Addy tilted her head.

"This might just be a field trip, when you get down to it. And I only have elective classes this term. I've already completed all my core units, but they wouldn't let me graduate early."

"Wow," Addy said. "Did you get a good primer from your House, before you came to academy?"

"It's not that impressive. We're small— House Lederer, I mean—and engineering isn't as glamorous as it sounds. We work with police houses mostly, and a few Primarchies directly. It's enough to fund Academy Fourteen training," he said glumly, before suddenly changing the subject, "It's just nice to get out, even if it's under—special— circumstances."

"Right," Addy replied, not really understanding

what he meant. She was nervous. "I don't like this kind of attention."

Nate nodded, though he seemed expectant. Addy realized it was impolite to learn about another's House without offering news of your own.

"Oh, I'm being rude—House Pershing—we focus on biology, applied biology mostly. I'm destined for a lifetime of designing crops to hold off starvation."

Nate nodded, his brows lifting. "That's very noble. You seem like a scientist."

Addy reddened, wondering if the comment was aimed at her appearance.

"I just mean you seem intelligent and self-conscious: the mark of a good scientist."

Addy laughed awkwardly, wishing she was back in bed and well-hidden beneath the covers. She had little practice talking to males.

Nate stood, as far as his restraint would let him, and he asked the other students, several of whom had shuffled aboard by now, about their houses.

Grateful that he was distracted, Addy felt quite ridiculous. Here they were, being legally abducted, and she was panicking about her appearance, and nervous about sitting next to Nate.

He's handsome, quick-thinking, and assertive, and here I am, with crazy hair and an unwashed face.

Addy sank into her seat and gave up trying to find her reflection in the window.

A female student was answering Nate's question, "House Fallbrook—we're a policing house."

"We do agriculture, House Topanga, I mean,"

another student added.

"Our Houses specialize in different professions," Nate said, looking to Addy. "What else might connect us?"

"Connect us?" Addy repeated.

"There's a reason for this. Something the Primarchy knows about us—something we don't."

Addy nodded, about to mention her conversation with Lynette, but a sudden outcry silenced the bus.

"You're a joke!" a voice bellowed.

A large student, burly and half-dressed, struggled with a pair of guards. They struck the student with their stun batons as they pushed him onto the bus. His unbuttoned shirt slapped against a visored helm during the struggle.

Addy caught a glance of the loud student's uniform as the mess of struggling bodies lumbered nearer.

"He's House Serrano," Nate said. "They're a little coarse."

Serrano continued struggling and insulting his captors as they forced him onto a seat, "Looks like you're having some trouble—call in a few more friends!" he moaned as they struggled to restrain his arm.

A blonde girl sitting next to Serrano recoiled, pulling herself as close to the window as she could.

"That armor's looking a little tight around the waist, trooper," Serrano said, mocking the struggling guards.

He received a gloved clout to the face in reply.

"Do you think he needs another restraint?" one guard asked, whether earnestly, or to punish Serrano, Addy couldn't tell. The other considered the question.

"Please—let me sit somewhere else," the blonde girl pleaded, still hugging the wall.

"I'm not that bad," Serrano insisted.

Nate stood again. "Just let him be. Once you're off the bus, I'm sure he'll calm down. Come on, Serrano, tell them to step off one more time and it'll be out of your system."

Serrano looked over at Nate and laughed. "You heard the man! Step off, boys, and hit the weight racks—you should be ashamed."

The comment aroused some laughter and the guards shrugged. "Let A-squad deal with them—I should be on patrol."

The other agreed and the two left.

"You recognize me as a Serrano?"

"I recognize the attitude," Nate replied. "House Serrano guards our compound."

Addy watched in wonder as Nate caroused so easily with strangers; his confidence was somewhat alluring.

He'll rot away in engineering—he should be a liaison, or maybe a professor.

Elements of A-squad arrived and took position on the bus. Motorcycle guards flanked the bus on both sides and armored cars formed up ahead and behind them. The motorcade rolled off the campus just as the sun emerged in the east.

"Nate," Addy started, "I wanted to tell you," she

paused as he was distracted.

"Look," he pointed at Serrano and the blonde girl sitting next to him.

Addy peeked over the seat and saw the girl, laboriously brushing her bright, blonde hair, and holding her head at an odd angle to catch the reflection off the chromed seat lining.

Addy forced an awkward laugh, recalling her own attempt to find her reflection. "Wait, how did she get that hairbrush?" the girl was rifling through a bag for makeup. Despite the rocking of the bus, and one restrained hand, she carefully primped and preened.

Addy felt envious, then angry that the blonde was allowed her bag, and finally pained by the whole circus. "Why does she care what she looks like? We've all been abducted."

Nate nodded. "Priorities vary, but, look at Serrano."

Serrano glanced at the blonde and crossed his arms as well as he could, lending some bulk to his biceps in the process. He tried to look nonchalant and uninterested. His restrained arm hung awkwardly, despite this, and he glanced again at the girl, who was busily unaware.

"We really are an embarrassment," Nate said.

"Indeed," Addy replied. "Listen, Nate—" He looked her way, and she brushed the hair away from her eyes, "—about what connects us. I was talking with Lynette and mentioned my parents."

Nate's brow contracted, then his eyes suddenly brightened. "Let me guess, you have a parent off-world?"

Addy blinked. "Both, actually. They were on Four."

"My dad works up there too. We haven't heard from him for years."

Addy tried to put a hand on his shoulder, but found it still restrained.

Nate chuckled sadly, seeing what she intended. He grasped her restrained hand with his, giving it a comforting squeeze before releasing.

Addy's face was suddenly hot, and she feigned interested in the window.

"Wha—where are we?" she gasped.

"We're in old L.A., near the Pit," Nate said, leaning over her to look. She knew she shouldn't, but Addy couldn't help herself. She took a deep breath and detected a hint of his aftershave. It was pleasant.

"See—the Pit," he said, drawing her attention.

Craggy, jutting walls of stone rose from the ground, so high that Addy couldn't see their peak through the windows. Over a century ago, the buildings and streets had been abruptly ripped apart; no one was quite sure how it happened. The land sank, as if a seam beneath the city had split, but there wasn't just one split seam. The Pit was a central point of the cataclysm, where the many chasms converged. This pit was famous for its tarry patches, which glittered on the sections of rock that flanked the road.

"Primarchy-exclusive territory—I've never seen it before," Addy whispered.

"It looks different on the screens," a voice commented.

The students had their eyes glued to the windows.

Though the sun was rising, it became darker as they followed the road descending into the Pit. Fortified ramparts and compounds lined the ragged cliffsides. Rotating radar dishes, missile batteries, and domed chain-guns featured prominently.

The motorcade approached a broad, steel barrier, which opened as they neared. The rugged cliffs were replaced with the smooth walls of structures, buried and built into the Pit. Rumors held that L.A. built this central command around some secret of the old CC, but Addy thought that was just another piece of folklore, meant to intrigue children and teach history.

One detail made her doubt that logic. "Why build here, if an earthquake could destroy it at any minute?" Addy asked.

"Government people," Nate replied, as if that were answer enough.

On a massive lot, the motorcade passed a fleet of expensive vehicles: sedans, limousines, armored cars, and more buses and haulers dotting the tarmac. It reminded Addy of a sleek formation of panthers, poised for an ambush.

Finally, the bus came to a stop and the guards bent to undo their restraints, two by two.

"Hey, should I put up a fuss?" Serrano asked as the guards neared.

"Just sit up and behave," the girl next to him

said. Her hair and makeup were now done, and done well, to Addy's estimation.

They were ushered outside.

"That girl who got her vanity bag onboard is House Beverly," Nate whispered to Addy. "And look—do you recognize him?" Nate nodded towards another boy with a mop of strawberry-blond hair and a curious, nautically themed uniform.

"House Mariner," Addy replied.

"You're sharp."

"Every person in the Combine should recognize House Mariner," Addy protested.

"*Should*," Nate repeated.

The students were arranged in formation, and only now did Addy realize that a second bus had fallen in with their motorcade during the drive. Dozens more students approached, joining their group. Few had any belongings, though a couple were out of uniform altogether, with sloppy work boots and denim jackets over tank tops.

"Clannies," Serrano mocked, eyeing the couple's strange clothes.

The two oddly-dressed students bristled at the jeer.

"Clannies?" Addy whispered to Nate, who stood next to her.

"That's a clan patch on their jacket," Nate replied, almost annoyed. His focus was on the guards and Lynette, who convened before their formation.

Clannies, Addy thought. *You rarely see people from the Clans this far south.*

A Primarchy sergeant called out to them, "By my command, atten-tion! Right—face! Forward—March!"

The mass of students started marching. Though they came from different schools, most didn't miss a beat, and slipped into the ordered rhythm of formation marching. Two, however, were out of step, drawing angry glares. It was the clannies again.

Addy looked up at the yawning gulf of the Pit, and the blue sky, several hundred feet above. The height was dazzling.

"Eyes forward!" the sergeant called, his thundering voice striking Addy, who locked her gaze ahead.

"We're no different here—you march at attention. That means eyes forward," he explained.

Addy felt slightly insulted, as the clannies were making a mockery of marching, though not a glance was spared for them.

They were marched through two guard stations and halted outside a bank of glass doors. The words, "Intake Processing," glowed ominously above the entryways.

"We're here at intake. It's no different than at the airport. You will be scanned, and biometric measurements will be taken. Be prompt and polite and it will be over shortly," the sergeant said.

Their formation was split and they filed inside. A handful of guards looked aghast at the wave of students, who jammed the four checkpoints. More processing personnel were called, and the slog began.

Addy was weighed, measured, had her blood sampled, answered questions about where she lived, the names of her parents, teachers, and even the names of a few of her barrack associates. Finally, she was scanned by at least three devices, though she was asked to pass through one at least four times, as the operators stared blankly at a glitching screen.

Addy glanced at Nate, one line over. He gave her a pained eye roll. She smiled, but, before they waved her through a fifth time, an argument broke out at the next station.

It struck Addy that she had never seen a security checkpoint catch someone. What would happen if they did?

The argument grew as a student resisted an inspector who was interested in his shoes.

"Take off your shoes, sir," the inspector insisted once more, waving for assistance.

"But the scanner said they were fine!"

"They look bulky to me, and I'm using my prerogative."

Shockingly, the student ignored the inspector and cried out to the room, "They'll never let you go! You have to fight—" He fumbled with his watch as the inspector tackled him. The student deftly elbowed and subdued the inspector before rolling away.

"Just cooperate!" Nate cried out.

The student's watch hid a length of cable, which, to Addy's horror, he used to strangle the inspector.

Shocked, Nate stumbled backward over a rope barrier.

Addy blinked, unbelieving.

Screams filled the checkpoint. Several students ran for the doors but found them locked, as guards leveled their stun batons and charged into the mass.

"They'll never let you out!" the murderous student cried. His shirt nearly tore off in the struggle and he was stained with blood, his hands especially.

Flechette fire pierced the air and doors shattered. A guard fell. Addy realized that several other students had drawn weapons, attacking the guards and inspectors.

The murderous student approached her, somehow bearing a compact flechette pistol. "Are you Pershing?" he asked.

Addy stood, shocked and silent, afraid that he would kill her.

Nate slammed into the student and the two tumbled to the floor. Serrano leaped over a glass barrier, rushing to join the fight, but Addy saw the student leveling his pistol.

He was strong and pulled away, training the weapon on Nate. Addy charged and kicked it from his hand; it went spinning under a scanning machine. Serrano piled on, but the student sharply elbowed Nate in the jaw and kicked Serrano in the crotch. The two crumpled.

"On the ground!" came the voices of guards.

Realizing that she had been standing the whole time, Addy gasped and dropped to the floor. She reached out for Nate, who was rattled from the blow. The murderous student ducked behind another x-ray machine. The whoosh of flechettes and the crash of shattering glass filled the checkpoint. Other pockets of violence filled her peripheral vision, but Addy focused on the student who had disabled Nate and Serrano. She could see him in the reflection of a glass barrier, still hunched behind the machine. He was fumbling with his shoe and pulling free something resembling a shiny, silver thermal blanket.

Addy gawked, certain her eyes were playing tricks on her.

A canister rolled across the floor.

"Cover your eyes!" Serrano ordered.

A flash and explosion dazzled them and, in moments, the stream of armed guards regained control.

Addy looked back to the reflection, but the student was gone.

"He's back there!" Addy called to the swarming guards, pointing to the machine where he had, a moment ago, been crouching.

They rounded the machine, their weapons leveled. There was only silence as they considered the machine. A pair glanced at their sergeant, who directed them further into the room.

"Where did he go?" the sergeant asked, his voice metallic through the speaker.

"He was right there," Addy said, getting to her knees and peeking around the corner. All she saw was a small pool of blood.

Addy and the others were forced to sit still as paramedics arrived, hauling off the dead and severely wounded, before tending to the rest. Addy, Nate, and Serrano leaned against the bloody machine as the minutes wore on.

"I can't believe they're keeping us here," someone muttered nearby.

"What's to say more of us aren't infiltrators?" Serrano replied, before repeating his tale of shoulder-checking and downing the one who garroted an inspector to death.

Nate elbowed Addy and pointed to the floor.

"What?"

"That drop of blood. Was it there a second ago?" he whispered.

Addy, still shaking from the shock of violence, considered it, but one drop of blood looked much like the puddles.

Then, as she stared, another appeared, a few feet closer to the doors. Addy blinked.

Serrano bellowed a laugh as he invented a new detail with which to bore the others. Addy thought that his bloody lip, suffering loud guffaws, was the probable culprit of sudden flying blood.

Nate saw the motion of her eyes and put the same together. He huffed and scooted closer to Addy.

"At least the floor is clean—well, it was, before all that," he muttered, leaning as far back as he could and closing his eyes.

Serrano slammed Nate on the shoulder in a bullish way, "At least we don't have to go back to class!" He bellowed.

Minutes later, Lynette appeared, flanked by guards.

"Lynette!" Addy called out, catching the woman's attention.

"Ah, Pershing, Lederer, Serrano—check," she said, tapping away at her slate.

"Let us out of here, please," Addy insisted.

"We haven't completed the inspections," was the hurried reply.

Serrano laughed and Addy gawked as the woman, in her three-inch heels, stepped deftly over debris and puddles of blood to continue with her roster.

Addy sighed, closing her eyes, but they burst open in realization. *That student, the killer, he knew my name!*

www.ingramcontent.com/pod-product-compliance
Lightning Source LLC
Chambersburg PA
CBHW030800260626
47169CB00001B/128